Ron Clooney is an ex-journalist; ex-teacher of English; and ex-construction worker.

Ron lives in Southampton England with his artist girlfriend and two dogs, Daisy and Biscuit.

He spends his time writing novels and poetry and recording music.

At the present time he is working on another crime novel.

www.ronclooney.com

BY THE SAME AUTHOR

Pancardi's Pride

A Measure of Wheat for a Penny

Gothique Fantastique

mr. mojo risin

aint dead

Ron Clooney

Copyright © 2011 Ron Clooney

The moral right of the author has been asserted.

Apart from any fair dealing for the purposes of research or private study,
or criticism or review, as permitted under the Copyright, Designs and Patents
Act 1988, this publication may only be reproduced, stored or transmitted, in
any form or by any means, with the prior permission in writing of the
publishers, or in the case of reprographic reproduction in accordance with
the terms of licences issued by the Copyright Licensing Agency. Enquiries
concerning reproduction outside those terms should be sent to the publishers.

Matador
5 Weir Road
Kibworth Beauchamp
Leicester LE8 0LQ, UK
Tel: (+44) 116 279 2299
Fax: (+44) 116 279 2277
Email: books@troubador.co.uk
Web: www.troubador.co.uk/matador

ISBN 978 1848767 577

British Library Cataloguing in Publication Data.
A catalogue record for this book is available from the British Library.

Typeset in 11pt StempelGaramond Roman by Troubador Publishing Ltd, Leicester, UK
Printed and bound in the UK by TJ International, Padstow, Cornwall

Matador is an imprint of Troubador Publishing Ltd

For

The gift of
The Doors & the Music

Thank you

This book is dedicated to you

Everything you are about to read in this book is true:
Absolutely true.

However:
Some of the names and places have been altered to protect the innocent

Is everybody in?
Is everybody in?
Is ev-reeee-bod-deeee in?
The ceremony is about to begin.

One

Help...

The first time I saw Jim Morrison was in the summer of 1970. The Doors were playing at the Isle of Wight Festival, they were flying in from Miami despite the fact that Morrison was in the middle of a huge court case for public indecency, profanity and lewd and lascivious behaviour. I was fifteen – well just about to be. Morrison was twenty six.

The next time I saw him was in Paris, France. I met and spoke with him on a few occasions after that.

In a small bar at the back of rue something or other – there was a band playing: The Lizard Kings. A bunch of lads from East Germany and there he was; sometimes tapping on the bar and sometimes humming along under his breath. Occasionally a rich baritone came through in snatches and I knew it instantly, that could not be changed. The weight had gone and the face shape had changed, but it was Morrison alright. There were scars and the shape of the nose was wrong. It was the eyes that gave him away – they were slightly too close together and just that little bit too intense. The only trouble was he was supposed to be dead, and not old like me. I had a real problem with it because the records showed he died in July 1971; that he was buried around the corner in Pere Lachaise cemetery.

You see for as long as I could really remember, The Doors had been bubbling away at the back of my mind. From the time when we were kids and our freedom was about camping out, smoking dope and challenging the teachers of the 1960s. I remember playing 'Light My Fire' and the day some blue pills, which were some joker's medication, were found in the toilets at school.

Now, that was a place like something out of the dark ages. A terrible place, a place where boys with any spark of inspiration had it crushed out of them. A place where the strive for mediocrity was paramount; a place to subjugate and disintegrate; a place for you to, 'learn your place,' become a small cog in the big wheel. The best days of your life – were they? Nostalgia certainly isn't what it used to be and memories are always mixed and jaundiced by re-evaluation. When I look back now, it's mostly in anger, but with an understanding of how my nihilism took root and began to grow.

In 1966 I discovered pirate radio, The Beach Boys and The Byrds. In 1967 I discovered The Doors and in 1969 Ten Years After. Magical times which I remember as probably far better than they actually were. Still, for me the festivals and the nights spent sleeping in the rain could not have been better. There was no responsibility and the crushing weight of adulthood had not flattened me. My mother let me be free; free to think and develop my own ideas, a simple thing, for which I shall be eternally grateful. I don't know if I was anywhere near the garden but I thought I was.

Once I was talking to two ex GIs, Vietnam vets, somewhere near Colchester they had done their time and were now taking a long walk to freedom through Europe, picking grapes and olives and then turning on and tuning out. It was bizarre, surreal even. There I was trudging along with my military sleeping bag and a friend, when around a corner in the path up to the festival site sat two naked guys. All their gear was covered by a sheet of polythene and they were sharing a pipe. I was soaked and miserable, but they were laughing, wet and stoned. They seemed not to care about their flaccid nudity, and neither did the many girls who passed, but I was still of an age when it really stunned me. Naked flesh, naked girl flesh, that was what I wanted to see

2

and as much of it as possible. Looking back now I must have seemed young and naïve, and as one guy pulled out a harp and began to play 'Rollin' and Tumblin', the other sang. "I was smokin' and drinkin', stoned the whole night long." It was like I had stepped through the gates of heaven to hear Muddy Waters play.

When the rain stopped they put on dry clothes but I was still wet. They laughed and I was miserable. Sometimes I wonder if I ever existed at all after that.

* * *

"How long you been in Paris?" I asked as I approached the bar.

He shrugged and made hand signals as if he spoke no English; I could tell from his reflection in the mirror, behind the compact bar, that his eyes were alert and he was comprehending. I had found my ghost.

"I came to see Morrison's grave," I said. "Like all the tourists, I came too. I expect he'd be laughing his head off if he could see how people were reacting. Star quality, that's what he had and he didn't even know it." I was looking for any glimmer of a reaction. "There was a girl," I smiled as I talked, "well a woman really, who had tattoos all over her back. The first few lines of 'People are Strange' and two pictures of Morrison, one on each shoulder blade, and The Doors logo emblazoned across the small of her back. Amazing really, crazy but totally amazing, and you know what? She wasn't even old enough to have seen him live. Told me she was thirty four – makes her birth 1972. How could she be so in love with a dead guy?" I was watching him. "You know all this tourist razzmatazz. Hey maybe he started a new religion after all? The religion of fame and we all come to worship at the alter? A July heist instead of the Easter one?"

The stranger nodded, recognised the word tourist, and I wondered how good an actor he might be. He grinned widely, but still remained silent. I tried again to draw him out into the open. I had a real feeling about this guy; call it a hunch, a

3

reporter's hunch. But this was more than that; there was a real pulling in my guts. Sometimes ideas came for no reason and then zap, they worked and I got a big story. I was getting that feeling again, a sort of soft nudge in the groin – a nudge of expectancy and I wasn't about to get laid.

I had nearly pieced the whole story together. I had the endings and I knew which one I was going to use, and now, like a bolt out of the blue, this. I hadn't expected it – I couldn't believe it. That's the thing about a story, it just arrives and sometimes it takes over – like some giant leviathan, until it consumes you.

"You know today there were a couple of German girls there and they had thrown some flowers on his grave, a bouquet marked The Lizard King – all red and gold. They were listening to 'Light my Fire' on the headset of an ipod. Each had one headphone and they told me that they came every year. They'd been coming for the last twenty years. It was like they came to worship. They were only thirty six, but celluloid allowed them to worship, post mortem so to speak." I had a brief flashback of Jesus Christ on film and wondered if his philosophy or fame had made him. "One of them was crying and you want to know what the real irony is?" No reaction. "Robby Krieger wrote that song." I was trying to anger my listener, goad him, incense him – it wasn't working. "Yeah, Jim added the funeral pyre verse and Ray Manzarek played the intro and solo, but it wasn't really a Morrison song – it was a Krieger song. Like all the really popular songs were. Morrison the poet, front man, the exhibitionist risk taker; the exhibitionist needed Krieger, and marketing man Manzarek needed them both. Well maybe Dorothy knew what the real answer was, she was smart and stayed in the background, but she was their first sponsor. She was the real powerhouse and she had that thing which a man can hold on to, she was supportive; she believed in her man and boy she wasn't disappointed."

I stopped talking as the man ordered another drink; my goading was failing miserably. Either the guy genuinely didn't care or was just intrigued. There was no alcohol and no soft sweet coke, his drink was a fresh orange juice topped up with soda water. I'd seen alcoholics take that drink.

Somehow I needed to spark a reaction. Suddenly it came to me; I opened a pack of gum and started to unwrap a stick. Jim Morrison detested chewing gum and all those that used it. I was real obvious, made it easy to see, just like I was a habitual masticator. I was hoping that the reaction I got would happen. Casually he placed his hand over mine and said one word, "Non."

The gum went into my pocket and at that moment I knew I was right. I'd found him. You see, people can change their faces, change their clothes, they can even change their habits, but it's the little things that stick, these are the things that give them away. I read somewhere, I can't remember where, that in France there was this murderer who was a wealthy socialite. Hey I'm wrong! It was the Lucan case. That was it, yes. Lucan liked a certain wine and they found this guy in the Philippines, or somewhere, who had died. Well this guy had no past, but he loved this one type of wine and he is supposed to have looked just like Lord Lucan. Now some people might say that's a bunch of bull, but I kinda hung onto that idea and when I started on this case, oh yeah, it's a case – the idea sorta came back. You know, like when you forget the name of someone or thing and then like hours later it just pops up. It's like the window froze and then suddenly it's back online. Where was I? Oh yeah.

"Well," I joked, "Is that what happens when you've got your kicks before the whole shithouse goes up in flames?"

There was no reply from the man, but his eyes lit up and I wondered once again how anyone could simply walk away from a massive fortune and fame. I know I couldn't, I'd be fickle, I'd change my mind and maybe be riddled with doubt and guilt.

What if you did something that gave you no way back? What then? Jim was one of those people who tested the boundaries. If he'd been a prisoner of war, he'd have continually been up at the wire, looking, testing for weaknesses. He'd have been part of the great escape. Seeing which way the lights fell and where the gaps were, fearless to the point of lunacy, or bouncing his endless ball – Hilts Morrison, 'the cooler king.'

5

I mean, John Densmore said he learnt a valuable lesson on greed from Jim; a lesson about Buick and the 'Light my Fire' ad. Morrison was all for purity and non-corruption and like he said, it was only money. There was a sort of band of brothers attitude in The Doors, and that emanated from Mr. Mojo Risin. The cake got cut four ways – simple, whatever each member did they got just a quarter. He wasn't like Brian Jones in The Stones, taking that bit extra because he was the leader, or the front man. It was never Jim Morrison and The Doors and he hated when anyone announced them as such to an audience. Together they simply were The Doors, though The Doors and their music were never simple. The whole thing was like a diamond and each point was covered by one man, each needed the other. That was what made them so good as a team.

So could someone just give it up, walk away and never look back? Maybe Morrison was the man who could, a Rimbaud of the rock world and anyway, there have been others since. What if he really was, sick of his stinky boots? If he didn't care about the money? If the only really important thing was freedom? Not just mock middle-class, leisure play freedom, but real freedom; freedom to step outside of the bars of the prison and why not? He knew that iron bars do not a prison make; the only real prison is in the mind. Jim Morrison was smart, real smart; he managed to reach conclusions that some of us take a lifetime to establish, and he was only twenty seven years old. That is frightening.

This was 1971 and things were changing, the whole damn world was in flux. Vietnam was still going and they'd been shooting presidents for years. Maybe he could just walk away. Maybe he needed to put down the torch and sit in the dark for a while, let someone else have a go at being the standard bearer.

This was still the sixties and would be until about 1973. That sounds crazy but the decade didn't really start on the 1st January 1960, you know, like the opening of a new day and the new wave of global optimism? 1962 – 1973, that was the decade, well that's what I always thought anyhow. Maybe, just maybe, this guy had the guts to do it. Had the guts to let go. After all, he'd been the one that was the trailblazer, maybe he was already way out ahead, knew what television and fame could do. Even on the Ed Sullivan show he didn't capitulate; the wild and devil may care Rolling Stones did.

They altered their lyrics to avoid public outrage, but Jim didn't change his. Like Morrison said, it's only words. Maybe it is just a bunch of bullshit, but I had spent months piecing this together and suddenly, like a puzzle, all the pieces seemed to fall into place of their own free will. Yeah there were holes, great big ones, bloody great big ones, but the gaps were getting smaller and the sense was getting bigger. Morrison was more than Mr. Mojo Risin and I knew he was a very clever and highly observant man. A man who could start a religion, or commit a murder and if he did, he'd get away with it.

He smiled and I knew he understood. Understood the references to Morrison and the music. His attempt to stop me chewing gum, well I thought that proved it. He knew precisely what I was saying, and yet he was choosing to ignore me. His actions were speaking louder than words.

"Like Morrison?" I said nonchalantly.

He nodded and raised his glass as if giving a toast but still remained silent.

We talked for a long while, well I talked, gibbered really, and he listened – patiently. We drank, again that was mostly me, the band played and played and the crowd danced and finally I went to the toilet; had to, the imperative was too strong. When I came back, the man had gone and so had his glass. I checked the street outside, in both directions, he had vanished. It was like he had never been there.

I asked the barman about the man, he shrugged. Claimed he had no idea who he was, never seen him before, he said.

And me – I wondered what and who I had seen.

* * *

At this point I ought to explain what I was doing in Paris and why I had gone to Morrison's grave in the first place. You see I loved The Doors music; I thought for years that it had been well before its time. It was jazz and blues and rock and theatre and revolution and punk and goth and...well there were so many things I really loved about it. Then there were the influences that Morrison created in living form: Iggy Pop and the whole of the punk movement. Goths, the gothic and the dark side, that was something that my editor wanted me to explore.

Oh yeah, I was telling you how and why I was in this bar in the first place. But Iggy Pop, I mean he took narcotics on stage and antagonised the audience ten times worse than Morrison ever did. I remember he did some lewd exposing too. It was like the baton had been passed. And look at it now, James Newell Osterberg, topless but respected, respected because he broke the mould and pushed the boundaries. It seems like you can roll around in glass and chuck-up on stage, take heroin even, as long as you survive to tell the tale. Like everything becomes Ok in the end. Now his face is on advertising hoardings all over my home city, Christ, it's even on the back of buses. Take Oscar Wilde and his antics, if you don't believe me, and he's in Pere Lachaise too. Everything becomes acceptable if you wait long enough.

Anyway, as I was saying, I work for the *The Times* in London, well did work for the *The Times*; but I'd shouted my mouth off once too often and after I told the last editor to, "go eat shit", I was freelance again. The new editor, he liked what I'd done in the past and he gave me this assignment on Morrison. They didn't know where it would take me and neither did I, plus they didn't have to pay for a full time reporter and I was willing to push the boundaries – so here I was in this bar. And there it was, a bar behind Pere Lachaise cemetery. The end of an assignment which I thought would be fairly pedestrian. I couldn't have been more wrong.

* * *

Perhaps I ought to go back to the beginning: the Isle of Wight. But I won't, I'll go back further. To when I got my first guitar.

It was my birthday and I was eleven, and I kept on about

getting a box. My elder brother had bought me a violin when I was seven or eight, but I didn't really get on with it. That guitar, well that was a different story. Night after night, day after day strumming Bobby Shafto. My friends, well, you'd call them fair weather friends, they took, 'the mickey,' and did other things instead. But me, I kept on practising, practising on those nylon strings until my fingers bled.

We lived in a small town in the suburbs, in a place where everyone thought they were more than they were. The word I'd use now would be snob, and boy they were snobs. My father thought the noise I made was dreadful and my brother, he was the really gifted musical one, he still played his Mozart and his Beethoven.

Oh yeah, where was I? The guitar, the brown thing that cost about £10 and which I had to fight to get, that guitar went everywhere with me. Except school, there the school masters were old and stuffy and I, well I was a rebel. At least I thought I was.

I remember there was this teacher, who thought he was really, 'cool' and he asked us all to bring an album of current music in. I arrived with a Ten Years After album, Ssh, I think it was. Anyway, he was going on about how he liked it. I understood where he was coming from when I did a stint of chalk and talk myself; and that makes me smile when I think about him now. Thing is, and this is the really weird bit, I can't even remember his name. But I know we had a lesson called social studies, in the late sixties – it was rubbish, total rubbish.

Anyhow I'm meandering around here. I remember taking that guitar and getting round a campfire with my mates; remember playing 'Light my Fire' badly. I think they laughed, but they couldn't do anything, or play anything. It was the summer of 1967 and the other big song in my memory was 'Mr. Tambourine Man' by The Byrds. I loved that jingly twelve string sound. Maybe the dates are wrong, but I do remember the times as hot summers which were long, full of school vacations and swimming. Radio Caroline, that I do remember, Stuart Henry too. Somebody told me he was dead, MS got him. I loved that

Scottish accent and the new sounds. I didn't know it at the time but the same twelve string sound comes at the start of 'Hotel California'; years later and the sound still hooks me now.

At the other end of the street from where I lived there were some boys and one had a twelve string, Ken Austen, that was his name: I remember that. And he could play; well I thought he could, because all I could do was strum. So I strummed out 'Light my Fire'; didn't know who the hell Robby Krieger was or Jim Morrison the singer. Four years later I did, and when he died, I had the whole weight of it fall in. It was after Hendrix and the school assembly, but that's another story.

Well as we're here I might as well tell it.

It was 1970 and we, that's me and a few friends, the fair weather ones, had gone to the festival on the island. I'd been there the year before when Bob Dylan was headlining and he had let the whole thing down. He finished his set in forty five minutes and then left. People were yelling and screaming and I had sat next to a fence made out of corrugated steel sheet and watched a guy roll a joint. When he passed it around I took a toque. That was the first time I'd ever tasted dope. That was one thing, and then there was this guy, you know, one of the bigger boys, he had a bright yellow tee shirt and across the chest, in bold bubble writing, orange and red and fancy: Fuck. Just the one word and he had hair so long it was halfway down his back; blond, well kind of blond. I expect he works in an office now or he's an accountant. I didn't contemplate that then, but now, with experience, I accept it. Hey, I'll even take a bet on it.

Something happened between 1976 and now, and well, things sort of lost their way, me included. I married young and then all the responsibilities piled in on me, kids, mortgage, and my mind died: died inside my head. All that promise, all that passion and flair and fight and being on the edge, well it just evaporated. I spent my time trying to pay the bills, listening to the crap being spoken at me and smiling. I even smiled back, grinned an inane grin so I could put bread on the table – make a life for my kids. I didn't even have the balls to be a drunk or a poet. Nope, I just gave in, rolled over and switched on the TV and watched. Like

Morrison said, I became a spectator. I watched while the actors delivered their play. The thing was, I had two great kids, though one of them I haven't seen in five years, his choice not mine. The crazy thing was, I loved them. Survival gene or procreation gene or something; Jesus Christ, I lost fifteen years of me and I messed up – messed up big time. Regrets, I've had few, as the old Sinatra song goes, but mine are not too few to mention; mine are God awful and huge. I married when I was young and stupid and we split up when I was older and wiser; that was the best day's work I ever did. At the time I went through hell, but I'd been through worse when I was younger; now I'm so much happier. What's the old adage? What doesn't kill you, makes you stronger? Hey, I'm a super hero.

Oh yeah, where was I? September 18th 1970 and Jimi Hendrix dies. I was in the last year of school. I had this reputation for being off the wall and I had this house master, who's dead now, well he liked my weird drive and energy. I think he hated the stuffy headteacher too, and man, was he stuffy; wanted us to wear stupid schoolboy caps, the type of thing boys wore in the 1930s and 40s.

So usually we had to take assembly, like the kids do now, to break the monotony of what was a mock religious gathering with hymns and such. Most of us hated it. The teachers did too, that's why they made us do them. So we got together and decided to do a tribute to Jimi.

For the opening we played 'Purple Haze'; that set some of the teachers' teeth on edge. Then there was the story of his life and finally a minute's silence. Man we got into trouble over that. You only did the silence on Remembrance Day, you know, the 11th of the 11th; but we did it for Jimi.

I'd like to think it was my idea, but perhaps it wasn't; anyhow, the shit hit the fan and my house master, well he supported me against the headteacher. That was something to behold and I never forgot it – it was great to watch, 'the system' breaking down right in front of my eyes. It doesn't seem to matter now, the guy's dead and they shut the school. Sometimes I wonder what pain that cost him after we had left, but man I

11

respected him, learnt from him and enjoyed it. He wasn't the only one, there were two Yorkshire men. One was ex-coal mines I think, and he was a great historian, and the other was English. It was no surprise to me that these two got me the highest grades. What is it the propaganda says? 'Nobody forgets a great teacher'? Well for once, maybe only the once though, I have to agree.

When I start to ramble like this you'll have to stop me or skip. I'm trying to get the context into place here. Trying to let you know what turned me on to Morrison and The Doors. *The Doors of Perception*, Aldous Huxley's brave new mescaline world.

Everything seemed to be in a state of flux. Europe had come out of two wars and Vietnam was happening and change was taking place. We grew our hair and wore colour and no shoes and beads like women and me, I did too. My father once joked; that I'd have to walk twenty paces behind or twenty paces in front if we were walking into town. I thought it was a joke, but like Steve Morrison, he was serious and he was military too. And yeah I'd had the enforced haircut when he was on leave. Morrison and I, we sort of have an affinity on that one.

Now here I was investigating, investigating whether he was really dead.

I'd spent months on the case, and everywhere I turned there were clues and each one led me up a blind alley. Too many people had trampled over the tracks, so I'd diverted a stream to see where they got out. Like James Fennimore Cooper and his last of the true Indians, I got down in the mud and sifted for clues. I had to think like him and absorb everything about the guy; what made him tick. It wasn't the women or the fame, the money or the booze, it was freedom. That was the thing he was seeking, like all the beat poets before him; like Dean Moriarty, he wanted to see the place and more – be in that place. Get further out west, out beyond the frontier before it choked us all. And when you're down in the dirt there are stones, but there are diamonds too. There were red herrings and twists and turns and then finally there was this bar and the stranger. DNA had come into the frame and I needed that to confirm what I was thinking, what I had discovered. No point in an exhumation order. Nearly forty years had passed and Clara, Jim's mother, was dead. Andy, his brother, wouldn't do anything, neither would the family.

The graffiti had been washed away and I reckoned there'd be nothing left now. Like when they dug up Dylan Thomas in Wales to drop Caitlin in. The whole corpse had gone: no more Dylan. That was about forty years too.

The, 'True to his Spirit,' headstone had been placed with a great block of granite or marble, with a bronze plaque. A huge thing to hold him in, as if he were some vampire that might try to get out and roam the streets of Paris.

I'd taken nearly a year and the Morrisons were clammed up, the Coursons too. It didn't make sense. But I made allowances for family and the whole hype thing. They must have gone through hell, and they always had to take the blame. The horrid military man etc, etc, etc. Hey, my father was military and yeah he could be a real disciplinarian, but he loved me in his way. Well I think he did, hope he did, he just couldn't show it easily, maybe that was the Morrison problem. Or maybe I just got in the way. Anyhow, Steve Morrison put the stone there as if he had finally made peace with his first born.

It's just simple things don't make sense and me, well after all these years, I'd found out the truth. It was unsavoury, not the stuff of myth and legend and it didn't read like Romeo and Juliet, nor was it the stuff of giants. Morrison the myth melted into Morrison the man; so here I was – in Paris, in a bar, at the back of Pere Lachaise cemetery, listening to a bunch of kids – wondering again.

Two

For what it's worth…

When you are at school they tell you the best place to start with a story is at the beginning, then you move to the middle and that is followed by the end. Except in this case, where the end is the beginning, or at least it would be if any of the endings made sense – all of them are cleverly dubious. All of them are cleverly ambiguous, and none of them… well… just read and make up your own mind. But, and it's a big but, try to remember that what you have to do is unlearn what you have been taught. Break on through to the other side, so to speak, the other side of the socialisation process. Not easy to try and de-programme your brain, especially if it has been going on since you were born; and then to re-boot? It could almost drive you to the point of madness.

Smash the pottery – but be warned, when you try to glue it back together, some of the pieces don't fit, won't fit, but the pot is still a pot that works like a pot. Oh, and follow what the giant egg said. When I use a word, it means just what I choose it to mean, neither more nor less.

Everything you read in this book is true: absolutely true. Just remember that as you find the edges of your mind beginning to fray, trust your own feelings and thoughts.

The main problem is where does truth lie in comparison to fiction? When is everything that we see – everything that we know? Philosophically we could be here forever, so I'm not even going to start down that route. And when do we need to take a leap of faith? I will let you 'the reader' decide that one. All I intend to do is tell it as it was, not to try and be anything, do anything, or have a closed mind. The whole thing became an obsession, nearly drove me out of mine – but it's done now, and here it is.

When first I started on this, a friend said, with a groan, "Man you can't believe he did that, surely. I mean it's almost too simple and yet?"

"And yet what?" I asked.

"Well it's too weird…"

"Oh," I replied, "you want me to have reverence, be in awe? No, be overawed? Like all the rest. You believe the hype and misdirection, be one of the audience slaves. Morrison knew what he was doing and he also understood human beings and their need to have something else, a purpose in life. That's what made him different: he'd recognised that one simple human trait. He wasn't a god but he also wasn't your run of the mill manager fodder pop star. Engulfing people with their own needs and yet understanding their weakness was his intellectual gift. Like a giant magic mirror, he reflected back what people wanted to see. By chance or by choice he used it, that talent, and made The Doors out of it. Can't you see that was all part of his plan? He made allowances for our adulation, reaction, religion, took things to the edge, just to see how far they, or he, or you, or me, would go." I was getting angry – pissed actually. "He knew eventually, knew that he was out there on his own, out in the darkness, and knew they would lock him up and," I paused, "he knew that even Jesus got nailed to a cross."

My friend was shaking his head.

"So don't you think he worked you too?" he asked.

I reflected, "Yeah you're probably right. But," I paused, an 'erm' in my mind, "I think I saw where he was coming from when we spoke. If I'd been eighteen or younger he'd have swamped me." I waited for a reaction. "And the worse part is, he began to realise that he had fooled himself too."

15

My friend was listening intently and I, to my shame and self-loathing, said something cruel and unnecessary.

"You're a teacher, right?"

My friend nodded.

"Why did you become a teacher?"

The silence spoke volumes.

"Was it because you thought you'd make a difference? I mean it was for the money, right, or the ridicule, surely not?" I was really punching now. "So what are you, an evangelist? Or just a masochist that gets their kicks out of being sworn at? You know that all the propaganda you were given at college is a crock of shit."

Silence again.

I stuck the knife in. "Look, how long's it taken you to get to the truth? And on a wet February morning I bet you jump out of bed in the dark and rush to be at the chalk-face. A miner, searching for the odd nugget of understanding in the walls of rock and crap that are facing you. Once in a while you hit a rich seam, but be honest, not that often." I knew I'd gone too far but I sort of kept pushing. "It's like politics, everyone ends in failure at the end, failure and rejection. No matter how great you are, you always get rejected, so you'd better get used to it in teaching too. This ain't *Goodbye, Mr. Chips*, that's a story."

My friend was punching back, "What about JFK?" he asked. "He never lost his place in the public affection." He looked triumphant.

"Yeah agreed," I replied, "but he was shot before his whole womanising, war-mongering, Vietnam debacle was totally discovered. His time would have come. There'd have been a Monica, what's her name?" I paused and grinned, "Lewinsky in The White House, hell, there probably already was. He was supposed to have been doing Norma-Jean." I pouted a breathy line of 'happy birthday Mr. President' in a poor impression of Marilyn. "But he was like Morrison, gave the people what they wanted and he didn't sweat like Nixon did. Well, not in front of a TV camera at least; mind you, I bet he worked up a sweat at other times, pounding away. His sore old back," I laughed. "At least FDR had the good grace to sit in his wheelchair, Kennedy jacked up on painkillers so people didn't see him in public in one. Man he knew how to work those crowds. I mean wheelchairs equal weakness, don't they?"

My friend's silence was filled with the inner thoughts of how he hated his job. I knew that, it was written on his face. Don't get me wrong, he was great teacher. He taught with verve and flair and he got results – first class results. But he knew I had struck a raw nerve. I knew I had too and I kicked myself for my arrogance. It was that self-destructive streak which rose in me from time to time. Don't get me wrong, I was just the same with myself. At times I thought I was the complete nihilist and at times like these I dragged others into the maelstrom of my confusion and self-doubt. That was probably why I didn't have that many friends. I'm not the sort of person that you invite along to a party, just in case I drink too much and then launch.

That is my gift, the ability to turn everything I touch into crap. In relationships I was superb at it, did everything wrong and never really got the chance to say sorry, and when I did it was always too little, too late. And the worst part? You just can't stop yourself.

"Now how do you feel?" I asked, twisting the knife. "Disappointed, washed out, maligned and accused of every social ill and failure? I mean it's your fault, right? I mean you're a teacher? Nobody told you about that one, did they?"

His head was nodding. "It's all shitty."

"Who warned you that whatever you did it wouldn't be good enough?" I stabbed again.

"Ok, Ok, I get the message," he laughed. He hands were up in mock surrender. "But it's hard to admit it man," he paused, "really hard."

"Hey, I know," I apologised, "but it'll kill you in the end, make you crazy. You got to get out."

"I'm fine and it's what I do," he replied smiling. "Like you with the books."

"Well you don't see me taking pills to go to sleep cos I'm so stressed out," I manoeuvred myself toward sympathy.

"I just take 'em now and again, just to unwind," he defensively replied.

"Look, nobody came to save Jesus either. They just let the man die and wailed a lot. Human beings, damn human beings."

"Hey, I'm on your side, remember?" was his terse reply.

I didn't hear. "Those that tried to follow often failed, because they had that one thing he didn't have – fear. Most people fear loss: loss of money, loss of status, loss of property, loss of influence, loss of love. Just look at us," I paused again, "look at us."

He smiled back broadly. "Bought and sold baby, bought and sold," he laughed.

His voice had a mocking lilt but underneath I could feel that, like me, my friend mourned the whole essence of his youth, which had been sucked out of him. Sucked out of him by a system which programmed him to faux rebellion and then enforced conformity. The power came from economic necessity.

My voice rose in tempo and pitch, "Morrison simply didn't care, in fact he was scornful of those that did fear. He may have been a complete sociopath, an anarchist that really was an anarchist, instead of some university type playing on the political margins. You know the types, all middle-class and advantaged purporting to be a university communist; hell, we went there with them. Only they were supported by a rich mummy and daddy while they played at finding their own way. We, on the other hand, had all the crap jobs that we could find to support us. What was his dad, an admiral? I bet they didn't sit around in the cold on a winter night looking for another shilling for the meter. And those rebellious girls we knew? Most of them ended up marrying a stockbroker and playing the system. Playing the system? The system played them, just like it played us – just like it played Morrison. It's all shitty."

My friend remained silent and let me ramble. He was grinning, it was his turn to.

"And once they had too much to lose, they shut up, clammed up. Then the years pass and the rebellion too. Morrison is clever, real clever; we're not dealing with some dullard here. This isn't an Elvis was abducted by aliens story. I'm not a crazy fan on the edge of my own reason either. True, I admired the guy, liked his mayhem; good god, we lived it." I could sense myself ranting and tried to check my mouth. "This is how I think it could have been done, or how it was done."

My friend was nodding. But the nod was like someone who didn't really believe what was being said; a knowing nod full of irony and insight.

"How, if I had been him, I would have done it – got away with it. You know? Closed the doors behind me – like he did."

"What about the note?" my friend asked.

"What do you mean?"

"You know perfectly well what I mean."

"Oh yeah – well that's not going anywhere."

"But they'll want to do tests on the paper, or worse, they'll say you stole it."

"What, that I was the one who broke into Pamela's place after she died?"

"Yep."

"Or I was the one that shot the fatal heroin into her arm?"

"Yep."

"Listen," I was livid now, "they can say what they like, but in 1974 most of the world had forgotten The Doors and certainly Pamela Courson; her time was over. There were new gods on the horizon. Sugerman started the cult like St. Paul. Hell, they all need a St. Paul to get the thing underway; it's all about the marketing. Every generation seems to need a personal Jesus, someone who hears the prayers, someone who really cares."

"Is that what you are then? What you want to be? What you deserve to be?" My friend was scornful. "The personal preacher of our generation? Ron the Baptist?"

He was mocking and doing an excellent job of it. I was on the back foot now. It was my turn to be riddled with self-doubt and self-loathing.

"Nope," I replied indignantly, "I just want to get to the truth."

"What if you can't handle the truth."

I was taken aback, I hadn't considered that option. "Listen," I replied, "the truth has to be out there. We deserve the truth?"

"But why?" he taunted. "That's a luxury we can't afford. Surely the truth is nothing more than we are told. And they only tell us what they want us to believe. Truth is subjective."

"Well we just do. We deserve the truth, the whole truth."

"And nothing but the truth?" he mocked by completing the phrase. "Why, because we bought a few records from the marketing pitch around a bunch of lads from Los Angeles? That's a crock man, a pure crock. Just think about it. The public wants what the public gets. How few people control the money? The power?"

Now it was my turn to nod and listen as he ventured into his pet subject: politics.

"You know as well as I do that's why we could have stayed at uni until Hell froze over, we wouldn't have stood a chance; that was never enough. Oh, there are people out there who think they have been really successful, but have they? Have they really? It's all relative man, all relative. It's that glass ceiling and about never being quite good enough. We're the dangerous types, you see."

I knew what he was saying made sense, but it was hard to swallow. "Very dangerous being a teacher, very subversive." I was attempting to agree but also edge away from the bitterness which I knew would follow.

"We," he paused and realised he was warbling, "we are the kids from the wrong side of the tracks who don't get fooled. We ain't nice but we ain't stupid neither. Yeah we got a better life, but hey, as high as we are, or think we are, they always manage to look down on us. We could have become the President and they'd still look down on us. Unless you're really purty," he drooled the word, "and then maybe, after they looked up your skirt, you get in amongst them while they use you."

He paused again, almost knowing what I was thinking. His eyes were shining bright; he was far from defeated.

"Marilyn Monroe, Norma Jean Baker, it don't matter what you're called, as long as you fuck," he laughed, "let yourself get

20

screwed." He looked right into my eyes as he spoke. "The truth is simple, it ain't real, it's a power thing; that's my truth and it ain't pleasant."

"Is that what you teach those kids?" I was laughing and wagging an admonishing finger into his face.

"I tell them the truth," he smirked.

"Your truth?"

"Is there any other kind?"

"Well I'll handle the truth and I am going to publish it." I was adamant I was right.

"What if some readers can't though?"

"They will, they have to," I gasped. "Look, all they have to do is think the whole thing through like it was a crime."

"Yeah, the same fickle people who..." He was struggling for words.

"Read books?" I offered.

"No," he snapped, "run for cover. Hell, lots of people are going to want your blood when you put this out there. They'll say you're crazy. Say you're a liar, a fake."

"So?" I was almost laughing. "They said Morrison was barking. And," I added, as if to add gravitas, "they said the same of Jesus too."

"Well, you ain't either of them," he laughed back. "So how are you going to handle your truth?" He smiled and a wink came into his eye, as he threw the, 'your,' back at me.

"You have to get inside the man's mind," I considered, "think like him and see it from the perspective of the time, his time, 1971. The guy was dangerously intelligent; perhaps, as some have said, insane. You know what he said?"

My friend was nodding, because he knew exactly what I was thinking. I had no reason to repeat it, yet again, but I did anyway, I said it anyway.

'I play a little game, it's called let's crawl back inside my brain. The game is called – let's go insane.'

Three

If six were nine...

So where do I start? Everybody knows about The Doors, everyone in the music industry, or any music lover, and even the young kids have heard the music. Love it or hate it, or just be indifferent to it. It doesn't matter. 'Light my Fire' still gets played on the radio, even today; it's a classic, like 'Stairway to Heaven', 'Sunshine of Your Love', 'Smoke on the Water' or 'Hotel California'. That Bach-like start from Manzarek, his, 'Simple spiral of fifths ...' and then bam, Densmore and Krieger are in; and then Jim's molasses voice hits you.

Everyone knows about Morrison, the mythological figure and there are several theories about how he died, when he died, and who saw what – so I guess I start to unpick it there.

* * *

The official story is–

God's gonna cut you down...

That Jim Morrison died in the bath. Heart failure because of a weak heart, after years of debauchery and excessive drinking which finally took him. Died while Pamela Courson was asleep, after a night of drinking and possible drug taking. Not much new there then. The only account comes from Pamela herself and she's dead, but that's another story.

So here it is: during the day, the 2ⁿᵈ July, Jim hangs out with an old friend, Alan Ronay. Time is taken to sort a telegram, which is sent to the United States, to New York, Simon and Schuster, publishers, and then the hook up with his old buddy takes place about lunchtime and they spend the afternoon together. Ronay had been a buddy at film school, UCLA and they had a few beers and talked. Just how many beers we will never know. But not enough to send Mr. Mojo Risin into a coma. Maybe they walked, maybe they just sat in a bar. Maybe they sat in the sun and watched the world go by during that day in the Place des Vosges. According to Ronay, Morrison had several hiccupping fits, he looked unwell, and when he carried logs up to the Beautreillis apartment, he was wheezing.

Now the unanswered questions. Was Mr. Mojo Risin an actor? Did he know what he was doing? Why was Morrison carrying logs if he felt unwell? So unwell he collapsed on the stairs? Would you? If this is added to the fact that in early July 1971, Paris was in the grip of an abnormally hot weather spell, it makes even less sense. The notion of roaring log fires being needed to sustain those inside from the ravages of the storm is nonsense. But he may have had a fever and so needed the warmth to break it? Again nonsense.

Then Ronay leaves – the time is uncertain, he says in his police statement 6pm. Is Pam there? Or does she return later? Again we have no idea.

Pam initially says (in her police statement) that she and Morrison went out for a meal. She then corrects herself and says he went out and ate alone. Maybe an investigation would prove that she wasn't there at that time – once the police found the restaurant – and she feared a thorough police investigation? He was a famous rock star after all.

Or did she eat at all? Sometimes she fasted for a day or two to keep her wispy figure; or did they just not eat together, did Pam eat at the flat? If so, why? Did they fight? Was Pam there then, or had she been away visiting the Count? The other man in the fight for her affections – Morrison's rival; the drug dealer to the stars; the man who openly stated he had supplied the smack that killed Janis Joplin.

At 11pm Pam and Jim go to the cinema. Get back at about 1am, Pam does the dishes, and they play home movies and listen to music. Then it dawned on me – who does dishes at 1am? And what dishes exactly? Jim ate out. So were these dishes from the morning? They had to be because Jim was out with Ronay prior to that evening so they were not lunchtime dishes. Or maybe Pam had not been there for a while and Morrison had just left the dishes in the sink. Pam comes home and there are the dishes that need doing. But who does dishes at 1am?

I know this might seem strange but these little details are the ones which allow conjecture. Even gods don't leave dishes on a hot day – do they? They stink and attract flies.

They go to bed. They don't have sex and that I can believe as Morrison had his drink problem which gives a special impetus to impotence. Then about an hour later Jim is wheezing and gurgling. Jim is woken up and then gets up and walks around the bedroom. On feeling 'strange' he decides to take a bath. Then he feels sick and vomits; by now Pam is holding the orange bowl. It may be nothing but orange seemed to be the colour of the moment for Jim. His 'Orange County Suite' and now his orange bowl. Is this some funny little twist in the tale, like the elaboration of a poor liar? Jim liked to play tricks on people – it amused him. He was a merry prankster, if not an honourable member of that gang.

Jim vomits again, this time there is blood in the bowl. Pam says she wants to call a doctor – Jim refuses. He tells her to go back to bed as he is feeling better and she does so and promptly passes out. It's now about 4am or 5am.

Now we go to the Manzarek book account (*Light my Fire*) where he claims, as told to him by Pam some months later, that Morrison's last words were, "Pam, are you still there?" If Pam heard this then she hadn't passed out, or fallen asleep immediately as she claimed in her police statements. That too could not be both, someone somewhere was adding a few extras, perhaps for

24

plot exposition. Either she was awake and waiting or she was asleep.

Then suddenly she's awake. Now this bit I believe because I've done this myself. Suddenly she wakes and realises Jim is not there, so she goes to the bathroom. Finds Morrison and tries to get him out of the bath. He's too heavy. She panics and phones Ronay.

The confusion is worse here. Ronay says he phoned the emergency services at 8.30am, but the fire service record log says 9.21 am. I know which one I think is the more accurate.

When the firemen arrive they report the woman as being dressed in a gown which is very wet. So did she get dressed to get Jim out of the bath? Alain Raisson was the first official to write a report and he clearly states that Pam's dressing gown was wet and on the floor. So unless she was naked she had changed? Dressed?

Then there is Alan Ronay's statement given to the police. He says he was woken by a phone call from Pam at 8.30am saying Jim was unconscious. Ronay then says he got up and immediately went to rue Beautreillis; did he phone first? But he also states quite clearly that he met the firemen in the street and asked them what was going on. If he had phoned them, why would he ask? Surely he'd know? Once again the accounts and the recall clash. If Pam could not speak French, and was in a state of crying panic and Ronay didn't call the emergency services, who did? Ronay then goes on to say, in his official statement, he did not wish to see the body. Even though it was already out of the bath and on the bed. Was it covered? Was the face?

The problem I had with the Ronay statements is that they conflict. In one he says he called the emergency services, in another he says they were already there. Something wasn't right here. Usually in an investigation this could be put down to translation difficulties. But Ronay, Ronay understood the nuances of this language very well indeed – just as any native would. Then there is the issue of his viewing the corpse.

He claimed Morrison's body was on the bed when he arrived. Was he distressed, too distressed? Perhaps what he saw was a corpse, on a bed, already covered over with a sheet? And then finally the corpse is not taken away to an undertakers it is kept in the flat. The same dull flat which needed to be heated with logs, though copious amounts of dry ice were delivered to the flat that weekend to keep the body from decomposing before the coffin arrived on the Monday.

Then comes the crazy romantic notion that Pamela Courson spent the night sleeping next to Morrison's corpse. That I would suggest is highly unlikely. Much more likely would be that Pam went with Ronay and his girlfriend Agnes Varda to their apartment in the rue Daguerre.

The question then is why. Why not have the body removed to a mortuary, a refrigerated cool area? Why not? Perhaps there was a fear of identification? The fewer people who saw the body, the less chance of recognition? Maybe the police surgeons would have performed an autopsy and the real facts surrounding the death would then be known. Drugs? Or was this simply to make sure that Morrison was not identified and a dignified funeral could therefore take place? Not the fiasco that accompanied the death of Brian Jones of The Rolling Stones. That sounds plausible. Or was it just to hide some drug involvement – that sounds plausible too. Or was it contrived to hide, as I suspected… something else.

* * *

The nightclub story is –

Rollin' and tumblin'…

It's hot, it's July 1971 and Jim Morrison is bored; the muse of writing has left him and he is seeking the limelight of notoriety in the Paris Rock and Roll Circus. A hip, if rather seedy club in Paris, a nightclub where those, 'on the scene' hang out. He needs to be noticed and the owners will later claim that Morrison was a regular visitor to the nightclub; that he came there principally to score horse (heroin) for his long time lover Pamela Courson.

Already there is a considerable conflict in that one statement alone. Morrison hated Pam taking heroin and that is verified by Tony Funches, his bodyguard, and Danny Sugerman, his number one fan. In fact, it might be reasonable to assume that Jim Morrison only really enjoyed the one drug – alcohol. As Pam often said, that was his favourite. He didn't mind cocaine or an assortment of pills and potions some people advocated, but heroin was a no go.

Paris was awash with it in the summer of 1971. The city had become the central trading point for the white stuff and the cut percentage on the street was unusually pure – somewhere in the region of 86% pure.

Back in Los Angeles, Morrison had taken Danny Sugerman to meet Tim Hardin, the writer of, 'If I were a Carpenter', and the classic Rod Stewart hit, 'Reason to Believe'. Why? To prove to the young and impressionable Danny that horse kills. Jim Morrison would not have bought heroin for Pam, that much is certain. He may have taken it by mistake but he certainly wasn't scoring it.

Danny Sugerman gives a detailed account of the Tim Hardin encounter in his seminal work *Wonderland Avenue*. He tells of how Hardin literally shit his pants before them and then tried to obtain money from Morrison for more horse. Morrison would not have scored heroin for Pam and besides, he had no need to, Count Jean de Breteuil was a dealer to the stars and he was also Pam's significant other. She had left LA and flown into Paris with the biggest smack dealer in town, why would she send Jim out to score? That doesn't make any sense at all. But it fuelled the legend of Jim Morrison and that grew bigger than the man himself.

Pam liked to be on the edge as much as Morrison did. She was no shrinking violet and she would have been more than able to score her own substances. In fact, despite being much younger than The Doors, it was she who had obtained some opium and introduced it to them. The small demure Pamela Courson was in reality a human firecracker. Even Morrison said she was the cat to his mouse. Perhaps he liked that, perhaps the fact that she simply did not do what Jim wanted was the kind of response he needed. For years men had wanted to be Morrison and girls wanted him between their legs. Pamela's great power was that she could walk away and she had done; she had walked away to Paris; and Jim, like an obedient puppy, had followed her. Whatever the hold was, it was strong, extremely strong. I'm going to be a little tentative here and plump for that old chestnut of a reason: love. I strongly believe that Morrison may well have slept with other women, may well have betrayed Pam's trust, but he also loved her. Together they had starved in Los Angeles, often walking back at night from The Doors gigs because Jim had spent his share on booze. When the first real pay cheque had come in, it was Pam with whom he had shared the Chinese feast purchased on the profits. Every other girl lusted after Morrison the idol, the sex god, the front of house pathfinder. Pam, however, got to see all the weaknesses, all the insecurity. She also got to grow up alongside him and between 1966 and 1971 those changes could be seen. If you don't believe me, look at the photographs; she starts as a plain kid and ends as a painted lady. Jim had always joked with her that eventually she would end her life as a prostitute. He never qualified the statement, so we are unsure of his definition. It could have been a simple one, in as much as selling sex for security could be what he was referring to. Perhaps he saw a marriage of convenience as nothing more than that, prostitution? Perhaps he was just trying to upset Pam? Either way, he did. That must have hurt and perhaps Pam had finally taken enough punches. Morrison was, after all said and done, a literate drunk with a cruel streak a mile wide when he chose to use his acid tongue.

On the 25th April 1974 Pamela died. Supposedly a bloated shadow of her former self: a fat club gold star member. A heroin addict? Not according to the autopsy report, though heroin did kill her. Maybe she just committed suicide, a result of guilt, loss, or the sheer terror of continuing into the unknown alone. They were together for far too long for the good behaviour to last, however good an actor Morrison might have been. They knew things about the other which were never recorded, things only they could know – they were just a young couple.

Here is the acid test: if you had to identify your partner's corpse without a head, hands or feet, could you? I don't mean do you think you ought to be able to, I mean could you? Here comes your homework. Think about them now; no time to check in advance, you just have memory – can you remember any really conclusive marks? Check them out later, you might be surprised at what you missed, I was.

So the next part of the story is that Morrison takes heroin, snorts it to be precise, and in the club no less – hence the blood clot in his nose after death; then he collapses in the ladies' toilet. The owners panic when they know who is in the cubicle, so they take the body out through the kitchen of an adjacent property and take him home. They know where he lives?

They strip the body and draw a hot bath and plonk the body in the water. In the morning the water is still lukewarm – when Pam gets back and the fire service arrive?

Or was Pam there and she suggested the bath?

A nice neat simple story of a superstar overindulging and then coming a cropper. Death in the ladies' lavatory of some Paris nightclub... But where exactly was Pam? Not to mention the risky strategy of having the body of an American in the back of your van. Not only a body, but a heroin death to boot. Was she out of town? If she was, why was Morrison scoring? Why would she come home at either 2am or 8am?

Morrison lived on the third floor, so the body had to be lifted through the courtyard, which has many windows facing onto it, up the flights of stairs past other occupants and into the flat. How did these men know that Pam was not there? How did they know that Ronay was not there? He'd sacked in the spare room for a while. To me this seems rather risky, ill conceived and very tenuous. I get the mental image of two burly bouncers tiptoeing and a little old lady opening her door to put out the cat, while they casually explain the man is just dead. It's just the sort of average Friday happening in Paris.

The whole story makes no sense at all, unless the man who died in the club was not Morrison. But could there be two men who looked like he did? Perhaps in reality he had become a bloated shadow and not the Morrison everyone else saw front of stage, the one so easily recognised. The key lies in what he was wearing and that no one has even bothered to record. I say that because, unlike Pam and her Themis days, he cared very little beyond his stage outfits. In fact, he would wear some clothes until they became unbearable and Pam would sneakily destroy or launder them. He would then promptly do the same with his next outfit.

The firemen who entered the flat the following morning make no mention of clothes, though they do record a wet robe on the floor. So once again I get this image of Morrison's bouncers neatly folding his clothes over the back of a dressing table chair. Again and again I found this story just too ridiculous to stand alone, unless it is part of a wider jigsaw – yet to be completed.

Perhaps there was someone who looked like Morrison in those toilets. Perhaps the person was a fan, a fan who modelled himself on Morrison, that could have been possible. After all, is that so far fetched? These days it seems quite common. Did Morrison have a stalker, an impersonator or a crazy bunny boiler who had found out where he lived? Or more likely an opportunity was planned, planned to divert, to confuse and misdirect. Get people looking the wrong way and you can have the world, and have it now.

Or maybe Morrison never went to that nightclub at all.

* * *

The accident story is -

When you've got a good friend...

The official story is partially correct, if this account is to be believed, but bits have been added.

Morrison and Pam returned home at about 1am. Somehow Morrison discovered the heroin stash that belonged to Pam. Pam may well have told him it was cocaine and so together they took some before going to bed. Morrison may well have liked the idea of cocaine as a stimulant, but Pam clearly states that they did not have sex on that night. Well actually that isn't quite true, she says they didn't have sexual intercourse – they could have indulged in some sexual activity and then Morrison, having taken heroin as opposed to cocaine, became too lethargic to continue. What was desired of the cocaine, by Jim, did not come to pass; perhaps Jim's impotence kicked in yet again? That often happens with drunks, but maybe this time Pam, who had been used to it in the past, was more attune because of the heroin intake? That, of course, we will never know. But more importantly, why would Pam lie? Why – because she knew how Morrison felt about heroin. She was there at the time of Tim Hardin.

Jim had, according to Ronay, been feeling tired and piqued all day, so cocaine would be a nice pick me up; a nice way to end the day. Morrison had tried the stuff and knew what to expect. The only real variation here would be that Morrison waking in the night was him overdosing on heroin. He could otherwise have slipped into a coma; and the bath? That was there to revive him, or attempt to. The blood clot in the nose could also be explained by the snorting.

The immediate cure would have been a cold bath to lower his temperature. Standard procedure in the case of overdoses on heroin. It lowers the blood pressure and suppresses the overheat. Did Pam or Morrison suggest that?

Now – here comes the problem: in the morning the water would have been cold.

All the reports clearly state that the water was warm.

Like I said to my friend, I needed to get some answers, get inside the situation and work the problem. When I proposed my little experiment he thought I was a basket case, but being scientific I had a go at finding out what warm was. Warm enough to feel that the water was not cold and the body was also warm; so warm in fact that artificial respiration was attempted on the bedroom floor at 9.25am?

So we go to 1971. There were fewer plastic baths in those

times, not like there are now; cast iron covered in enamel was the norm and, furthermore, that bath was free standing, by that I mean not against a wall. The water was thirty-five centimetres deep (as the police report states) as measured by the fire department and the night was a warm one on July 2nd.

In order to get the experiment right I went back to the police report of Jacques Manchez. He said the body was in the bath, naked, and the bath was, 'Full of water,' Jim's right arm was resting on the edge of the bath and the head was above water.

Wow ! So the Oliver Stone image of Jim, head back, defiant, was not true, he was sort of slumped against the right side. Manchez calls the water 'lukewarm' and that is neither tepid nor just warm, that is lukewarm. So I reasoned the following: they measured the depth of water after the body was removed; that gives us thirty-five centimetres of pinkish fluid. The depth would have been greater with Morrison's bulk in it. I had to try and work out whether the water would keep the body warmer, or the warmth of the body keep the water warm. Scientifically, the body would not have heated the water enough to make it lukewarm. Pamela claims they got up at around 3.30am and Jim wanted to take a bath; then he was sick three times. I settled for a start time of 4.10am.

Pam goes back to bed – falls asleep. The firemen arrive at 9.24am making the gap five hours and fourteen minutes. I started with thirty-five centimetres of water which I could barely sit in and submerged up to the neck. I stayed for a while, once I couldn't stand it anymore I got out – lobster pink -and waited. That was the longest five hours and fourteen minutes of my life. Oh and I should mention, I did the experiment in August in England and the daytime temperature was twenty two degrees.

I can hear the laughter coming from the readers of this book right now. Crazy, that's what I hear being said, a crazy fan who can't accept the obvious. I can also imagine the number of baths that will be experimented upon after my scribbling. Lukewarm – what exactly is lukewarm?

Alcohol and heroin don't mix and in someone like Morrison, who was almost pickled, it could have induced a seizure. Heart failure could have been caused, but why the focus on respiration? Was Morrison asthmatic? Is that how he avoided the draft? Is that why in Florida he never took part in sports, or on the holiday island sojourn, during the trial, he became bored, eventually flying home to LA?

Perhaps Clara Morrison had used the bath remedy on Jim as a boy. It was certainly one of the remedies my mother attempted on me when I had serious bronchitis. A hot bath to clear the lungs and open up the airways. Why, I'll never know, because it actually made me feel worse. Funny though, Clara Morrison and my mother were roughly the same age. Maybe Morrison resorted to the things he knew when the chips were down? Sometimes that's what we all do – run for home. The simple mammalian instinct?

Then there was the incident which Sugerman recalls. February 1971, Pamela is off to Paris to find them a place to live, and Jim goes on an absolute bender. Sugerman states that, Morrison knew why Pamela was in Paris – that Pamela had not run off with the Count but was looking for a place for them as a couple. A place where Jim could write, get away from the image which was haunting him and be with her. Danny Sugerman simply states: he craved anonymity. That may or may not be true, because Danny Sugerman is dead and he is saying nothing.

But the issue of the blood from the nose and the shortness of breath might be explained by an incident which Sugerman recalls, an incident which occurred when Pam had already gone.

At the Chateau Marmont Hotel, Jim fell from a second floor window ledge. Jim hated doctors, but this time he supposedly went because of the pain. The doctor apparently told him he had punctured his left lung.

This is where it gets hard for me to believe. A punctured lung, punctured by a rib I suppose? Jim falls so badly that he breaks a rib that seriously and doctors do nothing? That doesn't make sense either. Sugerman then says Jim discussed with him the fact that he was like a cat with nine lives and that they had all been used up. That he was brittle and it was like a sign. This is all nicely romantic, but is it true?

33

There were too many holes in the story for my liking and the more I looked, the more I found. The police investigation was a shambles – a total shambles. Perhaps once the body had been identified the police were aware of just who was in the bath. Perhaps there were some Doors fans among them. Unlikely as this seems, it could be a possibility.

Perhaps the police just didn't want the scandal of heroin-laced Paris to become international news – whatever the reason, the investigation looks to me, as an external observer, like it took place in 1871 not 1971. The only problem then is that I am writing this forty years after the event and everything has changed. The places, the gravesite and all his haunts have altered; even the bar across the street from his Paris apartment has changed hands. Forty years ago we didn't even have a phone in our house let alone a mobile. Phone calls were made from a public phone box at the end of the street. I had to keep making allowances.

* * *

The junkie story is -

White Rabbit...

Morrison was a secret junkie. A man scared of needles was a junkie? Ah, but he snorted the stuff, I can hear my critics say; smoked it, hence the respiration problems, the coughing and the hiccups and the blood clot in his nose. What about the punctured lung? Yep, he snorted pounds of horse up his nostrils and the result was absolutely no clue, no facial rebuild after his nose collapsed. Morrison, I would suggest, wasn't high most of the time, as people have mythologised, he was simply drunk. That would account for the rapid weight gain and the bloated appearance, but he was only twenty seven.

When we look at the time span, he could have been drinking seriously since he was fourteen. At that age the damage would have been huge. That was what he had been involved in since his teens? In Tallahassee he had a run-in with the law, fuelled by alcohol. In the counter-culture of California he had played with LSD but both Pam and he had moved on to other kicks. She was renowned for bad trips, involving blood. Being a child of those times, I know exactly what she went through and it is frightening. Morrison just got bored, so they went down their own pathways – hers was opiates, it was she who supplied opium for the band to try, and Jim went back to booze.

So how do I get to my conclusions?

Music – Morrison knew nothing of music. When first he heard Robby Krieger playing bottleneck he wanted it on every song. Blues men had been using bottlenecks since Muddy Waters invented electricity. Morrison, however, listened to crooners, and in particular Frank Sinatra. Were these the recordings of his parents and in particular his mother, Clara? Paul Rothchild was taken aback when they first started work together on *The Doors*, the first album, because Jim recognised the type of microphone Sinatra used. When Jim was at home with his mother, did he listen with her while the younger siblings were in bed? As the eldest was he 'The little man around the house' when his father was stationed away? That makes sense, his knowledge of music being based on his parent's tastes.

Morrison was not musically hip. That came from Krieger with his blues and Densmore with his understanding of alternative rhythms. Surely John Densmore must be one of the most underrated drummers of his time, but he experimented. That was his gift to the band and it worked. Alan Wilson of Canned Heat was a friend of his and as The Doors grew in popularity they worked with the Byrds, Jefferson Airplane, and Crosby Stills and Nash lived just up the road in Laurel Canyon.

Ray Manzarek was classically trained and he was the backbone; Morrison knew words, that was his forte. He may have been hip with film but poetry and the 'beats' enthralled him. Ginsberg and Ferlingetti were residents of Venice Beach and Morrison saw himself as one of them. Just look at his lyrics – which openly steal from these poets. Kerouac and the character of Dean Moriarty, to whom Morrison bears a striking resemblance in his stage persona, those were hip to Morrison. His film making is obsessed with the road; the hitchhiker was a personal moniker. The road features in many songs – the road is America.

Clothes – those were a functional object, not an adornment. Pam liked the hip clothing, Jim just wore his armour, in this case the Lizard King persona. As a youngster in Clearwater he had often bought clothes from the five and dime to save money for books. John Densmore remarked that when he first met Jim he wondered if he owned any shoes, as he seemed to go barefoot a lot. At the time he probably didn't.

Just look at the pictures, each period is classified by what he was wearing. A close look at the tapes of the Ed Sullivan show highlights the grubbiness of Morrison's shirt. It's that simple to see it. Dirty and unkempt, he still managed to exude sex appeal through the television set.

Steve Harris, Vice President of Elecktra Records, openly stated in interview: if this kid can sing the phone book on key – we're all gonna be very very wealthy. And he could and that was precisely what happened.

Morrison was more dangerous to the youth of America than Mick Jagger and prettier than Elvis Presley – they couldn't fail.

But the dichotomy was always that Jim saw himself as a philosopher poet, an inheritor of the torch of Blake and Nietzsche and rock music was just a vehicle to reach a large audience.

Morrison's success was his undoing, in as much as in Venice he starved and existed on what people, mainly girls, fed him, but he was highly creative. He took drugs when available; he drank when available and slept on a friend's rooftop under the stars. It was the perfect place for the burgeoning poet. When he bumped into Ray Manzarek on the beach, he was drifting, writing and drifting. He had already lost fifty pounds due to his lack of money, and the lean mean Morrison was ready.

Morrison had the looks, Manzarek, or Dorothy Fujikawa, to be more precise, had the brains, and the result? They made lots of money. Something Morrison became both guilty and resentful about. He once remarked that it, 'all happened after Robby wrote that damn song.' The title: 'Light my Fire.'

Tony Funches, his bodyguard at the time, has given many interviews on the state of inebriation he and Morrison found themselves in on more than one occasion: The legendary drinking sessions in Barney's Beanery, resulting in them being thrown out on to the street bodily. The white rock star and the black bodyguard side by side in the gutter. But there was never any whiff of heroin.

In fact, Morrison tried other drugs and played with hallucinogenics, but his real love was alcohol. Everyone who knew The Doors knew it was booze. That was the elephant in the room.

All the records of his youth show that he drank to excess from an early age. Drank to the point where he passed out, and that usually requires one of two things: either excessive amounts of alcohol, or an allergic reaction which causes the drinker to become comatose.

So much for the junkie theory.

＊ ＊ ＊

The suicide story is –

Death is not the end …

This is the one that relies on some of Jim's notebooks and accounts which come from The Doors themselves, and the recollections of Danny Sugerman. Jim was, or could have been, a depressive, and the recollection of the creation of the song 'People are Strange' is a perfect example.

An evening and Morrison has had enough and he Densmore and Krieger spend some time together. Spending time together meant the drummer and the guitarist talking him down off the ceiling, or hilltop on Mulholland Drive to be precise. Memory is a strange thing, but both are adamant that Morrison was suicidal and they feared he might do something foolish, in this case self harm. This was not the first and it wouldn't be the last time. Which leads us to the question of manic depression. Was he one?

Some said Hendrix was, and he even wrote a song about the subject. In 1971 it wasn't discussed like it is today. Today we have a much more open and frank society – in 1971 they put you in a loony bin.

So they talk, cajole and generally keep Morrison entertained until his wave of depression passes and then out comes the song. As quickly as it starts, so it passes.

In my home town they had two great big asylums. There must have been many people who experienced the 'treatment', including electro shock therapy; many of whom might have been manic depressives. As children we were told to keep away, well away. Those institutions have now been converted into flats and the grounds sold off as building land. Nice little posh suburbs within suburbs. The tall fences topped with barbed wire have been torn down and the concrete posts bulldozed away. Strange how the world changes in the space of forty years. Only this was about twenty five as I remember. It sort of happened while I was away from the town and having a life; and the saddest part was the old graveyard.

There are stones there which mark a life less pleasant than any of us could ever imagine. I went there sometimes and stood, I don't really know why but I did. Perhaps I'd been lucky – my demons were all on the outside and the grass there was pretty green.

There were no flowers and no fancy marble headpieces and no fanciful quotes. They were the forgotten ones; grey, twisted, cracked and cheap, forgotten names like the forgotten people they represented. Sometimes it does us good to look at the truth, however difficult that may be. Call me weird if you like, but a cemetery says so much about everything that makes us human.

If you've never read *One Flew Over the Cuckoo's Nest*, get a copy now. You get to understand what Ken Kesey was trying to say. Like Kesey said, he was too young to be a beatnik and too old to be a hippy. But he did take part in experiments with hallucinogenic drugs whilst working at Menlo Park Veterans' Hospital. He seemed to like to talk to the patients there, many of whom he claimed were not insane, but just unconventional.

His book came out in 1962 and was an immediate success;

and the result: he met Neal Cassady (the man upon whom Kerouac's Dean Moriarty is based) who, in turn, introduced him to Kerouac and Ginsberg. Is it possible that Morrison knew about the book and about Kesey? They were both based in California after all. There are other similarities too. In 1965 Kesey was arrested for possession of marijuana and he promptly faked his own suicide and fled to Mexico. When he did return to the United States he was arrested and sent to San Mateo County jail for several months.

Now comes the strange part. On his release he went home to the family farm in Oregon, where he spent the rest of his life. The road trips in 'Furthur', a brightly painted ex-school bus, stopped; the merry pranksters slowed in pranking, though he was still involved with the Grateful Dead and the California psychedelic scene throughout the 1960s. In 1969 he declined involvement with the pranksters bus journey to the Woodstock festival, even though 'Furthur' had been the first of the psychedelic missionary vehicles in June 1964. Perhaps even the model for Morrison's blue bus in the seminal Doors song 'The End'.

I know I have digressed a little here but it's worth it. Like the film with Jack Nicholson. It's the story, narrated by Chief Bromden in the text, of Randle Patrick McMurphy, a man who avoids a custodial sentence by pleading insanity. In the mental institution he takes his rebellion against Big Nurse Ratched and...well you need to read it.

What the hell has this got to do with Morrison? Well was he suicidal in 1971, or did he just not fit? Was he mentally ill or was this just part of the act? Like all of us, he had his adolescent heroes; some of us had rock stars or actors, singers and entertainers, but his were writers and the writers he liked were the beats: beat poets. He certainly didn't fit at school – he was a prankster, a practical joker. I firmly believe he knew all about, 'the merry pranksters' and tried, in a lesser way, to imitate them.

Jim Morrison was a Randle McMurphy of sorts and perhaps not as unique as we might like to think.

Robby Krieger had a twin, Ron, who was a manic depressive; who better to know where Morrison was going with his life than

Robby? Robby, of all The Doors, was possibly the most relaxed. The reason for that, in my opinion, is that he was Morrison's intellectual equal. What has to be remembered about this band is that they weren't a bunch of country hicks playing some rock and roll. They were real musicians with a real intellect – they could think. That's what made them dangerous and that's what made them famous, that and Morrison's natural sex appeal and good looks.

So suicide? If Morrison had been left to his own devices for some time, perhaps a few days, then maybe he could have entered a depressive cycle. With no friends there to discuss the main issues of life, he could only sit in the bars and become more morose until eventually he passed out.

Danny Sugerman says that before Morrison left LA for France he often said, after the death of Janis Joplin, that they were drinking with number three. There are also recollections of Morrison discussing what happened after death. Sitting in darkened rooms, saying he might never return from Paris. Then there is the fabulous text dedication/inscription to Sugerman – about meeting in the afterlife. He seemed to have a morbid fascination with death. Was he a Goth then? He could have been the first of them, a precursor to the revival during the punk period of the late 1970s. But so too could Jimi Hendrix, whose lyrics also stray into the magical and questioning on immortality; just take a brief listen to 'Voodoo Chile', the sentiment says it all.

Morrison couldn't speak French and there were few friends there. What if Pam had told him their relationship was over? Told him that his time was up – perhaps that would have been the final straw. Perhaps, because of her own natural beauty, she was the only one who was prepared to stand up to him, rather than pander to him. That, it would seem, was what he liked – no more than that; that was what he needed, especially in a woman. Morrison was strong but Courson was stronger.

Strength is a measure of the soul and not the body, maybe she tipped him into the 'Paris Journal' and the creation of, 'As I look back'. That poem reads like a brief autobiography of his time at school and UCLA; the drugs, the songs, the money and the fame – his final goodbye to America: his suicide note. But it could also be his farewell note too. Saying as it does that the money from home would encourage him to stay out of trouble. That he would not be a singer, or a film maker, or writer. Then he asks, reflectively, which of my selves, spelt cellves, will be remembered? Perhaps he was hinting at a self-diagnosed, multi-personality disorder. Stranger things have happened when people try to analyse themselves, perhaps philosophise upon the nature of their being. Morrison was, after all, a thinker first and foremost.

Perhaps he tried to fake a suicide and it went wrong and he died? Perhaps he was so upset that his world fell in? 'As I look back' really screams from the heart as he talks of pissing it all away. Whereas in 'Paris Journal' he ends with the hitchhiker levelling his thumb.

Finally, let's examine Pamela Courson. She was burning something in the fire grate of the apartment, that was reported; she was witnessed, letters or something. Could that have been a suicide note that she didn't want anyone else but her to read? Was it the preface to 'last words, last words, out'? Something she must have read. If she was such an advocate of Morrison's work, why would she destroy this? Every word would have been precious. Was it incriminating? To say that people shouldn't read this would have been a travesty, unless of course she had never seen it before and it was fresh, new and not a work in progress. That in itself would suggest that she had not been there while he wrote it, that her examination of the text was post-mortem. That we will never really know as it remains locked between the two of them.

Many chroniclers of the time talk about Pam being a selfish millstone around Jim's neck. She had no income of her own. This in itself would not have been different from many other women at that time. Women's liberation was only just beginning in earnest and she had no real interest in political activity. She had champagne tastes, that we now know, and a passion for buying a new car every time one broke down. She created the Themis boutique out of Jim's finances, but it never was a serious business. In fact, it lost money and Jim merely subsidised it to placate and please her.

41

If he genuinely loved her and cared about pleasing her then he might well have done what he did. Perhaps as he worked she became bored, maybe his security blanket was her rather than the other way around?

Then out of the blue comes a playboy aristocrat, Count Jean de Breteuil. A titled man no less. Like Morrison, he was a risk taker. He supplied heroin to the stars and he had charisma. Pamela Courson would have been drawn to him, he was beautiful too and he had a title. This would then have created a tension between Pam and Jim.

Some people have said that Pam would never have looked at another man. Is that the case? Just take a gentle look at the Geldofs, Angelina Jolie and Brad Pitt. Famous people, pretty ones too, do leave their partners, despite their fabulous looks and wealth. Often one good looking star is replaced by another – why? I think the answer to that question is simple and easy – because they can.

If this was a suicide then it was covered up well. Of all the alternatives, this is the one I can take most seriously. That would also account for why Pamela Courson never had the gravestone installed. Mind you, the graveyard was swamped and still is, so the graffiti would have put paid to that. In Pere Lachaise there is a huge amount of graffitti, in Cheltenham, at the site of Brian Jones' grave, there is none. It sits by the side of the road, just like all the others.

Maybe Pam was so piqued, or upset, she just did not send the money for the gravestone to Agnes Varda, though Bill Siddons said there was money sent. The design was never installed and now there is just a huge granite block which cannot be removed. A previous sculpted bust was stolen some years ago, perhaps proving that the double depth grave is a necessity for the god's of popularity. Once again I thought about the Easter heist and realised that perhaps across the oceans of time people were never that different.

* * *

The murder story is -

Gimme Shelter…

Now this is an interesting one as it takes in the notion of artists being important subversives. Does it work? I'll leave you to decide.

The youth of America were being corrupted by a bunch of anti-war longhairs and people with communist views trying to bring down the 'system'. Black Americans were getting the vote. It was 1964 only three years before 'Light my Fire' reached that magical money spinning top spot. Hard to believe, even harder to conceptualise – but true.

Rosa Parkes starts it at the turn of the decade; refuses to give up her seat to an indolent white male and, after taking a beating, all hell breaks lose. Then with riots and civil unrest and a war in Asia, the whole of the fabric starts to come unglued.

Chicago was a power keg in 1968 – the Democratic Party convention was interrupted; Paris was in turmoil; London was full of demonstrations. The whole system was being questioned. Quite rightly so too. It was as if in 1971 we all stood on the side lines and watched the game unfold – watching the whole shithouse go up in flames. Sides were being drawn.

The dull tweed was being replaced and lots of kids were doing the horrific thing of listening to rock and roll. When I think how Little Richard must have petrified people, a black, make-up wearing, possible homosexual. It was a wonder he didn't end up like Jimmy Hoffa. He was the true king of rock and roll, wham bam boom. Not some sanitised part Cherokee kid from Tupelo Mississippi, who was almost fully white. At the time, being black was fine as long as you danced like some little 'spade nigger' for the quaint entertainment of the white folks – but the vote? Now that may have gone too far. The thing was, it needed to go that far. Why? Because it was the right thing to do then, and is the right thing to do now.

I was there at the time, not in the States but in the UK, and we were a bunch of kids, as far as I can remember, trying to find our way in the world. Post-war baby boomers with more leisure time and spare cash than any generation before them. My father left school and went to work at fourteen. I was still worrying about the latest chart success of Cream or busy reading *Lady Chatterley's Lover* as I remember. Obsessed with zits and teenage angst, whether I would ever get laid or whether I had the right type of flairs. I did have an amazing pair of royal blue velvet trousers which I wore with a canary yellow, granny style cheesecloth shirt and red clogs. I was a walking colour wheel and my hair was getting longer by the day, though not long enough. I think I even had a few porno magazines hidden in my wardrobe as well, as far as I remember.

My friend had found his father's stash of real porn; this was not the stuff of top shelf magazines, this was homemade and totally illegal but a great set of black and white stills. I can see them in my memory, clear as a shock wave. I think I was excited by what I saw women do, perhaps they made me revise the Snow White image I had of them in my head. It's hard to imagine Snow in the nude even today. They really were over the top. My excuse? I went to an all boys school.

I was about as subversive as chocolate cake. There were no Abbie Hoffman's on the run in my home town. My generation had not fought a war nor lived through a great depression, but my parents had. And they longed for stability and a nice home; a home without the threat of bombing. I longed for freedom, excitement and colour. Colour TV. They wanted peace and stability, I wanted excitement. They had seen enough excitement to last them the rest of their lives.

We were young and searching for freedom in art and literature, and I think we were right. Jim Morrison was one of our pathfinders and upon reflection I expect of real interest to the establishment. Unlike Hoffman, he had popular appeal, though I never really saw the power until the festivals grew. Country Joe Macdonald taught me that one – 'Fixin' to die Rag' says it all.

Then along came Bob Geldof and Midge Ure – Live Aid and the raising of millions to dissolve African famine. The power of the rock star was enormous, frighteningly enormous. Maybe the establishment had been right all along.

The 1960s was the era of protest songs, television satire and marches to ban the bomb. Everyone wore the CND sticker. It was the era of The Rolling Stones, the pill, nude swimming at festivals and generally challenging the old order; free love and we were good at the façade of that too. The era of hope and challenge and change, the Kennedys and Martin Luther King; times really were a changing.

There is little doubt that Morrison was being watched as a subversive, despite his father being an admiral in the US Navy. Much as Brian Jones, the founder of The Rolling Stones, was being watched and, as now has been asserted, murdered; murdered by an ex-army builder Frank Thorogood. Though this cannot be definitively proved as both men are now dead. Terry Rawlings has written a particularly interesting account of how Jones decided to go for a swim very late at night on the 2nd July 1969. The one time account of Jones' Swedish girlfriend Anna Wohlin has subsequently been retracted by her. She claims that she was frightened and that she had been drugged. Keith Richards doesn't buy the official account of Jones' death either.

Sometime near midnight he was found at the bottom of his swimming pool in the house at pooh corner – Cotchford, West Sussex.

Now comes the really interesting part. Both Brian Jones and Jim Morrison were heavy drinkers, both were bordering alcoholics. Both were supposed to have been involved in drugs. Brian with Durophet and Jim heroin. Both die on the same night or during early hours of the following day; the night of the 2nd July. By the early morning of the 3rd both are pronounced dead. One in 1969 the other in 1971. Both in water – one in a pool and the other in a bath. Both by natural causes and both under mysterious circumstances. Is someone playing a game here? Using a calling card?

A set of coincidences? If these men were murdered then why? Why pick the two most influential bands on either side of the Atlantic? The man at the forefront of The Doors, an architect of mass hysteria, and also the man responsible for the birth of The Rolling Stones. Both bands were considered dangerous, sexually subversive and intense. Parents were encouraged to 'lock up their daughters' when either band was in town. Maybe both were killed before they could move to their next project. After all, Brian was out of the band and extolling the virtues of world music way before others had contemplated it. Robby Krieger was doing the same with the stuff he knew, Flamenco, for one easy example. Just examine the pictures of Jones, his travel tape recorder in hand. Jim was just coming out of a six album deal and looking to develop into another artistic scene.

The opportunity presents itself, much as when Kennedy drove through Dallas on that November day. Maybe Morrison and Jones were the result of a lone nut, an Oswald who was on a mission, or maybe they were executed by a covert cell of MI5 and CIA operatives.

At first this can sound far-fetched. But the CIA has undertaken covert removals and so too have MI5. If someone wants you dead – you're dead. The question is motive – were Morrison and Jones dangerous enough? Were they the enemy from within? For this one there is no more than conjecture and supposition, but there would be nothing more – both organisations are professionals in their field.

* * *

This was where my friend kicked me after listening to my research.

"Listen man, you don't have the real basis of knowing what the hell happened and most of the people from that time are now dead." He was shaking his head. "It's impossible."

"Not if you unlearn," I replied. "You have to think like them, become them and that way you can understand what they did. Don't try to be overly confident and don't let some of the wrong answers throw you."

"Listen," he said, "there's all sorts of stuff here that's connected."

I was nodding.

"That stuff about Hoffman and how he was at the forefront of politics. He also had some involvement with drugs. Didn't he go on the run for years?" he asked triumphantly.

"Yes I know that and I also know he was bipolar. Which is manic depressive in old money, isn't it? He took 150 Phenobarbital tablets in 1989, perhaps he had had enough too. You know after a while it just gets too much and you want to let the whole thing go. Look sometimes, what did Jim say? Life is the hard bit and dying well that's easy. Maybe he was right?"

"Maybe as the conservative pendulum swung back, Hoffman was out of sync?" my friend asked.

Now it was my turn to nod.

"The counter-culture was dead? Maybe that's why Abbie Hoffman pulled the plug?" My friend was trying to reason the balance. "Maybe Morrison did too? I mean, he had wished to make a fortune out of his songs, become famous. He did just that, he got his dream and when he had it, it smothered him."

"So it wasn't murder then?" I asked.

"Not what David Dellinger said though, was it? He still says it was a murder."

"Why murder someone whose influence had waned? An act of revenge? So some of the right questions don't get asked? Everything is connected in some way."

"Example?" he barked.

"Ken Kesey and me – same birthday 17th of September."

He was laughing at me now. "Coincidence," he squealed, "nothing more. How can anyone get the right answers if they don't know the questions to ask?" He gave me a quizzical look. "Unlearn it?"

"The wrong answers to the right questions," I smirked.

He was shaking his head. "Look, you're looking for answers which are making things overly complicated. Don't."

"Morrison had influence but not enough." I continued. "The establishment is a very shrewd beast. Perhaps they could foresee

47

stadium rock concerts? They also knew that fashions change. That the pendulum would swing back toward them once again. If they got him locked up, the public would soon forget him."

"You know what, that's more like the truth."

"He asked questions of the sheeple, all the wrong questions."

"What wrong questions?" He quizzed me.

"Do you really want me to go through them now?" I asked.

"Might as well," he chirped, "we've come this far, we have to go on."

That night we talked into the night, drank wine and… and I convinced him that all of the six theories about Morrison were or had been designed to achieve two things: to make him into a legend by those who had admired him, or to demonise and degrade him by those who hated him. The reality was that the true story had never been investigated properly and I was going to do it.

The more I looked, the more I found, and the more I found, the less sense it made. I was convinced that something else happened on that night in Paris and I was going to blow the whole bunch of stories to hell and back. I was going to explain what had really happened.

"How, if you have no absolute proof?" my friend had asked.

And me, being very philosophical, had answered, "Just because you can't fully prove it, doesn't mean it didn't happen."

We talked about Muhammad Ali and how the greatest ever boxer could be stripped of the world title and made to look cheap. Why – because he refused to kill and fight?

The thing is, most of us never really know what we're fighting for. To protect our homes and our families? Now that really was a bunch of bullshit. Ali was made to look a coward, just as Morrison was perceived as a pervert. I convinced him that if Jim had come back for sentencing they would have thrown his arse in stir. That I am certain about – three years or thereabouts. Jim wasn't stupid either, he knew that. One thing he always was – perceptive. A perceptive thinker. Knew that his career would be screwed. They had to crush him.

Ali was a loudmouth and if you were black you had better

hush your mouth, or if female, learn to open your legs and drop those panties on demand. God only knows what happened to Kesey inside.

Eventually we agreed it was all a crock of contrived shit and he wanted to help me expose it.

Four

Before you accuse me…

Perhaps I ought to give you some more detail on how the Morrison 'case' got me. In 1971, when he was supposed to have died, there were lots of changes going on. I'd made it through school, learnt how to roll a joint and my parents were finally getting a divorce. I found it hard to believe. Mr. Mojo Risin dead – impossible. He was supposed to be an Achilles, a god, someone who didn't need to touch the earth. Now I know better: he was just a man.

My father had simply had enough, couldn't hack it anymore, he told my older brother and then he went. I was angry because my brother had found his sanctuary-he'd moved out and was safely away from the mental chaos which my mother then plunged into. My mother promptly went into melt down which lasted over three years, and me, I grew up real fast and learned how to survive alone. My guitar playing improved and I read everything I could get my hands on. I was the only teenager sitting in the park on a winter day reading D. H. Lawrence. That was my sanctuary, books and music, my only constants in a shifting world; just like Morrison, I lived inside my own imagination, was a loner, a misfit, only I wasn't beautiful to look at. Nature has not made me the object of female desire. You could have dressed me in the best and I'd still have come up smelling like crap; I wasn't a clothes horse. In consequence, I became even more isolated, but I was never lonely. I learned to live with disappointment as my ideas grew, needed the space to get my own head around what had happened, so I dived into books. It wasn't until I got older that I sort of grasped the affinity we, Morrison and I, had: the military, the loner, the lack of trust in fellow human beings. I'd had a few kicks in the teeth from so-called friends by then and I admired later the steadfast friendship of Babe Hill. The kind of friend who wanted nothing from an individual and took a person as they found them. That was what Babe Hill did for Jim. When older, my confidence grew and the damage of my youth was diluted, ignored even, and suddenly, like some liberated bird, I learned how to fly. Sleek coloured feathers lifted me high into the sky and then suddenly I was higher than the rest and squawking.

What really turned me on about Morrison was challenge. He didn't simply accept those ways in which we were supposed to do things. Just look at his poetry. Some people will say it's all over the place; there are others who will say the grammar's all wrong, or the words are too obscure, or it doesn't fit into the pattern of the accepted norm. All I have to say is two words: James Joyce.

Language is art, and art is about communication, sharing the human experience, one thing it's not about is a rule book created to hem us in. Hey, if we all played by the rules then there would never have been any Romantics. No Coleridge, no Wordsworth, no Goethe, no Chopin, no Liszt, the list just goes on and on. Then that too would have had consequences, no Impressionist painters, no Renoir or Monet, no Van Gogh and later, no Picasso. There always have to be people who are prepared to go out to the edge and look down, it takes guts. Jim Morrison was one of those.

Ray Manzarek said that everyone lived high on Jim's dime. Maybe he was right about some, but there were some constants too. Me? I didn't have that. I had winter walks in the park and days in the reference library in town, or wandering into warm art galleries and shops. I'd hop onto the train and try not to pay, unless I got caught, and I'd explore the neighbouring cities. Drift back late at night and be so tired I could sleep anywhere. Yeah, my youth evaporated like morning mist, but with a strange sort of irony, it did me good. It gave me the chance to hide away and of course most of my school and college buddies had better things to do than hit the libraries. Books gave me sanctuary, a place to hide; and I liked being alone – did Morrison?

We had this old flea-pit cinema, 'The Embassy', and once you went in you could stay all day. The film ran three times and you could stay and watch it over. Movies came after Rawhide and Bonanza on the old black and white Bush TV we had when I was a kid. A TV which stood on four legs, had two channels, then three and doors which closed like the concertina effect of an accordion. Little brass handles which opened the sliding doors of the cabinet and then the two minute warm up as the valves heated and the grainy black and grey burst into life. I thought it was fantastic. Now I get better images on my iPod, in the palm of my hand and in colour too. And the world? The world is ruled by television and computer games.

I did movies some Saturdays, just to get away and get some peace. Peace away from my nervous breakdown mother and her rage and fits. Peace to sit in the dark and escape.

I learned all about how and what a bastard my dad had been, as she spent nights waking me up to talk. Her mind was in meltdown and I don't think she ever really recovered. Sometimes, a couple of years later, when I was at college, I'd lay on the grass in the warm afternoons and go to sleep. Sleep then because I couldn't sleep at home. Nobody really knew what the hell was going on and I learned how to hold my tongue; learned how to withdraw when I needed to. I grew to know what a nervous breakdown was; learned the signs of drinking too much and scattered clothes; watched as the soul of someone I cared about was torn to pieces by self-loathing and self-doubt. When I started on Morrison's case file it all came flooding back; came back so hard that it felt like a kick in the guts. Here was a guy who had developed the same strategies as me and I began to think about his youth. His father, Steve, and mother, Clara, did they operate in the same way as my mother and father? Absent dad for long periods and a mother who gave free reign at some times and choking oppression at others. The more I thought about it, the colder my blood ran.

Anyhow, so Jim dies and there are rumours flashing about that he had chased his girlfriend to Paris because she was fucking some French Count and Morrison had been so in love that he followed her. That didn't make sense either at the time; it does now. I'd been one of those devil may care guys with women. I was young and dumb and full of come – one out, another in. I lost my virginity to a Canadian, she was nineteen and I was fifteen. I'd lied about my age to her and she had let me slam myself home like a tank. Blank as a lump of metal, with the feeling of a mating bull. It was over in less than a couple of minutes and I was bleeding because I'd torn my foreskin on her dry tightness. It was crap – no worse, worse than crap. All that teenage angst and anxiety about pushing myself into a girl and boom, gone. A few muscle contractions and then it's over. Rather like the first time I shaved, searching for the hairs that needed to go. Rushing to grow up, rushing to get something I thought I wanted. Like they say, perhaps you shouldn't wish too hard – you just might get it; and when you do, it might not be what you wanted after all. Morrison wished for fame and fortune and when he got it he hated it. A fine example of precisely that saying.

Like all the rest, I was riddled with doubts and mirror checking and looking for a girlfriend. That was all consuming and it had been the same for Morrison. I didn't want love, just a girl whose legs locked behind my back and who screamed when I exploded. No wonder I was often alone. But hey, that was life.

It wasn't until years later that I knew they had planned their escape together. Pam Courson had gone on ahead, while Jim Morrison stayed in LA to work on the last album – *LA woman*. The band had got the tracks down and then usually they all had some input into the final edit. Morrison seemed to have liked this stage of the production process, that's what the other band members said, but with *LA woman* he dropped the bombshell. Said he was going off to Paris for some well-earned R&R; said he was going to join Pam, and the rest is history.

Then you get into the he said, she said, no really he said kind of territory.

I didn't know any of this back then; all I knew was that Morrison had died in the bath. The pundits all went into whether it was a suicide, a death wish, an accident. In fact, the papers reported that he had chased her across the world to get her back after an argument, and then he had been taking a bath and the hot water had made his heart go into overload. I didn't get that either, until I'd fallen in love myself and lost her; then it made sense. A god falling for a mortal woman, who ran off with a Count because she was impressed by his title. Then I thought about that too, as she had been there at the start. She had shared the first profit Chinese feast so she'd hardly be seduced by the wealth of aristocracy. The political tensions caused by Pam, the love between them, got swallowed in the mire of complications which the myth continued to feed. I was as green as grass and had known for a long time that he had some kind of death wish. Falling out of hotel windows, balancing on the parapets of high rises; the man played with death, taunted it almost. So when he died, I kind of thought it would be with more of a bang, rather than a whimper. A Doctor Faustus descent into Hell, after five years of unbridled debauchery; lust and Dionysian orgies, a series of great golden copulations.

The thing is, he was just a guy; a clever guy, talented yes, but he still had to squat to take a dump and stand naked in the shower, that is when he took one. Even the President stands naked in the shower and has to wipe his own arse. Well I won't go into that one too deeply, but I know you get my drift. I mean, people like to think that Marilyn was a goddess, but she bled once a month and got 'the curse' and I bet she puked every now and then too. Hell, you can screw a President as long as you are both myths; that's the problem with humans, they seem to have a need for a hero. A Christ, a martyr, a figure that gets so big no tomb can hold them and that's a load of bullshit too. Elvis, Michael Jackson, the king of rock and roll and the prince of pop; but everybody forgets that these people are just flesh and blood too. Look! Cut them and they bleed. We're all just like Jim said, nude pastry for the worms to feast upon. Jim Morrison and Mercutio made into worms' meat and he didn't even have a wound the size of a church door. But his heart was as deep as any well – filled with despair.

Once you've died, you don't come back to life after three days or thirty days, but somehow Morrison knew what the crowds needed. It was like they needed to believe that the very best cannot be crucified. That Jesus was the son of God and as such, he could not be put to death. Morrison couldn't die a tub of alcohol-sodden lard in a bath. So the myth grew, as Morrison knew it would, he knew that others would feed it and gradually, oh so gradually, the myth became a legend and the real man disappeared. The starving boy from Venice Beach, the boy who stole steaks with charm, became something else. A male Norma-Jean, he had seen that happen too; first with Marilyn and the non-acceptance of an overdose accident. After all, she was found in the nude, so she must have been saying something – making a statement. Then with JFK, the grassy knoll theory as opposed to the lone nut. The goddess and the accident and the prince of the future destroyed and all those possibilities too, by a lone nut.

Then there was Brian Jones, dead in a swimming pool; accident, murdered? Morrison knew about that too. Just read 'Wilderness – Ode to LA while thinking of Brian Jones, Deceased'. Coincidence or playful prank – or real clever manipulation? What about the dates? Two of the most influential rock bands of the sixties? Both central characters gone under mysterious circumstances. Both prone to alcohol and drugs, though not heroin. That in itself was strange. But for both to die, at the same age, on the same day, during the early hours, both in water- hey, I was beginning to get the mystic vibes here. The sort of thing Morrison loved to delve into and play with. Even I was feeling uncomfortable. It was a Robert Johnson Devil's crossroad moment, and they were both responsible for lifting the blues into the lime light. Brian with his epic early slide guitar, a Cheltenham middle-class boy with a bottleneck and the admiral's son from Florida: brothers in the blues. Both dead on the same day, two years apart. Both twenty seven. Something jarred in my head – something was wrong. 'Cut off the head and the body dies'. That's what my father used to say, old military stoic that he was.

Morrison was highly intelligent and pieced things together quickly. He could have made a brilliantly observant defence council and made his mark there. Just listen to the interviews, there is no grunting moron there, just a well educated, thoughtful, philosophical almost, young man, searching for a way through; a middle-class kid with the security to think. Freedom was his thing, not a shabby mock-turtle freedom but real, on the edge, freedom. Even if the regime at home was military, he had his three meals a day and access to his wonderland – books. It was others that shaped him and others he stole from: Ginsberg, Nietzsche, Kerouac and 'the beats'. What about Blake and Huxley? The early rock and rollers, the blues men and of course the legends of the Native American Indians, regurgitated and sanitised for the silver screen? The list of credits was endless and he sifted and sieved the information until he produced his distilled version on the stage. All this poured into James Douglas Morrison and Jim Morrison, Jimbo and Mr. Mojo Risin poured out.

Morrison did it with individuals too, punched them below the belt and gave them precisely what they needed, or didn't need, depending upon what he analysed. He toyed with their minds; mind fucked them – a real clever bastard with a tinge of irony and devilish playfulness which bordered on the sadistic at times. You could just imagine him taunting those establishment folks out to make money out of the band. That's what he did in Miami. He was getting even with those greedy promoters, who had taken the seats out just to get an extra few thousand bodies in and make a quick buck out of deceit. Drunk, angry and fed up with the image he had created, the whole house of cards was out in the wind. Only those promoters hadn't calculated on a man who had been angered by Pam, fuelled by alcohol and then let lose into an unsafe venue – just to make money. You might as well have thrown some matches into a petrol tank. Boom, the whole thing goes up like a shithouse in flames and a lot of people get singed. When people lose money they get nasty and some want to get even.

Morrison may well have wanted to destroy Mr. Mojo Risin in one glorious evening but he also was drunk. That night Jimbo appeared on stage, just like Ray had feared, and Jimbo was the nastier side of Gentleman Jim. It was Jim himself who later said of the evening that basically he was calling the audience 'A bunch of fucking idiots'. Listening to a bunch of fairly good musicians when they, the audience, were really there for something else. Told them they should not be, 'Slaves', and go and find what they were really looking for. Did he mean slaves to the system? Wow is that political, or religious, or what? Whatever it is, or was, it was perceived as dangerous, dangerous inflammable incitement. That's the reason he was arrested, not because he supposedly took his dick out on stage. Which, by the way, he didn't.

So he is arrested and the whole of the established order personify him as the head of the demon snake. Cut off the head and the body dies. Only there never really was a demon, just a bunch of kids hanging onto some ideas, ideas which he helped to fuel and create. Funny thing was, Morrison knew that too, knew that they, The Doors, would be replaced, just as Elvis had been replaced, and rock and roll had been replaced – and he was right. By 1976 Punk rock was in, and the kids were doing 'The Pogo', and spitting and pissing on each other. Mob-rule violence was back and then that too passed into, New Romantics, Goths, Hip hop, Garage, and on and on. Now it's back to the plastic mass produced, bubble–gum music, just like the early sixties. The Monkees and the Archies all over again, until someone else breaks the mould. We get manufactured darlings of reality TV and viewer votes on Saturday nights; pale pastiches of originality. All it has to do is make money. Money was never Morrison's thing otherwise he'd have been a clothes horse, or a car collector, or someone with Real Estate.

1968 and The Doors and the Airplane, that's Jefferson Airplane, are on a double headline tour. Morrison had been drinking all day and, like Grace Slick says, taking every piece of gear fans gave him, on the spot. No holding back, no keeping something for later, no, he just took the stuff and then went out of his head. Then, like Kantner said, he started dancing on their stage, dancing to 'Plastic Fantastic Lover', until he collapsed, that is. Collapsed and was taken to intensive care, from where, the following morning, he simply discharged himself. See, both the bands took turns to headline and that night the Airplane went first, Morrison collapsed and Ray Manzarek sang the lyrics. Made a good fist of it too, according to Grace Slick.

Real Estate – he did have some of that, though nobody really knew how much and where. What exactly did he do and where did he go? During the 'Light my Fire'-Buick charade he disappeared for two weeks. No one, including Pam, knew where he was.

The story goes that while Jim could not be found, the remaining members of the band signed up to let 'Light my Fire' be elevator music to market a car. Jim is? When he gets back he is crazy. He threatens to get a Buick up on stage and smash it to pieces with a sledgehammer. Guess what? Buick decide that the song is not really for them.

Lesson learned about greed.

Everyone looks at the story and thinks how quaint. Me, I think where the hell was he? Pam was still around, was he alone? Where? Perhaps someone was handling his affairs and he didn't even know what he had? Perhaps investments were being made? Perhaps Max Fink, the trusted fixer, knew and did far more than he let on; perhaps a friend, a really trusted friend, a friend like Babe Hill, did too. The legend sort of swallowed that fact. Swallowed it whole and spat out the myths.

So it seemed strange to me back then that the mythology of the indestructible god of rock and cock should get into a hot bathtub and die. Die of heart failure; something old folks died from too. Come in like a lion and slide away like a lamb.

Years passed and my life took a series of twists and turns a bad marriage: shit jobs, going back to college and looking after two young kids as a single parent. Philosophy was dead in my head and all I needed was sleep and food on the table. I remember being tired a lot of the time. Everything on Morrison went onto my back burner and The Doors sort of vanished from the public eye. The seventies turned into the eighties and the eighties into the nineties and before I knew it, twenty years had passed. Then, from nowhere, the legend was fuelled and Danny Sugerman became Morrison's St. Paul, and the myth started to explode and the man began to be lost in the bullshit. Along came Oliver Stone, exploding the 60s with his conspiracy theories on JFK and elevating Morrison onto a pedestal. The band was back and now being inducted into the rock and roll hall of fame. You have to make it across the twenty year line and then suddenly everybody remembers you. Live long enough and everybody thinks you're a hero. Die young and you become a god.

We had taken over. The kids in the audience for The Doors were now running the show. The hair had gone and the rebelliousness had been tempered by mortgages and the need to get a kid-rearing career, but somehow we were on top. The age thing I guess – dead men's shoes. We were comfortable and still young enough to think back and pretend that we had made a real difference. We had stopped a war and now every home had a recycling bin too. We listened to fat men talking shit, we had all grown fat now. The rainbow warrior was free to roam and the threat of global warming was being addressed. It was time for the old gods to be honoured. Gerry Garcia was dead, so were Frank Zappa, Janis, Jimi and Morrison. But the gods had to be honoured, dead or not, remembered and then inducted into the hall of fame. Who remembers Al Wilson now? The blind owl. The bullshit was back, only this time it was thicker and more profitable, and it was justifiable – we told ourselves we had made a difference. More mass produced stuff, more pure technology, more, more, more, and all ours. I wanted to weep. No more Wavy Gravy, just a tribe without a people, for what it's worth. How far had we come to get here? Everything was made for me and you, all we needed to do was take that ride: get into the car.

Time makes illusions of everything and bends truth into legend. The past is the history of the winners, and only the winners are remembered. Once The Doors wanted to be as famous as Love – who even remembers them now? What once was fashionable becomes garbage and what was garbage becomes fashion and the line between the two is drawn, like a line in the sand. Morrison crossed that line.

So, after a long time I picked up the threads again; only this time I was sharper, less idealistic and less easily swayed by fashion, or fooled. I was out of the dark tunnel and running toward the light. Twenty years inside a tunnel. It was like someone looking for a reason to believe, not finding it, and then years later, bang. Chance gives a fine thread which when you pull it, hauls in a rope, which is tied to a tug, which in turn is pulling a liner. My liner came in when I got a gift of the six albums on smart new CD. Digitally remastered, enhanced and to be truthful, a damn sight better than the original albums I had played until the groove had worn right through. I had a vinyl copy of *Morrison Hotel* which was so thin you could have moulded a lamp shade out of it. Now I had the whole experience all over again. It was like coming home. In the centre, dancing his shaman dance, Morrison, leering, antagonising; not Morrison the myth but Morrison the man. The old blues man, the Muddy Waters of our generation and suddenly I understood. No more pretending, no more rubbish, no more bullshit: I was back – I was alive.

It was then that the pieces which I had fashioned into a palliative jigsaw didn't fit anymore. So I read a few books on it. They were the Sugerman and Hopkins bits, Densmore, Manzarek and Patricia Butler's *Angels Dance and Angels Die*, and every rag tag and bobtail bit on the internet. I surfed until my eyes ached and my arse grew roots into the chair. Like everybody else, I was searching for the big answer to the big myth, and then one day it dawned. A sudden Marcus Aurelius moment, a time of quiet calm when it did make sense: simplicity in all things.

What if Morrison wasn't dead? What if he and Pam had committed the perfect escape? Twice? So I went back to the Manzarek notion of Jim not being dead at all. Intelligent man, not convinced, why? Because he knew that Morrison could be crazy enough to try it and intelligent enough to succeed. I thought about it – the money. All that money from the band – where did it go? Hell, The Rolling Stones nearly lost everything to tax and bankruptcy. What if Morrison had already squirreled some away on his trips out of the country? Perhaps he had accounts in France already, or Spain. It would be around 1970. Man it would have been so easy. His Kerouac wanderings all over the globe – India and other places. Then that stuff in France, the passport, the holidays. That's what Tony Funches said anyhow, said he took off alone for places. And that was his bodyguard, man. But he'd done that before too; told people he was off to New York or Venice, and in reality he was starving on the roof of a house in Venice Beach – not Venice Italy. His father said he was a storyteller, a myth maker with a vivid imagination.

Morrison wanted to be Dean Moriarty and yet he also wanted to be Salvatore Paradise, a strange dichotomy in his subconscious. On stage he was Dean, Mr. Mojo Risin, Jimbo, stealing cars and starting fights, fucking women and taking off on his cross country road trips. He was hip and beat and wild. At home with Pam he wanted to be Sal. a.k.a. James Douglas Morrison, poet – and get it down on paper. Hell, he wanted to write the next great American novel. 'The' novel about the sixties; the novel which would define a generation – his.

There was, however, the personality split – simple.

The outsider, estranged from himself and society, cannot experience either himself or others as 'real'. He invents a false self and with it he confronts both the outside world and his own despair. The disintegration of his real self keeps pace with the growing unreality of his false self until, in the extremes of schizophrenic breakdown, the whole personality disintegrates. That's what R.D. Laing said; I looked it up for the research. Now that is probably as close to the truth as it gets. That diagnosis fits Morrison like a glove too.

Maybe Morrison was precisely that, an outsider who concocted a story in which to live his reality. I was getting in deeper now. It was like trying to swim in treacle: every stroke was laboured and painful. The more I floundered and tried to understand, the more I drowned.

He was really good at that, spinning unreality like a classic storyteller; like any entertainer, he lived a duality, a schizophrenic existence. A creator of myths and misdirection, a poet, a writer, a word man and not a birdman; not Robert Stroud. If he, Jimbo, committed a murder, he'd not be in Alcatraz. He would plan it. Was he crazy?

So I made the leap like Ray Manzarek, and let's face it, they started the band together and were intellectual equals, why couldn't it be true? At first I thought, hey Manzarek, you're just spinning the bullshit to keep a dollar fish on the line, you want the hall of fame, but something kept kicking me in the ribs making me think again. The guys in the band are wealthy, good investments would make life easy for them. He had Dorothy after all, the band sponsor: a smart cookie.

But what if Morrison's life as a child had made him? After all, we are all products of our upbringing – I include myself in that too and you the reader. You've been created, influenced and honed by your experiences. You could say it was the military life, the punching from place to place that alienated Morrison from his peers, or that his father tried to break his spirit. Even the bronze Greek plaque, fixed to the block of heavy granite which holds him down, can be open to interpretation, depending upon old or modern translation. *KATA TON DAIMONA EAYTOY* it says, and in ancient Greek the word daimon means spirit and is neither negative nor derogatory. Who drafted it? Most probably Steve Morrison. 'True to his own spirit' but then there have been other translations offered: 'down with his own demons' and 'with the devil himself' are just two which have been offered up.

Everything has a duality; everything is schizophrenic, it would seem.

After six albums you make a lifetime living out of it? Clever, I thought, real clever. Now that's marketing, living off a back catalogue for so many years. Only what if he, Manzarek, had been fooled just like the rest of us? He knew the head games Morrison could play and the clues he could leave. True, the man was obscure – just look at some of the poetry if you really want to blow up your head. Manzarek knew his limitations, that's why he asked Bill Siddons if he'd seen inside the casket. I began to think again and somehow things began to make sense – after forty years they made sense: crazy, perfect, stinky boot sense.

And that was where my writing came in. By this time I was a crime novelist and it was easy to imagine the way someone could cover their tracks. I did it all the time, became the criminal in my imagination, researched and made the impossible plausible.

I'd seen Pamela's design for the grave; some people have said that the cash for that went into her veins. But what if it went somewhere else?

Morrison could be very smart, smarter than the average bear. I knew I'd have to out think him if I was find out the truth. In my teens I had been sucked in, but now, now I was ready to get back inside Morrison's head.

Five

Plastic fantastic lover…

"Jim Morrison are you drunk?"

"Hey baby you know what I need." Jim's hands were fumbling around in his pants. "I get drunk to be able to talk to arseholes and that includes me."

"Don't you smart mouth me you mother fucker. Your mind tricks won't cut the mustard. In fact, nothing with you cuts the mustard. Call yourself a rock star? You can't even get it up. Washed up and wasted, pissing your talent away."

"Pam, I just had a few with Babe, we've been recording all day. Robby's been talking about another album and I reckon he's got some ideas for some really big songs."

Pamela Courson's voice lowered to a whisper. "But you said this was gonna be the last of music. You said the last of the six and then you were going to concentrate on poetry. No more albums, no more Doors, just write. Write the great American novel."

"I am, I am," Jim Morrison was pleading now, reassuring. "My Orange County Suite."

"You're a lousy fuck. A pig, a goddamn pig." She paused, "Hey Morrison, you shit head, what's grease for the gander, well that's grease for the goose too. I can fuck the Count and you can go to hell and rot. Take up with one of your stupid little whores."

"Hey baby, you know I'm comin'."

"Yeah and you better not be comin' inside some dumb arse

blonde that likes your meat." She paused again and her voice became soft. "Because, Morrison, nobody does it like me. I got what you like."

Jim Morrison laughed a guttural laugh, which echoed into the receiver and pumped into his girlfriend's ear. Her reaction was instant, sharp and decisive.

"Well you think what you like; you're nothin' more than a pound of floppy horse flesh. You can't fuck worth a damn, you're a lush, a burnt out, fucked up lush. Call yourself a rock star. Some fucking rock star. Sometimes I'd think you were queer the way you carry on. What, you got the hots for little Danny?"

Morrison voice lowered like an admonished child. "Look baby," he said, "I'll come to Paris just as soon as we finish. Hey, I'm not even gonna hang round for the mix. Ray can do that and John too. Pamela Susan Courson, I'm comin' to Paris and we're gonna have some fun times. Like back in the old days, down at The Fog. Hey, they were fun, weren't they?"

Pamela laughed, "Yes, Mr. Morrison, they were."

"Well then, Mrs. Morrison, we can have some fun again. Chinese food in cartons and." He paused and the slow Southern drawl of Florida interspersed with the, … erms, and ums and considered words returned. He had moved into interview speak and his guard was up. "You know what I miss? Heart."

"Heart?"

"Yeah beef hearts and Venice, and the real LA. You know we were happy then. Drinkin' and walkin' back at night. But we were happy then, weren't we?"

"Of course we were happy."

"Well we're gonna be happy again. Happy like Robby and Lyn."

"Oh spare me the Robby and Lyn speech. You're not like him. I'm not like her."

"Yeah, but he writes a good tune. Jesus I wish I could play."

"Well you can learn and then you won't need The Doors anymore. You're better than them anyway. You're the spirit of the band. Without you they'd all be nothing."

"Hey baby we're a team. A band of brothers."

65

"Oh fuck you Morrison. Don't give me all that military shit. They use you; they need you. Just get yourself on a plane."

"I need some R and R. I think my mind is blown Pam. I mean it. Robby will never get the credit he really deserves."

There was a pause in which she knew what he would be thinking. He would be wallowing in his own self-doubt and self-pity. She knew what he was like. Everyone knew the magic Morrison; the face at the edge of the cliff, grinning before he jumped. He could swing out on a rope over the crowd, wreck a stage, get arrested – but she knew his demons. The things that came for him in the dark. The fear of rejection, the pain of his family background and his own doubts about his poetry. She also knew that he could never control her, and now he was beginning to realise that too. Every woman in the world wanted the god of cock. But she had been with him before they, The Doors, were famous. Been there when Dorothy bullied them and pushed them into trying another try.

"Well I just hope you remember that this is it. You're gonna write and get away from those damn drinking friends of yours. That Babe and those Doors, they're killing you, killing the Jim Morrison I fell in love with. The intellectual, the thinker, they've taken your creative juice and poured you into a bottle and nobody gives a shit except me. You are better than all of them and they fight over you like a dog with a bone."

Jim Morrison's voice trailed a few words, most of which she could not discern and then she made out, "Honey and coming next week."

"And I bet those arseholes haven't even asked about me have they?"

Morrison grunted inaudibly.

"See, they just want you to stand up front and peel off for the crowd. They'll kill you. So you piss away your talent for the crowds, but don't expect me to be there when it all turns to shit. You're a writer, that's what; you're a writer, that's what you are. A writer, a storyteller, a…"

* * *

So there I was in the hotel room near Gare du Nord trying to piece the story of their last months together. Going back to 1971, in my mind, trying to imagine it. Was this a waste of time? I knew the answers were in his journals and his poems and his state of mind; I wondered if he had committed suicide and if Pam had found a note. Was that the thing she had burned in Paris? His final words to the world? The point when the nihilism had finally conquered him and driven him into a pit of total despair.

There was also the idea that he died and began to decompose while she was off cock sucking the Count. That man was seriously messed up too, heroin, and I drifted mentally into how fucked up he was and what he would do? What if he had been in Paris and then ran, thinking that Morrison was dead. Wow, what a brilliant smoke screen. This was *Eisenheim the Illusionist* territory; only this was better than a Pulitzer Prize short story: this was possible.

I had to get right inside Morrison's head and a complex head it was. He wasn't your usual fame fodder and he was one of the first. A trailblazer that others would follow. I was intrigued to see if I could think of something which the others had missed. Then I lost it for a bit and flicked on the TV. Like a friend of mine said, "Who cares anymore?" He burbled on about, "In a hundred years, Morrison, he'll be forgotten. Like Swinburne and the Victorians, man. And who the hell reads Swinburne these days? Matthew Arnold, who apart from the academics read him?"

Despondency set in.

I had to sort of agree and then I wondered what really would be said about us after we had gone. It was kind of sobering to realise that Morrison was right. He had read the fickle crowd and knew that nothing really mattered at all. It took me years to get there; years of self doubt. I mean who reads Rimbaud in French but the French, and times and fashion change. My mind was dancing all over the place and for some reason Bram Stoker leapt up. Bloody *Dracula*, a dead book, lost, gone, forgotten, until the advent of movies and then the whole thing goes stratospheric. *Lady Audley's Secret*, that came next, and *Precious Bane*, and then back to *Dracula* in one quick circle. Books about things that never really made the main stream. Very much loved by the Victorians, but now virtually forgotten. Fashion and fame and the fickle crowd and Paul Weller and the public getting what is given to them. I thought I was losing it, trying to hold on to all the disparate strands in my head. And then I wanted to write it down and explain it.

I knew Morrison was alive and I could sort of imagine the gaps. I sensed him, knew it, felt it; like some crazy psychic going mad. It was like I was him and not him and her too. Forty years it had taken me to get to this place. I had to learn it on the way. Had to have the things happen to me in my life to understand what the hell could have happened to them, what they did to escape. Age had given me an edge.

They were just two young people and they were finding their way at a time of flux. Everything was all turned up, churned up and there were people writing and the pill was there and women were changing. The whole thing was changing and everyone was trying to make sense of the whole shitty mess. I mean the war was still going and we were going to demonstrations.

Suddenly I had a brief picture of Marianne Faithful come into my mind. Not the one of her singing 'As Tears Go By' you know all grainy and black and white sitting on a cushion; or one of her in the Rock and Roll Circus – heroin induced, *Brave New World* somatose, and barely alive. I imagined the one where she and Morrison were supposed to have done some horse and he died. I could see the panic in the toilets as they, they being her and The Count, tried to get the body out. Was that Morrison or a doppelganger or was it all bullshit, smoke and mirrors?

No, the one I saw was the one that stuck, the one of a shapeless middle-aged woman on the South Bank Show, with the ever pretentiously arty Melvyn Bragg. He was talking bollocks through a nasal congestion of snot; talking about Marianne and how she made it through. Made it through what? Fucking Mick Jagger and being dumped because she was out of her tiny little mind most of the time? Made it through the aristocratic hell that was her upbringing. My heart was bleeding.

She had, as far as I could see, never worked in her life. Unless you can call being an ornament for The Rolling Stones and singing a few songs, work. She was being interviewed about her new album. She was wrinkled and older and her figure had gone and the once lively smile, was replaced by a stern cynical sneer. Like the rest of us, I thought. Then she sang a song and it was awful, droning on about some terrible injustice that had been done to her. All about being able to smell another woman's cunt (her word choice not mine) in her bed. She seemed to love using the word cunt. She was breaking boundaries, only she was trying too hard. A cross between a tortured Edith Piaff and some street singer with an accordion in Place de Pompidou.

I shuddered and wondered what Pam would look like now. The cinnamon hair would be gone and she'd be fat and grey like the rest of us. Or she might look like one of The Rolling Stones, wrinkled and lightly smoked, like some Whitby kipper. Her time as the queen of rock would be over. And once, a long time ago, she had been beautiful. Red hair and green eyes and passion and power and intellect and wow!

* * *

"Listen, Pam, it's over. John's had enough, he's got that skin thing again and he's really un-nerved. I kinda feel sorry for the guy. You know once, when we went to the draft board, I kinda thought he had a thing for me."

"What kind of thing?"

"You know," he paused, "a thing, thing."

"Morrison, you're mad."

"Ride the snake, to the edge of the lake, baby."

"Listen you dip shit, don't start all that nonsense with me. I spoke with Alan and I've found us this place on Rue Beautreillis. It's really nice. It's in a building with a courtyard and the people here won't know you. You can write and be free. We can go down to Charleville and then on to Corsica and Africa. Take some time to feed our heads."

"White rabbit territory, huh?"

"Don't even go to that place. Grace motherfucking Slick. She is a real fucked up poor little rich kid. And you slept with her didn't you? On that tour in Amsterdam? You fucked her. You're a pig, Morrison. A first class pig."

"She came on to me."

"What, like she did to the whole of Airplane and everyone else? Fucking plastic fantastic lover."

"That was over two years ago. Anyway, what's this place like?"

"It's small and like our place…" she checked herself, "small and nice, like the Norton apartment."

"I'd like to have a good look around Paris and see what's happening. I'm kinda tired, blown creatively."

"You're gonna write the next great American novel."

"I want to get my poems up together." His speech was beginning to slur and Pam knew now was the time to quit the call.

"So when will I see you?" she asked.

"A couple of days, maybe a week. We got a few bits to add to *LA woman* and then I'm on the plane."

"You just make sure you are. Don't you fuck up again." There was a click and the phone went dead.

* * *

Why did I use the idea of red hair and green eyes? Why did my first delicious villain have these things and why was she a bitch woman? I was trying to think it through, trying to get my head around the Pam and Jim thing when the phone rang. I wrote *Pancardi's Pride* and made Alice Parsotti a strong female – just like Pam. Yet she was vulnerable and highly manipulative, just like Pam. Pamela Courson was more than a moll or a groupie, much, much more and only twenty four. And why Alice? Lewis Carroll, Humpty Dumpty and all that fantasy, my head was going to explode and I was in so deep now it was like quicksand.

"I thought you said you'd phone?" said the voice on the other end of the line.

"Yeah I was," I offered apologetically, "but I kind of got caught up in the mess of this Morrison thing. Out by the grave and then there were all these people milling around. It was kinda weird to see the thing. I sort of felt helpless, messed up."

"You're obsessed by Jim Morrison. It's like you worship the guy or something."

I could feel myself becoming defensive. "No, I just like The Doors."

"Are you sure you're not all screwed up by it? Maybe you've got a thing for him?"

I started to become aggressively defensive. "Look, I liked that band and their music still does it for me even now. I liked Ten Years After, no, I still like Ten Years After but I think I like this lot better, especially as I get older. Morrison was edgy and punchy and didn't give a stuff. I like that in a person – balls of steel. When I saw them he stood like a statue, like a stone gargoyle on the stage. They sounded tinny but his voice was soaring like gravel washed in a roaring river."

"Yeah, poor little rich kid that he was," she snorted. "Never did a day's work in his life. Nice life if you can get it."

For some unknown reason I was beginning to get angry, frustrated, and I had found him. "Look," I said, "you may like Take That, but it's bubblegum music. My stuff is real music. Nobody played the guitar like Alvin Lee, nobody. Never mind Clapton and Hendrix, that guy was, is, the dogs bollocks. Morrison was the voice. It's my time, my clan, my people. If you had ever seen Ten Years After and The Doors live you'd know, feel the electricity. Morrison put a rocket up everybody's arse. Those were great times. "

"So what have you found out then sleuth?" She was mocking me and turning the conversation. It worked.

"Well, who keeps a body in a flat in the middle of summer for three days? Why didn't she let him go to the morgue? Then he would have been frozen."

"Perhaps she thought he'd be identified and then the story would get out?"

I was laughing now, loud manic laughter.

"What's so funny then?"

"Just this," I was speaking calmly. "The body in the flat wasn't Morrison, that's so obvious to me now. It was someone else. The grave gets bought quickly, the body is interred and there are no mourners. Just Alan, Agnes, Bill Siddons, Pam and some professional mourners. A sad end for a giant star."

"Yeah, but they were his friends?"

"That's bullshit. What nobody wanted was the Brian Jones thing. The man was a god."

"You always look for things that aren't there," she replied. "You are a sceptic and septic too. You always look for the worst in things. Just like your brother, not a good word to say about anything. Not everything is poisonous."

"Don't be so simple," I was saying, listening to my own voice. "Don't be so bloody naïve. One of the best known icons of the western world, cast down in a deep grave and then nothing. No headstone, no plinth. Pam may have shot the money for that up into her veins, but you'd think there would have been more. More to him in death and more to her in mourning. So she goes home to the States and becomes a virtual recluse. She is so messed up and yet no one looks to get a headstone made up. Bullshit, it's all wrong."

She was laughing now. "Oh my God," she was saying, "and you think I'm the crazy one? I'm not in Paris chasing a ghost."

"He's alive, I'm sure of it. The money was not spent on the grave either – he didn't want it to be. Why? Why would he want that?"

"Why not be cremated like Janis then and scattered along the beach? Why didn't they have a cremation? That would have destroyed any evidence once and for all. "

"There's the idea of a suicide – maybe Pam had a note. A killer note that explains it all."

"Spill the beans?" She was obviously eager to hear what I had found so far.

I should say at this point who *she* is. I'd done a few short stories and then she said to me, "Why don't you write a novel?" So I did. That was alongside the journalism. Two years of blood and sweat and self-doubt and all the things that make you spit. But I did it. It had been a good seller and the second one followed it. I was extremely pleased and loved the acclaim. Like my ex-wife had sneeringly once said, "Well you always wanted to be famous." Like that was some kind of sin? I had this fantasy that I'd be buried somewhere and people would come and stand at the foot of my grave and say, "What a shame the guy's dead. He could write a story." Anyway, I was now a novelist, a proven novelist and I'd been thirsting to get my work out and published. The Morrison thing was bubbling away at the back of my head and now I'd cracked it, or it had cracked me.

"If you really do well," she had said, "why not write a book about Morrison?"

"Well I am supposed to be doing an article."

She cut to the chase. "Look, you're freelance, they're not even paying you decent expenses are they?"

"True."

"So it's your story?"

I nodded and thought to myself, she's right.

"If it's your story, you can do what you want with it surely?"

"I suppose I can," I replied.

"You're a pushover. Far too easy going. Look, you're a writer and..."

I hoped she was going to say good one. "You're biased," I interrupted her.

"Ok, you're a shit one then. But shit or not, you're my crime writer," she paused and then suddenly blurted, "so write up the crime."

That was what I loved about her. She didn't feel the need to try and put me down or deflate my ego to make her look or feel better. In fact, she always did the opposite. When I was getting shaky and doubted myself, she managed to kick me back into reality and lift any despondency. For me that worked.

It seems kind of weird, a crime writer finding a way to unearth the Morrison mystery. At last I'm beginning to get inside the guy's head. I don't really know if there was a crime, or if there was, what it was.

"I don't know if there is, was a crime," I answered.

"Well there must have been even if it was only to avoid the Miami sentencing."

"Bingo, that's it."

"What is?" she was momentarily lost.

"Motive. That's the missing angle."

"Glad to be of service," she chuckled. "When do you think you'll get back?"

"I don't know," was my honest reply.

"Well I think as you are not on expenses we should get off this phone line before it costs us an arm and a leg."

"So practical."

"One of us has to be," she chuckled, "or we'd be skint."

The thing I was always looking for was motive. I mean, what makes people do the things they do? Even if the motive is skewed, it's still a motive; the real thing is trying to work out what someone else thinks. I was talking to one of the behavioural people once and he said that the mistake everyone makes is judging people by their own standards. People who don't lie find it hard to evaluate liars. Like the American Indians, they signed treaties and believed they would be binding. When the whites broke the treaty they could hardly believe it. See, the Arabs are the same, they have a kind of loyalty. Lawrence of Arabia found that one out real quick. Anyhow, to get the answer to Morrison, I had to think like him – be him. It was harder than I thought. Even watching old copies of Rawhide and Bonanza gave me the shudders. The kind of moral code which came from the silver screen and was pumped into all of us. Self-determination, self-reliance, individual freedom; the frontier and the ability of the sacred Indian shaman to be more than a lice-ridden aboriginal who hadn't even learnt to smelt metal. Someone who would swap a pint of gold for a handful of crap glass beads. Then there was the other thing about bigging up your enemy so that when you beat them you felt and looked better.

I started to reason carefully, because she was a levelling influence. She'd read my novels and had given me some valid ideas. She asked me all sorts of things and then criticised the final copy. Not in a nasty way, but in a kind, constructive way.

"Look," I said, "I think I know how they did it."

"Who's they?"

"Pam and Jim."

"Don't you mean Jim and Pam? He was the brains."

"Yeah, but she was his Lady Macbeth. I think he was dangerous, but she was lethal."

"There you go again with your misogynistic viewpoint on women."

"No, just work it out. Morrison needed someone to make it work. Make it look plausible. Who better than the vulnerable little redhead from Orange County. Only she wasn't quite the little meek thing everyone thought. I mean look at the Oliver Stone movie, what does she say? 'Pamela Morrison – ornament'. That's the biggest load of bullshit. They started as equals, with her being the little kid in the city, but by the end she was controlling him."

"So you reckon?"

"Yep I do. And I think they planned a murder together and then…"

"Oh come on. You don't really believe that, do you? A murder, that's far-fetched and people won't buy that unless you have absolute proof."

I wondered if she was right. Maybe I was crazy. Cruel in the head – spiteful.

"Why not?" I asked

"It's crazy, that's why not."

"Look, what if the body in the coffin was not Morrison, but the identified corpse was?"

"What on earth are you going on about?"

"Or vice versa, misdirection, like a magic trick. Like the Easter heist?"

"And you think you know how it was done?"

"Almost. Well nearly almost," I paused, "perhaps if some of the detail comes together."

Six

California Dreamin'...

When I woke up I didn't know how long I'd been asleep or where I was. Confusion reigned and I was beginning to think that a prolonged derangement of the senses was making my judgement flawed. I stumbled into the bathroom and took a leak. Morrison was taking me over, messing about with my understanding. Was he alive? Was I awake some of the time, all of the time, or in a dream? If he was, as I believed, alive, had he buried someone else in that coffin? What precisely did happen? Perhaps it was just an accident, or a suicide? My head was spinning, throwing me off balance. It was like being on my own trip and falling the through the cracks of reason, like water slipping into a drain. It was like that crazy thing he said about being a shaman, a medicine man of his age, a conduit for the wrath and rage of a people locked into an unpopular war, led by a corrupt government which had a front man who lacked the Kennedy charisma.

Like me, Morrison was obsessed with cowboys and Indians, and why? Because the Jewish dominated film industry of the forties and fifties needed to show that they were 'in tune' with Americanism. They had to prove that as new immigrants they were Americans. I was scrubbing my teeth now, looking at my face in the mirror over the sink. And what was more American than the fine upstanding cowboy? Somehow morally righteous and good and clean-cut and clean-shaven, the white face of the new world. After all, this was the land of the free and the home of the brave. It wasn't until I went to university that I understood the truth around the propaganda. As a kid I'd sided with the oppressed Indian, the noble horse warrior beaten by the even nobler cowboy. That was a load of old bull too. "Always big up your opposition if you wish your triumph to seem more significant." The sage words of my drunken history tutor rang in my head. Clever bastard, he was, and I enjoyed every dissenting moment; I identified with his disenchantment of the system and felt myself his 'friend'. I found out that most cowboys were illiterate, that Billy the Kid shot most of his opponents in the back and that most eulogised cattle herders were either ex-Confederate soldiers, dispossessed by the war, or just black. But Hollywood churned out the myth for the sake of the immigrants who had to belong and who sold the rights to TV stations in England. Morrison was a sponge, he soaked up the movies, the myths and then added the beats over the top, poetry for the rebels. Like a mirror he reflected back out what the watchers wanted to see. In England the same thing was happening to me, and to this day I love a good western. Not the Audie Murphy type, but the real thing, the *Dances with Wolves* and *Unforgiven* variety. That was why Morrison was so popular, he was a mimic for the masses, a bringer of the new religion – fame. Man, he was what Warhol said, he was a man who brought the possibilities of fifteen minutes of fame to all, developed and honed the image and understood what the voyeurs needed. Morrison and Warhol had that gift – the pathfinder gift.

Somehow, I don't know how, he was giving the answers only most of the time; I was too blind to see it. It felt like some sort of elaborate game of cat and mouse, or catch me if you can, was going on. And then I wondered, at what point did he decide to give up, get out? At what point was he so pissed off with people that he turned his back/ He had already said he was too old to be a rock star, too old at twenty seven. Jesus, with The Rolling Stones it's a case of lock up your grandmothers; too old, what is too old? Or it was so obvious that it didn't make sense. A Campbell's soup can, well, when did that become an icon for a generation? Petulance is a gift bestowed on the few for the annoyance of the many – and Morrison he had it in spades. He really was a 'Clever Trevor'. I knew he would be in that bar, part of his personality, a very small part, was still with The Doors. He had to be there, that was him.

I knew that I needed to go back to the start and think the whole process through all over again. Breakfast, I needed breakfast and then perhaps a visit to the Paris records office.

"No damn good, you numpty," I said aloud to my reflection in the mirror, whilst I clung to the side of the sink like a limpet to a rock. "That's where everyone starts, and then they go to the doctor, then the cemetery." I paused. "That is why they always fail. Think it through... properly." I slapped my own face and the stinging sensation brought me up sharply. "Call yourself a journalist? Wake up."

I needed to work out the whole process, as if it were a crime, that was the only thing that made logical sense. I'd done that before when I was a stringer. Years on *The Times* and working for IPC magazines as a crime reporter had forged a cynicism which gave me an observant eye and a sceptical brain. Now I needed to think like him. Start from the end and then work backwards. I had the motive, now I had to work on the means. In any crime there are fifty ways to mess up and if you can foresee forty nine of them, you're doing well. Christ, just a drop of blood would give me the DNA. Perhaps the Morrison family would let me have some, then I could get a bore into the grave. My mind was running riot.

"Bloody ridiculous. No sane person is going to let you get a drill bore into a cemetery."

I thought about a night raid over the wall.

I had to start again at the beginning: LA, or the ending really, as it was for the band. So I set to re-reading my notes – the accounts of The Doors themselves, well Ray and John, because Robby said he wouldn't write anything yet, not until everybody was dead. That way he could avoid the libel and litigation.

I drank coffee; I took a shower; I walked and finally, I gave in.

Later that day I was sitting at the laptop and began. That's the hard bit – starting.

Murdering Jim Morrison, who really was responsible? Like who killed the Kennedys? When, after all, it was you and me. I'd heard those lines before. 'Sympathy for the Devil', and boy was I dealing with a Devil. A demon, perhaps someone who was down with his own demons, or brought down by his demons.

Try as I might, the mess wouldn't flow into a coherent story. Morrison had managed to confound and confuse his audience – once again.

Then it struck me: what if Morrison had planned it all, every last little piece. His great talent always seemed to be that he could reflect back to people what they wanted. He could be the perfect southern boy, the poet, the rebel, the drunk, the bum, the academic. But what was he really? Who was he? And if he could be these things then could he be a murderer, a murderer of himself? Well his image anyway; but a murderer, an actual murderer? I could see the law suits and injunctions flying before I wrote it, it would be like taking on a machine, a money grinding machine. If he wasn't in the casket, who was?

Then it came to me. I would have to think like him and not follow the reaction he would most expect from the public, the sheeple.

So in LA the six album contract has been fulfilled. The first album was quick, the second and third still drawing on the original material of youth, not just Jim's but Robby's too. Like his poetic influence Rimbaud, Jim had finished his creativity. *The Soft Parade* had lapsed into the pretentiousness of the age; I mean, even the cover looks like that. Everyone was answering the criticism that pop was pap: there was The Who's rock opera, *Tommy*; The Kinks did *Albert and Victoria*; The Beatles, *Sergeant Pepper* and even the Stones were *At His Satanic Majesty's Request*. Popular music had gone mad. Yes had morphed into Rick Wakeman's *The six wives of Henry the VIII* and cloaks and progressive were in, fashionable nonsense trying to make rock into the creditable music of intellect. Thirty five minute tracks of noises and suites and musical pretension. Crazy doped and LSD soaked stars started talking about elves at the bottom of their garden and J.R.R. Tolkien had written a bible years before, which now everybody read. It was the book of the time – the Zeitgeist.

Then out comes *LA woman* and pow! We're all back, back on the whore of Babylon with Bo Diddley, and Little Richard and the blues and that, that was Morrison. The music of raw sex and passion – The Punk: The fore-teller.

So Morrison, yet again, had seen the need. Only this time he wanted out. Paris!

Pam goes to Paris, and Morrison? He takes that in his stride, knowing she's gone with the Count, not so easy a thing to do for a guy who is becoming increasingly reliant on the cinnamon redhead. She had been there from the beginning and, strangely, would be there at the end.

Morrison was a strange person, he loved the fame and yet he hated it too. Like Gollum, he loved and hated the ring in a strange dichotomy of being. But he was constant with the band. He was the first, the front man, but they were all equals. Equal pay and equal rights, until near the end when the rot set in. John Densmore always said Morrison taught him a valuable lesson in greed.

* * *

"All we have to do Pam, is work on misdirection. They have a legend, all we have to do is feed it with myth. I seen it with Marilyn and Jimmy Dean, everything gets exaggerated and we just keep fuelling the flames. Give them what they expect and do what they don't expect."

I could hear Morrison's voice inside my head.

"Give the people what they really want to hear. Give them a Lord, an idol, and they'll do anything. They're all a bunch of fucking slaves."

The phrase kept coming back to me. The Miami concert, the first stage of self destruction, 'You're all a bunch of fucking slaves' over and over again. Why? Why would he do that? Maybe he had seen fame for what it was, a vacuous shell, a candle in the wind, loneliness on a stick. Perhaps he really was insane and the money meant nothing – really meant nothing. If that was the case and Densmore was right, perhaps he could walk. That's the thing if the world has become oppressive, you have to get off. He'd seen sycophants trying to screw him and the band over for a percentage, heard the girls offering themselves to him. Listen to the live recordings and you can hear it too, they are there in the audience.

I couldn't have given it up, but then I wasn't famous. Imagine it, being famous enough to walk down the street and, in consequence, not being able to walk down the street. Tony Funches, his ex-Vietnam marine bodyguard, said Morrison was happiest just talking to people, normal people. Perhaps he could do what others couldn't – walk away.

Pam was replying now, "Hey, Morrison, I love it when you go on a mind fuck. People can't stand that, but it will make us into gods not lords. All we need is to be free, be on the perimeter."

In my mind I could see her laughing, her green eyes alive and the mischievous glint taking hold. I bet she was a hell of a kid to control and good in the sack too. The intelligent ones usually are, especially if they can see through all the bull, and she was manipulative, little girl manipulative, and he was sucked in. The mouse that caught the cat, that was what he called her, a cat. I could see her in the Brownie pack, in her floral dress, refusing to conform and I knew; knew that Morrison loved her, loved her for her love of freedom. She was Yang for his Ying or something like that; two halves of the same coin, only not one thrown into il Fontana di Trevi.

"I need to do the album and you could hang out for a bit and then I could come over and join you. It will look like a vacation and it will give us time to think and travel."

"I love you, Morrison," she was saying and then the phone rang.

My mind cleared and the bond with the 1970s snapped. I was back.

"How you doing?" her friendly voice asked.

"Not too good," I answered. "I've been trying to get my head around what happened, trying to imagine myself into the situation, was it a murder or suicide? And now I think I've seen him, actually seen him in a bar. "

"Well was it?" she was dead calm.

"Christ knows."

"Well it's not me writing the article, is it?"

"I know, but I keep jumping from suicide to murder to accident and then back to escape plan and none of it makes any real sense."

"You know what you're missing?"

"Don't even go there," I laughed, as she began the flirtation.

"Well you need to think things through carefully."

"I know, I'm going up to the cemetery again this afternoon, and the public records office. Need to take another look at the death certificate. There's something wrong, I can feel it."

"You mean you'd rather look at the grave of some dead rock star than look at me in my nice lace panties? All moist and inviting."

"I'll be on the next plane home," I said. "Just a few more hours and then…"

"And I'll be waiting," she laughed.

* * *

The alarm began to buzz and I woke up. I thought I was already awake and for a few moments I had to adjust my brain to see where I was; find out what was real. I'd just been to the toilet, but I could feel the tightness of a full bladder, telling me I had to go again. Was I awake or had I been dreaming? I was losing it.

I was beginning to lose my grip on reality. I thought that I had just got up; was I losing that to? It was the weirdest feeling of déjà vu. So I went to the bathroom and peed. From the time I was there I knew that the night had only just ended and that I had experienced some very vivid dreams. It was like a prolonged derangement of the senses; like some kind of weird night trip.

Thinking about Morrison, I knew I had to focus on two things: motive and means. The motive was easy: escape. The means was the one that proved a little more difficult; just how did he manage to fool everybody?

Seven

A woman left lonely…

Outside the Morrison apartment in rue Beautreillis, Paris, I sat in a bar across the street, trying to get a feel for the guy's mind. That was probably the hardest thing of all, like trying to get inside the mind of a serial killer. What I needed to do was be him, think like him. If I could become him then I could piece the puzzle together. That was going to be the hardest thing of all trying to establish precisely what he wanted, even if he didn't know himself. The man was a mirror who had perfected the perfect deflective reflection – gave people what they wanted to see. That was a perfect disguise and a complete millstone too, which hung around his neck and dragged him under the water. That way he never had to be himself, unless he was with the band or Pam, or the faux Doors. Then he could be Jim the poet and lyricist, Jim the husband and also Jimbo the drunk, but that was also part of the images – the 'cellves'. The real key here was Pam and she was dead. That was a certainty.

I sat drinking, watching the sun against the brickwork of the building and tried to shed the years which had passed. I was falling between the actual and the subconscious conversation – losing me. My memories were changing and my attitudes too, I was going back, always going back, like a taxi from Africa.

Her body had been formally identified by her parents, who maintain to this day that she was murdered and here there is little conjecture. The thing that always puzzled me was why she would have chosen to inject heroin. It's not the heroin that would have got me, that was believable, but the process, the injection. You see, Danny Sugerman also said that Pam had no veins, said she always snorted and that needles scared her. Whatever is was, murder or suicide, death ended it. That was the final curtain call.

Many people have claimed that this fact alone unequivocally proves the death of Jim Morrison. If Jim were still alive then Pamela must be also, and, ipso facto, if she were alive, he must be too. Pamela Courson/Morrison died of a heroin overdose, whether that was self-administered, a suicide or otherwise, no one will ever know. Things vanished from her apartment after her death, notebooks, clothes and other things which were principally Jim's, just how much and who took them we will never know.

Danny Sugerman, years later, donated items to the Hard Rock Café, things like a set of lyrics for *LA woman,* which are now framed, along with Jim's leather trousers complete with crude stitched repair. The same brown trousers he wore to the Hollywood Bowl concert in 1968 and which he continued to wear until they, quite literally, fell apart. Pamela Courson is supposed to have, 'stolen' these, 'leathers' or to have removed them for destruction at the very least.

It was no secret that Morrison often refused to wash and as time passed his habits in this quarter got worse. Those pants have paint splashed on them and are ripped and repaired, albeit crudely; perhaps he did a little freelance painting and decorating just like Muddy Waters supposedly did. Whatever happened, he wore those trousers virtually continuously until they fell to pieces. As Pam loved fashion, Jim was scathing of it, often opting to stand against the flow of the tide. The world he inhabited was one of challenge and opposition and he was the candidate least likely to swap one accepted uniform for another. Maybe Danny Sugerman rescued those trousers, repaired and kept them, much as any sincere fan might. I'm not saying he took things, but as the head of the 'official fan club' he would have had more access than most to things which Pam possessed. Indeed, he kept in contact with her after 1971 and until her death in 1974, when he would have been 19 years old, if his recollections in *Wonderland Avenue* are to be believed. In that book he claims they even had sex together and that her post-coital reaction was both odd and bordering on mental instability. Something akin to the notion that her old man, presumably Morrison, would kill him if he found out. And there that story would end, but for someone like me. The outburst, recalled by Sugerman, could be the result of mental instability, but it could equally be the unguarded outburst of someone who knew, emphatically knew, Mr. Mojo Risin wasn't dead.

In that bar, on that day, I had deep feelings that things were not as they should have been. I felt like a cop with some deep-seated gut reaction to what really did happen. The more I thought, the more determined I was to get to the truth.

There was that inner scream again: 'The thing is, the truth is often ugly.'

At the time of Morrison in Paris, Sugerman would have been fifteen; seeing as we shared the same year of birth, that fanaticism I could understand. I had the same sort of mentality about what was one of my favourite rock bands at that time. I went to as many of their concerts as I could, tried to copy the style of the lead guitarist. What I should have been doing was trying to develop my own style. That's the key, be different, and Morrison had worked that out and simply done it. The result: music which is a mixture of nihilistic doom and fairground frivolity – scary clown music; and hey, aren't clowns scary? That they are there for kids is amazing, because they look terrifying.

The thing is, you grow up. When I was fifteen I thought the greatest novel in the world was *Lord of the Rings* and anyone who didn't think the same must be 'strange'. Hey, I'm in my fifties now and if someone my age still thought that was the best novel ever, I'd think them 'strange'. The thing is with The Doors, the music is still as good as it was then, simply because it is different and has timelessness. Some of the songs are truly products of the 1960s but the vast majority are still innovative and fresh; maybe that's why even the younger audiences still buy the albums.

Danny Sugerman had the knack of collecting those things which had once been Jim's, things which others might have cast aside. Perhaps, like Morrison, he had learned the art of iconography, or perhaps he had simply learned the lesson from observing Morrison at close quarters. His mission and transition from fan to manager, and his unwavering loyalty, clearly helped to establish the mythical status of his idol Jim Morrison. But the other thing has been time and history. The Rolling Stones, The Beatles, The Who, if any of these guys had been asked how long their music would last, none of them would have predicted forty plus years. Mick Jagger once said, around about 1969, that the band might last four years. Apart from the period in the wilderness of the 1980s, they go on from strength to strength. There are always those that survive fashion and those that fall from grace and there are legends in music – Glen Miller is a prime example.

I was engaged in an internal monologue with my voices now. The beer and the warm afternoon biting into my brain. Those voices, the ones which make you question things, were getting louder; my state of mind less controlled.

Just take the time, if you are on Hollywood Boulevard, to take a look at those leather pants. You can't miss them, encased as they are in a glass case, mounted on a full life-size manikin set of legs and adjacent to a life-size portrait and display. 'At 5ft 11in he wasn't that tall', I've heard people say that, but for 1968 that was tall. The kids today are taller, with boys topping out at 6ft 2in as an average and girls at around 5ft 6in. He weighed in at 145 lbs in 1966 after the Venice hungry months. He was lean, perhaps a little too lean.

Pam was 5ft 4in and painfully slight at 90-95lbs, but for the time she would have been the epitome of chic. Ultra slender. By 1968 he was near to the fighting weight of 170lbs, which would give those leathers a 36in waist and a body mass index which would be medically nigh on perfect. In that sense, Morrison was perfection, both he and Pam would have fitted into the glamorous world of West Hollywood with consummate ease – they looked the part. Their challenging attitude, however, made them very square pegs in decidedly round holes.

Morrison's weakness was that he didn't really know what he wanted; he was drifting, drifting on Venice beach. Perhaps he could have done something with the movies, but he lacked the discipline to work at it. Perhaps he could have become a truly great poet, but once again he lacked the discipline to hone it, even though he clearly had a prodigious capability. He was pretty and he was lucky; and for one brief moment in 1966, The Doors came together and the Zeitgeist was with them.

Fate and destiny have a funny way of biting someone on the arse sometimes. What was it David Bowie said? 'I was an overnight success after fifteen years of hard work.' Maybe Morrison was one of those rare creatures who happened to be in the right town, at the right time in history. But I shouldn't forget that during 1966 and into 1967 they toured, mostly California and the east coast. If *Light my Fire* had not been that successful in the summer of love, perhaps, just perhaps, the whole shooting match would have been different.

He certainly was lucky to get a group of musicians of that quality who locked together so well, and who tolerated his crazy artistic ways.

I looked up at the apartment window and thought about the nature of luck. Like his sister was later to say of him, the family thought Jim was going to end up a bum. My mind quickly switched to the down and outs around Venice and Santa Monica pier. A lot of those guys have mental frailty issues and a lot of them weren't lucky and the 'what if' scenario sped into my brain.

On those beaches there are restrooms which are free and places to get water; there are places to sleep too, under the pier and on rooftops if you know a friend in the building. The weather is nearly always good and there's the beach, and if some girls feed you 'cos you're a good lookin' southern boy, maybe you can survive, for a while at least.

The Hard Rock Café at 6901 on Hollywood has other Morrison memorabilia. The leather jacket, the highway jacket, the one with the fur collar, that is in Las Vegas and the record company have donated things too. There are things which people came by, by a variety of means, and I'm not saying Danny Sugerman was involved; but The Doors, continuing legacy was fuelled by his unflinching loyalty until his death at the age of 50 – lung cancer.

The ugly truth is Pamela Courson is dead and her ashes are now interred at Fairhaven Memorial Park in Santa Ana, California. Many fans have asked why were her ashes not placed in the Paris grave. That is the lynch pin which has hung up most investigations, for a while it did me too.

You'll read stuff about how the Coursons and the Morrisons could not agree and how it took eight months before Pam's ashes were finally laid to rest. Believe me you will find loads of this stuff, I did, and most of it won't be true.

Whatever discussions took place, we will not be party to them, even if both families continued to share equally Jim's portion of the royalties due. Having sold ninety million albums worldwide and with the other band members having been made multi-millionaires, that is some small fortune. Nobody really knows what goes on in families and back then, before we all became used to the open and frank television exposé, family things remained behind closed doors. If we then add on top the popular media perception, fuelled by the Morrison legend, of a set of dreadful families hell bent upon usurpation; a sort of skewed logic begins to prevail and I knew I needed to strip that out if I was going to get near the truth. I couldn't let my perceptions get all twisted by trying to judge others with either standards they had set or ones they wanted to impose. Once again that 'family thing' was something people wanted to believe; that made sense, especially when trying to fathom the 'real' Jim Morrison. It sort of neatly ties up the corners and corners don't always tie neatly. Perhaps there is no happily ever after, and no reason for being – there just is.

Pam was his rock, I have heard journalists say, without her he could not continue, and I've also heard the same applied in the opposite direction. It's true, she probably saw more than anybody

Jim's grave as it is today. The grave has a security
attendant at all times.

A typical pathway through the cemetery.
In this case the one up to Jim's plot.

The rooftop in Venice Beach. Jim slept and starved here after leaving UCLA in 1965. Though he told Ray Manzarek he was moving to New York, he remained in Los Angeles. Renamed 'The Morrison' in his honour.

The mural of Jim singing, on Speedway immediately behind the Venice Beach boardwalk. The original beachfront rehearsal space (The Mondrian Window House) has either been demolished or extensively remodelled.

Venice Beach – looking back toward Santa Monica pier. The original
Muscle Beach is centre frame. In 1966 all beachfront properties had
open access straight onto the sand. The concrete boardwalk now
used by cyclists and roller skaters is a recent addition.

A typical Venice canal vista – A Bohemian centre for artists,
poets and musicians in 1966. Still a lively place today.

The Alta Cienega Motel on North La Cienega Boulevard. Jim's regular room is top left above the entrance way.

Jim Morrison's Room (32) clearly marked. The room remains the most rented room in the motel. People visit from all over the world. Advanced booking though is an absolute must, as is a love of graffiti.

The Laurel Canyon store on, 'Love Street, the place where the creatures meet,' as seen from the Rothdell Trail. Graham Nash and Joni Mitchell shared a house on the street, as did John and Michelle Phillips of the Mamas and Papas,

Even today the store serves as a focal point for the Canyon and the "stars," who live either in the area or above it. Though the musicians may have moved on, the location, just below Mulholland Drive makes a great stop for early Sunday morning coffee.

Jim and Pam's apartment on Love Street.
The brown building to the right.

The Whisky a Go Go on Sunset Strip. The club at which The Doors had a residency and the place famous for cage dancers. Many famous groups have made their mark here and gone on to international fame.

The Chateau Marmont Hotel located on Sunset Boulevard. A favourite hangout for stars visiting Los Angeles. The window from which Morrison fell onto the roof of a car, shortly before his departure to Paris, is located centre right, second floor.

Place de Vosges, Paris, showing the apartments overlooking the square which was a favourite 17th century duelling spot. Doug Prayer's apartment – above the arches on the right.

Sausalito City, on the far side of the Golden Gate Bridge, north of San Francisco. A favourite hideout for Pam and Jim – the exact spot as indicated.

else, knew more than anybody else, after all, she slept with him and knew his deepest secret fears.

I immediately thought of my mother, a widow at twenty two with two small children in the middle of a war. Luck, or fate, or destiny, she survived, though she cried so much when she got the news of her husband's death that a bath towel was sopping wet. Well that's what my brother remembers and he was four at the time. She carried on, maybe because of the kids, maybe because she had to. Anyhow, she met my father, a younger man and a soldier of an occupying army. Fell in love, though he was years younger than her, eleven nearly, and along I came, her last chance child before the menopause set it. The truth is, people do carry on and things happen.

When my father left she did nearly go crazy and then wanted to kill herself. Christ, the times I spent talking her out of depression were endless, so I kind of felt, rather than knew, what real depths people can go to. She survived, but only just, and then went on, though by the end of her life she kind of was disappointed.

I could write a book about what she told me of those times and maybe one day I will. It's all filed away in the memory palace somewhere.

We all heard the stories of just how wild Pam had been as a child, and if you compare Jim's childhood, she was the wilder of the two. After all, Pam did leave Orange High School in her junior year and transfer to Capistrano Union High School for her senior one. This was a school some eighteen or so miles from Orange; however, she did not graduate – why? Pamela Courson had become a beatnik who truanted frequently, caused her parents considerable turmoil and anguish; a fact mostly overlooked by commentators and more importantly, she was bold and independent. Capistrano was in another district and there Pam would have been less likely to embarrass the reputation of her father – the principal of a junior high school. But precisely what did happen in that last year 1964? Did Pamela make a mistake? She hung around the beatnik bars, she hitch-hiked and did and went to places which other girls of her age would not have been allowed to do. Did her parents simply let her go? Pam was, 'difficult' as Jim was 'difficult'; they were, as a result, allowed the freedom to roam. Jim from his basement world within the family home, which his father clearly encouraged. Steve Morrison gave Jim space; did the Coursons do the same with Pam?

Is there a Courson child somewhere? Sudden strategic disappearances happened for many girls then, as did illegal terminations. My mind was running a riot of possibilities. Pregnancy and adoption? And just why did Pam never get pregnant by Jim? He would never have taken precautions, of that much I am totally certain, and they were together for a long time. I thought of the possibility of someone becoming pregnant too young, terminating and then being unable to conceive at all thereafter. He certainly was supposed to be a fully functioning, fertile male, if the claims by other concubines are true; that is until the alcoholism kicked in. Pam would tease him about his flaccidity, if we are to believe the stories of their tempestuous arguments and various incidents of her throwing his possessions out of windows.

For a fleeting second I thought I saw a flash of red at the window and heard some girlish laughter. The window, in the smart enclave of Paris, had been theirs. My mind was wondering, chasing the demons of the rubbish which other people had made the stuff of the Morrison legend. There were those who said that Morrison wandered the streets of Paris to try to regain 'the muse'. I thought about the idea of him wandering Midtown and Downtown Los Angeles on foot, something he was supposed to have done from West Hollywood. Or taking afternoon strolls down to the beach in Venice or Santa Monica Pier. Once I got there, I was certain that was a romanticised view. Jim spent most of his time in West Hollywood around and within his college, UCLA. Like any student, he frequented the bars and nightspots, only these were the happening ones in the 1966 USA music scene. There were equivalents up the coast in San Francisco at Haight and Ashbury and in London in Soho and the Kings Road. Luck or destiny had placed Morrison in the right place at the right time. If the truth be known, Morrison and his continuous theatrical antics had got The Doors noticed. Outrageous bad-boy reputations made the band infamous, with little additions like Robby appearing on US national television with a black eye etc.

His death would make them a legend, and Morrison knew that too. But I suspect that even he would not have expected what happened over the next thirty years. Everybody likes the bad guys; the good guys are quite often dull, unless they are bad to be good. If that makes sense?

Suddenly I thought of John Denver, don't ask me why, I just did. He died and yet he has not reached the iconic status of other musicians. That was simply, I would say, because he had no Danny.

The more I sat, the more the voices appeared. Hollow voices. Was I just another fan? Was I deluded? Was I doing something sacrilegious? I knew I'd get some real kicks in the teeth for everything I wrote. I'd gone past the point of worrying. The truth just is.

The question of whether Jim could ever be happy with Pam kept bubbling in my mind. Mary Werbelow, the pert-breasted beauty, went the same way as his father. They both had the temerity to say The Doors would never amount to anything. Admiral Morrison was a success, the youngest ever admiral, and Mary, well she was Queen of the Sunset Strip dancers in 1966, the best dancer in the Whisky a Go Go, but that was it. Her brief fifteen minutes came and went and her future went with it – but hey, she didn't have a crystal ball and didn't know it at the time. The Doors music was shit, she told Morrison, and she was a hit, well that's what she thought. He warned her they would go all the way and they did. Perhaps he had a real feeling of destiny, unlike the rest of us who are just insecure mortals. Perhaps she should have done more with her painting and then she would have been Pam and maybe, just maybe, the whole Paris thing would never have taken place. She would have been the enduring widow now, a tortured artist pining for her lost love. Portraits, multi-layered portraits of Jim: Jim the idol; icon of the 60s; the boyhood sweetheart with the tortured soul of a poet; the Che of the music world. But Mary Werbelow told Morrison that his band weren't any good; the result: Morrison, Mr. Confident Morrison, Mr. Mojo Risin, Morrison was gone.

Even his own sister thought he would end up as nothing. Why? Because she had lived with him. To her he was no idol, no sex god, to her he was simply Jimmy the elder brother. Who, for all we know, she considered had serious mental health issues.

Hindsight is such a wonderful gift; the gift of endless pain, played out on an empty hollow canvas. Even prime ministers regret; perhaps Tony Blair now regrets his choice. I saw an interview once and he wondered, publicly, for the camera, if 'he could have made it' as a rock star. He had charisma?

Life is full of ifs and buts, and Morrison was bound to chance just like the rest of us. There is no crystal ball, no certainty, no fears, no ruined years, no clocks. Hey, I was now transposing our lives and words, because everything was too late, far too late.

I thought about trying to get a look inside the apartment there in Paris, but I knew that the things inside would have been altered. Morbid curiosity made me wonder if the bath, in which he was supposed to have died, was still there, or whether that had been sold to some souvenir hunter.

Her silent voice said, "Get into the courtyard, at least to take a look."

Creatures of habit – Morrison liked red hair; all of the significant ones were redheads. There was a trigger there that I needed to explore. What in his young life made him secure with redheads; what made me make my first female crime villain a redhead? I needed to see her eyes – green. I examined the photograph from the Themis shoot, pulled it out of my bag – green, jade-green, striking green. Eyes that could so easily be Bernie Taupin's blue if they weren't green. She was beautiful, striking in fact, another Lizzie Siddal, another redhead. Pre-Raphaelite beauty and truth and sex and poetry being wound into the hair of the dead body and Dante Rossetti getting fat and indolent. It was all in those eyes – Pam's. Rossetti's head going after he had reached the pinnacle, laudanum, opium, sex, fame, rebellion and finally a stroke at fifty three. Broken. That could have been Morrison, especially as he lived like he was on a thousand mile an hour jet ride.

I remembered the statistics about red heads being the first women to get picked in male preference; I read that somewhere too, and yet the ginger headed boys at school? They had a hard time; they got the little Irish red and green leprechaun thing. They just got bullied and reviled, but the girls, they got picked first in gym activities, got laid, got married. Morrison was just like the rest of us guys – bingo! There was something, he wasn't that different after all. Maybe he was just a man and not a god. That's the problem with fame – the public image. Someone is famous so they have to be exceptional, be different, so different as to be awesome.

Cinnamon-headed, white-skinned Pam, walks into a beatnik place like the Rendezvous Ballroom. Pretty, slight and full of confidence, she's the beauty from Orange County who everybody wants. Just like when she walked into the London Fog on Sunset. Different place, same reaction.

Now I'm going to upset people, but what the hell? So you get this guy, a good guy, with some nice ideas about how to live a decent life, and the vested interests get him nailed to a cross. Money honey, if you wanna get along with me. Even the chief outsider and spectators want the ceremony truncated, want the gentle man with the peaceful demeanour set free. He ain't doin' no harm, in fact, he's a kinda nice guy; he gives the crowd something to see and talk about. Hey, he entertains them; but the vested group won't let go, can't let go, they have too much to lose. They need the man pulled down a peg or two, need to keep those spectators amused, they need him dead. He asks too many questions and upsets the apple cart, so they get their man nailed to a cross. Even after a public washing of hands and the symbolism of blame removal, they still want him dead. The fame cult begins.

So the man dies and three days later the body disappears – the Easter heist. He must be the son of God or a god, or something unbelievable, because he is a legend. But maybe, just maybe, someone took the body away? And Adolf Hitler, well he must be the anti-Christ, that's why there's no body. Just a few shards of bone. A man so evil could not possibly be just a man, who rose by luck and chance. He had to be a demon, or a god, or … Hey, it's all luck and chance, just like Bob Zimmerman says, 'I can't help it if I'm lucky'.

Danny Sugerman went on to say, 'My personal belief is that Jim Morrison was a god'. What, they have to be able to drink forty pints of beer in one night? As Dylan Thomas openly boasted in New York, that's six gallons or three two gallon bucketfuls. Now that is a lot of fluid for a man who was only 5ft 4in in height. There was a man fuelling his own legend, just like Morrison, he needed to be a god. And Morrison, he could drink a whole bottle of brandy by lunchtime, and not the weak stuff, Courvoisier no less.

"Then there are the voices," she said, though she wasn't there in person.

"I know," I replied. "I hear them all the time; only they're not real, are they?"

"As real as you and me, unless we're dreaming. Are you dreaming? How do you know you're even alive?"

"Because, I'm talking to yo… I'm talking to myself in a bar in…"

"Precisely," she blurted and was gone.

Challenging religious education, wild poetry, oratory and civil rights and pop music and philosophy, it's a kind of circle; and then Miami – it all rolls and tumbles into Taupin's 'communistic politics and negro blues'. The complexity of it is enormous, maybe that was the thing – the complexity. Beat poetry, Dylan Thomas and Bob Dylan, and being different, and constantly rebelling, but, and here was the big one, Morrison liked red heads too.

Caitlin McNamara, now there was another one of those strong and wilful cinnamon beauties, the one who tormented Dylan, or was it he who tormented her? Romeo and Juliet, Caitlin and Dylan, Pam and Jim. It came as a sort of revelation, a freedom. Maybe that is what love is, a kind of constant intense torture, a rollercoaster ride bordering on insanity? A success – my piecing together of so many disparate strands to make even less sense than I started out with. Finally, I wondered if Jim and Dylan liked cinnamon pancakes like me too.

I had copies of all the documents: the death certificate: the fire brigade report and even details from the American Embassy. Like a giant jigsaw, it had sat on my desk and rolled around in my head, forever changing places. One minute I believed it was the perfect crime, then a suicide and then an accident; but try as I might, the one thing that kept returning was murder.

Years before, in this bar, the locals told me, the owner would play The Doors music whenever a fan came to the place to pay homage to his memory. Maybe this story was no more than that? A story. But the guy, who had owned the bar back in the seventies, had sold up and the new owners didn't seem that interested in Morrison. In fact, the youngsters, now pulling the sweet beers, were just that, youngsters. Too young to know the story of the man and his sudden death.

Alcoholics don't die suddenly, unless they have other ailments, ailments which they don't tell anyone about. Alcoholics die slowly and usually in a great deal of pain, unless you count the sudden *Leaving Las Vegas* style death of Nicholas Cage. I was getting the same feeling that I got in Brown's Hotel in Laugharne and at the grave of Dylan Thomas. There was a Caitlin moment here. Pam and Caitlin, only Pam didn't drink, she did heroin, and after Morrison died she didn't dance the Can-Can down the high street with no knickers on, Pam became a recluse, for a while. Only Caitlin Thomas made it into the same grave as her one true love, as she claimed him, whilst Pam is in California still and Jim in Paris. Well, that is if we believe the story which we are all supposed to – the official line.

Vitamin B12 deficiency brought about by a form of diabetes which made the sufferer collapse and sleep heavily, a coma of sorts, that was Dylan Thomas, the secretive Dylan Thomas. He had morphine and other drugs administered by Dr. Milton Feltenstein, administered to someone who may have been diabetic and an alcoholic. A death blow, as opiates and alcohol don't mix.

"Morrison's mix, alcohol and heroin?" That damn voice again.

Dylan Thomas, the man who hadn't even told his wife of the diabetic possibility, or had he? The man who got the clap and managed to hide it from his mother, despite still living at home. Had social stigma colluded to make him silent, while he ate dolly mixtures in the bath? Why didn't Caitlin connect the awesome headaches, which only went away after Dylan had eaten, with some medical issue? Inexperience or her own battle with alcohol? Caitlin Thomas, like Pamela Courson, had her own set of demons to fight.

My mind raced through the possibilities and similarities; John Densmore's account of his and Morrison's visit to the medical board prior to possible draft into the Vietnam War. Morrison was so certain, so absolutely certain, he could avoid the call up, just like Thomas had done in the Second World War. I read that piece several times in his account of life with The Doors, *Riders on the Storm*. It could simply have been a poor recollection on Densmore's part; the mind has a terrible propensity to play tricks on people. Memories fade and meld into what the mind assimilates as a form of truth. Sometimes, according to R.D. Laing, the renowned psychiatrist whose seminal work *The Divided Self* exploded the myths of schizophrenia and multi-personality disorders, the mind plays tricks. I had thought about Morrison and sanity as well. Dreams and reality merge and the actual becomes a dream and the real a myth. For no related reason I suddenly remembered the interview I had seen on TV before Laing had died. A simple story of adultery recounted; I couldn't explain why I remembered it, nor what made me write that here. It just came to me. Like some mystical hand was guiding my pen – now that is a crock.

Jim's voice now, "It's all a bunch of bullshit – mysticism."

A woman comes home and finds her husband on the couch with her best friend. They are naked and the husband has the friend's ankles behind her ears, while she is screaming a hefty orgasm to his full depth thrusts. The wife is so shocked that she feints on the spot, due to sensory overload; the two copulators quickly dress and the friend leaves. The husband then tidies up, and pretending to come home early, rouses his wife. She confronts him but he simply says that was not happening, there is no evidence in the room. The wife becomes confused, doubts her own sanity and due to the severity of the disbelief of possibility, falls once again into apoplexy. She is so 'in love' she cannot comprehend that the husband is having any affair. Her mind cannot accept reality and instead concocts a truth which makes her 'crazy'. The husband continues with the illusion and the wife, fearing her mind is delusional, willingly accepts a period in asylum. It must be her, for her love object never lies to her, she is the imperfect one, and she cannot see things as they are, merely as she wants them to be. A fantasy delusion, R.D. Laing's simple take on the confusion of self-delusional love. Ridiculous as this sounds, Laing's argument is the absolute trust which the wife has; she is unable to accept such an act of betrayal and therefore it cannot be true. Therefore if it is not true, she must have imagined it, dreamt it, transposed it. Her mind must be deranged. The resulting collapse of the personality is therefore so devastating that nothing can piece the fracture together, and as the malady deepens the chasm widens, until the delusion becomes reality and reality a delusion – result: insanity. And all the people are insane, lost in a wilderness of pain: The End.

Hero worship encapsulated in adulation, idolisation, a perfect god complex, Madonna on a pedestal; whore in the gutter... religion; Freud. It made sense when you balanced that on the masturbatory knife-edge insanity of Nietzsche and his superman theory. 'And man created God in his own image; because man is God'. Well, some men at least. Suddenly again I thought of Danny Sugerman, loyal fan and believer in gods. He had loved Morrison, and right on the nail head it was true, no one gets out alive. We all die, we all go the way of all flesh; we truly are billion year-old carbon.

Jim's voice again, "The ultimate product of a recycling philosophy man."

Sometimes I thought I was going mad, trying to piece together bits and get it down into a sort of stream of consciousness, a dialogue, one that a reader could get into – dig. Critics say 'weird," and 'tortured unhappy soul'; I kinda enjoy that – I was cutting the crap out. Things aren't wonderful anymore, but they aren't awful either, they just are. Said I had a sort of 'jaundiced' view of humanity, a hopelessness which must make me miserable. But hey, I feel fine, and I get to laugh a lot, mostly at myself.

There was Jim's baritone in the background, "Me too man, alright, alright."

Some said female characters in my novels are either portrayed as sex objects or users of men. Doris Day jumped into my mind's eye, for absolutely no sane reason, right there and then, in one of those ridiculous hats too, sporting her effervescent smile.

The more I tried to separate one life from another, the more the links kept forcing me back. Morrison, with his high IQ and constant wish to make sense of it all, must have been going, or gone, crazy too. No god? Himself as a god?

"Let's rock," he screamed from my subconscious. "Do it, Ronnie, do it."

Just what excuse had Morrison devised that day to avoid the Vietnam draft, or what medical condition? Was he asthmatic? Was he diabetic? Was he mentally unstable? Did he have a heart condition which even his parents didn't know about, or perhaps his parents did know about? Maybe he had an adverse reaction to alcohol? Like Dylan Thomas, he replaced food with drink and literally starved his body of nutrients whilst gaining calories, which made him both fat and impotent. The whole thing was battering away at me. Strands and diverse thoughts were flying in from all directions, and I was having trouble holding them together. The more I tried to delve into Morrison's mind, the more confused I became. And that, I decided, was precisely what Morrison had wanted, and that was how he had managed to fool everybody – red herrings and double twists. Playing with people, reflecting back at them precisely what they wanted to see and all the while keeping his inner most thoughts for himself. I began to wonder just who he spoke to and who could keep up with him. Then maybe he did get drunk so he could talk to arseholes, just like he said. Maybe pissing in a punchbowl at some ridiculous function was a statement which we could not understand. Perhaps Pam did though, maybe they weren't so far removed from each other.

Mozart and autism, a spectrum beyond comprehension? Practical jokes? I could see his genius ripping into Salieri, poor Antonio. Mozart precociously showing off; vexing him with his talent; mirroring back. That was Morrison. God, was he autistic? ADHD? Then I saw the graveyard in Saltzburg, Christ knows why, all rain and October and chocolate Kugeln in a violin shaped box; just gone and nothing but a pauper's grave. Nude pastry! Nude pastry!

Instruments in a house where once the family had been, not even their instruments, just instruments of the kind they would play. And a town, singing along to Rogers and Hammerstein's *The Sound of Music*.

Ray Manzarek said that Oliver Stone had directed Val Kilmer to play the guy all wrong. That was twenty years later. And Manzarek said Morrison was fun to be with, that he liked to joke and to laugh. A fun guy and my friend, he said. He wasn't always down in the despair pit; that film played the guy all wrong. Maybe he was the smartest kid in the class and the fool? Maybe a genius? Like all good thrillers, it made no sense until the finale.

There was always this idea that Morrison was going to write the next great novel. Let's take away the pages, think about the 1960s and the rising role of the famous rock star. Maybe he had not written the great American novel; maybe he had lived it instead. A crazy idea? Why? Art moves on and eventually the printed word will have had its day too. Like the tank has become an obsolete weapon of war, the written book may well now be on the wane. The great American soap opera, acted out on the daily stage of super-stardom, televised; until finally it sickened him enough to kill off the character he was playing. Like Mary Shelley, he created his own monster – alone; alone in the dark, just like she did. Morrison cut up the pieces of other people, philosophers, poets, subculture idealists, novelists, artists and dramatists, then stitched them together to create a new god. A god without a soul, a god asking, who am I? James Douglas

Morrison, poet, thinker and educated sensitive southern boy creates Jim Morrison, songwriter, lyricist and spokesman for a generation.

Only he doesn't write him down like Kerouac did – he lives him; lives out the pages of the fiction for others to chronicle. Then he found that it consumed him, and like Victor before him, found that there was no end to the beast. A beast made up of cellves; there was no father, no mother. Jim Morrison was just a creation, hungry for knowledge and understanding, ready to push the possibilities. In what part of the image does the soul reside? In which one of our cellves?

That was Morrison's legacy and when I watched the obscene ritual of the golden coffin concert for Michael Jackson I understood. Poor bastard! A kid who had lost his way because there had been no childhood, all there had been was the road. The endless road, which rolled on into the endless night, and somewhere along the way he lost himself and cut up his monster. The big nose, so derided by this father, replaced by the smaller white one. A man lost in his own identity crisis; a corpse over which other less popular performers shrieked and wailed. But always remember, no one can kill a god. God's don't die... Gods don't die.

Morrison had seen the fiasco with Brian Jones, wailing girls and trophy hunters, that's why he was buried so deep. Jesus, people would dig the body up? I began to feel sick, until I remembered they stole the bust. Someone stole the bust from Jim's grave. How sick is that? Thankfully, when they opened up Dylan's grave there was nothing left, but they posted a guard at the site anyway. My God, what are people like? Like? Morrison knew and he spotted that when Hendrix went. They've been rattling Jimi's bones from grave to grave ever since, over these past forty years. Just for one minute imagine what they'd have done with Jesus now.

Janis they cremated and scattered from a helicopter.

Down at Clouds Hill they stole, the worshippers, well one of them, stole a sleeping bag. Meum and deum they were, hand stitched by Lawrence, Lawrence of Arabia. Some sick minded individual stole it. Why? Perhaps because they too had fallen into the hero worship cult which stardom brings.

"Only they stole it after the movie came out," a female voice said. "1962 and Lawrence died in 1935, nearly 30 years later." It was her mocking voice.

There was Jim's voice again, "Television rules the world."

And David Lean re-made T. E. Lawrence, repackaged and re-sanitised him, just like Dracula got 're-branded'.

"You see?" Jim's voice in my head again, "We're all slaves, man. Power to the Sheeple…" There was a laugh – his laugh.

Peter O'Toole and Omar Sharif, another couple of really good looking boys, prettified the past and made heroes. Only this time, Lawrence's 'relationship' with Salim Ahmed, a.k.a. Dahoum, was conveniently obscured for the possible homophobes in the audience. In T. E. Lawrence's lifetime, homosexuality would have ensured his complete fall from grace, much as it might have done for the frequent and erstwhile love interest of Doris Day, one Rock Hudson. Masculinity, Hollywood style, did not allow reality to creep in, that has become a more recent phenomenon. Hollywood, the stomping ground of The Doors, is, after all, nothing more than a fiction factory. There is less to it than meets the eye and what meets the eye is seldom the truth.

Anthony Quinn's portrayal of Auda abu Tayi verges upon the ridiculous when a close look is taken at the real historical events of the time. Cinema and television takes the world, chews it up and spits it back out – regurgitation.

"See," his voice again; or his head in my voice. I was losing it.

Dylan and Caitlin get just a simple wooden cross. One side, one name. Some great monument for a poet, the most popular poet in 1953; a poet who had courted the company of presidents, no less. A drunk who happened to be good with words. Man, I was finding my way to Morrison. All the fine threads were fixing into a web now. It was twisting and turning and finally it stuck. Did Morrison know about Thomas? I wanted to ask myself the questions. When did Dylan die in New York? When was Morrison born? When did the muse get him? Did he read Thomas? Of course he did. He read Rimbaud, he would have read Thomas too. He knew the beats, Manzarek knew them too, they both must have known about the drunken idol Thomas, impoverished for his art. In mid-fifties/early-sixties art, Thomas was a big-hitter. Dylan Thomas to Bob Dylan and thence the protest song. Venice Beach – beatnik heaven; Morrison and Manzarek had been weaned there too.

My brain was frying. The booze was kicking in now. One more beer and the understanding was really coming, or going, or neither. I stood up, crossed the road and walked through the large gates and into the courtyard in rue Beautreillis.

Number 17. I didn't know what I'd see, or even why I'd want to see it. Dutch courage pushed me on.

"Come on man," his voice from the stairs. "Take a trip with me…"

I passed unhindered up the staircase. The imperative to run was overwhelming. Needed to get to the right hand side and up to the landing. I hoped none of the residents would come out to stop me. Third floor on the right. Staircase A. Dutch courage; Dutch courage. Needed to see how high and steep the stairs were. Mounted them two at a time, breathless, quickly and with purpose, until I reached the double doors.

Then I stopped dead.

"And they all told me to turn around and face the crowd," his voice boomed, "I screamed man, screamed my scared-shitless lungs out."

I was petrified and despite the drink, my legs wouldn't work. Never before had I experienced anything like it. On that staircase it happened, the transmogrification – I lost it in the understanding, the connection. I was feet away. Bottled, choked and instead of knocking, walked away; now how puerile is that? Stage fright of the very tallest order, all I had to do was knock and talk. Do it, just knock.

That was all I had to do – but I didn't.

Eight

Shapes of things…

The years have deadened the responses and time has begun to heal over the deep wounds of the past. The graffiti too has been removed from the adjacent gravestones; a sombre silence now clings to the air. The raging against the dying of the light has waned and the world has spun on.

It was warm and July, though years had passed since Morrison frequented the place, and he would have frequented it; why? Because it was close and all of his haunts in LA were within a very short walk of each other. The Doors, offices, Themis – Pam's boutique and the cheap room in the Alta Cienaga Motel, room 32. His habits would be the same.

'He lived like a bum,' Tony Funches had said. Cared little for himself and just thought about his art, his poetry. But what if that poetry got the Werbelow and Admiral Morrison treatment and he reacted; not in public, but privately. There was another thing he reacted to: criticism. I knew that one. Had that in school, you know, when I had the wrong hair, or the wrong albums, or I wasn't cool enough. When I wrote my first novel, some now forgotten publisher wrote to me and said, 'It didn't grab me'. That was hard enough to bear, it stung, but the guy was just a stranger. What if the person making the criticism was your father? Christ, that must have stung.

"Father, I want to kill you," I could hear it plain as day. It was in the wind."

I could feel it, remembered what it was like. That is a killing blow, a below the belt blow. An unnecessary hurt to a sensitive artistic soul.

So you cover that hurt, like you've done all your life – by withdrawing. Years of learning to be alone, in books, inside your own imagination, crawling back inside your own head; crawling back to a place where you can go insane, but at least there you are safe.

"We spent a long time alone didn't we, Jim?" I asked. "You and me?"

I could hear him nodding. "Out there on the perimeter – observing?"

I replayed our lives in parallel, saw the similarities and then understood Morrison even more: Jim needed love. He needed to prove that there was something worthwhile in him to love, that he was worthwhile. Jim chose words. The one thing he knew well, the music of language and the depth of the imagination. The one place that you cannot be broken or imprisoned. There you can become The Lizard King and there you can do anything.

Mary says The Doors are a waste of time too; says she's going to be great and he is going nowhere. Morrison turns in on himself and the personality splits for self-protection, just like Laing foretold, and bam, it's like petrol and a match. All the energy he has goes into The Doors. The stage persona takes over and the real James Douglas Morrison is engulfed, swamped and swallowed whole by the music making machine. Sometimes people get what they wish for, only they don't know what to do when the wish comes true. The Doors, wish came true: they were bigger than Love. And while the other members of the band rolled with the ride, Morrison saw it for what it was.

Everybody hurts – sometime, and he hurt more than most. Then to top it all, 'Light my Fire' goes to number one and the band becomes international. The walk of fame beckons. Suddenly he's alone in the dark with all those demons. The only constant is Pam; she's been there from the start when they were no where. She believed in him and told him he could be a great poet, not just a singer in rock and roll band. Danny Sugerman did that too;

maybe ego stroking was precisely what Morrison needed. Maybe Morrison's protégé Sugerman, the writer, was what he would rather have been. Reassurance and encouragement are fundamental to any artist when they create, especially if they are out there in the vanguard. Now I understood why Pam was so important. He relied on her; yeah they fought, but they were intertwined, they were soul mates.

Being a beautiful god, he takes to the stage and enjoys what he never experienced before: being loved. But with Morrison, the guilt kicks in. Was it luck? Does he have a talent, or just an image? Money guilt? Success guilt?

The water's full of sharks and along comes Robby Krieger's dad's lawyer: Max Fink. Mr. fix-it Max Fink and…

Well the rest is history.

But what do you do when you've been the best? Been the first one onto the moon? The pathfinder? Where do you go next? Is there anywhere else to go?

The answers must seem like questions and the questions like answers and I was on my second large beer. It was hot. It was July. I'd been to the cemetery and seen the grave and watched the tourists. I'd seen strange things with strange people. Tattoos and taboos on girls old enough to be his daughter. I had been amazed by the strength of feeling about this one man.

Back in the same bar, after my 'experience' in the apartment lobby. Strange as this may sound, paranoia? Voices? Was someone watching or following me? I'd been feeling like that since the cover band was playing. Felt ridiculous; all the way there and then stage fright? Totally irrational, absurd and very out of character. Me, I'd batter the door down and make a complete nuisance of myself for a story. I wrote one word in my notebook: Twat.

* * *

There was an old man in the doorway. A Spike Milligan look-a-like, gaunt, thin, drawn, possibly seventy, maybe older, most likely younger. Long grey hair and sandals though he had a tweed jacket on, one too warm for the day, like some long lost country gentlemen come upon hard times. I could smell the stale sweat on his shirt as he came closer and saw the ingrained dirt which had produced blackheads in the folds of his wrinkled face.

He stumbled toward me.

"You the guy who's payin' for information about Mojo?" he asked.

Let me explain. In some vane hope that I might get information from some aging hippie about Morrison, I'd posted a reward in several of the local watering holes around the 4th district and around the cemetery area. That might be crazy to you, but it had worked in the past. In San Francisco I'd been on a bus with my girlfriend trying to find the house which belonged to the Grateful Dead. The legendary house in which they'd been busted. We were looking at the map and this older couple got on. Everybody wanted to help us and the result was a discussion about us going there. Almost an argument ensued when one old guy said there was nothing to see. The older couple dutifully explained that they had lived it, told the guy to 'let the kids go there'. They had been in Haight and Ashbury at the time. They came alive again when we said we wanted to go. Their old teeth and stiff joints were forgotten. It was like we were trying to get back to their world of lost youth, on this time-machine of a bus. More helpful people you could not get, right down to the correct bus stop and directions for a walk. It gave me a buzz at the time too, because I was well into middle-age. It's a long time since someone called me a kid. I hoped the same 'luck' might happen for me in Paris.

I first got the 'spiller' when working as a full time journalist in London. I was doing articles on the anniversary of the blitz and the old folk, who had been there, loved to talk. Talk? They spilled their guts out to me. Somebody ought to get out among those people and record it all, before their memories are lost. Same with the sixties and the hippies.

I nodded in reply.

"Well I knowed a few," he said smiling. His teeth were yellow. "You payin'?" he asked.

I placed a $100 dollar bill on the table.

"First you got to give me something," he blurted.

I replied, "Drink?"

I ordered a bottle of tequila.

"Classy." He nodded, and as if on pre-record, he began, "That year it was hot," he said, looking at me. "1971 was very hot and no one carries logs in the hot summer. That was a really big lie. Out of breath my arse."

The barmen caught my eye and rolled a finger at his temple. "Crazy," he said.

I made the universal sign for two and he began to pull the beers into long glasses.

"I heard that," the old man barked. "I'm not mad. I was here in July 1971. I was here the night Jim died."

I couldn't believe my luck. I thought, my God, I've got an eye witness. Who the hell is this guy? I knew the answer to that one. He was a bum, a street derelict and I'd let offers of money onto the streets for information. Now some people might think that strange, odd, but I had an idea. If they knew anything, they'd let me have it. If they didn't, they'd try to lie, but they wouldn't have enough detail – so I'd find them out instantly.

"I played guitar with him you know," the old man burbled as he slurped on the cool beer I had ordered for him.

He is a crackpot. I suddenly realised my mistake. I knew that Robby Krieger had been the first and only guitarist in The Doors. Hell, I was now trapped in bar with a nutter, drinking beer, beer I had bought him.

"He does this to all the tourists," the barman smirked as he wiped the bar top. He spoke at the man, "You tell them that you knew that Jim Morrison and it's all shit, isn't it? All one great big fairy story?"

"It's Ok," I said, "he's not bothering me. I'd pay to hear a good Jim Morrison story." And that was precisely what I got. A story which could only mean he had at least met the man.

"Agnes Varda was working on that film," the man started. "The one about the Tango in Paris. Sort of watching Jimbo as he disintegrated. They all said he was finished and washed up but that ain't true. He had a whole book of ideas and songs ready. Only he didn't want to sing them with The Doors, he wanted to speak it."

That I'd heard before, but I ordered another drink for him anyway.

"So how was he?" I asked.

"Clean and his drinkin' was gettin' better."

I noticed the accent and was trying to place it. It was from the south and then I remembered – Miami. But there was something else there too, surfer speak. It was a hybrid a mix, which gave his voice a sort of laconic lilt, warm and rich and full of vibrato; pleasant on the ear, easy to listen to.

"He was singin' like an angel man, the last time I seed him. But he weren't no angel and he weren't dead."

I wondered if the man was stringing me along. We had another beer and then a tequila or two. After that he seemed to relax and then he delivered the one piece of information which threw me off balance.

"See this," he said, as he pushed a scrap of paper toward me. "It's from Jim's books."

"Are you sure?" I asked.

"Listen man, you can check that if you like."

It certainly looked like Morrison's hand. Big flowery letters with abbreviations all through it. It might have been a lyric.

"Look at the fucking date man," the man shrieked loudly.

Heads turned in the bar. The man raised his glass and said, "Here's to all them chickens." Then downed his tequila like it was water. With abandon he started to chant the old George Formby song 'Bless 'Em All'. Only he had changed the lyrics to fuck 'em all. Sung loudly and with attitude.

I checked the piece of paper, there was no date.

"There's no date here," I squealed.

"Man you really are a dumb arse, ain't ya? Look at the date you cock sucker."

The problem was that the man's speech was beginning to slur and the barman clearly didn't like the idea of a drunk passing out in his bar. Much less an abusive drunk. And I didn't want to order another bottle of tequila.

"Look at the date," he barked hoarsely

I lifted the page to the light. The writing was feint and in pencil.

"What's it say?" he asked.

I read the words 'Ten, y/s on', that was underlined, the rest, 'get some kicks in 76, ferocious feline/s fix', was not.

I couldn't clearly see an actual date as part of the faded script. I said nothing but knew that this, if it was Morrison's writing, could prove beyond a doubt that he was still alive; I could barely contain my excitement.

"Listen," the old man continued, snatching the scrap from my eager hands and stuffing it deep into his pocket. "You know nothing. If you knew that, that you knew nothing, it would be start, but you're so fucking stupid you can't even think, can you? Can you find your arse with both hands?" One, two tequilas gulped. "I played the fucking guitar with Morrison. We recorded together, 1971. Look at all these cunts in here," his arms were flailing and then he bellowed, "they're all a waste of a perfectly good skin." He stood up belched and yelled, "You should all be put to death man. Put to the sword. Burned at the stake and turned into rat shit." Then he lurched backward and stumbled into an adjacent table, knocking both a customer and his beer to the ground. He raised his hands in supplication as if seeking inspiration and then laughed. "It's all crap baby, this is all there is and it's all crap. Could there be any fucking hell worse than this? And you fuckers." He was pointing at each customer in turn. "Yawl a bunch of fucking slaves." His voice reached maximum power, "Fucking slaves. Too stupid to see what the hell is happening to ya. Dumb, fucks, shit lickers." He grabbed the tequila bottle and drank deeply.

"That's it, out!" the barman was yelling, pushing the man toward the door. "Coming in here and upsetting all my customers, swearing like that. I told you last time not to come back."

"But I was in the band," the man was yelling. "This is Jim's bar. I knew The Smoothies. Fuck off me you dumb bastard."

The barman was pushing him now.

"We recorded the Orange County Suite. I heard all of his really great poetry. You motherfuckers," he turned back to the few occupants of the bar, "you mothers don't know how great that man was. I did. He was fucking great. Real fucking great and he died across the road, well that's what you dumb arse-licks think."

The barman was ushering the man out into the street now, "And don't come back, ever again," he called, "you're crazy."

Strains of "Fuck you" and "go eat shit" could be heard as he stumbled away. "You're all a bunch of slaves," he yelled, "slaves, motherfucking slaves."

"He is, how do you say, crazy," the barman said, taking up his position once again.

I could hear the crashing of bins and the stumbles as he fell against dumpsters and dustbins.

"Who is he?" I asked

The barman shrugged.

"Do you know where he lives?" I asked.

"He is one of the street people," was his nonchalant reply as he shook his head. "He lives where they live."

I hurriedly paid and left to follow the old man.

I could hardly believe my luck. My adrenalin had gone through the roof. Here was someone who could identify Morrison, had spent time with him, and had recorded in a drunken afternoon a tape which would later be sold for thousands of dollars. And then there was that piece of paper. If that were genuine, it would be an earth-shattering revelation. I cursed the fact that I had let it be snatched back. He'd lifted the $100 too.

Luck and circumstance were on my side. It was the kind of coincidence which novelists concocted and journalists hoped would happen on every story, and I wasn't writing a novel.

My heart was racing as I left the bar and made my way after the man.

I wasn't going to let Jane Eyre bump into her cousin on a moor in the middle of nowhere. Nor would my heroine mysteriously inherit twenty thousand pounds from a long lost uncle, who had inadvertently stopped my marriage to a potential bigamist by housing his brother in law in Madeira while enroute to Jamaica. This was a coincidence like that, just as far-fetched; but this was a real one. This was a no shit, one hundred percent lucky lead.

And I was one very lucky journalist.

Nine

Itchy coo Park...

At the Place des Vosges I sat and waited, studying the tourists who made their way to the small enclave, which had been one of Morrison's favourite spots. It was mid-morning and I had a hunch that the man I was after would turn up here. This was wino heaven, a place which would have a photograph in the memory of anyone who sat there and observed. There were kids playing, kicking up the gravel and the dust; a couple of youngsters were kissing with their legs and arms wrapped around each other. It was Paris and warm and summer, for all I knew it could be 1971 or 1612. The place felt timeless; like the summers of years ago, when I had been young and full of idealism. The days when we believed that love could rule the world and flowers could fit into the barrel of any gun. Now, after years of thought and disappointment, I realised that idealism was a leisure activity, a pursuit of the young and something which eventually dashed the hopes of everyone. An activity which was the preserve of those who could afford to think, to create, to examine.

I wondered if my mother's generation had experienced the same hopes and fears. Man, now that was something which we, I, never had to go through. When I think of it sometimes I realise just how cheap and easy freedom was for me. There were no 6th of June beach parties, no Anzio landings or war.

Years of looking after children and struggling had taught me that much. In order to think and really piece things together you need time; in order to create you need time, and peace? Well that costs, unless you are wealthy or prepared to starve for your art like Van Gogh. We had it easy, no civil war, no bloody despots, no genocide. Jesus, Morrison was really getting inside my head now, dragging all the nihilism out into the open. The Nietzscherian superman all messed up with trying to make sense of chaos, and like we all really know, chaos just is. You can't make sense of it. Our generation was blessed with the last of war and death and yet we screamed about it. Vietnam was the last of the big, bloody conflicts and what the hell was it all worth? All those men, all that potential: gone. And still they go on – the cost of freedom is the loss of innocence. Experience has been a bitter pill to swallow; what if someone had got there too?

What if Morrison was like Rimbaud, produced all his best work in his teen years? I remembered what Peter Cook said about his comedy, that he hadn't written anything new or fresh since his Cambridge days – now that is a burden to shoulder. Knowing that at twenty seven all of your best work has been produced and it isn't getting any better. Knowing that however hard you try the muse has gone. The creative spirit has been pissed away into a meaningless public punch bowl.

Where the hell was this guy?

As I sat, I looked at the old buildings and the history which they encapsulated. I dreamt of duels at dawn on the grass, after all, this was a favourite place for people to duel, well it had been in the past. Now here I was duelling again. It was enchantment personified, and I knew that Morrison would have felt the same way. He would have found the place beautiful and yet tragic, and he would have read about the use to which the place was put. I could imagine the sound of flintlock pistols firing and the screams of men as their vital blood leaked into the green of the grass and it was – truly magnificent.

I missed my girlfriend and I felt more alone at that present moment than I had in a long time. I couldn't speak French and I liked to talk to people, talk about life and art and religion – the way of the world. Pass the time of day – like a student on an endless quest for meaning and knowledge. Then it struck me that Morrison and I were similar, we were searching, searching for maybe something that couldn't be found. Then I was thrown back to his interview in 1970, when he talked about leisure time and revolution and I knew he was right.

At about ten thirty the guy from Jomo and the Smoothies turned up. He was not at all what I expected. First he was sober and second he was clean. He'd had a shower and he looked kinda normal. His hair was tied back in a ponytail and he looked fresh. In his hand he carried a beer, and not just any beer, but one of those extra strong ones that taste of alcohol. Like they've been spiked.

I watched the man enter the park and sit on a bench and then walked straight over to see him. At first he didn't notice me, but as I stood before him he lifted his eyes from the paper he was reading and focussed on me, though he had to squint as I had my back to the early morning sun, like some ancient gunfighter duellist.

"Morning. Remember me?" I asked.

The man shook his head.

"The bar?"

"What fucking bar?" he growled.

"The bar, Morrison's place?"

He shook his head.

"I go in a lot of bars, especially that one."

"I can see you like a drink, mind if I join you?"

"Look buddy, I ain't in no mind to be jaw waggin'. Why don't you just go and set yerself down in the sun and… "

His voice tailed off in the long laconic drawl of his State of origin. I tried to place his accent again. It was definitely southern. Carolina, I guessed a second time, though the years had stripped out the 'yawl'.

"You said you played with Morrison. Played guitar." I sat down next to him. "Strange because I thought that the ambassador's son or someone played with Jim."

"Listen buddy," the man took a deep swig from his beer, "that's what everyone thinks. You know the tape of drunken ravings in a studio. Morrison's last great work. That is until *American Prayer*. Though by then times had changed and punk was in. All Johnny Rotten and The Sex Pistols. Though what does he call himself now? Well no one wanted poetry. No one wants poetry now, only the academics. Now television rules the world. Just like," he paused, thoughtful, drinking, "Jim said it would."

"What are you saying, there's more?"

"More?"

"More tapes of Morrison and songs and…"

"Listen buddy," he drank again, "Jim Morrison did a lot more than go on holiday when he was in Europe. I know, I recorded with him. I played guitar, oh and I ain't no ambassador's son. I ain't no WASP." He spat the words with real contempt. "You ever been to Washington?" he asked with sudden fury. "You ever been over to Arlington?"

"Well I have actually," I replied.

"Funny ain't it, making a national cemetery out of General Lee's garden? Sick bastards that they were. It wasn't enough just to win, they had to make the whole thing into a gross act of vengeance. And you know what the funny thing is? Grant, he kept slaves, and Lee didn't. It was all a load of bullshit. And everyone believes that the war was fought to preserve freedom, when all it was, all it was, was to preserve the union. The union? Some cock-a-mammy idea that no one really understands."

I knew then that this man drinking heavily was no numbskull. When sober, he could think.

"Been to the Lincoln?" he asked

I nodded, wondering where this conversation was headed.

"Well that's where all the smucks go. All the singers of the battle hymn of the republic." He took an even deeper draught of beer and finishing the can, tossed it deftly into a garbage bin some twenty feet away. From his coat pocket he produced a second, which hissed as he popped the ring-pull. "Breakfast. I woke up this morning and I got myself a beer," he chanted rhythmically, "the future's uncertain and booze is always near." He laughed; a deep rolling laugh which had a real edge of warmth to it. "The

Jefferson Memorial, that's the real place to go. 1943 they put that up. The same year Jim was born, now there's a coincidence, him being an admiral's son and awl." His accent was becoming more pronounced "The superman of the declaration of independence and freedom, Thomas Jefferson. And Morrison, and freedom and..." He began to recite, "We hold these truths to be self evident, that all men are created equal," he paused to drink, "now that is a doozy." He laughed as he guzzled.

I wondered how old he was, I guessed late fifties and his face, his face had suffered some major trauma. Like he'd been beaten hard and a surgeon had put him back together, only the seams were a little blurred and the broken jaw bone had not quite set back into the groove. His teeth were bad and his hair was thinning. All in all, he had been handsome once, but the ravages of time and pain had eaten into him like bugs on an apple. He caught me looking a little too long.

"It ain't pretty is it?" he smiled. "Kinda puts people off. One windshield can do plenty at the right time. No one wants to take a hard look at damaged meat. I mean, even liberals turn away, after they steal a look. You know, like the Guinea Pig Club?"

I immediately thought of the ex-pilot from the war who used to deliver milk to our house. He had a face made of plastic, a reconstructed face, only it wasn't all right and this guy, he had the same problem.

"I'm doing a story on Morrison," I suddenly blurted.

"You a reporter then?"

"Yep."

"Well what d' yawl wanna know then?" he asked.

"For a start, I'd like to know how and where you met Morrison?"

"Easy, me and a friend were busking. We'd been olive harvesting in, Jesus I forget just where now, down south somewhere. But we were busted and trying to get enough for a place to sleep or a meal. So we were bluesing in the street, me on the guitar and him on the harp, outside the cafes for the tourists. There was this guy listening and he passes us a hundred dollar bill and asks if we know 'Crawling King Snake'.

"So that was Morrison?"

"Sharp ain't ya?" he snapped, "for a reporter an' awl."

I loved that southern drawl, which in the mouth of a women seemed to scream the words 'fuck me, fuck me now'. My first experience of it at close quarters had been two southern belles who a friend and I had met in Frankie and Johnny's steakhouse, just off 5th Avenue and 42nd Street in New York. They chatted and I listened and now I was doing the same again. Letting the musicality of the sound carry me away.

"Of course it was Morrison," I replied. "And he recorded all sorts of stuff with you, didn't he?"

The man nodded. "And you know what? Because he recorded with lots of people, buskers, guys in bars, street musicians. And you know why?" He didn't wait for an answer. "Because he liked the normal people. He preferred the company of bums to all those record executives and hangers on, who just wanted to use the band. It was never about money, man." The man almost snarled. "It was about being out there on the edge, exploring the possibilities. And hey, that's a god awful place to be." He opened a third can and his voice began to take on that edge of intoxication. "Sure the man liked to drink and awl, but he was a genius. You ever listened to *American Prayer*? Why do you think he recorded that? Poetry gets written down man. Then it gets spoken. He was way ahead of you man, way ahead, way ahead of The Doors too. 1978, before they got round to get a track around the words. A vehicle, a new way to see art. Jesus fucking Christ and everybody else is playing big stadium gigs or wearing fucking spandex and back-combing their hair. You know the Spinal Tap rip, a courgette stuffed down your pants. A fucking courgette instead of your meat. Yeehaa, Jimmy was there man, Yewah, way ahead he was there."

The man tossed the fourth can and then produced a paper wrapped bottle.

"Do you think…"

He interrupted me, "What that I can't think? Listen sonny, I like a drink, Jimmy liked a drink, hey fuck," he shouted, "hey fuck, hey fuck," and standing up, yelled again, "the whole fucking world needs a drink." He sat down again, or collapsed down to be more accurate. "The whole world needs a drink to kill all the bugs it has up its arse; and every rag-tag and bobtail hates a drunk. Ain't that the truth honey? Hey honey I'm home," he yelled again, before suddenly becoming intense and morose.

"So you played guitar with him?"

"We did several sessions. Me and two other guys and we weren't The Smoothies. That tape was the result of some drunken afternoon and because he left the tape at his friend's house with his notebooks, it was found."

I was finding the whole thing slightly intangible and yet completely plausible; the more I thought about it, the worse or better it became, depending upon your viewpoint. I was sitting in a park in France with an American who was gradually becoming more intoxicated as he spoke and yet when he did, his reasoning became intensely appealing. Morrison did walk and wander the streets, everybody knew that. He was a voyeur, a voyeur of life, and as he absorbed things so he regurgitated them. Regurgitated them in a way which made them more palatable. This guy was right.

He could so easily have experimented with musicians in the street, he had the time and the money. Why would he just hire a studio for one afternoon for a few ad-hoc hours. Unless of course his creativity had been completely spent. Pam was busy with her heroin Count and he was free to roam. Like he had done in Venice in the early days. In fact, he did that a lot, disappeared. That was how he lost weight – walking, constantly, that and not eating. Just like he did in Venice Beach in the summer of 1966. Starving and writing poetry and dreaming songs and scrounging a meal here and there, that was when he was at his creative peak. A strange kind of freedom which could never be repeated in Paris. The city was there and the history and the art, but the deprivation was not.

Everything was going well creatively until 'Light my Fire' took off and then, just like Robbie Krieger said, 'All hell broke lose'. Excess kicked in and the creative juice that was in full flight was swamped by alcohol and endless nights of idle talk and nonsense. The soul was washed out of Morrison with booze and success. I wondered what might have happened had he not been quite so successful; maybe he would have struggled to get the next great American novel out. *Fame and fortune and the American dream*; or *Success and the Rebel* – that would have been a great title. I could imagine it; now the years had passed, I could almost ghost it. But would he have written it? Been the first piper at the gates of dawn. He lived it certainly; maybe that was his art form. He did say that he thought the interview was the new high art form and you know what, he was probably right.

The rooftops of Venice Beach, must have been a wild place to live and sleep, and off them he comes –The Adonis. The rock god of revolution, chaos and cock; the girls loved him, and the boys wanted to be him.

The admiral had given him his own space as a boy and he could come and go as he pleased. In Paris he had the cash and the time and maybe he had explored other things too. He loved the Louvre and had spent hours in that gallery.

The Prado in Madrid had enthralled him; Velasquez had intrigued him with his secrecy; Bosch had captivated him with his vision: Heaven and Hell.

Morrison was an intelligent man, an artist and a trailblazer. Why not try the marriage of poetry with pop, who else was trying that in 1971? Where were the beat poets? Yeah there were poetic songsters like Dylan and Neil Young, but this thing Morrison had was something avant garde, more toward literature and performance art, before the phrase had ever been coined; the stuff out there in the perimeter. Neither music nor song but story and music combined with philosophical thought. Andy Warhol was experimenting, or had been with the Velvet Underground, why does everyone think Morrison would not?

"Morrison never settled for a goddamn thing," the drunk yelled "he was always ahead of us. Movement like a snake, man, a predator."

"What do you mean?" I asked.

"He was out there man." The bottle followed the cans into the trash and the man promptly stood up and started urinating where he stood.

"I've still got the tape man," he snarled. "I got the Morrison tape of uncut songs. And they are good – really good."

He was laughing now and touching his nose and hushing his mouth with his finger, as if he had a secret to hide. "Me, I got the tapes of me and Morrison and they're better than anything you've heard I bet." He was struggling to put his penis back into his trousers, and then I noticed the absence of underwear and the dribble stain at his crotch.

"Just like Morrison," I said aloud.

"What the fuck?"

"No underwear."

"Yeah man," he blurted, "and the guy took his pants down in Miami. Fucking bullshit. A real crock of shit. That was all designed to make sure all the truths are self-evident, baby."

The man slumped back to the bench and his eyes rolled. "Jail, damn jail, that's what they wanted, because they knew that the public would forget him. The fickle public that had a revolution and then chilled out with downers in the 70s. Jim knew that too, he knew they were slaves to the system. That's what he meant in Miami. Don't any fucks understand what was being said?"

He was yelling now "Sunday truckers, Christian motherfuckers, yeah." Then his voice dropped and the power subsided "Cocksuckers," he hissed.

"My name's Ron," I said.

"Like Robby's twin brother?"

"Yeah," I replied. But I was taken by surprise by the weird reply. It was familiar and yet odd. Odd for a man who would so obviously be Robby Krieger's rival.

"Fuck," he snorted, "they're all a bunch of fucking slaves."

"What's your name?" I asked.

"Me? I'm Mr. Mojo Risin, baby. You can't tell by my beautiful face? Woo," he drawled, "am? I'm bath-time Bertie. The suicide swimmer man."

"You got a real name?"

He was now roaring drunk. His penis still exposed by his failure to close his fly.

"Wow, you are real heavy baby. You sure you're a journo and not a pig?"

"I'd like to hear that tape," I added. "What's your name?"

"Sic em pig," he yelled, "take that boy away and throw him down a well man. Who do you love? Who do you love?"

He jumped to his feet as tourists passed, nearly knocking one to the ground.

"So do you have a name?" I asked again. "A real one?"

He jumped onto the bench and turned to the passers by as if they were an audience.

"A name, what's in a name?" He was shouting in a rich deep baritone. "A rose by any other name would smell as sweet."

"Romeo and Juliet."

"Clever boy," he smirked. "Only the plan went all wrong and she died. Corky said she was murdered. CIA or some covert group man, designed to pull us all down, man. She wasn't meant to die. Nobody really was meant to die." He was yelling again, "Oh happy dagger, here is thy sheath."

"So do I get a name?"

"Cool Hand Luke,"

"So you're Paul Newman now?"

He paused, examining me, looking down, as if making a vital decision.

"Doug Prayer. Any good?"

"Pleased to meet you, Doug."

I offered my hand.

But it was too late, the man, whose name I had yet to verify as correct, had fallen from the end of the bench and promptly passed out on the grass. On the other side of the square I could see the gendarmes, and they could see me. And worse, they could see the drunk and were beginning their long walk over.

"Shit, now I'm gonna get arrested," I said aloud.

Meanwhile, my new interviewee was out cold.

121

Ten

The Hunter...

As a reporter I learned real quick that every action has a motive, even the most banal things have some form of motive. It could be the things we were taught in childhood, or it could be a need that had to be served; and that was just the same for a crime, a deception, a heist, a fraud, a whatever. Crime reporting teaches you that very very quickly. The thing is, nobody thinks of the possibilities – why? Because they cannot conceive them and thereby cannot accept them, and the result? Confusion. That's what I was finding the hardest thing to do – think. Trying to keep a clear head is difficult when you have admired someone for so long. I was seeing Jim Morrison everywhere and not getting any closer to finding the guy. That was my problem. I wanted to be the reporter that discovered him, found him alive and well and living some great life of Riley.

Maybe, like Manzarek said, Morrison was in the Seychelles; happily married and out of the rat race. Maybe that keyboard striker of genius and befuddlement has enabled the band to live off their back catalogue for years. I agree the music is timeless, well some of it anyway, and that the kids who want Morrison are the same kids who wear Che Guevara tee shirts, without having the slightest understanding of what he did or stood for. I have even seen Che on a coffee mug in a local chain store. Now that is irony, the beautiful revolutionary who adorns the dorms of would be accountants and architects while they are at college. Who the hell has a picture of Andreas Bader or Ulrike Meinhoff on their walls? Marketing men were able to exploit one and not the other two, and yet all terrorised in their own fashion. The whole game was riddled with bluff and double bluff.

Then finally some rodeo horse breeder in Oregon pops up, says he is Jim Morrison and you can buy the video story for just $29.95. Just overlay one acetate image onto another and there you have it. Cool as you like, Morrison pops up and in Oregon too, rather handy that one. Now that has to take the biscuit for sheer nonsense. Only the guy's eyes don't look right, that's the bullshit – like the dummy pass that Manzarek says Jim raised with him, a month before he left for Paris. Apparently he showed Ray some pictures of the Seychelles and quipped about faking his own death to escape. What if that was a double, double bluff designed to fuel the myth long after he was gone? Morrison was really good at that, throwing red herrings into the mix, he was, by his own admission 'a prankster' whenever he wanted to confound and confuse. Or it could have been a Manzarek and Sugerman myth, concocted to keep the spirit of Morrison, and The Doors fortunes, alive. Christ I was getting, or had got, cynical in my old age. Did everything come down to money?

Now here's the problem: who in 1969 would have taken a long bet on bands like The Beatles and The Rolling Stones still being in existence, let alone performing live?

The youth counter-culture now becomes the granny culture. Would you have bet your shirt on this simple fact in 1984? My shrewd guess is no. We have to judge things by the time they were in and not from the perspective of hindsight. Nowadays we can visualise bands remaining, reuniting, often repeatedly, and doing more farewell performances – repeatedly, but back then we couldn't. Who the hell listened to Little Richard in 1984? The teddy boys had come and gone like a morning mist and the folk revivalists too and the bluesmen – fashions had changed and quite dramatically. The age of conspicuous consumption had well and truly kicked in, while ecology had become main stream. Now though, forty years later, all the old gods are being resurrected, because the generation that made them gods in the first place is beginning to retire. They have made their dosh and now they splosh on toys and joys which once they could never afford. Those people have brought up their kids, paid their mortgages and finally bought that little Harley for weekend road trips. They go on cruises and travel and they go back to their youth. Some of us never really changed at all, we just put on an act to get us through. Economic necessity ha, and we fooled ya.

How do I know this? Simple – because I'm one of them, one of those who actually got their dream car. Though they may be far too old and tardy to enjoy it as they once could.

The world is populated by fat old men on Harley Davidson motorcycles. Driven by grey-haired ex-accountants trying to relive, or should that be relieve, the rebellion of their youth, which wasn't a rebellion at all. 'Three days man' does not make a revolution. That takes twenty five years in Robben Island prison during the heat of oppression and apartheid. Or walking through the streets of Alabama getting stabbed, shot at and maligned, until eventually you end up with a bullet through your brain on a lonesome balcony one April morning. The fashionable opposition of the Woodstock generation speaking out against the madness was nothing more than that – fashion.

What was it Jac Holtzman said? Something about being the best selling group that is no longer around. Somebody somewhere was taking a nice slice of that pie, and the pie was getting bigger, in fact it was getting puffed up in the legend. A conspicuous legend, with a conspicuous price tag attached.

And then there was the grave marker. Why didn't Pamela get a headstone made? She drew a design for Siddons, didn't she? A traditional design with the little porcelain photo holder and some Morrison lyrics from 'The Soft Parade'. Why that album?

I had found out, during my research, that Pam was not tasked with the job at all, even though she had some involvement with the design. She couldn't speak French so to get her on the organisation would have been nuts. Morrison also always talked of a shallow grave for which we sweat and slave, that's in 'The

Soft Parade' too. Perhaps he had that in mind and wanted no marker. That would be ironic, wouldn't it? An unmarked grave slap bang in the middle of all those monuments to the great and the good. An unmarked grave which has now become a most visited site of Paris. A most visited site, with nothing to actually see – that is Morrison the prankster poking a single finger salute to all voyeurs, the spectators. I sort of found that very funny, it made me smile.

Did Pam ever go back to Paris between 1971 and the fatal 25th April 1974? I made a mental note – why this date, coincidence? How about this one: this was the date she first met or slept with Jim. Where did they meet? Some say The London Fog on sunset strip, others say UCLA, when Manzarek and Morrison were studying film. Some say Pam was a cast off, a previous lover of the American actor Tom Baker; others say they met at the beach. Wherever they met, that date is significant.

Pam did enter a period of mourning in Sausalito. But then there was the real question: was this mourning, self-imposed guilt, or a pact, a tryst with a very clever lover? Maybe they were both just kicking old habits? Out went the heroin and out went the booze. You might think I'm crazy, but just for a minute, think it through. Hindsight gives perspective as long as we don't judge; is that even possible? And hey I'm not judging here, I'm just ticking off the possibilities.

The whole thing was turning messy in my head again. Motive, motive, motive came screaming back at me. It had to be one of two things: either she and Jim had pulled it off, faked it and then gone into self-imposed rehab, or she was so wracked with guilt that she became a recluse. Had a sort of mental breakdown for nearly a year and then tried to bounce back. After all, she was only twenty five and youth heals more quickly than age. Just for one wild moment though, think, imagine this: Diane Gardner gives her soft asylum, a place to hide and together the pair heal each other.

Sausalito is very similar to Venice Beach, a little cooler admittedly, but just as quaint. It's the kind of place where you could vanish to. The Doors were full of other issues and Pam had never been their favourite person anyhow, so they were not likely to come visit. Take a look at Issaquah dock and the house boats. Who's to say that Morrison hadn't bought one, they had the boutique and the Norton Avenue apartment in West Hollywood. They could have had other places too.

It's true that Morrison wasted money, but he also was unpredictable and he had advances – big advances.

Morrison quits booze, Pam ditches heroin, the old friends, the trusted friends, who themselves have dropped out of sight – are they only the ones who know? And just where is Babe Hill now? Who knows? The most likely scenario is just Pam knows; that would certainly be the safest.

Agnes Varda was the contact for Bill Siddons and he has no idea why the grave marker never got installed. And an interesting fact immerged as I delved she too claimed not to have had sight of the body. My mind was screaming now – what? She didn't see the body either? Who did? She arrived with Alan Ronay after Pam had phoned them in a panic, they were the only three at the flat, she must have seen the body – a body.

Years later, Robby Krieger claimed, in an interview, that The Doors had given Pam money to get a memorial headstone made up, but that had me guessing too, because I had found out about the lawsuits. Especially the one in 1974 trying to get the $250,000 back from Jim's royalty share, that had been advanced against potential album sales. Strange that a group of people who were negotiating via law suits would calmly discuss a grave marker. It didn't match. Then there was the matter of that amount of money in 1971- a lot. Where did that go? Who was handling it? Was it one lump sum? That was a problem, motives needed to match if I was to make any sense of the investigation.

Finally, on the matter of that grave marker, or any marker come to think of it, are we really expected to believe that The Doors management and the band really didn't do something to get a grave marker in place? That, even to this day, seems to me like a callous act, an almost indecent act. An act I can't understand if, as the remaining band members claimed, they missed and loved Morrison so much. Some things don't gel and in this case there were too many. But there I go, judging others by the standards that I have inside me, ones put there by either my parents or social conditioning. So here's the question: would you leave the place unmarked, unrecorded? You see, that's the problem, it's not just one person, it's a whole bunch of them. Even Danny Sugerman claimed that he had to make sure Jim's memory lived on as a pathfinder, a god, so why disregard the grave marker? He had taken over the management of The Doors Inc. by then and could have got a marker placed.

I thought again about the Paris apartment. A neighbour saw a corpse, clothed on the floor or dressed in a gown. A Monsieur Chagnol, who was there by chance; he had followed the fire brigade up to his apartment and he didn't know who Morrison was. But the official report said that the fire brigade lifted the heavy body out of the bath, because Pam could not. So who put the clothes on the corpse? Or was Monsieur Chagnol just mistaken? Is everybody just mistaken? Or are we all supposed to be?

Strange that Robby Krieger seemed adamant about money being given for a grave marker; was that for the bust which eventually got stolen? That couldn't be, because the Mladen Mikulin bust did not appear until 1981, the tenth anniversary which in itself ties in with the *Rolling Stone* front cover scandal. The notorious dead and sexy story. The sculpture was stolen in 1988, now what sort of numpty steals a tomb stone? A fan – some fan. Robby Krieger had his Gibson SG guitar stolen too. And they buried Brian Jones fifteen feet down in Cheltenham? People! It's one thing being Suzy Creamcheese and wanting a belly full of arms and legs as a baby anchor, but collecting body parts from your heroes? I began to feel slightly sick at the human race. That gave credence to the whole idea of getting Morrison underground quickly.

My mind jumped to the Catholic relics in the churches all around Italy, bits of bone encased in gold and jewels. In some churches they even have mummified body parts and whole corpses under the altars. In the Church of the Holy Blood, in Bruges, people queue up to chant and then kiss a vial of what looks like dried red powder. The church claims the vial contains the blood of Christ, collected whilst he was dying on the cross. But he didn't die. Another Turin shroud moment? Then I thought of Mary Magdalene and my mind jumped to a comparison with Suzy and the other groupies. There are those who expound the intellectual idea that Mary Magdalene had in fact been his wife, or a principle architect or collaborator in his philosophies. Ok I can buy that, Caitlin with Dylan, for example, but what if she wasn't his wife? How about she was a groupie? I can hear the screams of 'heretic' from the Catholic Church as I write. Hell, I've managed to alienate just about all of the religious types anyway. The thing is that the truth is often far more ugly than we can bear, so we clean it up; easier for the mind to swallow.

But if speed was needed and forensic evidence erased, say an overdose of heroin needed to be covered up, cremation would have been the only absolute way. So why not go down that route? Pam could have done that and taken the ashes back to the States on a plane. Why a grave? Motive? A focal point? A red herring? A slight of hand? She herself ended up in Santa Ana in an urn, though the memorial there covers both her and Jim. Why both? Was that their last resting place? Or going to be? Unless of course the wishes of Morrison had been pre-discussed, pre-determined, but with who – Pam? Who does that at twenty seven? Decides that they want internment, that he wanted no marker, that he wanted secrecy? That he wanted to create a legend, and knew precisely what he was doing? Was that why he had visited Pere Lachaise only days before his death? He'd been in Paris a while and it's easy to walk from rue Beautreillis to the cemetery and Morrison walked, just like he had done in LA. He seemed to know that you could see far more that way; learn far more too. What did he learn? That for an idol and a pilgrimage there has to be a place and he chose it; a clever and wise choice. Janis was scattered above the beach and there obscurity beckons.

Maybe the Santa Ana site was designed for two? Then why a double grave plot bought, if Pam never made it into the same grave after her death and cremation? Did he know he was dying?

Was he preparing to depart? Or was he busy constructing a myth, a religion? Then we jump again to the why? The motive? Exhumation would be the only way to reverse the quick descent into the soft earth, to become nude pastry. But a relic, a bit of bone could be… worshipped, just like a grave could be the site of a holy pilgrimage. That's the weird thing, Morrison's grave is a popular Parisian tourist attraction, one of the most popular. After all these years? Human beings never cease to amaze and confound me.

The thing is, who, as next of kin, could get an exhumation? The father? The wife? That in itself could have been a long legal tussle. The Courson family still own the legal rights over Jim's written word. Jim's parents are dead. On the day of the memorial service for Jim and Pam, her place was burgled and some of Jim's stuff stolen. Not lucrative in terms of comparison with the back catalogue sales of the six albums. In a few years items might surface in some auction room somewhere, just like John Lennon's old school books.

Rumour would not be enough, I needed to have proof, absolute proof. There was a death certificate, signed by a doctor, and the French authorities did not want to open an investigation. Why? Because the heroin supplier was a French aristocrat, who subsequently died of an overdose?

Maybe, if there had been more time, someone could have chopped Jim up and distributed him to his fans – made special little boxes; sold him as a 60s relic.

Human beings are dreadful and now I understood the Christ thing. Hauling the body out of the tomb under cover of darkness: the Easter heist! That's the funniest thing – Morrison did too. That alone is what made me think, one coincidence too far, one little message left on the wall. More and more it seemed like the elaboration of a poor liar.

Suddenly the word suicide popped into my head. Did Morrison choose the date on purpose and check out? Did he choose a date on which to depart? That was of course one theory, I had another. The more I stirred the water, the less clear everything became.

Then I thought about publishers and the cut that they got, and the shops and retailers in books and the whole thing turned into a mess. Christ, the royalties thing was the same for singers as it is for me. Morrison and Krieger had the talent and the result was they made Holzman rich. So rich he could refurbish the Los Angeles Elecktra offices and then sell the company to Warners and still walk away with more than a Shelby GT 500. He had given Morrison 'the blue lady' after the success of 'Light my Fire'.

Motive: Morrison wanted to get out of this crazy money trap. He had had enough and no amount of money or fame could have made him change his mind. Christ, he flopped in the Alta Cienaga Motel, down the street from The Doors, office. Money didn't matter to Morrison – it was a means to an end. Clothes – meaningless. He had left his mark with his poetry and with possibly the best album they had done in years, and he didn't even know or care.

So I started to think, what would I need to pull this misdirection off, if I were him?

A body – someone, who looked similar to me. Or someone I could pass off as me.

A passport – one that gave me a chance to disappear.

A chance to kick the booze – that was going to be the hardest thing of all. There was no AA, no Betty Ford clinic into which I could check.

A group of people who I knew could be silent, or just one person, a co-conspirator, someone who wanted me all to themselves, that person had to be Pamela Courson.

Then it struck me, if Morrison had all of these, where would he go?

* * *

At the drunk tank, Doug Prayer had disappeared and I was kicking myself. I was half an hour too late and I didn't have an address to find him. Call myself a reporter – I was a dope. The man had spent a night in the drunk tank and then simply walked.

The Parisian cops knew him and picked him up regularly, they told me; if that was the case, they would know where he lived. I needed to get a look at the arrest file, and for that I would need charm; for all I knew, he could know where Morrison was and I had missed him.

Twenty minutes later and $200 US lighter, I went for a coffee.

"You bum." I was talking to myself. "Work the problem." I was drifting into the realms of possibility. "The man decided to fake his own death. Work out how he did it first and then…"

I needed to check out those tapes and where they went – why did he leave them behind? Were they legitimate or were they a figment of this man's imagination? If Prayer was legitimate then he could show me the tapes or better still I could listen to them; once I heard Morrison's voice I'd know if the tapes were genuine. There was so much out there, but that voice was distinctive, not so much in the rich baritone but in the phrasing. I could get one of those sonic trackers on the voices, even after time they should match. Like Sinatra, he had a certain style and he milked it well. Once, when I heard the two albums from the remaining Doors, after he died, I knew precisely what he would do to them – how he would work them. Some of them would undoubtedly have been classic songs but, as Manzarek said, Morrison was the fourth point of the diamond and the diamond only worked when all four points were present. The whole thing was pulling me into a morass of mixed up thinking and gluey clay and my boots were heavy.

One guy in a bar, listening, another who claimed to have recorded with Morrison and yet he was treated like… My mind was racing. "What if there is more than the one tape?" I blurted out loud. A couple of locals gave me a strange look. A look which said 'loco'. "First ditch the music." I was talking to myself again. "Motive and how it was done."

A corpse – a corpse was needed first. So that when the doctor came there was something to examine. That body had to be dead.

I looked at the address on the scrap of paper the desk officer had pushed to me, after he pocketed the two bills I had passed to him. He smiled and for a moment I wondered if he had given me a bum steer. I ordered another coffee and checked a street map. It was at least a twenty minute walk if not longer. I decided to have another coffee first. I wanted to solve this thing once and for all.

The first thing Morrison needed was a body. Where the hell did he get that?

I pondered, maybe he found a bum who looked like him. Maybe the bum came back to his place and a drunken Morrison or Pam fed him some smack and wallop, his heart stopped. I mean, that's not murder – is it? Maybe the guy even died by accident and suddenly opportunity knocks. Morrison knew what heroin, when combined with excessive alcohol, could do to the human heart.

They had a valid passport which ran out in August, but that was the old one and the one which they also reported lost or stolen in Marseilles. But, and here's a strange fact, it was that passport which was used by the police to identify the body. An old passport to identify someone, who a primary witness claimed was her boy friend. A lot of facial changes in that time. Would you start to delve any deeper on the case of two foreigners? I mean, it's not like he was known there. He was known but not well enough, essentially he could move around easily; plus, knowing the French and their propensity to dismiss anyone who did not speak their language, I can understand the cursory checks. Was there a second one? Once that old passport turned up again, did they get another made up? Had one already been made?

So the body in the bath is a bum? Washed down, cleaned up and clothes gone and dead. That is the body which the doctor sees and pronounces dead. That is the body which the firefighters lift from the bath.

Then came the switch.

"So simple," I laughed out loud.

Other customers in the café looked at me as if I were insane. "Got it."

I slammed the cup into the saucer.

"One of the neighbours said there was a strange smell coming from the Morrison's flat." My immediate reaction was to think putrefaction. "But then the body would have to be in the bath for days." I was voicing my thoughts.

The other people in the café were staring intensely now, waiting for me to perform some form of weird seizure or some such. Perhaps seeing someone having their tongue pinned to their lapel held a strange macabre fascination. There they were again, the spectators, back at the auto crash site, slowing down to see a headless corpse draped over a bonnet, after a nosedive through the windscreen glass. It was time for me to shut up and think.

The fire brigade would have reported a rotting body. The doctor would have noticed. Unless of course he had been paid off, or there were two bodies? But could the fire brigade be paid off too? The more I thought about it, the worse it got, well not worse, ludicrous would be a better choice of word.

Then suddenly I remembered an account of Christopher Jones, the actor, I think it was him, who had visited Pam at their Norton Avenue apartment. He claimed a smell like sheep was permeating the place. Bearing in mind Jim did not shower often, could it simply be BO? Unlikely though, his natural pheromones were attractive to most women. Most women I have known have a highly developed sense of sexual attraction based upon smell. Put simply, men that stink don't get the girls. Pam supposedly showed Jones a fridge full of beef hearts, with the caveat that 'Jim likes hearts. Jim always eats hearts'. That could have been what Chagnol and the other neighbours smelt, the decomposition of offal in a hot Paris apartment. The lazy clearing up of a variety of meals. I don't suppose any local butcher would remember, forty years later, a tiny emaciated red-head with a tendency toward anorexia and a long-haired drunken American buying beef heart.

But what if there had been another body?

The neighbours could also have got the timescales wrong. The memory has a strange way of twisting time sequences out of line. I'd learnt that one in relationships where two people tell the same story from different angles, and both of them resolutely believe they are correct.

What if Pam and Jim had had a massive bust-up like before Miami? That sent him crazy then and he blew the whole thing out of the water. One glorious night of madness, where he goaded the crowd by calling them 'Fucking idiots'. Telling them that they were at the concert for another reason beyond the music. Maybe he was right, maybe they were worshipping; maybe the whole thing was some kind of quasi religious ceremony. Perhaps his audience were there for more than a concert, but telling them that they ought to get out and seek it caused a riot. Pam knew how to goad him, the mouse that caught the cat.

I thought about how, during the early seventies, other bands stepped up to the plate and the stadium concert arose. The picture that kept arriving was Robert Plant, screaming out 'The Lemon Song' shirt open and hair flowing as he strutted his meat.

Morrison was on the cusp of that, could see it coming; hated it and wanted to end it.

Then there was the weird idea which also struck me again; what did Morrison say or do at the draft board? John Densmore stayed outside, so he never actually heard what was said. What if Morrison actually had a weak heart? What if Clara Morrison knew? Perhaps the parents kept it secret from everyone so that the young Jim was not perceived as weak? Then my mind made a sudden and quantum leap. What if Jim guessed what was wrong and he was dissecting hearts in an attempt to learn. A man with such a high IQ – would that be such a wild step? This was not your average piece of stage pulp; in fact, he was a record company nightmare. Holzman loved him because he was successful but also saw the self-destruction which followed him in every stride. A step of exploration into the dissection and inner workings of himself. I dismissed that idea as absurd, but try as I might to banish it, it kept bouncing back.

Holzman loved him and hated him too.

The smell at the Norton Avenue apartment and the smell reported by Monsieur Chagnol and the other families, both like decomposition. Or were they both just like a butcher's shop? I recalled the sickly sweet odour of blood tempered with sawdust.

It was such a distinctive smell in my small hometown when my mother went shopping. Now in the big supermarkets meat is wrapped in cellophane and not paper and the smell, which is unusual, or off-putting, is disguised. No longer are there carcasses which look like animals split in half hanging or thrown onto beech blocks for dismemberment with saws, axes and knives. Now bits of flesh sit in white trays with absorbent pads to catch the flow of residual blood. The cellophane wrap hides the smell and the labels entice the buyer. The result: you'd hardly know it was dead flesh at all.

I needed to get to this drunk. Needed to piece the whole thing together.

Morrison died on the 3rd of July between 1.00 am and 9.00am and the coffin arrives on the 6th. Originally the body was naked, so the funeral directors get the body ready for burial? Or was that Pam? What was he buried in? On the 7th at 9.00am the funeral cortege arrives to collect the coffin and take it to Pere Lachaise. So where was the body between the 3rd and the 7th? On the bed? In July in a hot and sultry Paris? Could that be the smell, could the police arrival have been confused by witnesses? Maybe the witnesses were just confused and their recollection skewed?

Then there is the real knock-out punch. The death is registered at about 3.00pm, the same day, complete with burial permit. Pam and Alan Ronay make their statements to the police. But, and there was the really big but, the doctor views the body at 6.00pm.

No autopsy, no enquiry, just bury the guy?

Did Pam stay at the flat with the body on the bed? Where did she sleep? Did she go elsewhere? Questions, questions and more questions kept buzzing around in my brain. Why not let the undertakers take the body? Press? Rumours? The wish to have a quiet funeral?

Finally, I knew that it didn't make sense; panic and calm don't make for fine bed fellows. At times things seemed so regimented and ordered and a series of strange coincidences, and at others sheer chaos.

The grave was a double, bought on the 6th, The Tuesday after Jim's death and he is then buried as early as possible on the 7th at 9.00am. Why? Had Morrison hinted that he would have liked to be buried in that cemetery? Why was he there only a few days before the 3rd ? Morbid curiosity?

I can agree that coincidences occur but in this case there were too many, far too many. It just seemed like the unnecessary elaboration of a poor liar. If it was a lie, why?

"Conspiracy theory?" Her voice reassured me. "That'll make them sit up and listen, it always does."

"I know," I answered her imaginary voice in my head. That voice which was getting stronger day by day, confusing me. "If I get to the core of this and it's just…"

"Just what?" she asked.

"I'll go crazy."

"Why? You said all you wanted was the truth. Well maybe it's not what you want after all?"

"Shit! Shit! Shit! It just can't be an accident. Can it?"

Her voice came back again, louder, stronger. "Why? Why not? Why?"

My mind was racing and my heart beating. I needed a drink; I was losing it.

* * *

Sometime later I was calmly looking at my map, trudging the streets to find Doug Prayer and, if lucky, find the real Jim Morrison, in the flesh.

Eleven

Teenage head...

I found it – what a dive.

The place was dark and dingy, a series of corridors and rooms which overlooked garbage strewn back streets that reminded me of Hell's Kitchen in New York. The buildings were old and tired, though once they had been prime residences, but now rooms had been converted into what looked like bed-sits. Many windows were cracked and hallways were brown and almost sticky to the touch. It was an unpleasant place.

I spent ten minutes knocking at a door on the second floor, one with the number 32 on it, which had at some stage broken into pieces, each of which was attached by a single screw. Before I gave up, I tried some other doors, which in retrospect was not wise. I met an assorted bunch of people. One seemed to be a girl who was on the game and her eyes told me that she had a habit. She was slight, emaciated some might say; once she would have been beautiful, now, however, she seemed worn and threadbare, like a carpet that had been walked upon too many times. Her hair was thin and greasy and carried the beginnings of grey, but once it would have been a cinnamon red, lustrous and glowing with the vibrancy of youth. Her face certainly put pay to the idea that sex for sale is glamorous. Selling your own body for sex is not, and never will be, glamorous; in this case it was necessity. A necessity driven by a habit which would eventually kill her; she, like all addicts, was powerless. The selling I could understand – there had been many women I had known, friends and relatives of my mother, who had to do just that. Their reasons had been simple: the men were dead and they had hungry young to feed. There was a war on and the world was starving their children. Basic mammalian instinct had driven them to sell the only thing of value which they had left to sell. I immediately thought of Jim's prediction for Pam, that eventually she would end up a prostitute. He may well have been right, but her death had put that notion to bed.

The woman's face was tired and the lines around her eyes were ingrained with heavy make-up, which looked as if it was applied thickly and removed scarcely. One front tooth was yellow and I could see that the inner decay was about to break through the thin veneer which constituted the front enamel. Once she would have been pretty, but now she had passed even the depths of the hog-ranch and was barely alive. I could see her corpse in her eyes.

"What you want?" the woman asked in French.

She looked as if she were in her fifties, though she was probably in her thirties. Her off-white tee shirt was riddled with those small holes which appear on all hash smokers' clothes. Those little burns spoke volumes, as did the greyness of her laundry.

"I'm looking for a friend of mine," I lied in reply. "He lives down the hall near the back." I pointed.

"So?" she snarled.

"Well, I was wondering if you knew where he was?"

"No," she snapped, "why should I? Do I look like his keeper?"

I felt like a sheepish little boy asking a mother if her son were allowed out.

"I've tried his door and he..."

"Look, I don't give a shit." She was beginning to shut the door as she spoke.

I let it go.

"He's a no good anyway," she snarled as she slammed.

That told me she knew him at least.

I crossed the hallway and knocked at two other doors. One was answered by a bleak teenager who looked like a young mother. She said she had not noticed a man who lived down the hall, but that if I was looking for an afternoon of relaxation she could oblige for a fee. I began to understand the neighbourhood I was in now. This was the kind of place where men appeared and left swiftly, where faces were not remembered and money could get you any service. I declined politely and moved on to the final door, which was opened by an older woman who was only partly dressed. She seemed confused and disorientated and I detected the early onset of Alzheimer's. I had seen that behaviour before, in my own mother. She did the same flitting in and out of understanding as her mind disintegrated. Once, she too came to the door half naked, though she thought she was fully dressed. It was sad to watch that in a person that you cared for and this woman looked lonely and on the edge of capitulation. What a place to end your days.

I began to wonder what kind of society we lived in, where the kindness and decency had gone and what the future held. Suddenly I noticed the television blaring in the background; my questions had been answered in the instant and I sensed, rather than knew, that this was her only friend. I wondered what her life might have been like and what circumstances reduced her to such penury. Had she been loved, had she loved herself? I asked a couple of questions, but the combination of my French and her mental state made for a very disjointed conversation. I learned nothing except that my quarry was extremely elusive.

It's very strange, faces do come out of the rain and sometimes if you think too hard it can have you reaching for the razor blades. That is also something many people don't take into account. It doesn't matter how much money you have, how much you give away, loneliness is a drag. God this place made me maudlin, if this was where I lived, I'd drink too. Boy would I drink and probably shoot up, until the despair or blood poisoning got me. I could hear the cries of 'What's the bloody point' in the graffiti on the walls of the halls. Man, this was just like Jim had said; I mean could any hell be worse than this? But there is something about the people, an honesty, if corruption is honest? At least these people don't lie about it – they'd fuck you over if they could. It's the lack of a façade, lack of politeness and falsity of manners. Here, at the edge of the abyss, everyone clings to everyone, there's a vague hope that someone has still got hold of the rope that's tied to the stump at the edge of the precipice. In fabrication world above, the lemmings run one by one, biting each other on the leg as they go. The faster you run the more you get bitten, but somehow you all end up going over the edge. No one gets out alive and no one gets a free ride, whatever the odds.

Outside in the sunlight I looked at the Paris skyline – it was a different place. Tourists were milling and there were groups of musicians on street corners, they weren't too bad either. I had another coffee as I watched them play; they played real good and for free. They could probably have made it, with the right promotion and the right company image behind them. Perhaps if a billboard were hired in downtown Los Angeles they too could be made into stars. All they needed was a raw natural beauty, some sexual chemistry, a poetic and rebellious spirit and they'd be halfway home.

They seemed to be able to sing well enough, but drive, or will, or circumstance, or just plain luck had not come their way. Much of life is about being in the right place at just the right time. Los Angeles and San Francisco were the places to be in 1965/66 and that is precisely where Pam and Jim were. They were in the eye of the storm, and boy what a storm, it came right across the Atlantic and landed in my lap – soaked me to the core. The problem is, I'm too cynical, I mean how many talented songsters have gone to the wall because they didn't have a backer, and how many slubbs have made it to headline act because they did?

Four times that day I returned to the place, four times I received no answer; eventually I gave up and returned to my hotel.

The next day I did the same, and the next and the next, but I also walked the streets around the area. Much the same reception always occurred. I knocked, no answer, I left. I spoke to whoever I could and I got nowhere. Doug Prayer seemed to have vanished like a mist in the sunshine. I began to think that the $200 I had spent was a complete waste of money. The man seemed a ghost.

* * *

"Well you tried."

"I know but something's not right here," I was saying to the voice back home. I knew she was sensing my despondency, she knew me too well. "I don't usually get the bums rush like this. I usually get my man. I've been at the place at night, in the evening, early and at midday. Nothing. No damn answer. I'm just chasing my tail like some puppy running around in circles."

"Hey, are you a mountie or a puppy?" She was mocking now.

"A what?" I'd misheard the link.

"A Mountie," she repeated, "you know," she put on a deep voice, trying to sound like a man. A comical effect which only a really feminine voice can achieve. "A member of The Royal Canadian Mounted Police," she snarled deeply, "we always get our man."

"Ha, ha, ha," was all I could muster in retort.

"Witty," she laughed, "very witty."

"Look, I just can't find him. It's annoying the hell out of me," I pleaded, looking for some balance.

She gave it to me. "Look, maybe the guy," she hesitated, "maybe he doesn't go there very often," she offered.

"Grasping at straws love," I replied, with despondency in my voice. "That is grasping at straws. This whole thing is going to get right inside me and destroy us if I'm not careful. I think I'm going slightly mad."

"Listen to me Freddie Mercury," she seemed serious, "you're not going."

"I know, I'm gone?"

"Gone for years." She was giggling, "I mean, who else would put up with a crazy like you? But the show must go on."

"I'm not though, am I? Even though my make-up is flakin'."

"Not what?"

"Crazy?"

"You're a basket case Virgil Caine. Best get back home to Tennessee and start choppin' wood." Her giggle was very pronounced now. We were trading verbal blows.

"The money's no good," I replied.

"So? You take what you need?"

I answered her with, "And you leave the rest?"

"Hey I know," she giggled again, "why don't you go back to that park and see if he turns up, he might be somewhere else and then just come back there. He could just have disappeared for a little while; maybe he's gone on a bender. "

I grunted a reply, "Maybe he's just drunk somewhere?"

"It's worth a try. So try another try," she sang at me.

That was what I loved about her. Never once had she told me I was a waster. Never once had she rubbished my research. As I drifted off to sleep, I thought about where this man would go and, encouraged, I had a brain wave.

And then there were the voices, always the voices. They came more frequently now. I was beginning to wonder at what point imagination forced out reality. If you could hear Morrison and me sometimes too; but there were other wails in the wind. Fiercer, darker demons that belonged to me alone, ones that must be cleansed. Only they wouldn't, couldn't.

Maybe in that space between consciousness and sleep – the crystal ship, as Jim labelled it – it all made total, nonsensical sense.

Twelve

It's never too late…

Eventually Doug Prayer wasn't that difficult to find and he certainly wasn't Jim Morrison in disguise. I can hear you asking how I did it. The simple answer is usually the correct one; so I tried to distil down those things I knew. One, he was clearly a Doors fan; two, he had known Morrison; three, he was still in the area so many years later; four, he must frequent the area, bender or no bender he'd turn up again; five, then I caught the fish alive.

What I did was simple. I returned to the Place des Vosges where I had first talked with him. With all of the wonderful buildings that surrounded it and the atmosphere of the place he was sitting, reading, drinking coffee this time, though there were a couple of beer cans near his feet. It was almost as if he were waiting for a lover's rendezvous. Though I could see no clock and no flower in his lapel. He wasn't drunk and he wasn't loud, he was just sitting quietly. He looked different, sober. I was quick in my approach.

"Nice to see you again," I said, and plonked myself next to him on the bench. "Don't mind if I join you do you," I continued, "I believe you promised me an interview and some information."

"Did I?" he quietly replied.

"Yes you did," I was more emphatic, "and you gave me a fool's errand with that address. That was very slippery of you."

He turned to me and I could see a deep sadness in his eyes.

"Look, you want to know about Jim, well I'll tell ya some things and even give ya some things, but you got to leave me the hell alone – right?"

His accent had changed and I wondered why. There was the very slight southern twang, which gave his voice a little mocking tone. But this time it was warmer and felt, rather than sounded, friendly. He was clean and his hair and clothes brushed. It didn't make sense. First he appears as a bum and now as a quiet respectable older man. He caught me studying him.

"Fooled ya, didn't I?"

"In what way?" I asked.

"In every way honey," he smirked.

"Well not totally or I wouldn't have been able to find you here, would I?"

"Maybe you just took a lucky guess? Maybe I meant you to find me?"

That brought me up short and I raced to tell him why I was back there.

"Not really, you see, all of the apartments that face onto this park." I stopped and tried to reason. "If you had been the son of an ambassador then you'd have money," I hesitated, knowing it was a long shot, "probably." I thought of Jomo and the Smoothies, thought of long lost tapes and confusion and I shot an eye contact at him. "So I checked them all and it took me ages," I lied, "but eventually I found it." I waited for a reaction. None came. "You might have changed your name though to make it less difficult."

I didn't know why I was saying this but it appeared to be effective. Perhaps he thought me better at my job than I imagined. The bluffers guide to journalism and all that – but it was working.

"You thought I was drunken bum? A loud mouth with bottle and living in that dive?" he replied.

"Do you mind if I take notes?" I flipped open a pad and scrawled some shorthand down.

He looked dubious, but then just nodded.

"At first maybe," I said, in a noncommittal reply, "but if

you'd been drinking that heavily for all those years, you'd be mush by now. It made no sense. So I reckoned you were a guy who had come to Paris and then ended up staying. The thing was if you were an American," I was bullshitting at my very best now, "you'd have money and then I remembered."

I stopped the waffle and out of nowhere it just came. It was that Frost/Nixon moment when everything turns on a knife edge. When the least little thing provokes an intense reaction and then boom. To this day I still do not know why I got through his guard. Did he see something in me, much as Nixon saw something kindred in Frost, something not based on, as he labelled it 'snobs'. This drunk had made the choice, not me. Luck really, I was just in the right place at the right time. That's the thing with zeitgeist, it just is.

"You know how many idiot researchers have been looking for me?"

I shook my head in response.

"And how many found me and tried to get me to say where Jimmy was?" He didn't wait for an answer. "Hundreds."

"If you want to find out the real story. you gotta be a bit smarter," he paused, tapping his temple with his forefinger, "like you," he continued. "I been watching you askin' around."

My jaw fell open. I thought about how he might have watched me. Had he been following me? Or was he just doing to me what I had done to him only moments earlier. I felt uncomfortable.

"Bullshit," I mocked. "No way Jose."

"Mmm, interesting reaction from a reporter," he laughed.

I tried to reply, "But the…"

"Reward?"

"No that was…"

He interrupted again, "To get someone out into the open?"

"I just thought that someone might be in need of a few bucks."

As soon as I had said it, I knew it was a totally lame thing to say. A stupid thing actually. He let it go with just a blank stare. But he had done what he intended, threw me off balance, unnerved me, and I thought I was the one conducting the interview.

Then the flood gates opened. It was as if I'd passed an invisible test of some sort.

"See you were right, I came here in 1968, back-packing, only I never went back. Me, I learned the language and married a local girl. That's when I saw Morrison for the first time, in Europe, Amsterdam. They were playing a gig with Jefferson Airplane, Grace Slick and awl. Man she was good lookin' too and with the morals of an alley cat. I bet you could wear her like a necktie. Hey, they were times." He started to sing, "Sex and drugs and sausage rolls are very good indeed."

"The Blockheads?"

"Absolutely, nice and edgy," he chuckled. "Bands that are edgy are the key. Don't you just hate all that bubblegum niceness or the lethargic ketomine of laid-back prog-rock. Give me the boys with razor blades in their ears and glass in their teeth every time. Something with some bite and kick, something that lets you know you really are alive – that you are something more than just a number. That's what Jim did, you know, he made us feel like we really were living."

He was smiling broadly as if recalling a long lost past. I had seen that before in interviewees, especially ex-service men. I did a piece on Cambrai once, and the early tank battles of the First World War, and this veteran glazed over as he spoke, as if he were back there. He must have been sixteen at the time, and eighty five when I did the interview. He stank of piss, but boy he gave me detail for one of the best articles I've ever done. Douglas Prayer had that same look. The Scots have a wonderful expression for it: glaikit, pronounced, glay-kit. To be glazed over, and that is the best word I can use here. Only this guy was no half-wit, he was firing on all cylinders.

The strangest thing was, I knew precisely what he meant. That was what I liked about The Doors. They were the bad boys of American rock, just like The Rolling Stones were for Britain. Nobody likes the nice guys, nice guys are boring, nice guys don't bite.

"So you were in Amsterdam?" I asked.

"Wasn't everyone?"

This, I thought, was my chance to test the guy. To see if he really was on the level.

"So how was the gig?" I asked, expecting him to say fantastic, even though I knew Morrison had collapsed on stage whilst dancing to an Airplane song and then spent the night in hospital.

He was laughing now, "Hey, that was one wild gig."

I stopped writing, thinking I was about to get a story of Morrison in full flight, even though it had not happened. I hoped I wouldn't, because I so desperately wanted the contradictions I was hearing to be true. But, and it was a big but, that would have given me an excuse to terminate the interview as a useless waste of time. However, I was totally wrong; what I actually got was far better and obviously the truth.

"You see," he continued, "I only got to see Airplane play. Somebody gave me something and man I crashed out. Ended up in the hospital and guess what?" I shook my head. "In the bed next to me, Morrison. Jim Morrison, apparently he'd done the same and we laughed about it."

"So you're saying that on the night Morrison passed out, you did too, and that you spent the night next to him in hospital?" I was finding this hard to believe but engrossing. "So what happened next?"

"Well," I could tell he was relishing the story, relishing my enthusiasm. "Cool as you like, Morrison says, hey buddy, what's your name? So I say Doug, and he says wow my middle name man. Let's go get a beer. As cool as you like, we check out and take to the streets, we don't wait for the doctors, cos he says he doesn't trust 'em anyhow. Anyway we were young and full of life, so what the hell, we went. A few beers later, he's back at my place and I'm playin' the guitar and man he's singin'. That rich baritone still sends me man, still sends me." There was a pause in his recollection and a smile crossed his lips. "He had all these songs and ideas and bits of phrases in this notebook. Poetry and stuff all about celebrating lizards or something and then boom, he meets Vanessa. That's my wife, well girlfriend then, and she has red hair and man he's really freaked now and talking about soul spirits and doubles, voodoo and fate and chance and all that

147

shit. Tells me about this girl he loves, that's what he said, she's my girl. Turns out she's from Orange and has red hair just like Vanessa."

"So you married a local girl?" I wanted him to continue, so I started scribbling again. That seemed to reassure him, he relaxed and I knew I had the scoop.

He changed tack, "You were right," he said.

"About?"

"My father was a diplomat. Well a secretary or dogsbody would be the best description. Still, he punched all around the world. There was no way I wanted to end up in 'nam. You know, mostly it was poor kids or black kids that went. Loads of the middle classes didn't get drafted, but I did. Anyway, my ole man, he wanted me to go, dumb schmuck, said it would be character forming. I think he fixed it so I did go; see he was a company man. He'd been in Korea and the Pacific before that, said it would be life changing, a valuable experience. Christ Almighty it was just that. Changed my damn life forever." Suddenly he pulled his left trouser leg up to reveal hideous scars. "Got this for my trouble too. Cong love bite I call it."

I was stunned at the mangled yet healed calf and knee which was more scar than flesh.

"I got a nice couple of holes in my back too, where my lungs got punctured, and one of my balls is scattered in that jungle. But hey," he was bitter, "they send me a pension every month."

I was taking notes like mad now.

"You wanna know how they got me? The gooks."

"Sure," I wanted more on Morrison but knew I would have to let the story play out.

"We set down in the chopper to pick up some wounded in a rice paddy and there was all these guys yelling and runnin'. It was damn chaos." His eyes were fixed now as he replayed the image for me to note. "Suddenly there's a kid runnin' toward the chopper and one of the guys he's screamin' shoot him, shoot him." Tears rolled into his eyes. "I had the kid marked and I coulda dropped him but I didn't cos he was a kid; he could'na' been more than nine or ten and he's yellin', his hands up above

148

his head. When he's up next to the chopper, I see the grenade he's holdin' but then it's too late. Bam, the whole damn thing goes up and the kid's head comes apart in the blast. Blood and metal everywhere, it was like hell. Then came the gunfire and I knew I was hit."

"So the kid was the…"

"Dummy? No that was me, I shoulda…" He stopped dramatically. "You ever been in combat?" he asked.

I shook my head.

"Well it ain't heroic. What would have been heroic would be to cut that kid down. Six men died there that day because of my mistake."

"That wasn't a mistake," I reassured. "It's what any decent man would have done."

"Yep, I thought that once. But was I a decent man? I killed people who I shouldn't and all because the government said I should. There ain't a day goes by that I don't think about that damn war and the wrongs I done. I will carry that with me until I die."

In his eyes I could see the picture, the torture of a mistake. He would forever be on the horns of a dilemma. Damned if he killed the boy and damned if he didn't. The cost of his decency he had already shown me.

"You know what Morrison said to me?"

I shook my head.

"He said, it didn't matter. That we only see things through the jaded doors of perception. The restraints of things placed upon us by others. If the doors are cleansed then everything will be as it should be, infinite, immaculate."

"And do you agree with that?" I asked.

"That's the weird thing. At the time he'd lost me, but now, thirty years later, I kinda see where he's at. Man he was one clever mother that Morrison."

"Can I quote you on this in my notes?" I requested.

"Yeah, if you like notes." He paused and then, as if throwing away a casual comment, said, "I got a note I might show you one time. I been keepin' it safe. Just in case they said I was a crazy."

He let the trouser leg fall. "So I got healed and went off to Europe and I ain't been back to the States since. Except the once when my mom died. She stuck by me, though her only son was chopped into meat. Then one day I get this letter and all the old man had," he paused, "it comes to me. Mom's dead years before and now the stupid bastard leaves it all to me. Maybe he was sorry and that makes the whole shit even worse. Be the first one on your block to have your boy come home in a box. I nearly made it – I come home on a stretcher."

"Inheritance?"

"God damn inheritance. The poor bastard sends me off to be shot up and then he damn well leaves me everything. Worked like the devil to be a someone and ends up alone, life just ain't fair for some. Come in with nothin' and left the same way. Only, even his son blamed him, when in reality he was just a cog in the system. You can't beat the man. Can you believe that? And me, shit that I was, I just walked and he, he had the love to let me be. Man I made some big mistakes – damn monsters."

"Maybe he changed his mind about you, people can do that you know."

"Yeah and that makes it worse," he became reflective, "far worse. To think that he let me run free; man, the guilt I carry is like a ton of chain wrapped around my soul. I should have been a better son. "

"In the end it doesn't really matter though," I placated, "nothing does. I think I was the same to my father as he was to his; history kind of repeating. My father sided with his mother when grandfather went on the booze. He came to regret it and be ashamed of himself, especially when his father had a stroke and simply refused to speak. Can you imagine that? My dad telling me that his father had collapsed into the fire grate and then not speaking again, his wife just left him there. That's what my old man said, but he added the killer, when he told me, that he was sure his father, that's my grandfather, never spoke again," I paused, "because he simply chose not to."

Doug Prayer was listening intently but saying nothing.

"The man simply gave up the will to live; the disappointment killed him I think. Jesus Christ, what a way to go. And my father was sure he could speak, but that he just let go. I think he kind of blamed himself for the whole thing, as if being a kid in that could have made a difference? And then when he started shagging around, because he was so messed up with the baggage of his crazy wife, I sided with my mother – hell, I should have made more of an effort to be a better son. "

Doug Prayer and I connected that day. There were no bonds, no exchanges of cash, what happened was precisely what really matters, that two human beings find something in common. Morrison had his demons, Doug Prayer had his and I had mine; the thing is, we all had a connection. Hey! Call it shared experience, call it karma, call it coincidence, call it a crock, call it what you like; the truth was it was there and none of us could do anything about it.

"You know that's what Morrison said too. Kinda let the whole of life wash over him. Like it didn't matter, and he was…"

"Right," I interrupted. "Maybe he mellowed, you know, like we all do eventually."

"Yeah, I have," he replied.

"Me too," I laughed. "Now things that once were important aren't important anymore."

"Kinda feels good, don't it?" he laughed back. "All those things we used to worry about, hell they ain't worth a fart in a hurricane."

I changed the subject, "That place is yours then?" I had no idea where or what the place was like. I was rolling the dice.

"Yep, all mine. For what it's worth."

"Yours and your wife's."

"Yep and she died, ten years back. All that I did to make things right and it all goes to hell in a handcart."

"Kids?"

"No but we wanted them. Now they got IVF, but we just had each other and then that was stolen from me. She was too young, too beautiful, and too perfect."

"What happened?" I asked with sincerity.

151

"Cancer," he paused, "fucking cancer of the womb. I seen that before too – Agent Orange and all that. It ate some of my buddies down to the bone, but hey, I'm the lucky one, I'm still here." He became reflective. "Maybe I ain't lucky at all, maybe she was the lucky one. My life ain't worth a dime. I mean what have I got left to look forward to in this life? I spend all my time looking back; maybe we'll meet in the next one if I ain't too late."

I thought he was about to cry. Thought I had re-opened the oldest and deepest wound he had, much deeper than the wounds on his leg and back, those were superficial.

"She was a beauty too, my fiery red head. There ain't a day goes by that I don't think of her either; I loved her."

"So how did the friendship with Jim continue?" I tried to steer the conversation, lest he suddenly become absorbed in grief.

"Morrison was the perfect gentleman. He never once tried it on with her; he had a kind of respect for marriage though he didn't believe in it himself. Well that's not really true. There ought to be a better way to put this," he paused, deep in thought, searching for words to explain the concept. "Morrison understood the sanctity of the relationship but hated the ceremony and the idea of an establishment of rules and roles via marriage. Does that make any sense? He understood the cosmic connection, that two people could be one and the same under the skin, but he didn't know how to control it. See I think he loved Pam and she did him but the relationship transcended the physical. It kind of was on a completely different level, and I don't think they even knew what it was they had. That's what I thought was the problem with him and Pam. One of them always had to have the juice."

"The juice?"

"Yeah, the power man. See with them it was like he'd met his match. He always got his own way, except with her, she was small but man she was strong. She knew what made him tick and that made him weak to her."

I was listening intently now, because he was confirming with fine detail what I had always suspected.

"Look, if Jim fucked a girl, she'd just fuck someone else, just to get back at him; sometimes one of his friends, just to make it sting a bit more. Then she'd tell him and watch the reaction. It was like each one of them was trying to control the other with cruelty. In the end the damage they did to each other just about destroyed them both. Somebody shoulda banged their damn heads together. They had it all and they didn't even know. You know some people jab a vein to get it, or dive off buildings with parachutes, and all the while they already had it. Every day man, every day, was a white knuckle ride with both of them. Thing is, I don't think I could have lived like that, on the edge all the time. Eventually if you dice with death, one day you're gonna lose man, bound to lose. It's the law of averages, every gambler knows that."

"Were they really in love?" I asked.

"Hell, I don't know," he snapped back. "If he said slower, she went into dead stop. If she said faster, he'd go right to the edge. But they were good together, so good together at times you'd wish you could get that close. Hey, I liked her."

I changed tack, "So how did you meet up again after Amsterdam?"

"Easy, one night in the bar he was just there. I was singing with a guitar, Crosby, Stills and Nash, for what we had when the hat got passed. He didn't speak French then and we sorta hit it off musically, him bein' a good ole boy and awl, he sang some songs too but nobody really knew who the bluesman was. We laughed about how the drugs got us and, well, he just appears like a ghost man. Then there was that damn admiral father of his, wanted him to have a career. Hell, who'd send their boy off willingly iffen they had a choice? Damn Uncle Sam and all who sail in him."

I tried to pull him back, "So how did the music work with Morrison?" I asked.

"Luck I suppose." He reflected, "Yeah, luck."

"You said you played guitar. Who else was there?"

"There was Josh Blaine, he played the bass, his older brother Jon, who played drums, harmonica and keyboards, sometimes, and Miguel."

"Miguel?"

He nodded.

"Miguel Alvarez."

"Mickey A. Morrison used to call him."

"What did he play?" I asked.

"Hell, he didn't play, lessen you call a tambourine playing. Did backing vocals though and Morrison liked him; I don't even think he could see straight most of the time. You know I don't even think that was his real name. He didn't look Mexican or Spanish to me either, but he had a Mexican name. He was a dealer, cocaine mostly and Jim liked coke, but, and this is the bit that fascinated Morrison, he looked a bit like him. Well except for the fact that his hair was lighter and short. Standing next to each other you'd have trouble telling them apart – sometimes. If Mickey had been dark haired, well they could have been brothers. Morrison liked that and he joked that Mickey could wear his clothes and be Jim Morrison for a while, so he could take some time off and go be himself. He joked about that a lot. Sometimes I got to thinkin' that Morrison wouldn't mind if someone else did take on his character. Said he could disappear and go on holiday." There was a pause. "Look, people think that Morrison was down all the time. Man he was funny, clever and funny, though sometimes he could explode, but most of the time he was a laugh. Hell, he made me laugh a lot. There was something that made him seem like he could turn anything into a chuckle. He wasn't down and drunk, he was fun to be with. He could tell jokes and be one of the boys and he had a warmth man. When he was on the bottle he was supposed to be real bad. Only thing was, I didn't see him like that when we worked on music, he was always buzzin' and changing things. But he had ideas, ideas that worked. Some people didn't see that in him but I did, and he loved to joke around, especially with people he liked. I reckon he must have liked me cos he joked around a lot. He even brought Pam to the studio once or twice. Man she was lovely first time I seed her, all red hair and thin like a waif, but her smile was the killer."

I stopped him abruptly, "Studio?" I asked.

"Yeah, just like the mystery Jomo and the Smoothies."

"Are you telling me there is a proper tape made in a studio?"

"Sure am," he replied.

"A tape with Jim Morrison singing with another band?" I was finding this hard to take. "Next you're going to say that it was recorded after July 1971," I nearly choked on my words. My heart was pounding now, I was so close.

"Nope, because it ain't," he replied. "It was recorded in 1971. It's the last recordings he ever did."

"What, before he died?"

"I didn't say that. All I said was the music was over before July."

I think he noticed a slump in my shoulders.

"Look, Jim wanted out and when the chance came he took it. Hell, he just took a chance and it worked."

"So the tapes are from 1971, while he was here in Paris?" I was pushing hard now, trying to force the pace of the story along.

He turned his gaze full upon me and his eyes wide, they made contact with mine. "I loved him ya know. Really loved him, and he hasn't been around for a while so I reckon it's 'bout time."

"When did you stop seeing him?"

"He wasn't burnt out you know," he replied. "He just had enough and a lucky chance came his way. A real lucky break. Sometimes everyone ought to have a lucky accident." He reflected, "You know I seen a interview with a guy who missed one of the 9/11 flights because he got caught in traffic. See that must have been fate. What is it the Arabs say, your fate is written?" He continued to ramble, "So you take your chance in the circus ring and dance."

"When did you stop seeing him?" I repeated.

He didn't answer me. I asked again.

"Man you really are persistent ain't yah?" he growled. "Just listen man, stop trying to get the story out for your damn paper and listen to the man's mind." He grinned. "You might even learn something.'"

"But without proof this could all be a crock of shit." My voice was reaching falsetto.

"Bullshit," he exclaimed

"That room, in that place?" I squeaked. "That's all a game, an illusion."

"That's my Alta Cienega man." He laughed, "My little bolt hole, a place where I can dive down." He started singing, all bluesy and slow, "You know if the river was whiskey I'd be a diving duck. I'd dive to the bottom and I'd never come up."

It was baritone rich and dark, nice and easy on the ear.

"So you rent a place that is a shit hole so you have somewhere to what?"

"Work myself up before a performance, man. Somewhere to hide," he smiled.

I didn't smile back. I thought I was being played.

"It works on most people." He started singing again, "I got my mojo workin', got my mojo workin', but it jus' don't work on you."

I thought he was playing with me. I was struggling to see the logic, but I understood the idea. It was like a multi-personality disorder. Like there were separate existences lived in parallel in one place by the same person. Doug Prayer was a drunk, in another he was Douglas Prayer, respectable what? He hadn't told me and I hadn't bothered to ask. He had a veteran's pension and inheritance and lived in… where? I didn't know that either. All I knew was that in each place he could be someone different. Like a performance, he took the persona that suited him. Had he learned that from Morrison too?

Then to my utter amazement he said, "You wanna see the note?"

"The note? What note?"

"Jim's note to me, written after he was dead."

He might as well have offered to introduce me to the man. I couldn't believe it, "Why me? Why now?" I asked, "Won't Jim be mad?" As soon as I had said it, I knew the inflection was wrong. Knew he would be offended by what appeared to be a hint of sarcasm. I knew that must have stung his pride.

"You don't believe me, do ya?" he asked.

I must have looked stunned or something.

"Look, if you want to you can listen to the tapes too," he continued.

"You are kidding me right?"

"Nope, deadly serious man."

"The tapes with Morrison singing?" I asked again.

"Yeah the tapes…"

"The tapes with you?" I interrupted.

He shrugged, "Who else?"

"When?" I asked.

"How about now? Hey, I'll tell you all about us, the apartment, the heist and the hoax. You see, I was there."

Thirteen

You can't judge a book by the cover...

The apartment:

I followed him dutifully and very closely this time. I was careful not to give away the fact that I had no idea where he might be taking me, but I wanted him to think the exact opposite; think that I had tracked him down and discovered his secret.

The place was a palace; it was an amazing contrast to room 32 and an amazing home. Chic and tasteful with a beautiful opulent feel to the furnishings, this was a place that spoke of wealth. Everything was chosen to be in perfect unison with the next; the walls were off-white and clean, displaying paintings which became the focus of each space they inhabited. It was open in the central part, with a square of deep enveloping sofas which invited you to sit around the central coffee table. That was strewn with books, several of which held markers within the pages. There were also magazines, including *Rolling Stone* and *National Geographic*; American magazines and French newspapers. It was clear that the man could both read and comprehend the French language. This room was designed for conversation, for human discourse, for reading, for relaxation. There was a large music player and quadraphonic speakers which dominated the corners; also there seemed to be rooms, which were themed, that ran off this central space. I couldn't get a full view but I could see matching décor.

A bedroom, which appeared to hold a heart shaped bed with trimmings of purple and gold – unmade. We passed through the central square to a room which was opulent and warm, rich in reds and gold.

"My rest room," Prayer said, as he motioned me to sit. "My sanctuary, my place to hide."

"Not exactly what I expected," I said in reply.

"Do you like it though?" he asked. "My Vanessa designed all of this and she had so little time to enjoy it. Life's a real bitch, don't you think? Those that deserve a chance seldom get it."

I tried to take in the décor. "It's wonderful, no beautiful," I corrected. "So why the rented room?" I asked. "That place looked like a dive."

"It is," he laughed, "a total dive, but it keeps you lot at bay. It is there to remind me of what my life could have been if not for Ness. She saved me you know."

"Saved you from what?" I asked profoundly.

He laughed. "Saved me from the worst thing, the thing that would have killed me if it went unchecked."

I was racing through the possibilities, drug addiction, booze, crime, but in the end just simply asked.

"And that was?"

"Me, dear boy, me."

"So that place keeps you grounded?"

He became thoughtful. "Well for the past few years it has. I seem to use it less and less now. Also, it keeps the gendarmes happy if ever I go on a bender. Alcohol is a real bitch to kick and well..." His voice tailed away. "I miss her so bad it hurts like hell. I shoulda been better to her when she was alive. Man I regret that. If I could turn back the clock, I would. Hey, if I could have taken her place in the queue, I would. By rights it should've been me anyway, not her. She didn't deserve that, but I did. Life was, for her, too short." He reflected, "You know on one score at least Jim was right, none of us truly get what we deserve in this shit house. That's the real truth of chaos, there is no deserve."

I could see his face quite clearly now. It was the face of an old man, but there was something else there. Sadness, a deep sadness, brought on by the ancient enemy- defeat. Perhaps he had chosen me, rather than me choose him. Even now when I write this account I see him in my mind's eye and ask, why me? Just why did he choose me to tell this to. He had others he could have spilled to, but fate, or luck, gave me the opportunity.

"Why not check into a rehab centre or something. Maybe they could do something for you."

"For what I got, they ain't got no cure, they cain't do nothin'."

"But in rehab they can do marvels. Perhaps with some therapy."

"Therapy, fuckin' therapy. Man, for what I got they ain't got no cure baby."

"But there is always hope…"

He cut me dead. "That's a bunch of bullshit man. That's what they tell ya to keep ya quiet."

"But what is there without hope then?"

He became jovial, whistling a familiar tune. And then laughed, asking, "You like Amy? Everybody likes Amy Wineshouse surely?"

I nodded, knowing that strand of the conversation was dead and buried. He would never go to a clinic; that much I did learn, he'd rather die first.

"Misdirection," he continued. "Hey, you want a beer or a coffee?"

"Coffee please," I spluttered, quite overcome by the place and the fact that he had kept up with the modern trends in music. Then without thinking, I asked, "Can I take a look around." I knew it was rude and I expected a sharp rebuke, but the answer I received stunned me.

"Sure," he said, "knock yourself out man. I'll make us a decent coffee, might even drop a little harsh into the mix to mellow it out. You might as well start in the kitchen." I followed him like a puppy. "The terrace runs out through those doors." He nodded. As his hands worked on the coffee grinder, the fresh smell rose into the air and spoke of home and comfort. "The balcony looks over the park, it's the first place I saw Jim. We were busking for a few cents here and there, just to get some scraps of bread. I was a California kid, on the road, free and lovin' it. We had some real good times then, kinda wild. Take a look around, there's not much to see really, it's just a pad."

This was now the third version of how he and Morrison had first met. So far I'd heard Amsterdam, a club, in which Crosby, Stills and Nash songs were being worked, and now this: busking. There seemed to be a great deal of confusion in the mind of my contact, so much so that it threw all other things into disarray with it and subsequently made me doubt his whole story. Memories can become confused and cross over. I wondered if I was getting one or several different persons accounts. I wondered how many previous journalists had experienced much the same and then simply given up. The problem for me, as always, was the sifting. Sometimes the act of talking to eyewitnesses or the old, after a long space of time, makes the work extreme, but occasionally you get a gem. He was confused, or attempting to confuse me, either way I couldn't be sure, but I was certain that some of what he said was true.

I could imagine Morrison as a busker. Knew he would be equally at home as a street musician as he would a superstar, the trappings of stardom didn't interest him. In fact, that might have even suited him better. After 'Light my Fire' all hell broke loose, and that success probably sealed Morrison's fate. The old adage of not wishing too hard for something, just in case you get it, should be applied here. All of us might wish to be famous, but is it all it's cracked up to be? And why does it destroy so many?

The thing was, the man didn't really know much detail about his three stories, though he believed each and every one – that disappointed me. Perhaps he had learned them from some sources, as yet unspecified.

So I did look around. It was functional, clean and wholesome, but it also had the feel of a place which someone had settled in, finally settled in. The other rooms were much the same, only as I passed from room to room, I noticed the total absence of a TV. Unless one was tucked away in a cupboard, there was no visible sign of one. Music however, and books, they were everywhere. Wall after wall of texts, ranging from modern fiction through Ancient Greek; history and philosophy, natural history, arts, sciences and even math. I was stunned by the sheer complexity of the material. This was a man who read widely and clearly had an intellect. Then it dawned on me that this man and Morrison would have a lot in common. Their conversations would have been interesting and perhaps Doug Prayer and Jim had discussed the Easter story, much as Jim and Mary Werbelow had done so many years before. I had a sudden flashback vision to the Oliver Stone movie, where Jim supposedly follows Pam back from the beach, Venice Beach. That surely was how Jim met Mary on the beach at Clearwater, Florida and not Pam.

In the Stone movie Jim follows Pam back to a house with The Doors tune 'Love Street' playing in the background. There he climbs a tree to get in. That, I'm afraid, is pure fiction. Pam's place was on Laurel Canyon, about a twenty five minute drive with no traffic. And if you go between the two at a busy time allow forty five minutes drive time at least. Venice to Sunset and then up to the canyon is one lengthy walk.

Pam and Jim's place on the Rothdell Trail, a.k.a. Love Street, is just behind the Laurel Canyon grocery store, which is still trading today. That was the place where the creatures meet. The 'creatures' being the hippy long hairs, of which Morrison spoke. Morrison may well have been around at the time but The Doors were not 'hippies' though they did sport long hair and were part of the 60s rebellion subculture. The Doors were something else, something unique. The English equivalent being The Rolling Stones or The Who. The Doors were a darker edge to the endless summer of 1967.

Even today, on a quiet Sunday, the canyon store, plays host to the odd 'star' who might show up for coffee. Renee Zellweger, George Clooney and Steven Tyler of Aerosmith have all been there. A little further up the hill is the old, and reputedly haunted, Houdini mansion. Once used by The Doors and others for promotional photoshoots, it's within walking distance of the store, only now it's been sold and is being renovated.

Further up the hill is Mulholland Drive. The twisting road which runs through the hills between Hollywood and Malibu. Along this 'Drive' Frank Sinatra, Marlon Brando and a list of stars too long to mention either have or had their homes. Morrison's college, UCLA, is nearby, just below Sunset Boulevard, but don't be fooled, you need a car to get around in anything like normal time.

Jim liked the beach; the infinite possibilities which lay within and beyond the ocean both intrigued and excited him. Los Angeles is a beach and in the water there, there are sharks.

The first song he is supposed to have sung from his imaginary concert, which he held in his head, was 'Moonlight Drive'. That appears on *Strange Days*, the second album, proving two things: one, Jim liked the ocean – he was a good swimmer; two, that the band had many bits of material to choose from. He liked to be near the sea, it was part of his psyche, and 'Moonlight Drive' says it all.

The idea that this man and Jim might be soul brothers with the same tastes in women did not escape me. I suspect it had not escaped Jim either. Morrison was the kind of man who would have been very sensitive to any 'cosmic connection' to another human being. Doug Prayer was getting more interesting by the minute, and more credible, and for some reason I was beginning to like him. I should have found him utterly exasperating, but I didn't, I actually found him entertaining and sincere. I know you as a reader will think I'm nuts, but honestly you had to hear the guy. He was a strange individual, but mesmerising too.

His music collection was vast with records in vinyl, tapes and CDs spanning an array of eclectic tastes. There were the old crooners from the 1930s and 40s and the big bands too, plus early rare recordings of rock and roll and blues artists long forgotten. There were also modern singers like Amy Winehouse. This was a collection of items which spanned the decades and had taken a lifetime to amass.

The balcony was something to behold as it reached out and overlooked the ancient park below. This was a space which had charm and beauty. From the moment I stepped out into the air, I

163

understood the choice of this location; it was central Paris, but it was also something else, something old and timeless, a space in the history of the world and we were, at that moment, in it.

"This is amazing," I remarked as he handed me a coffee.

"I had to wait a few years to get my hands on this place," he said, "but eventually one of the apartments became vacant and the rest is history man. I wanted to be near this park and told Jim that too."

My ears pricked up. "It is stunning."

"Sugar?"

"No thanks," I replied.

"Well if you like this, come this way." He seemed pleased that I noticed his taste.

"You like the early blues and rock and roll?" I asked. "I noticed all the records."

"Yep, that's virtually all I listen to these days. Mind you, that took me time to get them together. I hate that bubblegum crap that they feed you on the media. *American Idol*, star factory or whatever it's called; reality TV pop star show, call it what you like, it's karaoke singers to vote for. It's just like Warhol said, in the future everyone will be famous for fifteen minutes. He didn't mean that literally, you know fifteen minutes, though some folks think he did, dumb schmucks."

"Yeah, I agree," I replied. "He meant that being famous was going to become shorter and shorter, surely?"

"Precisely 'and if you ain't got talent baby' it's gonna be real short, reeeeal short; that's what he meant, and," he paused, "we live in the future."

"I noticed you don't seem to have TV?"

"Yep!" he exclaimed.

"Any reason?"

"Do you watch it?" he asked accusingly.

"Yeah, but not that much, mostly when I'm away from home in some hotel somewhere."

"What, porn? Girls? Boys?"

"Sometimes," I replied honestly, I thought it might engender trust. "Though I'm for the girls me, strictly for the girls."

164

He became apologetic. "Look man I don't care what you're into, it's all the same to me. You do who you like, I mean what the hell. I just can't stand the endless drivel they serve up for the spectators, that's you and me." He paused in thought and then continued, "They can make you believe what they want and get you to believe you want it. Hell, they can get a President elected; influence public opinion, whatever that might be? If you wanna watch a girl sucking cock at least that's honest and we could do with a little more honesty in this world. Most of what we see is bullshit anyway. Nope, I don't watch the damn TV." His eyes burned with passion as he continued, "Hey, it's hard to get political truth and no spin on that mother fucker. Everyone wants their fifteen minutes and that damn machine entices people into it. Sucks them up like a vacuum cleaner, swirls them around and then empties them into the trash."

"So you don't watch it at all?"

"Try not to." He became reflective. "But you know the funny thing?"

I shook my head.

"When we were kids," he continued, "we all wanted a colour one. A great big glass eye cinema that spat garbage at us. And the funny thing is we didn't know it was garbage, but now we do – and we still watch it. It's true, successful hills are here to stay."

"So you'd rather have music and books?"

"Yeah, much nicer for me and I don't have to swallow that crap that they dish up to make me somatose. See I can think – that's education for you."

I picked up the *Brave New World* reference to Soma and thanked my college tutor for that one. I knew I'd have to keep my wits about me as he threw references in from all angles.

"You like Huxley?" I asked. "Well I suppose you would do, *The Doors of Perception* and all that?"

"That's a must read and yep I get where the man's coming from. *Brave New World* has come true, well some of it and that scares me shitless. It's not 1984 is it? Huxley spent time in LA too. Mescaline and LSD before it became illegal. Did you know the US army experimented with that stuff to see if it could be used to heighten aggression in combat? That's ironic, because when us hippies got hold of it we chilled out in dream world and it got banned. One law for you and one for them man. Ain't that just the whole damn mother of a truth? That's why they hated Jim, because he said it as it was and so they wanted to put him on a chain gang."

"I know," I agreed.

"Just because he told them some of the things they didn't want to hear."

"Just because he saw it as it was." I agreed again.

"Yeah, and the truth is hard to swallow. Right?"

"Right," I agreed, "but the truth always triumphs, always comes out in the end."

"What a bunch of bullshit man," he was laughing, "the thing is, most people can't handle the truth. So they run away."

"You know Huxley's buried in Godalming, in Surrey, England. In a nice middle-class plot. All that rebellion, all that experimentation and he ends up in a tiny place like that."

He shrugged as he responded, "All our lives we sweat and slave, saving for a shallow grave."

"Maybe we're all destined for an anonymous grave?"

"Yep, ain't that the truth," he confirmed. Then, turning and looking me straight in the eye, he said, "You know what kid, you're alright."

I couldn't believe that sudden statement. It was as if I'd passed some invisible test known only to my interviewee. Doug Prayer visibly relaxed, as if a switch had been flicked.

"Let's smoke a joint and chew the fat a while," he smiled.

I nodded, though not wishing to get stoned. I wanted to keep my wits about me.

"I wonder if Jim ever visited the grave site when he was in England?" I asked almost under my breath.

"Of course. Huxley and Blake were two of his great heroes like Rimbaud in France, though I don't know about Nietzsche in Germany. " He reflected as he pieced together the papers for what looked like an impending Camberwell Carrot. "He was a smart man you know, that Morrison."

I smiled broadly at him. "How do you know though?" I asked.

"Man, you don't listen do you? He told me, Jimmy told me. Told me lots of things about people and places that he'd been. His mind was thirsty man, real thirsty for knowledge, always pushing."

He roached and then lit the joint drawing deeply, holding the smoke in his lungs. It popped as the seeds exploded. I didn't recall there being any tobacco mixed in with the grass.

"This is good grass man, skunk weed, A grade, quality."

He passed me the finger thick joint, I drew deeply and almost instantly the numbness started. He was right.

"He was a naturally clever man then?" I asked as I exhaled, passing the joint back.

"Worse, he always wanted to see what was around the next corner." He drew deeply once again and paused, holding the smoke to him. Then exhaling said, "Like a cat man, he was curious. Curious as hell."

I took another draw and another and we talked. Sometimes about The Doors, mostly about me and my life. In that Paris apartment on that bright and sunny day I unloaded more of my demons than I had ever done before. It was as if I was the most important person in the world to Doug Prayer. To this day I don't know how he did it, but he managed it, made me feel I was unique. It was better than therapy and one of the most pleasant afternoons I have ever experienced. Doug Prayer told me about his wife and I really began to feel for the man. Marijuana helped with the pain, he told me. When the wine appeared I was eager to drink it and after that and a second huge joint, the conversation became confused. I'd shed the notebook but I do remember laughing a great deal. I was comfortable.

At one point he made lunch, I think. Corned beef or pastrami with jalapeño peppers, fiery as hell and yet absolutely my favourite sandwich on that day. He had chips and melted cheese and guacamole, fruit, Hershey's too and some kind of peppermint patties that were heavenly and moreish. Then there were the lemonheads, only they were mixed fruit, but boy were they sweet; and I mean sweet, real roof of the mouth wow sweet.

We talked a great deal that day, laughed more than I had in a long time – well into the afternoon. The funny thing is, I don't remember that much of the detail, just an overall feeling of well-being. But I do know I was there.

I was alive, I was free, and I was flying – until I crashed.

When I came round I was back at my hotel. How I got there? I kind of remembered a taxi ride but not much else. My mouth felt like the inside of vulture's cage, my head was pounding and I needed to drink due to the dehydration.

Fourteen

Dear Mr. Fantasy…

The second visit:

I was in the red and gold room this time, that was where I thought we were going to stop. Ready to continue the interview, I had my notebook out and was poised. I hadn't come back the next day or the day after that; I'd given us both some space but I was eager and he knew it.

Finally, after several phone calls home and many casual and not so casual morning and afternoon sits in the park, on the off chance that I might, 'bump into him', I'd summoned up enough courage and enough time to finally knock on his door. The first time he hadn't been there, though I tried several times; that was yesterday. Today he was in and the reaction I received was warm and welcoming, though he didn't look that well. His skin was pale and his eyes sunken; his footfall seemed a little wobbly. I thought he looked hungover and a bit sickly.

My first reaction was that he wouldn't want me hanging around if he needed some recovery space; I couldn't have been further from the truth. Instead, I was guided to a door on the furthest side of the room, a small door tucked away within an L shaped alcove; once through it, I understood immediately. It was a door I had not noticed, an insignificant door.

"This," Doug Prayer said, "is my studio. If you didn't know where to look, you wouldn't know it was here. I bought the extra space from the apartment next door."

On the walls I counted seven guitars. There was a full drum kit and a piano, one occupied each corner and a glass partition separated the fourth corner from the main room and behind the screen there was a bank of dials, knobs and sliding mixer keys.

"Your own studio?"

"Yep. All mine. This is what my inheritance and my pension pay for." He lifted a guitar down from the wall hanger. "1957 Gibson 335 Cherry Red, Unique – the roll n' rollers guitar. Beautiful isn't it?" He pointed. "1964 Gibson Les Paul custom black beauty – priceless. SG cherry." He pointed again.

"Just like Robby Krieger," I replied.

I heard a click as an amp hummed into life. There was a crackle as the jack-plug hit the female socket. The guitar burst into life. His fingers flew over the frets like lightening and the rock refrains he reprised were quick and easy on the ear.

"Exactly the same. And before you ask, it wasn't his or the one that got stolen."

Placing the red guitar back, he moved to the acoustic models. A Martin parlour sized guitar set with mother of pearl and finished to a buffed glow; a twelve string version of the same and an all steel Dobro style guitar named Ozark hung in another corner. It was a truly impressive collection of instruments. Finally he picked out a 1950s Gibson J45 deluxe in gold sunburst. The rounded shoulders gave the guitar a distinctive appearance, the gold burst bled into a high polished black; the sound was also distinctive and I was immediately thrown an image of John Lennon and The Beatles. There was a twang to the sound which made for easy listening.

He sat with the guitar on his knee and tuned it. It was clear he was no novice. When he played it sounded truly professional. It was then that for the first time I noticed the disparity between his fingernails. On his left hand they were neat, cut short and clean; his right, however, sported what might best be described as talons. They flashed from string to string as he picked the familiar opening to 'Love Me Two Times' and then, with the same smooth ease, he started the driving thud of 'Roadhouse Blues' followed by 'Spanish Caravan'. It was obvious he was a player, and a good one too. He knew the guitar lines of Robbie Krieger so well that he could have been him.

"I didn't have any of these when I first knew Jim," he said, pulling the Martin OM 25 down and replacing it with the Gibson. "Jim gave me these as a leaving gift."

"They must have been worth plenty," I replied.

"Yep, but hell, he didn't care. Money and possessions didn't matter to Jim. Probably because he had so much of it by the end."

"Did he have that much then?" I asked.

"Oodles man, oodles. He had squirreled away a few dollars over those years."

"So it's not true that he had nothing then?"

"No, when I knew him," he paused, "he never carried cash but he did carry a card."

"That is some leaving present" I blurted.

"Yeah, back in 1971. This guitar belonged to Paul Kantner I think or, was it David Crosby? I forgot. Anyway, when they messed around together up in the canyon, they wrote 'Wooden Ships' on it. One of them, I think it was Kantner, gave it to him when he said he was gonna learn to play. See, Jim didn't play a note, not on any instrument. His instrument was his voice. And the 335 over there was Zappa's. Apparently he'd given it to Jim when… "

Then with sudden abandon I interrupted, "Why tell me all this?" I asked, "And more importantly, why tell me now?" I paused. "You said that loads of people wanted to find out about you and the music which Morrison might have made in Paris in 1971."

"There's no might about it. We made music and I don't want it forgotten," he snapped. "I'm the last one left now man. If I don't say, it'll be gone forever, and it's too good to be lost. It'll be like the stuff Brian Jones was supposed to be working on when he died, where the hell did that go? Our stuff is the stuff of legends and hey, it'll get burned or sold in some junk shop and nobody will even know who it was. His guitars all got sold, you know, maybe these will go the same way." He pointed at the walls. "Someone somewhere is playing one of Brian Jones' guitars and they don't even know the history, maybe they just bought it second hand somewhere in London. I think the builders took what was saleable and nobody really seemed to care, not even his father. Who knows? See that's what'll happen with my stuff too. I got some cousins somewhere who can't wait for me to be nude pastry. Hey, they'll all come swoopin', claws out. Only the dumb asses won't know what they got. You know after he died, all the vultures stripped the building of anything valuable. He had a studio too. They even took the gates to the drive. I read that somewhere, but it might not be true..." His voice tailed off.

"That's a cynical and sad way to look at it." I interrupted his train of thought. "People aren't always that cruel."

"Not cruel?" he almost squealed. "That is what people are best at, cruelty. Sheer, naked cruelty. Look at what they do to people man. We're not animals we're worse, we're human."

"Do you honestly believe that?" I asked. "Truly believe it?"

"Listen man, they stole the bust. Stole the damn bust from Jim's grave. What shit does that? Who the hell do you think got the thing put there in the first place man?"

"That was you?"

He didn't reply. "I loved the man. I mean, loved him. Didn't want a piece of him. He was my friend. You know what? You reap what you sow man, reap what you sow. Human beings are sheep man, fuckin' sheep, that's why Jim ran. He came to see them for what they were, no worse, what they are. He hated it in the end, hated every last minute of being a commodity. And you know what he said to me? He said that he had wished for it. He and Ray had wished for it, to be famous and make a million dollars and when they got it, the dream turned into a nightmare. He told me that after 'Light My Fire' he ceased to be a human being, ceased to be a man; that he became an image, a brand. Just like Marilyn, he was so unhappy."

I had a sudden flashback memory to Brad Dellevale. Who is Brad Dellevale? Brad is the guy who works the Laurel Canyon grocery store and a more helpful guy I could not have met. Gave me loads of information about the history of Laurel Canyon music while I was researching for this book. Gave me the inside track on some of the star visitors. Told me where the Houdini house was and who lived where. A researcher's absolute gift. And if the place hadn't been so busy, I might have got more from him. But the one thing that stuck in my head were Brad's simple words, "The last time I saw Jim Morrison he seemed so unhappy." Virtually the same thing that Doug Prayer was emphasising now.

He continued, "He said things to me that I couldn't understand, because I wasn't him. He was the Lizard King and he could have anything," Prayer paused, "except peace. Hey, and you know what else he said?"

I shook my head in reply.

"He said he was looking for freedom and you know what the real irony is?"

I shook my head again.

"The more famous he became, the less freedom he got. Now how does that work? Told me he was in a prison of his own device."

"That's in a song somewhere," I replied.

"That's why they wanted to jail the man."

"I don't get it," I remarked.

"To shut him up."

"I understand," I replied rather sheepishly. I couldn't remember the song but kept coming back to 'You're Lost Little Girl'.

There was a long and uncomfortable silence, and I had that sudden self-doubt as to whether I should leave this story alone and respect the...

"Music," he suddenly belched, as if snapped back from a dream. "I said I'd let you listen, didn't I?"

He walked over to a cupboard and inside there looked to be something which I could only glimpse, but I thought it might be a safe. It certainly was metal. He removed a canister and then placed it on an amplifier which stood nearby. A round tin which looked like a film canister.

"There," he said, "Jim's and my work with the band. I'll set it up for you if you give me a few minutes."

As he worked, I could feel my level of excitement and anticipation growing. Questions kept pouring into my brain about the detail. What if this was the next stage on from the 'Orange County Suite'? I thought the remaining Doors had remastered just about everything they thought was in the least bit viable. I didn't blame them for that. They had so little time and the fragments are not always good. What seemed great in say, a live performance, did not sound quite the same in the cold and clear light of day. I'd done the same when I went over what I thought were real purple patches of prose.

It all seemed so simple now and like some accident, or a piece of fate falling into place. This guy Prayer had chosen me to be the one who would reveal things to the world. Then the big question came. It should have been at the front of my brain, but had been smothered by my excitement – suddenly it resurfaced. A ten storey 'plook', as the Scots call it, or as the Americans say, 'zit'. Right slap bang in the middle of my forehead of an investigation. A flaw which no amount of lipstick and powder could hide; I had to burst it.

Motive, motive, motive; what was in it for this man? And why, after all these years, now? That was the one puzzle that needed a credible answer. Why be silent for so long and then open up now?

Could people do it, I was asking myself. Had people done it before? I thought of one name: Lionel Logue. Mouth as tight as a drum until his son released his diaries in written form. So many years had passed that it didn't matter anyway. A sudden belt of electricity shot through me. Was Morrison dead?

Doug Prayer had no son, nor daughter, as far as I knew, and he had referred to me as 'kid'. Panic hit my stomach like a lead weight and then the recording started.

My heart stopped.

174

Fifteen

Born Under a Bad Sign...

The motive:

As the music started, I heard guitars.

"You said you had a reason for divulging this now. Can I ask what it is?" I was asking nicely, well I thought I was, but his movements showed he was uncomfortable.

He shot me a look which seemed defensive and then paused the tracks playing. My mind went into *oh shit I've blown it mode,* but he quickly regained his composure. Like a prize fighter who had received an unexpected blow, he reeled, took a step back and then came again.

"Hell, that's easy." He was so matter of fact as he punched back at life. "Cancer."

He said the word with such abandon that I could not really believe what he said. I had to reassure myself.

"Cancer?" I confirmed.

"Yep, you heard me," he paused and became thoughtful. "Looks like I'm gonna break on through sometime this year. Break on through to the other side."

He saw the look in my eyes.

"What's the matter man?"

I shook my head.

"It ain't that bad, nobody gets out alive man, nobody. Hey, could any Hell be worse than this?"

"My father died of cancer," I said. For some reason I just blurted it out.

"Hey man, I'm sorry," he replied, with genuine concern.

I couldn't believe it. He was diagnosed and he was worried about my feelings. That I had never come across before. It startled me and also unnerved me. I wondered if I could come to terms with the big C if I had it. I had a thousand things left to do before I checked out.

"You know, most of us don't get to know, much less get to choose," he said with conviction. "So while it's bad luck, it's better than no luck. Hey, and everything's luck really, just luck, right?"

"Right."

"Go on then," he requested, "spill."

"What did you mean, choose?"

"Well I can do as I please now. Check out when I like. I don't need to stay there cos I can't find the door. I can leave the party when I choose; I like that fine – so far."

I could feel an affinity with this man and that was dangerous; dangerous because it made me want to say more than I ought and like him more than I should.

"That's what my father did," I said.

"Woa, man," he replied, "you mean he checked out early by choice? Cool."

I could hear the California surfer accent in his 'cool'.

"No, he didn't do that. Though that's what I'd do, I think." I reflected, wishing, I not said it. "No, he just decided on the last day that was his time. They had him on morphine and when I last saw him he was setting his house in order."

Bingo! The alarm bells went off in my head, that's what Prayer was doing, right here and right now. And I was getting what my father did to me, all over again, only from someone I didn't know.

"Did you love him?" he casually asked me. The Morrison tapes forgotten for the moment.

"I suppose I did," I replied, with open honesty. "But I don't know if he liked me, or if I liked him." His ears pricked up, it was my turn to open up. "He was a military guy and we kind of had a relationship which happened when he was on leave. It was weird. We weren't close and after he split it got worse. But when he died I cried."

"Hey man, we had some things."

He understood and that simple phrase let the dam burst. "I think there was love," I started, "but he got married again and the split sent my mum crazy. That was hard.

I kind of put all the blame on him for that. Perhaps that was a shitty thing to do. There must have more to it than that. Still, it was comin' a long time. He left me with a crazy breakdown woman and it fucked me up in the head."

I paused, thinking back and searching for the right words. He said nothing.

"But before he died we kind of chewed the fat a while," I continued, "and he apologised. Just me and him in a room and he apologised. Not another living soul there and we had never spoken together like that – ever. That was hard to take. It hurt, made me feel like I'd got it wrong blaming him. And you know what he said, he said, 'Sorry, I let you down'. There he was in his bed at home dying and I'd come to see him. Fuck, fuck and double fuck, I should have treated him better. Instead I just didn't, I said it was Ok and that I was grown up now and it didn't matter. Hell, he said he was sorry. He said lots of things to me in that half hour before the pain kicked in. Told me he wasn't going to die in that bed, but in hospital. His wife didn't like me; saw me as some kind of threat perhaps, or maybe she thought I was a shit. Which I probably had been, but I was just a kid. See, my life at the time was goin' nowhere. I had qualifications, but I'd fucked up all over the place. I was just starting to climb out of the pit and then bing bong, the time bell sounds for him."

Doug Prayer didn't say a word.

"So we cleared the air that day. I said it was fine and that I was grown up and that all the mess was in the past. Then a couple of days later I get the call – he's dead. On the last morning, real casual, he asked to go to hospital about 9am. So they come and get him in an ambulance and at 11am he's dead.

Just like he let go of a rope and fell. He knew and…"

I could feel the regret, the ridiculous mess I'd made of my life and my relationship with both my father and my mother and he understood. In that instant he understood. He'd done it too.

"Families man," he said, "families are shit. Jim had the same problems ya know. The horns of a dilemma, he used to say."

I felt kind of good about letting it out to the man. Why? To this day I don't know? But I was also full of guilt that he had cancer and there I was talking about me again. I was worried about my piece on Morrison and the man was dying?

"See, I promised myself that I'd say nothing and I trusted me," he said casually. "But now I'm not even sure if I'm still alive. They're gonna nail the lid shut on me and then there'll be no one left. But here's the real rub, you gotta promise me man. Promise me that you'll not do any damage. I don't want Jim's reputation destroyed; I just want people to understand. I think you're the one. You understand man. They can say what they like about me; believe it or not, I don't give a damn. But be fair to Mickey and the guys and cut Jim some slack. Pam's goin' hit him hard."

I did not know what to say and choked.

"Hey, it's not that big a deal man," he laughed. "No one gets off alive."

He waited for me to question him further, but I didn't have the heart to, so he filled in for me. The message had no false emotion, no hunger for pity, nothing; it just was. I admired him for that. There was an acceptance that his time was done and that whatever he said now was immaterial.

He began stoically, "Nearly six years back now I got this growth in my belly. So they chop it out and stitch me up and hey I'm fine for a bit. Only this year the damn thing's come back. This time it's in my rectum and kidneys and stomach and hell just about everywhere. They give me Chemotherapy, but that makes ya sick as a dawg."

I said nothing.

"I smoke a little grass."

I thought, a little?

"And it helps with the pain sometimes and boy I got a lot of pain to carry. I got mine and Jim's and all the other members of the band. I don't think I can carry it any longer. It's time to let go."

"So Jim's alive?"

He didn't reply to the question but went into what felt like a prepared monologue.

"The other members of the band, they're all gawn. One to an overdose, one to a crazy woman who cut his throat in the night, and the other, well he's inside a lunatic asylum. He flipped on acid man, and I mean like truly flipped. His brain is fried. Keeps claiming he was in a band with Jim Morrison. Says that Morrison's alive, but he's tried to kill himself four times and so nobody believes him. They got him in a padded cell on medication and nobody wants to know. They say he's a delusional psychotic because his brother was killed by a girl who he introduced him to. Kinda guilt complex or somethin' like that. They're full of shit, because he ain't delusional. He just can't be believed because of the other things he says. Thinks he's a vampire too, eats flies and spiders. Says he's collectin' lives.

Hell, Jim's been to see him twice. Came over here to see the man, risked it for a friend. Twice man and they don't take any notice, don't even know. He's right there talkin' to the nurses and because they don't expect it, they can't piece it together-dumb schmucks. What do they think, he's gonna turn up in leathers with a lion's mane of hair? He's older man, older and wiser. That was one of his other cellves. Nobody thinks he can do it – Rimbaud did. Jon's screamin' his shit, you know, like 'This is Jim Morrison'. He's running up and down and he's screamin' and they're tryin' to calm him and nobody checks. 'Cept Jim that is, 'cause somebody's payin' for the medical care and it ain't me. I been to see him a few times man, but he don't even recognise me. I never seed anythin' like it man, never in all my born."

"What about you, you could say?"

"Yeah me and the loopy, we could say alright. Yeah and they'd believe us, sure. I mean me I'm ill in the body and he's fucked. They'd be all over us like flies on shit and then what?"

I shrugged.

"The paparazzi man, they'd be tryin' to hunt Jim down like a dawg. That ain't right man. That ain't right." His voice was now more pronounced in the southern drawl.

"You could explain," I offered.

"Explain a body, an overdose? We'd be up on a murder charge then or some such. They still want his arse in jail for Miami. Everyone knows what they wanted."

"You tell the world the truth."

"The truth? What truth?"

"The truth about Jim and Paris."

"Say what? That Jimbo Morrison affected the greatest rock 'n' roll swindle of all time. Hell, who's gonna believe me? Doug Prayer the drunk or Doug Prayer the old cynical veteran? Hell, they'd lock me up too. Then one night I'd up and hang myself, or just die, and no one would give me a second thought, would they? What, a drunk and bum stoned and lame and screwed in the head. Who the hell would remember me?"

"But the tapes, the music, you could produce that much."

"They'd find a way to discredit that, come on."

"That's a bit naïve."

"Really? I think you're the one who's naïve. Nobody would believe me, even you aren't sure."

We exchanged knowing looks with one another.

"I have to admit I was sceptical. I mean, why choose me?" I asked.

"We had a feeling about you man, a psychic vibe; so we checked. Like you'd be true to the story and true to all of us. Money, that's not what turns you on. And I can't get to Jim because he doesn't want me to – he has another life now. That's if he's still alive."

"So tell me where he is and I'll go if you are unfit to travel." I threw it into the mix without thinking, and then checked myself with honesty. "I do like money though, but I suppose it's not the most important thing." I was searching to define what I meant. "Just enough for me to survive and not much more and I'll be fine." It wasn't enough; I tried again, "Enough to get me out of the rat run?"

"See, I was right man. I can tell. Oh, I can travel Ok," he replied, "only I don't know where to travel to man."

My heart sank. "So you don't know if he's alive for certain?"

"Oh he's alive," he said, "I'll show you the letter. Well more like a note really."

Out of the music canister he produced a note, folded in half. It appeared to be a page torn from what looked like a pad. The words were large and the hand scrawled, and it certainly looked like Morrison's. I'd seen enough of his poetry books and notepads. It was dated 25th April 1994. There was an envelope stamped and the postage was paid by franked mail, which looked like it said New York. The serial code had been erased but I knew it was probably a forwarding mail service from another location.

There are places in the world that specialise in the forwarding service, specialise so that things cannot be traced. I had no idea if the note was genuine or a hoax, but I could see a small line drawing almost like a doodle at the bottom of the page. A hitchhiker's thumb, Morrison's moniker. And there below it a doodled design with an owl and a pattern. It was the kind of doodle people make when they are listening to a long conversation with someone, or are bored in a meeting.

The pattern I recognised instantly as Greek. Anyone who has been to Greece would recognise it too, it is everywhere. Kind of geometric lines in squares, the type of thing that art teachers get kids to put around their work as a border. I don't know if there is a technical word for it, so I'll just call it the Greek pattern.

The owl I could not understand at first. So I discussed it with my girlfriend over the phone; she reminded me almost too simply that the owl was a symbol for the wisdom of Athena. Athena was the goddess of wisdom and the patron goddess of Athens. Bang, an explosion in my head. Athens? Had Dionysus simply gone home? I couldn't believe it would be that easy – that simple. Was this an elaborate ploy to put any pursuers off the scent? Or was it, as I suspected, an idle doodle as someone whiled away time, much as others would whittle a stick? Just a mistake, a silly little error? Morrison was like the rest of us, sometimes he simply made errors and I was hoping this was one such time.

If this note were indeed Morrison, he had taken a very big gamble. He had sent something to someone that could have blown the whole thing wide open. There had to be a catch, a reason that Morrison trusted this man. That I had yet to establish.

I digested the note, the contents, the pictures, the words. I turned it over in my hands. I couldn't tell what it really meant. Like many things that Morrison wrote, they were not always visible on the first read.

"It's genuine," Doug Prayer said, "absolutely genuine."

"Well it's addressed to you, but is it?"

"I suppose you want to test it, check it?"

I was nodding like a dog now, almost salivating at the discovery.

"Well you can't do that yet. But I'll tell you how it was done. How the whole thing went down and you can fill in the pieces. That's if you know them?"

"Really?" I must have sounded cynical because he shot me a look like thunder.

"I'll tell you how Jim Morrison fooled the world. Fooled the world and got away with it. But you need to let me sort my…" he paused, thinking before he spoke, "shit out. You come back in three days. But before you do, you find out what happened to all the advances that were made to Jim for *LA woman*."

"What do you mean?" I asked.

"Relative values and all that jazz."

"I don't understand." I was floundering.

"That way you might finally believe me."

"I do believe you," I blurted, "well I think I do."

"Thinkin' ain't being," he said. "Then you might be able to put two and two together man and make your five. Let's have some music."

A voice filled the room. 'Let's do I woke up this mornin' man.' I heard a bottle open. That first crack of a bottle seal being broken and someone pouring a drink. There was another voice, '3 and 4', and the guitar started.

Prayer turned up the bank of switches and a deep blues wail came into the air. A rich baritone filled my ears and I knew it was Morrison. Knew in the instant. This wasn't a scream, like previous early recordings, this was a wail. A howl like an animal in pain, but one thing I knew for certain. It was as if he had walked into the room and started to sing. There were two guitars and a bass and a drummer and harmonica. The sound was a kind of blue funk, but I had no idea as to when it might have been recorded. The guitars were descanting now and the rhythm pattern reminded me of Michael Shrieve from Santana, sort of 'Soul Sacrifice', punchy, filling the gap; complex and driving, with the skill of Densmore only different. That would be 1969/70, outside of the time span I wanted confirmed. There were early blues overtones and a sound which resembled multiple chanting in the background. It was blues but different somehow.

The singer's voice was clear and grave – I was certain it was Morrison. Like he had been rehearsing and his throat cracked in the strain. 'I woke up this morning,' he sang, 'and my baby was gone,' he sang with pain in his voice. 'I woke up this morning and my woman was gone. Now I'm so lonely baby, don't know if I can go on.' It was the standard blues fare lyric.

The next song was the one that convinced me this was genuine. The song was called 'War's Over' and the lyrics dealt with the ending of Vietnam. Only this wasn't glorious stuff about peace, this was about Saigon and the way the south had been betrayed. Classic Morrison on the attack. There was a parallel to do with the southern defeat in the civil war woven into the lyrics too. It was mature, political and it simply couldn't have been written before 1971. The war was still raging and Morrison wouldn't have known about the Saigon evacuations. This had to be after he was supposed to have died. Now I was convinced. A man singing about an event that happened after he had died – impossible. The more I listened, the more I gleaned. There were songs which were less introspective; less to do with Pam and more to do with others.

Morrison was coming of age in Paris and on this tape his mind was expanding even further. But Prayer had said the recordings were made in 1971, so how could Morrison be singing about events in 1973 ? Could he still be in Paris right up to 1973 and beyond? That would throw Greece out of the window. There was something wrong here. Like all investigations, the pieces just didn't fit and I ended up with more questions than answers. My head was starting to hurt.

Next came a rendition of 'Got my Mojo Working', the Muddy Waters classic, done with a real Morrison twist and clearly aimed at Pam. The sound had that slightly fairground feel that Manzarek added with his organ work. Only this was piano not organ. I thought of circus clowns, sinister clowns and of Stephen King and the menace behind the smile. That feeling I had when I first heard The Doors was back. There was a tingle running up and down my spine and it felt good. Now I was wondering if this was recorded sometime before Pam's death in 1974. Then I reconsidered, could they have faked that one too? Or was this after 1974? More questions, more, more, more.

"So he is alive," I stated.

Doug Prayer shrugged, "Maybe," he said.

"But you said he was," I pressed. "Are you now saying he's dead? I mean, is Pam dead? Or are you going to say that's another hoax, or that Morrison murdered her to get away? The more you say, the worse it gets."

"No. You don't listen man. I said he didn't die in 1971, you added the other stuff. You think he murdered Pam, now who's crazy man? I've seen him a few times since and that's all. Maybe you ain't listening properly man. Maybe that's the trouble with everyone, they don't listen. What the hell do people have to do? We all end up in a hole in the ground. Gone and mostly forgotten. What is the goddamn point of it all?"

I could sense his frustration.

"That is cynical," I said.

"It ain't half as bad as Jim used to say. Man he was dark when he was on a downer." He waited as if expecting a reply. "That's why Pam burnt the papers after," he paused and stretched out

Issaquah Dock Sausalito – showing colourful house boats, one of which Morrison owned. This is a Bohemian area similar to the Haight and Ashbury district of San Francisco and the canals of Venice Beach.

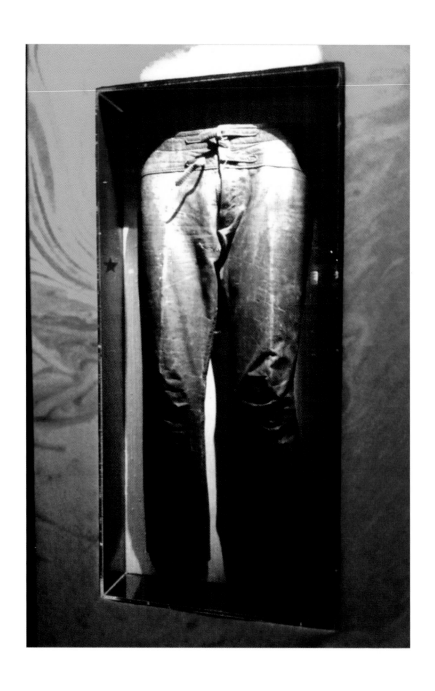

Jim's brown leathers, worn at the Hollywood Bowl concert in 1968. Now in the Hard Rock Café on Hollywood Boulevard.

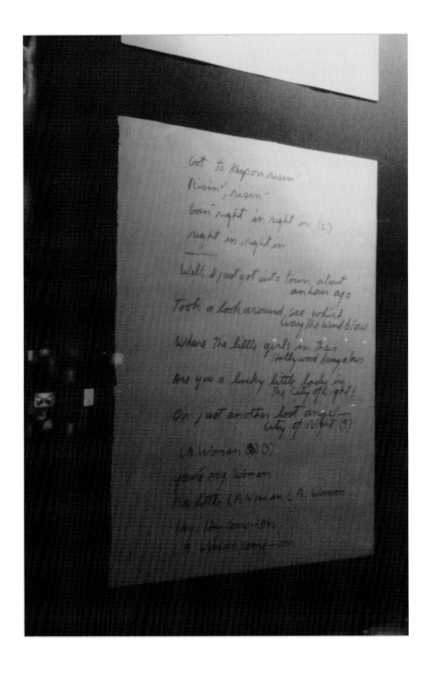

Morrison's hand written lyrics used in the recording sessions for
LA Woman.

Barney's Beanery, Santa Monica Boulevard. A frequent hang out for Morrison and his drinking buddies (The faux Doors, as Ray Manzarek tagged them). The place where Janis Joplin and Morrison had their infamous drunken run in/brawl.

The Norton Avenue Apartment (8216) shared by Pam and Jim, though he still retained the room at the Alta Cienega Motel throughout their relationship. Viewed from the street, the entrance is behind the gate and left.

The entrance to 8216 showing the shrine to Morrison and the memorial bust.

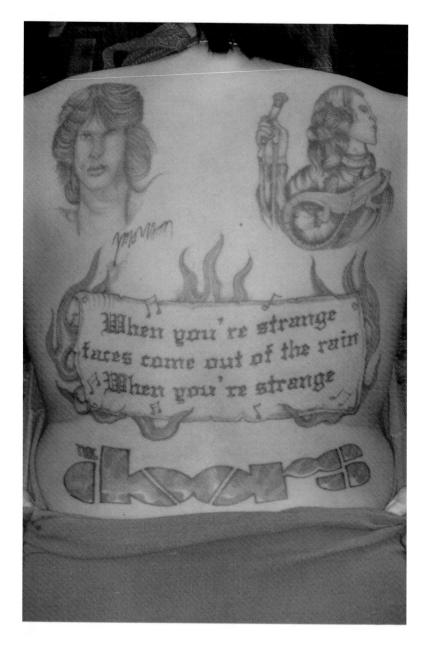

The ultimate Doors fan – Claire Stenning (UK resident) on her yearly homage to the Paris gravesite. Claire attends annually to mark the anniversary of Jim's death. Original tattoo. Image used with permission.

Theatre of Dionysus as seen from the Acropolis, Athens. To the right and down, the remains of the Temple of Themis; the name used for Pam's boutique at 947 La Cienega Boulevard North.

The pergola and concrete jetty at Kalamaki Athens. Taken with a telephoto lens from South Beach Bay – the frontage of The Lucky U. Jim Morrison on right.

Gold record award for the sales of *LA Woman*, located at The Hard Rock Café, Universal Studios, Hollywood, California. This proved to be the most popular of all their albums,

The Doors' star on the walk of fame, Hollywood Boulevard.

the final two words, "heeee diiied. She knew how deep his mind plummeted when he was down. Know what he said once, to me?"

I shook my head and issued the customary, "No."

"Well one day he's says, cool as ya like, 'Doug, there's a difference about a man waiting to die and a man unafraid to die.' Ya see, he just didn't give a damn. He'd have made a lethal soldier ya know, with an attitude like that. Fearless warrior, you know, like Spartacus. He didn't want to die, but he didn't shy away from the possibility either. That's what made him dangerous."

"He really was that devil may care?" I asked.

"Sure and that's what made him so different." He paused as if recalling an event. "One afternoon he stood on the edge of my balcony and asked me if I thought he was mad. Whether he should jump to see if he would survive the fall. How the hell can you answer that?"

"What did you say?"

"I said he was crazy to piss over everything good that he had. I told him, take all the money you've made and go buy a place where people don't know you. And you know what he did?"

"I shook my head."

"That's what he did too. A big grin on his damn face."

I could imagine Morrison doing just that. The trouble was, the story was riddled with holes. Balcony? Doug Prayer had told me he didn't get this place till after the death of his father. So that was wrong. He didn't live here then. Then he said Morrison went after 1973. That couldn't be right either. The whole story, or stories, had so many time frame inconsistencies that I began to wonder whether it was a compilation of a variety of accounts. Perhaps his memories had been overlaid with the press reports and things he'd read. The man knew lots of detail about Morrison but it was often skewed. On the other hand, I thought that might make it more credible, rather than the over rehearsed lie.

The music had stopped and there seemed to be some talking or poetry going on.

"You know the one thing he hated most of all?" Doug Prayer quizzed.

I had no chance to reply or guess.

"He hated being used. He rarely used people, though he did mess the women in his life about. They all wanted a piece of him or his child or his fame, Pam didn't, she wanted something else. Something they already had, but didn't know they did."

"A wanton world without lament?"

"On the barrel head."

"Enterprise and expedition?"

"Instead of trying to test each other all the time – pushing the boundaries – they should have just accepted what they had. They loved each other, but there was this weird competition thing they had, a test to see who was the stronger, who loved the other one the most. That wasn't pushing boundaries, that was mind fucking. She had been there from the start, from when they had nothing. The first Chinese feast, through the feast of friends to the final, fatal night. Well that's what we're supposed to believe. What's he supposed to have said, all romantically, 'Pam, are you still there Pam?' But hey, generally he was fair. If he went on the attack against somebody they usually deserved it. Greedy money grabbers most of them. You know what, if you wanted to be a friend of Jim's you had to be trusted, like Babe. He wasn't on the take either, and that's why he doesn't say diddly. You know Jim told me he used to arrive at gigs before everyone else, with Jim's clothes. He never said a damn thing – never. That's why Jim trusted me too; I keep my mouth shut man. You gotta promise me man. "

"But you're talking to me now," I quipped.

"Yeah, and I gave good reason why, didn't I?"

"Well if everything you say is true then I have a massive scoop story. I could go public."

"That doesn't bother me," he returned. "They'd say you're a crackpot looking for a big story. No one will believe you and you'll have no evidence. But if you give me your word then I'll tell you everything and then they'll believe you. Your choice man? It don't matter to me either way."

"Well it does me," I snapped.

"Your word man? Like you're givin' it to your dead father man. Your word."

"That's a cheap shot," I squirmed. "A shitty and cheap shot."

"Who gives a fuck?"

"Ok, I give you my word."

"No fucking good man. I want it properly."

"What do you want me to say?"

"Just say you won't say what's not true. And you'll wait till after I go."

"Go where?"

"Jesus Christ man. Go."

"I promise. I give you my word. Nothing until after you're gone. On my father's…"

He interrupted me and then continued unperturbed, "The Jim Morrison I knew was a nice guy, fucked up, but nice. Only it wasn't the drink that did for him, it was the audience. I think he thought he was on the cusp of revolutionary change."

"I thought that too," I coughed back at him. "At the time." I was off balance.

"He was a nice guy, a good guy and because he pushed, the man pushed back, and he knew that after Miami things would be different. Hell, he could smell their shit in the wind before they crapped."

"You think he would have gone to jail?"

"Listen man, even Jim knew he was going to jail. They had to keep the man down man. He told me that if they sent him away the audiences would simply forget him and he'd be left to rot. He wasn't no MLK and he knew it. With The Doors it was fickle fashion and the next trend was on the way. Make way for the Eagles baby. See, you can check out anytime you like, but you can never leave. The time of change was over and the time for mellow began."

"So what you're saying is he was going to carry on with music?"

"Yep, but mostly poetry too."

"And that something happened he wasn't expecting?"

Prayer nodded. "A bit of luck presented itself. And he was one lucky son of a bitch mostly. How much luck can one man have? It started as a joke, but it went sour and then turned sweet."

"Are you going to tell me about the other members in the band? The whole story?"

"Well I told you I was the last one."

"Precisely what happened?"

"That is if Jim's gone too now. But you're checking out the wrong things man. Use your mind."

"What should I be checking then?"

"Money honey, if you wanna get along with me," he sang.

"Money?"

"Yep."

"I don't understand what you're getting at."

"And you're supposed to be the journalist?"

I gave a nervous grin.

"Look, before Jim comes to Paris he gets paid advances of $250,000. Then he dies. Where's that money? Pam hasn't got it, because the other members of the band took out a law suit for the recovery of that money. All her credit cards are maxed out, and she's got nothing. Hey, the headstone never gets placed. So who's got the toot?"

"I knew about this," I said, "but I presumed that the money had been used."

"How?" Doug Prayer was leading me now. "What the hell was it spent on?"

"Themis and cars and meals and booze?"

He was laughing now. "Jesus, how much food can one person eat? And the booze, no way."

"So you think that's the link?" I asked. "What about Pam's habit?"

He shrugged. "You best get digging. But don't think Pam was a real addict. She was stronger than that. Yeah she liked heroin, but it didn't rule her. She controlled it and not the other way around. Well she did when I knew her. Man she was a beauty too. All cinnamon hair and white skin with freckles, little girl next door, they got that wrong about her too. A firebrand, too hot to handle, she looked like something out of the valley man, but she was stronger than she looked. A will of iron man, hard, tough."

188

I was beginning to believe this Doug more and more. I was certain he held the key to the whole story. He knew what had happened that time in 1971 and all the small details, which railed against the myths, seemed so much more credible. Morrison the prankster and Morrison the artist seemed of equal worth to that dark and sinister Lizard King which his stage persona portrayed. I saw pictures in my mind's eye of 'catalogue man' Morrison. Photographs I had seen of him in Paris. There was Pam in a hooded cloak and Morrison? No leather to be seen, just shirt and slacks and a sweater draped over his shoulders and tied at the front of his chest. The hair, the lion's mane, was still there, but this time it looked washed and brushed. I was trying to remember the sentiment of the photographs and then with crystal clarity it struck: defeat. These were the images of a man in defeat.

"The money?" I returned again.

"Look, that amount of money back in 1970, what was that worth and what could you buy man?"

"So everyone's missed a trick then?"

He shrugged, "Look, we worked with the guy. Then a series of things happen and it looks like the new band is in trouble. The court case is looming and then bang, happy accident. Morrison sees his chance and takes off."

"What do you mean, happy accident?"

"I said I'd tell, but in my own time. I need some days, I got things to say and people to see."

"Jim?" I asked.

"Maybe, maybe not."

"Can I come along?"

"No." He was emphatic.

"Please?" It was the only thing I could think to say at the time. Lame I know, for someone who is supposed to be a word man. But I defy anyone to think of something better at that time. I was clutching at straws and he knew it.

"Listen, you give me this time and I'll give you something too."

"What?"

"The Rock and Roll Circus is a club; Morrison goes there to

score horse? For Pam? That's a total crock of horseshit and it don't make sense man, no sense at all. Only what if this guy ain't Morrison, what if he's a look-alike, but he acts and tells everyone he is Morrison?"

I shook my head, thinking surely not. I was right in there now, the make or break point of the story.

"Look, today all sorts of people pretend to be stars that are famous."

I had to agree.

"I seen movies of a girl who looks like Britney Spears on the internet, only she's got some guy's cock in her mouth. That ain't her, it's a look-alike. It's staged. What about the Paris Hilton crap, arse-fucking and all. You don't actually believe that's them do ya. El schmucko?" He threw the idea straight at me. "What about back then? Nobody had thought about that. Hell, back then nobody wore a logo on the outside of their clothes man. The best you got was a tie dye."

"So it's not Morrison who died in the toilets then?" I pounced, finally grasping what he was intimating.

"Who can say?" He replied.

"You know, don't you? You know?"

"I told you, three days man, just three days."

I couldn't stop now, didn't want it to stop now. "And the guy dies and that gives us the story?"

Prayer grunted a response; I think it was in the affirmative, leaving me to piece things together faster than my mind could cope.

"So the two stories blend into one?" I was on fire, but Prayer had not confirmed anything. Then he threw me the curved ball.

"I'll give you the name of the man," he said casually.

"And you'll tell me how it was done?"

He nodded.

"Every last detail?"

He nodded again.

"And your part in this too?"

"Spectator," he chuckled.

"Spectator?" I asked.

"Yeah man, a voyeur in the process of death and idolisation. An observer man, a searcher. I'm the minnow. I'll tell you exactly how it was done. I'll even tell you Pam's part. She's long dead, so it can't hurt her. The thing is, you already know, or you can work it out. It's not complicated. And why? Because he's an icon, a god."

"But the world deserves to know." I justified.

"Why?"

"The fans deserve to know."

"That's a crock man, a pure crock. Just because someone is famous, you don't own them. They owe you nothing for being your idol man. Your idols are your idols. That's the thing with Jesus and all that jazz."

"But the public deserve to know the truth." I said it again like it was a mantra. Like I had the copyright.

His eyes went cold and grey as he spoke. "Listen man, deserve has nothing to do with it. Give me those days and I'll give you your story."

"Why me though?" I asked once again. "You've had your chances before."

"Yeah maybe," he replied, "maybe you're just lucky I'm dying."

"How is that lucky?" I asked. "How can your death be lucky?"

"Luck comes in all forms man, there is no proper way. It just is."

Sixteen

Money honey...

Research is the strangest thing, because just a little information can either prove or disprove a theory and a little knowledge is a highly dangerous thing. Doug Prayer gave me the big clue, set the snowball of discovery rolling and what a ball it was. $250,000 in 1970/1971, what would that be worth today?

The thing is, how do you even start to find out?

Using the consumer price index, a figure of $1,320,000 comes out; using GDP US economy deflator $1,070,000; then there are variables. Things, like I said, are never easy. It seems the more you look, the more you find, and everything eventually becomes as clear as mud. Money is a strange business, it attracts hungry strangers, and the world of rock and roll in the mid to late 1960s attracted plenty of them. It also attracted attorneys like Max Fink, a friend of Robbie Krieger's father and also a Mr. Fix it, should a blackmailer, a kook, or a paternity suit pop out of the woodwork. The Rolling Stones had them, The Beatles had them and bands today have them still. They are the managers, agents and other assorted backers who place money on the baker's table in return for a slice of the pie, sometimes the largest slice. Bands become more than the sum of the parts, more than creative people, they become a saleable commodity. As The Doors grew in notoriety and success, the money flowed, and as the money accumulated, the pressure began to build. Morrison was like an imminent earth quake, his antics made the band noticeable and his death would make them legendary, that much he did know. That was his gift: the ability to see and understand how a star is made; because they are made, not born. He had a myriad of examples upon which to draw: Dylan Thomas; James Dean; Sylvia Plath; Buddy Holly; Marilyn; Patsy Cline. The line starts on the right and just goes on and on and on and on. If the raw talent is there, it is for others to package it and sell it. Morrison was a clever individual, but he was also very good looking and that is what they sold: sex and as any advertiser knows, nothing sells like sex. The result: The Doors made a considerable amount of money in a very short space of time.

One thing you have to remember is I am not a numbers man. Look, I have to be totally honest here, complex multiplication is not a strong point for me, neither is long division. I did Ok at school and got my O Level math pass, but I've forgotten most of that now; basically due to lack of use I suppose. There isn't much call for algebra in my daily life as a writer – but words, now that's different. Language and languages, well they seem to come easier to me, though some people reading this will no doubt say they don't. My answer to them: go write your own book and then come back and see me. Those that can do baby and those that can't, they'll tell you, often repeatedly, what's wrong with yours, or that they could do so much better. Funny, but I have got to the stage where I don't care anymore. I suppose it's an age thing, what else can life throw at me now? It is what it is. Love it, hate it, this is my art.

As for those puzzles where you fit shapes next to each other at speed – that's a no brainer for me. That's logic and I don't think like that, I'm more of your crazy, off the wall, tangential type.

Taking the value of the consumer bundle I get $1,370,000; the unskilled wage comparator $1,310,000; the production worker compensation calculator gives us $1,530,000; the nominal GDP per capita $2,140,000; and then finally the relative stance of GDP to international norms and out comes – a whopping $3,160,000.

Confused? You will be – just like I was.

At this point I could go on about what was the most accurate basis for calculation and why and what precisely that would prove – but I'm not. I can't achieve anything on that score.

The point was, I wanted to see how things worked out and the more I thought about money, the worse, or better, it got. Once I had the notion, in my rather non mathematical brain, I got something of a buzz.

Then just to make things even more complex, in 1971 the Gold Standard and the US dollar parted company. So what had once been a stable calculation now jumped all over the place. I could feel worms coming out of my ears when I tried to compare then with now.

It was like Morrison was made of good luck, everything that could go right, did, while for the rest of us Murphy's Law tends to operate; he certainly was born under a good sign. For me, and 99.99999 % of us, if anything can go wrong it will and usually does. The story of my life that one. That makes 1971 and the Bretton Woods System and comparative calculation an even bigger variable. Like I said, the more you look, the more you find and to be honest I could have devoted a complete chapter to this subject alone, maybe ten, but I reckon I'd have lost the will to live. You might even too. And that says nothing about my inability to understand the systems and how to reach an accurate figure. So in the spirit of a journalistic good guestimate, I took an average, in the hope that you the reader would accept my reasoning that $250,000 in spring 1971 was worth a hell of a lot more than it is today. To be fair I have gone for simple figures, for the simpleton that I am, and the average is $1,700,000, give or take a few. Now that is not empirical fact, but it's not small change either. That is just a lot of money.

There was also a large amount of money from the first five albums. Jim often remarked on his money guilt, whether he deserved it or not. That, and possible plane death, did occupy his thoughts. Ok. There was Pam's shop, which was a loss maker, and her cars, another loss maker, the ones her father, Corky, and Preach Lyerla found abandoned all over the State of California, but unlike the rest of the band Jim supposedly didn't buy real estate. So where, then, did all that money go? That is an awful lot of booze, dope, smack and other substances. A level of parties beyond comprehension, even by today's standards. I know Mickey Rourke, the acclaimed actor, managed to kill off $10 million and return to prize fighting for a while, but he went bankrupt for all sorts of reasons. Morrison had a steady stream of cash from royalties due. Even if he had the Norton Avenue apartment on rent, and the Alta Cienega Motel, room 32, on a retainer and then stayed in the Chateau Marmont, that was the 'stars hotel' on Sunset, he still would have had change. Perhaps Themis was the filter through which the money went. A clever expensive smoke screen.

Pam wanted Jim to get out of The Doors, get away from his drinking film buddies too, as Ray called them, the faux doors. She was the driving force in trying to get him to stand alone and become a poet and writer. It may have been a pipe dream, but did they couple this with the fact that Jim had been trying to get away for perhaps a year? If this is taken into account, it all makes sense.

Morrison didn't stay at the Chateau that often, my reason is the steep climb up to it, rather than money. It was easier to walk downhill toward Santa Monica Boulevard, especially when he was drunk. Morrison was a man of the people too; he loved drinking in bars with normal guys. It that way he reminded me of Oliver Reed, Richard Harris and Lee Marvin, men who preferred to drink with working men. The case in point is, and was, Babe Hill, one of Jim's closest and trusted friends at the time. Babe Hill was a construction worker; Jim was from a middle-class background and, like Pam, he had hardly suffered a deprived childhood. The thing is, there are different types of deprivation, beyond the physical; somebody wake up and smell the coffee, and think emotional. Giving your kids absolutely no boundaries, because it was simpler to do so than otherwise, could be a weakness as well as a strength. Someone perhaps should take the time to define the difference between a reason and an excuse here. Sometimes the line of least resistance is not always the easiest or the right one. But what do I know? I had all sorts of stuff mess up my head and I was allowed to run very free. I think I'm Ok – well sort of though it's taken me thirty years to get my head around things that happened in my childhood.

Morrison didn't buy clothes like some 'stars' do, there were no constant changes of $15,000 shoes. Admittedly, he liked his French Carmargue boots, but they were often his only shoes. That attitude came from his transient military upbringing: travel light, travel quick. Clothes he liked, he wore till they dropped off. If you want to do a dating exercise it's simple, just like the bath water. Get the photographs in date order by the outfits he wore at that time – it's that easy. Though when Pam's boutique, Themis, was open, he did get clothes from there and encouraged her in the venture, naming her to the press as his favourite designer. I am convinced that Morrison had a hand in naming the place too. Themis is the Athenian goddess of justice; perhaps Jim was making a little jibe here? Perhaps he was giving a little clue to future plans? Ray Manzarek and the other band members will openly admit that whilst they did hang out together, some of the time, as the fame increased, they spent less time together.

Half of the time nobody knew where Jim was, or Pam for that matter; that includes their separate sets of friends. There was a continual stream of enigmatic secrecy which both Jim and Pam fostered. The same applied to their domestic lives together. True, we as the public would hear about the rows, the fights, the outrageous and public behaviour, but what we also have to take into account is this: was this part of 'the act' part of the Jim and Pam show. It's pure Hollywood, not everything you see is what you actually know; it's a construction, a fabric for the suspension of disbelief. Themis could therefore have afforded a chance to use money which was then filtered into other ventures and destinations. Pam chose fabrics and styles from India how? Items came from London and other European destinations? The internet did not exist, mobile/cell phones did not exist; CD, DVD, video tape all came after this period. Today we can view items online, pay by credit card to suppliers on the other side of the world and they then arrive. Things were so different back then, even in the USA, which was always at the forefront technologically.

He ate fairly meagrely too, liked Mexican food, his favourite places being the Lucky U, 1660 South Sepulveda Boulevard, now demolished, and Barney's Beanery on Santa Monica Boulevard. There is a bit of an irony here because Barney's has wall to wall TV now; screens stare at you from just about every angle. Mostly they show sport and the pool table has been changed. If you want to try authentic Mexican, much as Morrison would have eaten, get onto Sunset Boulevard, 7408 El Compadre. The place is full of West Hollywood locals and a nice little three piece band play Mexican tunes all night long. The margaritas are heavenly and I have little doubt Jim would have enjoyed a few of those in his time and stumbled to the nearest motel. That happens to be the Sunset Inn. History is often shaped by circumstance and luck-different hangouts equals different motels and offices.

This might sound like a travel brochure, but the only way to get into Morrison's motive is to understand him and the time he lived in. I still find it amazing and very strange that room 32 in the Alta Cienega Motel is virtually constantly booked. The walls are covered with graffiti, there's Jim's portrait staring at you and someone has written Woodstock in thick black marker next to the window. Another irony because the band didn't play there, the Miami trial got in the way. I found the manager really helpful, though he wasn't there in Morrison's time. Most of the other sites are gone or have been remodelled out of existence, including the house on Venice Beach ocean front, which was the rehearsal studios and Ray's home. If you go there now there's a concrete path which runs right along the beachfront, back in 1966 that wasn't there. The original Muscle Beach is further up the sand nearer to Santa Monica pier, that was where Ray and Jim tried to 'get fit'. The 'Mondrian' window/ rehearsal house, now remodelled, went straight out onto the sand. Venice is very different now from 1966, though the streets and boardwalk still have a hippie feel, with street musicians and traders selling wares.

That's the thing about time, it changes everything. My home town; I went away to college and when I came back the middle section, which I can still see in my mind's eye, had been demolished and a whole new shopping mall was in its place. The Los Angeles of today, is different to the Los Angeles of 1966 when The Doors were starting out. The London Fog has gone, The Doors' offices too, the Lucky U, Themis; in fact, it's all different. Hollywood has experienced a dramatic revival after the relocation of studios and the persecution of the McCarthy years. Things change.

Available on the internet, John Densmore produced his virtual tour of The Doors world, and it does give some insight into the places. But that came out on the back of the 1991 movie and even since then things have changed so dramatically as to make them unrecognisable. It shows the offices, or where they were, to be more accurate, the places of interest and just like he says, at the height of their success the other members of the band were buying houses and cars. Jim moved into the Alta Cienega – 'What a guy'. I have to reprise that with much the same comment; only I have to ask where did all that money go then? At $6 per night the Alta Cienega was hardly the Ritz, there weren't even pay phones in the rooms back then. Jim used to call Pam at Norton Avenue, the one bedroom apartment they had together, from a pay phone across the street. So where is that money? Can it be suggested that he simply spent everything on Pam, just to placate her, perhaps in lieu of marriage? The truth about that will never be fully known, but the fact remains that vast sums of money went to Morrison and through Morrison.

Maybe people have been taken in by the misdirection. Jim was good at that. As John Densmore said, on the net, when discussing 'Five to One' and the meaning of the title. Morrison's reply was 'That's for me to know and you to find out.' Where was he when the ruckus about the Buick ad took off? Nobody could find him anywhere. Everyone likes to think he was on a bender somewhere, drunk for two weeks. That fits in nicely with 'the image' and Jim would have been in no mind to dispel it. I think he may have been sorting out things elsewhere; at least I'd like to think so.

Sausalito has an area which is just like the Venice canals, a place chosen by Morrison after leaving UCLA. Creatures of habit are habitual; likes and dislikes can not be changed, faces can, mannerisms can, images can. As they can be created they can be disassembled? Venice: cutesy, bohemian, a haven for artists. Sausalito: cutesy, bohemian, a haven for artists. In the days before money laundering checks and infinite cross checking checks, he could have established a place there. A place where Pam disappeared to for almost ten months between April 1971, before resurfacing in Los Angeles at the start of 1972.

Jim could have flown to Africa, India, Italy – anywhere in fact – and bought real estate. He had the money and he had the means, he also had the motive.

The idea that both Pam and Jim used that amount of money in Paris, or on the few excursions they took, or indeed on booze or heroin, would be absurd. The figures, whether you use them then or now, just don't tally. If Jim had wanted to go to the Seychelles and become Jack, or Jordan, or Jiminy Cricket for that matter, he could have bought a whole island and had change over for a luxury cruiser. If he'd wanted to he could have bought the whole street that I lived in as a kid. He could be in England right now.

I won't go into the financial history of The Rolling Stones or The Beatles or even John Entwhistle from The Who and his impending bankruptcy. All I will say is when there is blood in the water, the sharks start to arrive. What I will add though is that Entwhistle lived high on the hog throughout the 1980s. He maintained the life of a rockstar when bands like The Who were no longer popular or hip; his was a Wonderland Avenue of excess. He continued to live that life well into the nineties. That is ten years, not three months, and he bought houses, cars and everything was lavish. Then the sudden revival of 60s' bands touring again made him vast sums of money. Like Roger Daltrey said, The Who went on tour to help him out.

I remember the 1980s and the New Romantics; I seem to recall Mick Jagger being refused entry to one of Steve Strange's , clubs, because he wasn't hip enough. I think Strange lives back in Wales now with his mother, while Mick Jagger has iconic status.

Now 80s' bands are out on the road again too, Duran Duran and Spandau Ballet. It seems that everything does go in cycles. At present we are in the bubblegum reprise again – the manufactured 'Sugar Sugar' Monkees, with Tin Pan Alley songsters churning out factory hits and number ones. Hopefully we'll get another group which is original enough to break on through on the next recycle. Maybe the pap which is American Idol will be seen for what it actually is. Things seem to go in circles, but who would dare turn away Mick Jagger today?

Sadly John Entwhistle had a heart attack in his fifties and died, but he had years in which to use the money he had. And my point is? Morrison was no clothes horse, his tastes were simple, he had no property and he had no cars – where did that money go? Or where has it gone since. The truth is, there can be little doubt that Morrison had the ability to be itinerant, but he also had the brain to have squirreled some nest egg away for a rainy day.

Jim Morrison was also a loner, he would come and go as he pleased; even at the height of The Doors' rollercoaster fame he would disappear. That would account for him using more than one domicile. Jim could conveniently be between abodes, between worlds. That was a lesson he appeared to have taught to his friend Doug Prayer and even while in Paris with Pam, he had trudged the streets, much as he had done in Los Angeles. Were there other bolt holes? Little surprise then that Morrison adopted a beatnik logo for himself, a hitchhiker by the side of the road. His homage to Dean Moriarty and Jack Kerouac perhaps? That much we can't prove, but the roots can be traced, just as some of the roots of Doors' music can be traced directly back to the windy city and Ray Manzarek. Like all good cakes, it's in the mix as well as the bake.

At Prayer's I heard music that should have been released in 1972. I knew in the instant, the same hairs on my neck stood on end as Morrison was in full swing. At times he sounded drunk, while at others he was perfectly lucid. It was just as I would have expected any alcoholic to sound. While I was listening, I kept thinking about Pamela Courson's role in the charade. That must have been vital.

I thought about the final Doors' concert in New Orleans, where Ray said he watched the performing shaman finally leave Jim Morrison. There he sat, deflated on the drum podium, after having slammed the microphone stand into the stage with frustration. But Ray also said that Morrison had been intrigued by Bonaparte's mural whilst in the hotel. He remarked how Jim had studied the work – could there be some connection?

Ray Manzarek has also said that Jim remarked on the Seychelles and that it was a beautiful place. That worried me more, because Morrison was a master of misdirection and if he had mentioned the Seychelles, that would be the last place he'd go.

Doug Prayer and I sat and listened, though my mind was racing with possibilities. We didn't talk much because there wasn't much more to say. I'd spent three rather restless days working in my hotel. I'd phoned home more times than was good for me and set up the possibility of having to go to Greece. Phone calls from hotels are usually at a premium, so as a sweetener I said I needed an assistant and that she should pack. That got me out of a hole in the short term. I thought of Morrison and saw the similarity.

I listened to Prayer's tapes, hoping that I would get a free copy when eventually the tracks were over. Doug Prayer was unusually quiet and very thoughtful and I wondered where he had been. I saw shades of Morrison in this man. I wondered if I had misread the whole situation and that he was him. Or whether Morrison was still in Paris and Prayer had 'nipped off' to see him. The truth was probably hospital, because he looked rather drawn. His face had that bluish tinge to it; that's the only way I can describe it. He looked sick – because he was sick. We smoked a joint, only this time it was a smaller version of his last makings.

Now at this point I ought to tell you as a reader that I listen to The Doors more now than I did when I was younger. Why? Well, because I like it and the new bands don't have any originality for me. One guy I know has no music after 1973 on his play list for his iPod. I'd get a bit tired of 'Smoke on the Water', however good it is, or was; The Doors have something else. They are unique and, like a piece of Cubist art, they take some aspects of other artists but punch it one stage further on. That was Morrison's gift: plagiarism with an original twist. I'm not that bad, but I am locked into the past. Somehow I've turned into my father. I don't know when it happened but it did. Now I'm old enough not to care, but I still believe The Doors were ahead of their time. The marketing was superb and that of course is the key. It's the same with books – that much I did know. The public wants what the public gets and all that.

A track stopped suddenly as the musical instruments sort of sputtered out without warning. It was clearly unfinished and needed to be refined. This was work in progress and I knew something had interrupted the process. The earlier tracks had sounded better. Why just suddenly stop? I could hear Morrison laughing in the background and words mumbled: 'I can change the course of nature.' I think I made out. That was what struck me about Morrison and the tales I had been told about him. Everyone seemed to be giving this picture of a deeply intense loner who rarely smiled – a man obsessed with death. In truth, as Doug and this tape confirmed, he had a wild, dry sense of humour and laughed a lot. That made everything more credible, much more likely. He had shyness too; perhaps the drink was an essential necessity against stage fright.

I once heard that Ian Drury used to get physically sick every time he was due to go on stage. Here we have, or should I say had, as he is no longer with us, a brash Essex boy with a tongue like a viper and a foul mouth to boot; legs held together with iron rods, handicapped – the epitome of challenge – getting stage fright. Could Morrison have experienced the same thing? Hence the nights before big concerts in the Alta Cienega, getting himself psyched up? When they started at the Whisky A Go Go, Jim sang with his back to the audience. Some say it was an enigmatic choice, a conundrum; what if it was just fear? Densmore's account of their first meeting in Ray's parent's garage was of a very shy guy with great and unusual lyrics. Darkness is always tempered with light and vice versa, he couldn't have been in a pit of despair all the time, or could he? Perhaps the drink was absolutely essential to the stage persona, and therein lay the seeds of destruction?

"That's it," Doug suddenly said, as if coming out of a trance. "The album that never was. Our first album. It's raw and has to be finished but I think it would have been a good one."

"Interesting."

"Interesting good or interesting bad?"

I didn't know what to say. This wasn't the work of street entertainers, this was the work of musicians who had worked together.

"I like the tracks with the two guitars; it reminds me of 'Been Down So Long'. But there is another sound, like Wishbone Ash when they first started."

"Yeah, but we're there first."

I knew he was probably right about that.

"I know this is probably a bit of a liberty," I was tentative, "but could I take another look at the note you've got?"

"Why?" he asked.

"I just wanted to take a second look," I said.

"What, to check if it's his handwriting?"

I nodded. I was already certain that the writing was indeed his, but it was the pictures I wanted to look at again. The patterns scrawled and the owl kept pulling at my brain.

Doug Prayer handed me the note.

There it was again, the symbols for Greece and Athens. But that couldn't make sense. I remembered the military junta and the Greek and Turkish conflict on Cyprus. The junta lasted until 1974, so how would that work? Also, it was only recently that the European Union had accepted Greece and that made the place more of a tourist haven. What I really remembered was the 1967 conflict, when my father came home from Cyprus after a six month stint with the United Nations Peacekeeping force. Admiral Morrison was in Vietnam commanding an aircraft carrier, while his son's music was blasting out anti-war sentiment on 'The Unknown Soldier'. I was helping to pick up my mother from the kitchen floor – she had fainted after listening to me play a protest song at my school music recital.

Actually that's not really true. What happened was my father was away for months and when he came home it was summer, so he took his shirt off and down she went. The reason was a series of bullet wounds which looked like he had been peppered with buckshot. In the same tradition of the active warrior, he said nothing. Only years later did I get something which was near to the truth, and to be honest, for all my anti-war sentiment, it was hard not to give a certain respect to a man who had survived combat.

I knew a guy once, when I was a student packing boxes in a biscuit factory, who had been on the allied Anzio landings. He, like my father, said nothing, but there was a deep sadness in his eyes. I asked him how he survived, why he survived? His answer has stuck with me to this day. It was just a single word, no pretence, no cosmic fatalistic approach; his word was simple: luck.

I handed back the note.

"So you have no idea of Jim's whereabouts?" I asked.

"He came to Paris several times. How crazy is this? He went to visit his own grave. How many of us can say that?" He laughed. "Hey, everyone should try out their coffin just to see how uncomfortable they are. They ain't cosy."

"You haven't?"

"Sure, why not? It's just a pastry box."

My mind jumped to when I went to see the corpse of my mother. There she lay in the small box, her body cold and lifeless. It may sound harsh, but I could only view it the once. It was kind of terrifying and reassuring too. I think though, had I been Bill Siddons, I would have looked at the corpse. Not out of morbid curiosity but out of respect. That way you know, it sets your mind at rest. Crazy as this sounds, I never got to view my father and for a while I thought, no, he's not dead. Sometimes he appears in my dreams along with my mother. People have told me that's a bad sign; perhaps it is.

Then there was the psychic I read once, who claimed that the reason Morrison had a room at the Alta Cienega Motel was because that was where he met the Devil. He got fame because of a Devil's bargain, she claimed. Same as Robert Johnson learning to be the best guitar player around, in only six months. For fame, fortune and longevity, both sold their souls and payback came when they became a member of the twenty seven club.

I didn't believe that myself, but I did laugh at the idea.

"When did you see him last?" I asked again.

"A few years now," he replied. "He sent me a painting that some artist had done about ten years ago," he pointed, "there it is."

There, as bold as brass, was the picture. A blend of green and grey with a Turner-style blurriness, but this was some ancient forum.

"Take it down, there's an inscription on the back," Doug Prayer said.

There on the back, in Morrison's hand, was a simple inscription: *To the only brother I have really known. Let's resurrect the old Gods and dance in great golden copulations until the sea rises to reclaim us.*

What did that mean? It was obvious to Morrison but not to me. I was having a Densmore moment. That was the key to all of his work. The ideas and the lyrics were intensely broad, but also highly personal too; that's what made him a poet. As to whether he was good or bad... well the jury's still out I suppose. I never really understood the meaning of 'A cold girl'll kill you in a darkened room.' I knew it referred to Pam and also to the sexual act, but it was also obscure and universal. Did he foresee his own death, or had he been planning the exit for a while and these were clues? Clues slap bang in the middle of his lyrics? That lyric appears on the last album, *LA woman* – why *LA woman*? Was the psychic right? I mean, was he referring to la petit morte, post orgasmic death, or to the act of murder which some say Pam was responsible for? Though of course she didn't mean to, so manslaughter I suppose. Then there is the notion that he engineered his own death at her hands. That then would ruin Doug Prayer's idea of a happy opportunistic accident.

If you believe some of the stories, Pam supposedly gave him heroin, saying it was cocaine. That she had a box of heroin sitting on a coffee table at the Paris apartment which people might dip into casually, as they would do a sweet treat, candy. That is absolutely fanciful and absurd. They were foreign nationals in Paris and known, if not to the general populace then at least to the authorities. Heroin might have been available and used freely, France was the heroin capital at that time, but not publicly. They could have been busted at any time and subsequently deported. France had an extradition treaty with the USA at the time, and that, combined with Miami, would have sealed his fate. There seems here to be cross over with Iggy Pop, who later did take narcotics on stage, but once again this was part of 'the act'.

The result of a heroin intake on Morrison: a hammer blow to the heart which killed him. If that was indeed what happened, was it murder or manslaughter? It now seemed totally immaterial, especially if Morrison knew that the item was heroin and let's face it, he would have known what the result might be. Then maybe it was suicide, intentional suicide, and that was why Pam burned all the pages of notes he left behind; and the reason? To protect herself or protect his reputation. This from the person most likely not to have placed a grave marker. My head was swirling as I examined and re-examined the facts as I knew them. Had Morrison been planning his own suicide off and on and given clues to it in the *LA woman* album? Every time my conclusion was different and the key lay with this man Doug Prayer; at times he too seemed confusing. How he first met Morrison was contradictory. Was it in the hospital or a bar or another place? Things were right but not right. The main issue was his honesty – his reliability.

There on the back of the painting was an artist signature which read *Kalamaki* and the single word *Dionysus* followed by an initial T.

"I like it," I said.

"He knew I would," Prayer replied. "Jim knew what people liked and he gave it to them – that was his forte."

A sudden thought flashed across my subconscious. Isn't that precisely what you are doing to me? I wondered if I was being duped?

"It looks like a Greek theatre," I remarked.

"Yep." He returned it to the wall.

"I suspect he got that on his travels. I mean he loved Greek ancient history," I casually remarked.

"Yeah, that's what they got on the grave now – Ancient Greek."

Then the whole hit me like another thunderbolt. His father liked Greek and studied it so he could read the Bible without it being translated, and then he has a grave marker placed on the grave? Once again things weren't making any sense – why? Why do that? Was that a final sign that the mistakes of the past were forgiven, or that after a visit to the gravesite, the pangs of despair at the loss of a child had finally hit the Morrisons? Or, as I now suspect, Jim Morrison had the marker placed.

We are all products of our parents. There it was again, Philip Larkin, and yes they do as he said, 'fuck you up'. But he was also right when he said, 'they don't mean to'.

Maybe James Douglas Morrison was an imitation of his highly intelligent father, whose passion for Ancient Greece had first surfaced in stories he told his impressionable son? Just a wild thought as I had the same done to me as a child. I listened as my father told me, and some of those stories still stick in my deep subconscious. The Minotaur, Medusa and the Golden Fleece are still there after forty, fifty years of data input. How Leonidas, King of Sparta held back the Persian hordes at Thermopolis – 300 against 10,000. Those were stories which I, as young boy, was reared on. That was probably why I liked *Zulu* as a film when it came out. Morrison had done much the same. I'd ridden in a tank and fired a submachine gun when I was thirteen. He had been on the bridge of the Bon Homme Richard with his commander father. I'd rebelled and he'd rebelled, that was our time.

The thing about education is that it gives people the opportunity to think for themselves – that much I learned when I did some teaching. So all things being equal if they have information and the ability to sift it taught to them, they might not necessarily reach the same conclusions. This might sound crazy, but think it through. I mean, history belongs to the people who are writing it.

Doug Prayer was giving me something akin to the truth. Just as my history teacher at college explained to me how the Russians destroyed the SS; just as they had crushed Napoleon a century before. Mind you, he was one of those dangerous tutors, edgy and influential. His claim that Russia won World War II seemed more than plausible. It seemed right.

I snapped back into reality. My thought processes were going so fast that I was finding it hard to evaluate.

"I'd like to come and see you again if I may?" I asked. "Like to talk to you about the band and the other members and what happened to them. I'd like to learn about Vanessa and how you and she and Pam got on. Is that possible? Would you mind?"

He was shaking his head but smiling.

I just kept talking because I didn't want him to refuse, "I'd like to get a copy of that music out in the public domain. I mean, what did you call yourselves?

"Shasta."

"Where did that come from?"

"That was Jim's idea."

"What does it mean?" I asked

He shrugged. "Jim came up with it."

"I really do want to talk again. Is that possible? I want to hear the full story. You said there was more to tell. The truth, you said." I could almost hear myself begging. Not a good trait in anyone, least of all a journalist. "I think the world could do with an answer."

"Yeah?" he sneered. "But is the world ready for it. The world may not like what it hears."

"But the truth is the truth."

It was a trite reply. A weak reply. He knew, like I knew, like Morrison knew, the world is built upon a series of lies and that often the bigger ones prevail.

"Well you're gonna have to wait," he replied. "I got an appointment with my surgeon again tomorrow and some chemotherapy is due, and then we can talk and talk man. Hey, I'll have nothing else to do. Day after tomorrow?"

"Fantastic," I almost squealed and then realised my mistake. "I don't mean fantastic about the chemotherapy, I mean…"

"Hey man, I know what you mean," he interrupted, "It's Ok. Like I said, we all got to die."

And that was how we left it. He'd agreed and I had more research to do. I had a few clues, an artist who came from Greece by the name of Kalamaki, initial T. That was an internet trawl job. I hoped he had done enough to be at least recognised. I visualised one of those artists who sold their wares on the streets to tourists, or some unknown artist who Morrison loved and had discovered. That, I thought, would be a disaster.

Then there was the link to Greece. Why would he choose that place to go as an American? I tried to follow the logic. If he wanted to disappear, what better a place to go. A military junta? He could just disappear into a country like that. Who would even suspect that as a destination? Everyone would be expecting him to run to Africa like Rimbaud, his own role model hero; but why not Greece? Athens had all the things he liked: history, culture, good food and beaches. Perhaps he could just have started all over again, especially if he had plenty of money, which of course he did.

If he had money in Greece, he could have come and gone easily. Business investment would have given him much more freedom too. The junta, as far as I could remember, encouraged outsiders in, but were more oppressive to their own citizens. What if James Douglas Morrison was no longer Jim Morrison the wild and crazy rock and roll front man, but simply an American living a respectable life in Greece? I thought of the possibilities. Even the boy who had a poster of Morrison on his wall and lived a floor below him in Paris did not recognise him. If a fan can pass him by, so could someone with minimal knowledge of him. There are many current popstars that could pass me by in the street and movie stars too. I simply wouldn't know.

I knew there were huge possibilities. The question was, could they lead anywhere?

Could I find him? I needed the final piece in the puzzle and only Doug Prayer had that.

And there was something not right about the picture Prayer

had shown me. It wasn't until I got back to my hotel and started to drift off to sleep that it hit me. What artist signs their work on the back? Every artist I know signs the front. It's a kind of in house advert.

I switched on the light and, despite the hour, my computer as well. I didn't get to sleep that night.

Seventeen

Reason to believe…

"Hi love, I've waited for hours to phone you," I was elated and buzzing and she could sense it. Sense it? She could almost taste it down the phone line.

I had spent a sleepless night on the internet. Tried to piece together all I knew about fame, love and possessive behaviour and I'd watched snippets of Pam and Jim, old movies, with them laughing a lot. I'd drunk coffee and then trawled from site to site looking at Ancient Greek myth. Dionysus, Themis and every conceivable clue which could lead me to any place in Athens.

Themis, I discovered, was one of the Titans, one of the great Greek goddesses. Had Jim given her, Pam, the idea for the name? Perhaps he had, because that was how he saw her. Well, Themis was the goddess of justice but also of communal gatherings and natural order. That much I had found out. Concerts? That was all I'd thought about. Did Pam become the lynch pin in what was going on in his life at the time?

"I was out walking the dogs," she said as I spoke.

"How are they?"

"Fine, though they do miss having you around. Daisy's got a new friend in the park, a great big Alsatian called Boomer. That's what the owner ought to be called, he shouts it enough. Boomer, Boomer, Boomer, it's funny really. Anyway, Daisy jumps on his head. She's totally fearless."

"You packed for Greece?" I asked.

"I thought you were joking, so no," she replied. "Aren't you coming home first?"

"I've found him."

There was silence on the end of the phone.

"And Doug Prayer is going to give me the whole story. Exactly as it happened in 1971, with all of the detail. With exactly how it was planned and executed. I shit you not honey, I've done it." I was whooping. "I've found Jim Morrison."

"How, what? We are going to Greece?"

"Yep, I'll be home in a couple of days and then bingo, off we go. I've been doing a load of research. Trying to find out where he might be."

"Isn't that Prayer chap going to tell you?"

"Says he doesn't know."

"I thought you said he was going to tell you everything."

"About when Morrison left yeah, but I don't think he knows where Morrison is right now."

"So you've not got it yet?"

"Well not exactly, not completely." I hesitated, knowing she was right.

"Not at all."

"The whereabouts of Jim Morrison is Greece."

"That much I gathered bright spark. Have you got proof?"

"I heard Morrison singing," I said, "and I've seen a letter written by him after the day he is supposed to have died. This will take the lid off the story and really make people think. If, and it's a big if, I can find him and talk to him and even get a photograph, then maybe everyone in the world will believe me. What a scoop."

I heard her gasp down the phone line.

"So you need to bring your cameras and a tripod and long lenses. The whole shooting match. If I get close, I need it recorded."

"What about Pamela Courson?" she asked.

"She's dead, I'm sure of that. But you know, I always said there was something funny about the fact that she's in Fairhaven

Memorial Park, Santa Ana and he's in Paris. Why do that, unless there was a specific reason? And her ashes were not interred for eight months. It's like T.E. Lawrence said, 'After my death they'll rattle my bones in their curiosity.' It's like she was his Mary Magdalene; you know, the rock on which he sat?"

"Jesus didn't sit on her – berk."

"No what I meant was she helped him. You know, like Caitlin did with Dylan's poems. Perhaps we'll never know the influence those two exerted over those men. But the fact is, they are not in the same graves. Maybe the Coursons know and maybe Jim wanted to be buried with Pam later, because he isn't in Paris at all. Maybe that's a diversion, a misdirection? Morrison was bloody great at those."

"Yeah? Well maybe it's just that the Coursons wanted somewhere in the US as a focal point. It's hard to lose a daughter and then just get rid of the body. It's like they didn't exist or something, and you told me they were really cut up about her death."

"Yeah, they tried to get a police investigation opened to look into it as a possible murder."

"That's the grief, see?"

"Still, things went pear-shaped and Pam's mother was on the phone to Cheri Siddons frequently, that's The Doors' manager's wife, after Pam died."

"Understandable. If you love someone, it's hard to let them go. Somehow they are always there."

Shit, I was being a shit, totally insensitive. Her father had died, died young of cancer and here I was talking about loss, like I written the rule book. I thought about apologising, but instead just turned the conversation away. Sometimes the least said is the soonest mended. I cursed my own insensitivity.

"Look, I'm sorry," I said. I'd changed my mind and come clean. "Sorry about your dad."

"It's Ok," she replied. "But I understand where they are coming from, don't you? Didn't they come from Orange or live near there?"

"Yeah."

"So maybe that's why?" she replied. "Just simple, plain, naked grief. It's Ok to cry you know."

"There's a double plot in Pere Lachaise."

"So?"

"Well I thought…"

"You thought?" she interrupted. "Did you think though?"

I was not put off. "Well tonight I think I made sense of it. Finally I've nailed it. It wasn't about the parents at all. It was all about her – Pam. Look, he loved her, that much I do think. I know he fucked other women, but I still think he loved her. She fucked other men – they were wanton, without lament. That may be crazy but it was something to do with philosophy and the time they lived in; he just couldn't get married. He didn't think it was necessary."

"Or maybe he was just scared?" she added. "That's another thing, it's Ok to be scared. Perhaps he was scared shitless."

Bang, the simple answer is often the correct one. If Jim wanted to destroy his sex-god image, what better way than to become Mr. Married, Mr. Nice. He could have married Pam and shot the image to bits overnight. Some say he was advised by The Doors' management that getting married would be financial suicide. Personally I don't think he would have cared. Even while *Waiting for the Sun* and 'Hello I Love You' were at the top of the album and singles chart respectively and jointly, he wanted out. Ray Manzarek states this repeatedly in his account of The Doors, *Light my Fire*. Why? Why? Why? There must have been something he couldn't handle? Is that why the Alta Cienega Motel room was so vital to work himself up?

"And she, she was the stronger one," I said. "She went off to Paris and he followed. We all thought it was because she was planning ahead, but what if she was actually leaving him for the Count. Leaving him for good. Could you imagine what was going through his mind? The same insecurities, the same desperate attempts to get away that he exhibited in Miami after they had rowed. Perhaps she thought that she could just go, maybe that's precisely what drew him to her. It's all in the lyrics of the songs. 'We could be so good together'; 'Hyacinth House';

'Cars Hiss by my Window'; nearly all of them are about her. Or at least they make reference to her."

I was on a roll now.

" 'The End' is about Mary Werbelow. The end of their 'elaborate' plans to become famous, the end of their relationship. Mary and Jim – what exactly was their elaborate plan? Her to be a dancer and an artist and him to go to UCLA and become a famous director like Orson Welles? What about when his class mates laughed at his work or thought it rubbish. Even worse – what if Mary was having a modicum of success on the strip, and she was, but then told Jim his life was going nowhere. What a body blow to someone who had issues with his father about both the course he had chosen and life in general. Let's not be under any illusions here, Admiral Morrison paid for Jim to go to UCLA and gave his eldest son an allowance to live on. Hardly the act of a rabid demagogue I would assert. The only proviso was that he, Jim, should write home on a regular basis, which he dutifully did. Even his own sister says the letters were obviously fiction and fantasy, and that everyone in the family thought Jim would end up as a 'bum'. That may be Anne's take on Jim in general, but it was she who first noticed the success of her brother. Those letters – where are they now? They would be worth a fortune, not only in the monetary sense, but as an entrance into the mind of a highly creative individual. Whether they were kept, perhaps none of us will ever know."

"You're not expecting me to write this down, are you?" she asked. "You're the one supposed to be writing it, and I hope you've got this down on paper."

"What, not just talking it away like he did?"

"Yeah, it's like you're in a bar and talking to some major fan," she quipped.

"I know," I laughed, "and you don't even like them that much, do you?"

"They're alright but not my favourite."

I stopped and we talked about things at home and then she said, "Go on then."

" 'The End'," I almost barked, "it talks about the desperate

215

need for a stranger's hand – was that a scream for reassurance? The song finishes with his, I want to kill you, line. Maybe that's Jim's response to a fatherly comment that a possible musical career was a crock. But the line about his mother? Perhaps we'll never know. What do you reckon?"

"Go for the simple answer," she advised. "Look, it's always served you well in the past, why not now?"

I sighed, "It's just…"

"Too simple?" she attacked. "And why not? He was just a man. How many times have you said, even the President has to stand naked in the shower?"

I grunted an affirmation.

"Didn't you say to me that even Marilyn had to wipe her own pretty little arse, or something like that?"

I knew she was right. That took the mystique out of stardom for me, picturing Marilyn Monroe wiping her arse. I thought about it some more just then and experience told me now that some people would get a great buzz out of it – the scatological especially.

"Don't get caught in the celebrity trap. Dumbo," she jibed.

I could visualise her singing: I seen just about everythin' when I seen an elephant fly. A line from the Disney movie. It made me snort aloud. I also knew, of course, she was exactly correct. I might admire the person, think they had a talent, but they were just a person nevertheless, no more than the rest of us.

It was like a joke. Imagine all the parts of the body discussing who was really in charge. Just for a minute, suspend the objections, the outcry and disbelief and go with the scatological flow.

So here they all are, body parts having an argument about the meaning of life. The brain pipes up that he's in charge, because everything is controlled by him. The heart says it's her because of emotions. The arms, the legs, even the stomach puts up a good case, as do the lungs and the liver. Finally the arsehole pipes up. It's me, he says, and of course all the other body parts laugh uncontrollably. The arsehole is so miffed that he decides to teach the rest of them a lesson and promptly goes on strike.

After a few days, the brain is sluggish, the heart is erratic and the arms and legs don't work properly. The poor old stomach can't eat a thing and is nauseous. The lungs are working twice as hard and the liver is causing black spots before the eyes. Eventually all of the body parts call a meeting to resolve the arsehole's strike and they reluctantly concede: arseholes do indeed rule the world.

Even Mozart, however talented, had to crap. So I had to be able to stand away from my investigation and take a very cold look at Morrison the man, rather than Morrison the image.

We hold these truths to be self-evident that all men and all that. That was why I loved her. She could cut right through to the quick and level me out. She'd done it again.

"What if Morrison was shy?" I offered. "Like Densmore said. Shy but someone who got drunk so he could talk to arseholes, or perform for the sheeple. Maybe he needed her. Maybe Pam was, in his mind, his only friend. It's easy to think things about people and then talk yourself into an understanding of them. A sort of self-delusional thing, like Laing says. We begin to believe the things which we use to fool others and ourselves. That's the thing, it's really hard to see things as they actually are, rather than as we want them to be. Maybe Morrison was needy and weak? Look, we can talk ourselves into being in love and then as time goes on we begin to realise. Or go crazy."

"Realise what?" she asked. "Think carefully now."

"That we may be wrong. It dawns that we have not been right all along. Kind of deluding ourselves in the euphoria of the orgasm."

"Familiarity does breed contempt, Ron Clooney," she laughed. She'd used my full name too. She never did that unless she was truly angry. "Hence us – we do see things differently with time, don't we?"

I was lost and unsure as to whether that was her repayment for my rather unguarded remarks.

"Remember Gloria?" she asked.

I was straight back. "Yeah, she thought she was lovely, and she was, until you got to know her. Shallow and vacuous I'd say, but pretty as hell. Everyone wanted to screw your friend; but as I got to know her more, I kind of waned from the idea."

"Bloody good," she snapped.

"I'm just being honest," I replied. "She said the girl pupils at her school wanted to be her and the boys wanted to fuck her."

"Well I'd rather you lied, you bastard. You wanted to screw my friend?"

"No, I just thought about it." Shit, my mind and mouth were all over the place and I was tired and making an ass of myself. "No, I didn't screw her, or want to screw her. I wanted to screw you. Remember she warned you that I did. You are prettier." I was redeeming myself. "What I meant to say was that beautiful people can get ugly if, as you get to know them, you see things in their character you don't like."

"Go on," she replied.

I was out of the hole. "Well look, the more I got to know you, the prettier you became." Damn, I'd thrown myself straight back in.

She coughed.

"Ok you were already very pretty, that's why I fancied you like mad, it was the arse that got me. But you got prettier in my mind's eye. Whereas your mate got uglier."

"And?"

"Well that's what I mean. You get to know someone and they just get better and better – like me?"

I could hear her laughing; I'd redeemed myself and the sweating stopped. I was out of the hole again.

"I know I'm not good looking," I continued, "but I'm kind and considerate. Generous, and I know how much meanness in a man turns women off. And I don't mean just with money, but with emotional output too. Like a meanness of spirit."

"Who are you now then? Clement bloody Freud?"

"Don't take the piss. I've worked it out. Jim needed Pam like a crutch. He gave her everything, money, clothes, cars. And what did he get in return? A Mary replacement. He and Mary had plans, long term plans and elaborate plans. Maybe if she had hung on in there the whole shooting match would be different and Pam would have been just another girl in Hollywood. Mary was an artist and a dancer. I don't think Pam had any talent."

I paused in thought and then considered my take on Pam – I'd read Densmore, Sugerman, Manzarek – and then punched for the KO.

"People said Pam was the most vulnerable and manipulative woman they had ever met. Maybe Morrison met his match – what do you think?"

"Oh please, spare me the nasty user woman speech," she sighed.

"No, he needed her as a crutch. And better still, she made him feel like a man by looking vulnerable. The classic passive aggressive, tiny with a girlish voice, perfect for the image. She was the named peg he hung his life on. That says more about him than her; perhaps he was more like his father than he thought; maybe that's why they clashed so much. Not only did he have an alcohol dependency, he had a Pam dependency too."

"And you believe this?"

"Why not? Look, it's in all the songs, well, the ones that he wrote after Venice and the rooftop. But he could have met her earlier, we don't know for sure, do we? What if he met her at UCLA, at a party before the band really got started? I get this vision of him approaching a very pretty girl in his shy manner; and why so shy? Easy, inexperience and lack of confidence, things he would later get from a bottle in spades. He said he was the mouse that caught the cat. She was one hell of a 'Wild Child' back in Orange. She wasn't Mary, and Jim needed someone to cry to down the phone. Pam got into trouble in school and not like he did, you know, a desk in the corner for a smartarse joker, she was out – booted out. He's doing the middle class rebel thing, but still goes to UCLA to study. She's not even graduated high school and she's off into Los Angeles as a young woman at seventeen. Hitchhiking and, I suspect, screwing all sorts of men. We, the public, get told the fairy story of the wild man who introduced this little, lost, lovely valley girl to the world of drugs and debauchery. But she got the opium for them – remember? She was no shrinking violet – she was poison ivy."

"So you're now going to tell me that it was her who planned the death?" she asked.

"Why not?"

"Bollocks!" The exclamation was totally emphatic.

"Mmm, interesting retort my dear," I laughed. "But think Lady Macbeth here, she's one of you lot. She drives Macbeth to murder…"

"So Pam murdered someone?"

"No, she just planted an idea," I said calmly.

"Really? This is absurd."

"No listen. He needed her and she managed to pull off the act for the cops and everyone. She's this little girl who needs protecting because she can't speak French. She's still doing the manipulative thing in Paris. Just because she's small doesn't mean she's not strong."

"I know, strength is not a measure of the body," she said blandly, "it's a measure of the soul. Is that what you were about to say?"

"Now you're even repeating back my own lines to me. See, you're doing it too."

She waited for a moment and then asked, "How long are going to be in Greece for?"

"A week?"

"So I put the dogs in kennels?"

"Won't your mum have them?" I asked.

"I'll ask her."

"Ok. It would be great if she could."

"I'll ask."

"Great."

"What are you going to do now?" she quizzed.

"Sleep, I've been up all night and I kind of feel zonked. I need to do a bit more about the 27 Club and this Robert Johnson thing. I stumbled on it last night. There's some crazy stuff in there."

"What like?"

"Like Johnson was supposed to have been born in 1911 or 1914. He dies in 1938 after making recordings, forty one tracks in 1936/37. Songs like, 'Sweet Home Chicago'. He dies and the record books want to show that he sold his soul to the Devil for fame. It was a kind of legend he created about himself. Once a dancer and harmonica player, six months later a great guitarist. Legends are funny things, they take on a life of their own and expand and grow. It has to be true because lots of his songs have references to the Devil in them."

"And you believe this nonsense?"

"No, but I've got to take account of it – don't I?"

"What's the link to Morrison then?"

"The link is they all get to twenty seven, so history goes to 1911 for Johnson's birth year. Oh and there's a J in the name. Johnson; Janis Joplin; Jimi Hendrix; Jim Morrison, oh, and Brian Jones too."

"What nonsense," she spluttered.

"There's an article that goes on about Morrison having to pay his dues to the Devil by raising him in room 32 at the Alta Cienega Motel."

She was laughing now. "What did he have to do then? Sleep with the Devil?" she mocked.

"Look, I think it's mad, but there was a guy inside that motel room for six days. I have no idea what the hell he was trying to do. Commune with Jim's spirit, get the Devil back and be famous himself, who knows? Speak to Jim's ghost? The Alta Cienega Motel is on a crossroads though. Santa Monica Boulevard and La Cienega North, I think. How weird is that? Maybe Johnson's song 'Crossroads' is right?"

"Yeah, and they buried suicide victims near crossroads as well. You're going there, aren't you? You are off on a wild goose chase because some woman back in the late sixties had an idea about a blues man who sold his soul to the Prince of Darkness. Please," she mocked. "Or was that the black magic woman who married Morrison?"

"It's in LA."

"I know where it is. You're mad, totally mad if you believe that. What about all the other places Morrison lived?"

"Ah, but the Alta Cienega was his space, the space he kept private. What the hell did he do in there?"

"How about he got sick and scared and drank. How about he just hid before a performance. Maybe he took something we don't know about. Maybe there's a secret space under the floor, something only the Devil and he know about. Maybe he took acid to dream himself into a concert state, like back in Venice Beach. What is it you say? The simple answer is probably the correct one? I think it was stage fright."

"Wow," I exclaimed. I was stunned at her understanding of my book, but more so of me. "Look, I'm not going to LA again," I reassured. "I've done that part and I don't think there is anything else I can get out of that place. It's all plastic and all a façade. Not everything you see is real."

"Exactly," she snorted.

"I just think it's an interesting attempt," I continued, unperturbed, "at justifying his meteoric success with music and women. Anyway the Devil doesn't want my soul, I'm not much use to him, am I?"

"I bloody hope not," she laughed. "Mind you, you are evil enough."

"But it's an interesting take on the whole thing, don't you think? It's like the human need to explain things. Like everything that happens has to have a reason; when in reality there often isn't a reason. I mean, what made the kids like 'Light my Fire' so much? Why did the band do a shortened version? Luck, chance and…"

"Interesting I'll say," she offered. "Nuts. The world is full of kooks and bunny boilers."

"Bunny boilers?"

"Yeah."

"Well there is a case in point," I philosophised. "A character from a movie does something and then the phrase becomes common speak. I've seen people use it who don't really understand the origin. Like the *Where's Wally* books. I think that came from the Wheely festival in 1971, near Colchester. Crazy I know, but a microphone announcement about a lost guy called Wally turned into a piece of popular culture. And I was there."

"Max Boyce now are we?"

I laughed. "Precisely."

"And I bet you were stoned too?"

"No comment m' lud."

"Mmm," was all she said.

"How did you know it was a woman?" I asked.

"I guessed," she replied, "just guessed. Besides, aren't all witches women?" she goaded.

"Wow, I'm impressed."

"Don't be," she laughed again, "it's just luck."

I caught her drift immediately and thought smart, real smart.

"Look, I know it's a crock," I agreed, "because at the funeral in Paris, mock or otherwise, there was no man of the cloth. Nor, for that matter, a woman priest either. And the reason is simple: Morrison didn't believe."

"So?" she asked.

"Well if you don't believe in God and Jesus, if you think the Easter story was just that, a story – a heist, you can hardly believe in the Devil, can you? That's one that people like that conveniently forget."

"People like what?" she asked.

"You know, the Jesus freaks."

"Jesus freaks?"

"Well that's what we called them back then. Now they wear a name band thing with WWJD on it. Supposed to mean what would…"

"I know what it means," she barked, "I'm not stupid you know."

"Well stupid is as stupid does," I drawled out the words in a bad imitation southern accent.

"Don't," she snapped. "I hate that stupid film. Don't get the point of it."

"Like I said…" I was chuckling at my own joke.

"But what if you're both wrong, clever clogs? What if there really is a 'Devil' and the 27 Club is true. You're gonna look real stupid when you get up there at those pearly gates to argue your case."

I laughed loudly in reply. "I'm gonna need a really comfortable pair of shoes I suppose? Running shoes?"

"You're gonna need a really good lawyer. Now who can we ask I wonder?"

"You are so funny," I quipped.

"Well your phone bill is not going to be funny. How long have you been chopsing away to me?"

I looked at the clock. "I better go," I said. "You're right, I need to get some sleep anyway. Just an hour or two."

"Call me later," she said in reply, and with a click, she was gone.

Eighteen

Subterranean homesick blues…

On the edge of the bed I sat towelling my hair. I felt thick headed and knew that a shower would clear the cobwebs from my brain. I had tried to assimilate all of the information as I let the water pour over me. Water in a shower has a very soothing effect, like it washes away all of the troubles and sins. That in itself is a quasi religious experience, rather like good sex. Then I stopped myself; sometimes the strangest things get you to 'understand'. My mind wanders all over the place but when it wanders things get picked up and tumbled, like flotsam and jetsam in surf. The thing is, when you burn that driftwood it burns clean and blue flamed, extra pure. Well that's my excuse anyway: it justifies my warped take on things.

I'd slept away the morning and the afternoon was drawing to a close. The 'Do Not Disturb' sign had not worked and I think the maid had a fright when I came out of the shower with nothing on but a handtowel. Unfortunately I was towelling up top and was not being modest – she left hurriedly.

I lay on the bed with my hands behind my head and my eyes closed and then, as if someone had dropped a large lead weight onto my chest, it hit me. The name on the painting had said Dionysus and Kalamaki. There was no signature on the front, why? I thought it was a Greek quirk, a tourist thing. But even in Florence, street artists sign their work. I was wrong; I was so wrong.

The Dionysus theatre is a place and there, as bold as brass, was another – Kalamaki. I wondered if there was a link between the two places. Perhaps the original theatre of Dionysus had some links to Kalamaki, was in Kalamaki. I knew there was a theatre on the way up to the Acropolis. It was close to the Temple of Themis, perhaps another coincidence. The problem with this investigation, book, novel or whatever you'd like to call it: there seemed to be too many coincidences. Perhaps I was like all the rest and had to believe in design. Is that a human condition? Why couldn't I accept chance and luck?

Kalamaki is a beach suburb of Athens. A beautiful little place with a character all of its own. A tranquil place, a place where someone could be alone, but also a summer hot spot. I had a map up on the screen now. I was on a virtual reality website looking down the streets and there was a beach, a walkway and sand. Shacks for the tourists selling the standard cheap tat. Highly printed towels, teeshirts, fridge magnets and postcards, sweets, ice-creams and candies. There were coffee huts and bars and several kinds of restaurant – perfect Morrison territory.

* * *

The trouble was that as I researched a little, very disturbing historical data kept popping up. Data which was interspersed with my own personal knowledge. My father had been in Cyprus during that period. He had been wounded in Nicosia, while acting as a member of the United Nations Peacekeeping Force. I remembered the bright blue beret and white cap badge he wore; it was vividly different from the sombre black of the tank regiment he belonged to. That fracas in Cyprus had almost resulted in his death, but also prompted the popular reasoning that an all out war was likely between Turkey and Greece.

Crazy as it seems, history does keep repeating itself. I could see a pseudo religious war staring all over again as Christianity fought Islam on the basis of validity of belief. That is why I have no religion. I kind of think it's just a good excuse to kill. I couldn't get past that thing that said 'Thou shalt not kill'. I still can't find any sub-clause to that, you know, like 'Except in the case of political expediency or capital gain, or for the preservation of vital oil resources'. The thing is, there is a difference between a reason and an excuse – isn't there?

Morrison disappeared in 1971; Greece had a coup d'etat on the 21st April 1967. That, I thought, was the end of the idea that Morrison was in Greece. Morrison, I believed, would never choose to go to a country which was run by right-wing nationalist generals and which imposed severe draconian measures against its people. His motives would be higher than that, they had to be, he was a god. But I wondered when he had gone to Greece. Had he invested money there? Did his father know about the Greek strategic importance? He was, after all, an admiral and Morrison himself was no turkey.

The Communists were the reason for the military government and while many civil rights issues did exist in the political field, many Americans were free to come and go at will. Truman had since 1947 seen Greece as a bastion against Communism, and large amounts of American money had been poured into the economy to discourage Communism. The Lyndon Johnson administration also cared little for the human rights violations and continued to see Greece as a vital NATO ally in the ring around the USSR. This was still the time of the Cold War and America needed allies. Not until 1999, when Clinton apologised for supporting the junta as part of the Cold War tactics, did some of the truth emerge. That's what I love about politics: people die, people starve and the whole world goes to hell in a handcart, but as long as somebody apologises, it's Ok? Politics, like sex, is a messy business, especially when it's wrapped up in dollar bills.

Publicly the junta praised and encouraged religion and nationalism and attacked western culture. Hippies and Communism were considered anti-Greek. But the film *Woodstock* was shown all over the country in 1970 and several hippie enclaves and colonies were left completely to their own devices. Probably because they posed no political threat as they were not Greeks, but usually the travelling American kind. One on the island of Crete, Matala, played host to Joni Mitchell in

1971 after her Laurel Canyon, 'playing house' days with Graham Nash. That 1971 stay produced 'Carey' for the album *Blue*. Nash's 'Our house' was one of the classics on *Déjà Vu* and refers directly to the very intense relationship the pair experienced a few houses away from Morrison and Pam. Love Street a.k.a the Rothdell Trail, produced many classic pairings.

There were also beach community hippies in tourist spots on Greece – Paradise Beach in Mykonos being just one notable group which continued to function throughout the rule of the junta. Function is probably not the right word, flourish is more applicable. These were bohemian hot spots, much like Laurel Canyon had been, or Venice Beach, or Greenwich Village even.

The irony was that despite the oppressive coup, tourism was encouraged, with nightclubs being opened at the whim of the junta. Inevitably corruption flourished, but unless political activity took place at a venue, the nightlife was vibrant.

So between 1967 and 1973 unemployment fell and economic growth increased. Foreign investors were encouraged. Even Coca Cola ploughed money into the country. By November 1974 the junta had fallen and democracy had been restored.

For several years it was a mess, but Morrison could have found a place to hide. As an American he could have come and gone easily and with a passport he could be anyone; anyone except the Lizard King.

Maybe he left Paris in 1971, there were plenty of sightings, and returned quietly to Sausalito. There he and Pam could heal, get well, before planning a new life together. Maybe Pam's death in 1974 is coincidence. Maybe it was an unfortunate accident; maybe the Coursons were right all along. The file on that one is firmly closed. Pam was dead then and remains dead now.

I wished at this point that my father was still alive; I'd have quizzed him about his time in Cyprus. Instead I had to hit the books and try and piece together something which might be possible. Information overload was happening and my jigsaw had become a full blown novel, which was getting bigger, and I needed to get back to Doug Prayer to find out exactly what he knew.

I wondered about the guy, how ill was he exactly? Was he playing with my head like Morrison had with his audiences? Was I giving Morrison too much credit for his actions and was he simply burnt out and hiding?

So I placed Morrison in Greece. Somebody would recognise him surely? Again I went back to the exile in Paris. Like Oscar Wilde in his time, he would have been known to some, but not to all. He had to change his appearance. How? He'd have no passport. Even if he had two in the name of Morrison, they'd still be Morrison; one old and one new – both James Douglas Morrison. He needed a new identity and that would require a passport and a false passport and a military junta. Man that was a risk, a really huge risk, one that could have cost him his life. Then there is the matter of being out of context, you know, like a teacher being seen shopping? Kids find that a shock cos teachers live at the school, don't they?

When I did a story on Princess Diana once, before her accident, I found out that she went shopping in Northampton with her bodyguard. She walked around the department stores quite normally, no dark glasses or furtive glances. They simply posed as a couple and she wore jeans. He had a gun, but nobody knew, why should they? They had no pattern, no one knew they were there – simple. If anyone stopped them she said, 'Oh lots of people think I look like her, but I'm not her, sorry to disappoint.' Then she walked. I mean what can you say to that? Cool as you like, she said, 'Oh no I'm not her.' I mean what are you going to say to someone, 'Yes you are, prove you're not'? That is crazy and most people aren't that crazy. It that situation you'd feel like a total schmuck and want a hole to open up for you.

So that seems like a good way not to be challenged – brazen it out. The only real risk is meeting a crazy. Jim Morrison, despite his fame, wandered around West Hollywood and many stars still do today. They have to eat too after all. It's only the giants like Elvis or McCartney or Michael Jackson who might not get away with it. Thing is, they are so distinctive. To blend in, all you have to do is be bland and bold. Look, generals and kings and even presidents have done it, walked around their encampments listening, learning. The trouble is, the eavesdropper seldom hears good things about themselves. I could hear Morrison's take on it: 'But hey, that's the risk man, that's the risk.'

Turn up unexpectedly too – no warnings. The simple thing about stars is they don't look much like their image when they're out. They look like you and me, some look better but some look worse. It's all in the packaging.

You see, it's image, an act. Perhaps Morrison changed his act and melted away into the crowd. I was beginning to believe that anything is possible in Hollywood. Dreams can become reality and reality can descend into a dream; the key, I suppose, is holding on to some sense of yourself and that ain't easy.

* * *

Kalamaki is a small enclave to the south of Athens and yet part of it. It is warm and the blue waters of the Aegean lap against the sands which are the same colour as those on Venice Beach. It feels like an island but historical Athens is at your back. There are palm trees and olives and brightly coloured flowers, orange, yellow and purple; flowers from Africa, flowers from the Mediterranean. The pace of life is more relaxed; buses run from Syntagma Square down Singrou and out along the coast road to Kato Sounio. There, on a rocky outcrop, surrounded by beaches, is the historic temple dedicated to Poseidon. Summers come and summers go, but when it rains it rains. Unlike southern California, there are bleak, cold seasons and tourists come and tourists go.

Sausalito house boats sprang to mind; Venice Beach and the canals; Santa Monica pier. There it was, the pieces of the jigsaw suddenly made sense. Jim Morrison was in Greece, in Kalamaki or near it, walking distance from it perhaps.

That was where I was going next.

Nineteen

Casey Jones...

Third time lucky:

When Doug Prayer came to the door he looked terrible. I'd done exactly as he asked and left him alone. It was one of the most difficult periods in the whole of this investigation. Besides thinking up the trip to Greece, mostly over the phone, I was also busy researching the possibilities of people escaping. I avoided POWs and things like Colditz Castle; instead I concentrated on civilian men, because it was mostly these men who never gave up. Very little is written about female escapees, but there must have been some, maybe many more than we shall ever know. I wondered about Ravensbruck and the holocaust.

Frank Morris, the bank robber, and his two accomplices, the Anglin brothers, the only men to ever escape from Alcatraz, they figured too. I'd been there so I could visualise the whole escape plan and the possibility of their success. It was daring and it worked. And as I walked around the cell blocks, I really understood that if I got out of there I'd never go back. What a place 'The Rock' was – it helped me to understand what Morrison might have been facing if he had been sentenced. I know Alcatraz was not Raeford but Raeford was nevertheless a very unpleasant place in 1970. Prisons in his time were not hotels and certainly not the stuff of *Cool Hand Luke* movies. Morrison was a sheltered middle-class kid who was out of his league.

I could also understand the absolute cruelty of man upon man and why anyone in such a terrible situation would kill to escape. I read the account of Henri Charriere, all about Ile du Diable, that's Devil's Island to you and me. You see, there is a real point to that one; 1970 was the year of the phenomene *Papillon*. It would have been all over the press and hot stuff in Paris. In 1970 it was first translated into English. Put simply, Morrison probably read it and digested it. He was, after all, a voracious reader with a capacity for intellectual debate and *Papillon* reads like the work of a master raconteur.

"Christ, not you again," Prayer growled. His face was slightly green and his eyes appeared to be sinking into his head. Put in absolute terms, he looked very ill.

I smiled sheepishly.

"You said you'd tell me the whole story." I stated nervously.

"Never give up, do ya? Still, at least you let me be in peace for a while. You know how many journalists have been after this story?"

I ignored the remark. "I thought that was what you said." I continued.

"Come in then," he motioned. "You can roll us both a joint. Christ knows I could do with one. Let's have another drink while we're at it."

He stepped aside and I sensed a stumble. I wondered if he was drunk.

"Get a bottle of wine out of the kitchen," he said, as he made for the large inviting couch. "And make it a real good one. I ain't got the time..." His voice tailed off to a whisper.

When I returned he had a needle on the coffee table and a vial of some clean liquid which he was preparing to inject into his arm. I panicked, thinking the worst – that he was a junkie. Doug Prayer was astute if nothing else.

"I'm not a fucking junkie man," he squealed, as his voice rose in pitch, "iffen that's what yawl think." The accent was pronounced.

The southern accent was back. I would have thought him Tallahassee through and through and wondered when the California 'dude' had appeared.

His hands worked quickly as he self-administered the shot. The plunger down, his eyes rolled and he leant his head back against the headrest of the couch. Within a few minutes he was back to his former self. Whatever he had taken had boosted him.

"So what are you taking?" I asked.

"Just a little morphine man. And it's on prescription baby. Thing is, I add a little cocaine man, you know, to give me a lift."

"That's a bit dangerous, isn't it?"

He laughed. "Don't give me a load of bullshit about how it's bad for my health now."

"I wasn't," I lied. "I came to hear the story of Morrison."

"Yeah?"

"You said that you'd tell me the truth."

"Did I?"

"Well I think he's in," I paused waiting for a reaction, "Greece."

"Well done Mike Hammer." He stopped short. "Sorry," he snorted, "you're English, erm," he hesitated again, "Sherlock Holmes."

"I just followed your clues and did a little research."

"Well if you've done that you should be able to find Jim's place real easy. What the hell do you need me for? Go see the man."

I panicked. "What if he's not there?"

"He was the last time I was there."

"But you told me that you didn't know…"

"Hell, I lied," he chuckled, leaning forward, "so serve me. Are you going to roll that joint or do ya want me to?" he asked

"You do know exactly where he is then?"

"Sure and so do you."

"Kalamaki?" I blurted like some schoolboy in a test.

"Got it in one, man."

"So how did he do it?" I asked.

"First give me the makings man; otherwise we'll never get that smoke."

He was right, I was all fingers and thumbs. Once he had the papers and the weed in his hands he set to making another of those thumb thick joints he had made previously.

"Get a couple of glasses," he barked. "I hope you chose a good 'un."

"1964 Chateau Margot, is that good?"

"Mouton Rothschild. Pretty good, pretty good," he muttered. "I was savin' that for a special day. Suppose today is special. Today you get the story, you know, like the whole nine yards. So hey man, let's get to it before the morphine wears off."

I poured as he began.

"Jim Morrison was a difficult man and his girlfriend man, she was worse, but he was my friend and I loved him. We had a lot in common. The story about Amsterdam is absolutely true and so are the others. You see, we just kept bumping into each other over the years. Jimmy said it was destiny."

"Jimmy? I've never heard anyone refer to Morrison as Jimmy before."

"That's what Pam called him when she wanted somethin'. Man she knew how to play him, she kinda went into little girl mode and then he melted to her. She didn't do baby speak or call him Daddy or nothin', but she gave off this vulnerable air. Man he loved her and he said we shared a common destiny. I thought that destiny thing was a crock, just some piece of weird luck, but there was no way man, no way he was goin' to believe me. He had the shaman thing you know. See, Jim had this thing, you know, like Pam being born near Mount Shasta and all. Some sort of old Indian story about lizard people under the mountains at the beginning of time. Anyways, he said we were meant to spend time together."

"So Pam, she manipulated?"

"She was lovely, kinda had this vulnerable thing and her eyes went gooey and moist. She had him tagged and when she called him Jimmy it reminded him of when he was a kid. I think that's what his mom called him. Well that's what he told me. When she was really pissed she called him James Douglas Morrison, you know, like a mother would. Wow she could handle herself too and man couldn't she punch."

"The incident?" I reminded him.

"Yeah but it weren't no incident."

"So what happened?"

"I was livin' in a place like that crap hole back then and a neighbour comes in, wakes me up and says, 'Hey Doug there's some guy on the hall phone, says his name's Jim, askin' for ya.' Now we had a phone in the hall then and it turns out Morrison's been tryin' for half an hour. It's 2.30am in the mornin', the 3rd July 1971, I think it was Saturday. Anyway I'm stoned and I get up and talk to the man. He's real excited and he says to me come over – now. And I said in the mornin' man I'm fucked up, but he says now because this could be a really important day for all of us. He was kinda cryptic, talkin' in riddles. Said he was sending cab to get me. Man he had a persuasive way, he could have been a real good salesman.

Well I threw some water over my face and combed my hair. I wanted a shower but I knew that would delay me and Jim sounded like, freaked out. Seriously freaked out."

"What happened?"

Taking a deep mouthful of the rich red wine, he lit the joint and took a deep toke. "So I get to their place and he's down in the courtyard behind the oak doors. Kind of in the shadows where no one can see him. I arrive and he motions up to the door, slips me some money and then steps back so he can't be seen by the driver. When the car's gone I ask, what the hell? I ask and he makes for me to like be silent, man. Only this ain't no joke, he's real serious and he's studying the windows and all, like he doesn't want to be seen. Then we go up real quiet to the apartment. Pam's there only she's freaking, talking fast about a plan she's got and how lucky they were. Then they take me into the bathroom and there's Mickey Alvarez in the bath; in the nude man. Only it didn't look like Mickey cos he had dark hair. Morrison says they were havin' a joke man, you know, playin' a prank and Mickey had gone down to the Rock and Roll Circus. Turns out he'd been goin' there for a couple of weeks. Mickey seemed to like that, dumb bastard, you know, pretending to be Morrison. He'd been getting blow jobs, joints and getting laid in the ladies' restroom too. Both he and Morrison thought it was fun. Jim thought it was a perfect crazy prank. He'd even talked about Mickey and him swapping places, swapping lives, only Mickey couldn't sing man.

You know, someone else being Morrison, that kinda appealed to Jim's dry sense of humour. Jim even gave him some of his clothes man and they were a perfect fit. It was like they were doubles only Mickey had a bit more weight on him man.

What the fuck? I ask and he says that Mickey's dead. Now it was my turn to freak.

What yawl mean dead? I ask. Well, says Pam, Mickey'd gone down to the Circus to score some coke and someone give him horse instead, only this is like crazy shit man, super strong and all, cos it's been hardly cut. He tries some and then he dies. Right there in the shithouse at the back he dies. How crazy is that?

They bundled him into a car and brought who they thought was Morrison back here. Only the real Jim's out cold in the bed, they don't see him and think Pam's got someone with her. Thinking that's her shit to sort out, they dump the body in the bath and go; they go real quick."

"So what did you do?" I asked.

"I just stood there and listened," Prayer continued. "That really did freak me out. Pam was the mastermind. She said if they did it right, nobody would know. Mickey has his clothes taken, well they belonged to Morrison anyway, and then they filled the bath. Pam said it was to keep the cadaver warm so time of death couldn't be established with any certainty. You have to remember she was one smart cookie too ya know. So she fills the bath with hot water man and Mickey goes kinda pink and there's blood comin' out of his nose and drippin' into the water. He's leanin' against the ride side of the bath man and his eyes are wide open." He paused and passed me the joint. "I can tell you man, I was scared shitless, but Pam and Jim, they were kind of enjoyin' seein' me freaked. If I didn't know any better, I'd say they were gettin' off on it. Look, she said, if the authorities don't believe us, then we can say it was a practical joke played on us. Mickey's dead and he would have loved it anyway.

Mickey didn't have family so it wasn't really that bad. Pam said they'd found a cemetery, which I thought was odd at the time cos it was like three or four in the morning by now. Jim's clothes were on the bathroom floor and Pam said she'd take care of the police. They wanted me to get Mickey's passport from his place. They said neither of them could go, they couldn't risk it, and that if I helped them they'd make sure I got looked after – she said. At the time it made sense man, I swear.

Man that was one crazy night, Pam laid it all out and they had Mickey's keys man. They were in his pocket, so all I had to do was go there and get his stuff."

"So they wanted you to get Michael Alvarez, passport? His American passport and then give that to Jim?" He was nodding as I spoke. "Did you?"

"Look, Jim was unhappy man."

"Did you though?" I pressed.

"Really so unhappy. Mickey was dead and…"

"Oh my God," I squealed, "that's how they did it. The old doppelganger ruse."

He drew on the joint once again. "It seems like it don't matter now," he said. "It all got fucked up when Pam died anyway and Jim sort of fell for a while. Yeah I went for the passport and his birth certificate, and drivers licence."

"So what happened next?"

"I went over to Mickey's place and it was easy," he continued. "I found the stuff and took it to Jimmy. Got back there about 5 am and left about half an hour after that."

"Who had the keys?" I asked.

"What keys?"

"Alvarez's?"

"I gave them to Pam I think. Anyhow I don't have them."

"So where was Alvarez's place then?"

"About three blocks from Morrison's, only it was like one room cos Mickey didn't have that much stuff, so he didn't need much space."

"So let me get this right," I quizzed. "Jim Morrison put Mickey Alvarez in the bath and then the story carries on from the official one?"

I paused for a response – there wasn't one.

"Morrison is in a closed casket and buried on the Wednesday. Why no cremation?" I asked.

"I don't know. I think that was Jim's idea. He kinda liked the idea of fooling people. Something about giving a focal point. Janis had been cremated and scattered and he knew that he didn't want that. Crazy, but I think he wanted to create his own shrine, his legend. Don't ask me man, I'm only guessing. Only the grave had no marker for years. Like he wanted to be dead and yet he didn't want to be forgotten as the Lizard King. What's that Iggy Pop tune? 'Nice to be dead'? Man, he was a strange mix of things and ideas. Who wants to be a famous dead man and not be dead? It was all crazy and mixed up and Morrison. See I don't think he really knew what he wanted. He didn't love life that much, like most of us do; for him it was like a daily trial with sanity. He did some weird stuff and boy when he drank man, he drank. I never seen anybody drink so much that they went into pass out mode and he did that a lot."

"So where did Morrison go?" I asked.

"Nowhere man. He stayed in the apartment with Mickey and Pam. It was all too crazy. Then after the funeral he simply left. I think he went to Mickey's place for a while, stayed in Paris and after that I didn't see him for a space. Pam went back to the US and hid out for a bit, did the grieving widow. Bill Siddons went back too and the legend was born. That's when the shit hit the fan. One day Josh and Jon pay a visit to Mickey and his place is empty man and he's like split."

"They didn't know?"

"Not then."

"But you said he came to Paris and visited them."

"Yeah that was after he knew about Josh's murder. He came to see Jon and boy he just flipped."

"Who, Morrison?"

"No, Jon. Went crazy man, called the cops and said real crazy things."

"So he stayed in your apartment? This apartment?"

"Who, Jon?"

"No, Morrison."

Prayer was nodding.

"But I suppose he could have gone any place," I suggested. "He could simply have done anything because nobody knew he was alive. The neighbours didn't know who he was. I suppose he was just another American to them."

I was reasoning aloud. It was all so utterly simple. A body which looked like Morrison and yet wasn't. Pam identifies the body as Morrison. Agnes Varda and Alan Ronay get called after Doug and Jim have left, or Jim stays hidden in the apartment. Where in the apartment? The closet? My mind was racing, was it a hoax? A joke, or a serious attempt to get away?

Early on the Wednesday a corpse gets buried. Simple. No autopsy, no embarrassing heroin-fuelled rock star death. That didn't make sense though – no autopsy. But what if a few bucks passed from hand to hand. I mean, there were two people saying that someone dead was who they claimed. No one would dream that they were telling a lie, why would they? A prison sentence, a deeply unhappy man and an exit. Mix them in the shaker and out comes a perfect cocktail. The perfect cocktail; the perfect crime. Like the perfect song – simple.

A piece of luck, good for some, bad for another – simple.

Doug Prayer drew in the smoke deeply. The whole story had taken less time than it had taken to smoke a joint.

"I once heard a story that Morrison and Babe Hill had swapped lives," I said. "The story goes that Babe was Morrison's best friend and he came to visit him in Paris. I've seen photos on the internet of this guy who could be Morrison as an old man. I mean, it was possible until I read this. This sounds even more incredible than that. It's like the ending of a novel."

"Well maybe good stories don't end they just develop," He replied. "I never met Babe so I don't know what he looks like. All I know is what I saw at the time. Jim Morrison was buried, only it wasn't Morrison in that grave. What do you think, they a kept double space for in Santa Ana? That Corky Courson was no fool and Pam, she was the apple of his eye. They liked Jim too and why, because he was nice to them. "

"Well Babe shared a place with Tom Baker once," I said,

"and he's dead now too. Back in 1974 they had a place in West Hollywood and Pam was going to meet them for breakfast and next day she's dead. Someone said that she was killed because she'd be able to see that Babe was in fact Morrison. I mean, there are wild stories going around and maybe that's what Jim wanted. In fact, everyone around this whole thing is either silent or dead. It's like all those people in the JFK conspiracy theory, they're dead too. Seems like…"

"A legend?" he smirked.

"A mess," I replied. "Why leave it like that?"

He laughed, a deep throaty laugh which reminded me of Morrison himself.

"Let's go get some tacos man – I'm stoned," he said.

Twenty

On the road again…

Excited – wouldn't you be? I'd landed in Greece with the one person who truly believed in me. When I'd started on this project as an idea, she said go do it. Everybody else had called me a crazy or someone who was looking to regain their youth. Not only that, she had trawled around Los Angeles with me as I researched. She had a bag full of cameras and memory cards and now we were going to see Jim Morrison, a man who had been dead since 1971, or was supposed to be.

We checked into our hotel, The Atrium, and freshened up. I'd flown back home from Paris and then we had gone on from London to Athens the following day. I was running on empty, but the adrenalin had kicked in and I was almost there; the finish line was in sight. There was no way of knowing if Morrison was alive or even still there, plus I'd never been to Athens before.

My simple idea was to talk to Morrison and get an interview and pictures. Then perhaps get a follow up a couple of days after that. The assumption that he didn't want to talk to me was not even on my radar.

* * *

We took a cab out to Kalamaki.

It was a small beach with a few rented loungers dotted along

241

the sand. Quiet and pleasant, though I was there when it wasn't the height of the tourist season, it was a nice place, pretty and a suburb of the larger city, with apartments which faced out over the ocean. I knew it was the kind of place which would have suited Morrison.

Like I wrote earlier, people can't change their habits easily, unless perhaps an experience comes their way which alters their values. At the start of the beach there was a turnstile and you had to pay to get into an area which was fenced off. That's where the toilets, showers, restrooms and other amenities were. There were also places to eat. Hotdog stands, burger bars, places to buy beer and at the far end a place called The Lucky U. A Mexican place where you could buy tacos, burritos and fajitas. A small surf shack made of sawn timber, with loads of colour and old surf boards for a bartop. The place smelt of cedar and salt. It reminded me of the typical offering you could find in Santa Monica or along Venice Beach. A kind of hippy coloured Amsterdam café with loads of razzle – dazzle.

Jutting out into the water was a finger of man-made rock. It stood at the curve of the beach and on it there was a path, and at the end of that a hut. It was a palm-covered structure under which people sat. Sunlight danced across the water and made me wince.

I stopped at the bar and a dark-haired girl appeared from behind what looked like bead curtains. She was sleek like a cat and moved like a snake. Striking is the only word I could use to describe her.

"Yes?" she asked in English.

"I've come to see the owner" I chanced.

Her ears pricked up. "He's not here, day off, but he'll be back tomorrow."

"Have you got a number for him?" I asked.

"He doesn't like me giving out numbers," she replied.

"Well does he live nearby? Perhaps I could go see him?"

"No I don't give out his address. He's the boss and he wouldn't like it."

"Can you give him a message then?" I asked.

"Sure, when he gets back."

I was convinced that someone was listening beyond the curtain. I could see a shadow but couldn't make it out.

"Can you tell him that I've come from Paris and I'm a friend of Doug? I think he'll want to talk to me."

"Ok," she said, and then went back to serving the queue of customers that had built up during our brief conversation.

I went back to where my accomplice had sat with a camera in her hand ready to take any photos she could.

"He's not there," I said, "all this way and he's not there. Bollocks!"

"Oh good," she replied. "That means we can go for a swim and have a sunbathe. "Did you get us any drinks? I could murder a coke or something nice and cool."

I was nonplussed.

"God, I can't believe that," I said.

"Neither can I, why didn't you get us a drink while you were up there? Now you'll have to go back, that's a bummer."

She smiled dreamily.

So back I went.

At the bar a man with grey hair came out from behind the curtain. His hair was thin, like it had had one too many applications of dye in his youth. His face sported a full beard with a heavy moustache. He was overweight, but not so much as to call him obese. About six foot, give or take an inch, his skin was a nut brown colour like he had spent way too many hours in the sun.

"Can I have two lemonades please?" I requested.

"You came to see me?" he asked.

"I came to see the owner," I said.

"Tha's me," he replied. His voice was thin and shrill and I knew instantly that this was not Jim Morrison.

"I got a message from Doug."

The man shrugged.

"Doug Prayer?"

He shook his head. "I don't know this man."

243

The girl with the dark hair appeared again. "Papa, the barrel needs changing," she said.

"Ok I'll do it now," the man replied, and was gone.

"He's your father?" I asked casually.

"Yes."

"I was sent here to find the owner of something in Kalamaki." I continued, floundering.

"What was this something?"

"Well I thought it was this bar as it serves Mexican food and …"

"Who are you trying to find?" She was patient, yet probing, like an insistent lover.

"I came to find a guy named Mickey Alvarez."

Her face lit up like beacon. "Oh the Americano. He's gone."

To say my heart sank is an understatement. I was gutted. All this way, all this work and all I was likely to get were two lemonades on a Greek beach.

"I have a painting," I said.

"What a coincidence, that's his hobby, the Americano. He told me once that he learnt it from a girlfriend he knew in America. Said he wished he had a talent like she had, but she became a dancer and they drifted apart. He has a shop in Plaka now, selling tourists pictures and hand painted pots. We bought this place off him about two years ago. He still comes out here to paint though, but only on the weekend."

My spirits rose instantly. "Do you know where the shop is?" I asked.

She called to her father to confirm the address and I took the lemonade back toward the sun loungers. I was ecstatic.

"It appears our bird has flown," I said as I sat down. "Apparently he sold this place some years back and now has a shop in Plaka."

"Where the hell is that?" she asked with genuine distress.

"Apparently it's a district of shops and a flea market behind the Acropolis. The place is on the corner of Nikodimou and Voulis."

"What's it called?"

"Get this, apparently it's 'Ninety Leaves' Or something like that. I couldn't quite get the accent, but I can't be far off. How difficult can it be to find?"

"And I suppose you want to go there right now?" she asked in disappointment.

"No, it's alright; we can sunbathe for a bit and go tomorrow."

"Really? You can wait that long?"

"Yep – I haven't finished my lemonade."

* * *

That afternoon we found the place. It was a small shop which sold Greek tourist materials. There were pots and vases dedicated to a variety of gods and deities, and other assorted items including sculptures, both classical and modern. All were hand made and all had a real feel of art about them, rather than the standard tourist schlock.

The name above the door said Ninth Life Gallery and below it in Greek: *OY OPONTIS.*

I walked in to be greeted by another dark-haired young woman.

"Hello," I said. "Is the owner here?" I asked.

"Out the back in the studio, probably," she replied. "But if you're selling stuff, he won't buy. He hates reps and we only have items from authentic artists here – nothing is mass produced. So if you're trying to get us to stock things – we won't. It's policy, though I've tried enough times to get him to change his mind. We could make far more profit."

That, I thought, was a strange thing for an employee to say. Perhaps she was some kind of relative – a daughter? I made an attempt to move through the shop.

"Can I go through?" I asked.

"You can, if he lets you," the girl replied, hitting some kind of buzzer under the desk as she spoke. "But the woman stays, she's got cameras and there is no photography allowed."

A man came through the doorway at the end of the gallery. He was quite lean with very thin hair and a swaying walk. I noticed that immediately and surmised a broken leg which had not healed properly. His hair was white and long and tied in a ponytail. His eyes, which looked slightly too close together, were piercing. The same broken nose, the same facial scars, only this time I could really see the depth of them; the tan had accentuated them. It was the same man I had seen in the bar near Pere Lachaise in Paris. The same man who had vanished in an instant back then. His hair had grown and his size changed, but I was seventy percent certain it was the same man.

"Not pretty eh?" he said smiling.

I didn't know what to say. I stammered, "What's not pretty?" I lied.

"This face man. Not what anybody expected is it? See, a car windshield can play havoc with your face man – havoc. And things happen that make changes."

I cursed myself for not having pursued the matter with Doug Prayer. How could I have missed that one? I wanted to ask if they had been in an auto wreck but had no questions prepared and simply clammed. When had the accident happened? Who? Where? Those questions came later; but right then I clammed up.

"So what do you wanna talk about?" he asked nonchalantly.

"I'd like to talk about your time with The Doors, I said."

He started to laugh.

"Doug Prayer is ill and he told me where you were," I lied. "He said it was time for you to talk to me. Set the record straight. He gave me a painting to look at – Dionysus." The face staring back at me gave no reaction. I upped the bet. "I've heard the tapes. I know about Mickey Alvarez and I know you're not him. You swapped identities, didn't you? He's the man in the coffin – Mickey A."

The man had stopped laughing now.

"You've been a very busy little bastard," he said. His voice was cold and flat. "Was it worth it?" he asked. "Did you find enough to base a movie on it?"

The teeth were all false and seemed small for the jaw line. But the voice was immediate – a smooth baritone with a lilt to it. That had not changed.

He paused and then looked straight into my eyes and simply asked, "Why?"

"Why what?"

"Why do you want this to be true? Why do you think I'm Mr. Mojo Risin? Why me? Why now man?"

"Because the tru…" I could hear my own voice falter as I reached for something I had never considered, until this moment – my own motive. "..th always comes out in the end. People deserve the truth."

"Does it though and deserve," he paused thoughtfully, "tha's a hell of concept."

"Well I think they do." There, I'd said it.

"So you're one of those who are swift to deal out justice. You wanna be careful man, that's the realm of gods." He paused and thought again. "There are many who deserve life but get death and vice versa don't be so swift to deal it out. Those who deal out judgements are often not wise enough to make those decisions; why would you be any better?"

"I'm not saying that," I was struggling to give a reason. "It's just that…"

He interrupted me, "You just wanna be the man who shot Jesse James? The man who exposed Jim Morrison and why," his head tilted thoughtfully, "so you can get notoriety?" He laughed out loud. "You wanna be famous man?"

"I just think…"

"Bullshit man, that's a bunch of bullshit. Hey man, you shouldn't wish for those things too much, it might just come true and then where would you be when the summer's gone?"

"Well I know that you are Morrison and I can prove it." I sounded ridiculous, childlike. "I have spoken to Doug and he said that you'd…"

"You know it ain't all it's made out to be man. It nearly destroyed me, and Pam's gone. Whatta you want fame for?" He put on a Hispanic accent, "Cars, money and girls? I traded all that for peace of mind and…" He paused again, "You know nobody's gonna believe ya anyhow? They'll say it's all a crock and that…"

It was my turn to interrupt, "Well I'm here now and I know who you are and I know the truth. Perhaps I could get an interview and a few photographs? "

"Listen kid, everyone's dead man. The ride is over. Why can't they just leave me be? I don't wanna sing memories, past glories; I'd rather drive a truck."

I nodded. "But what about your fans?" I asked.

He shrugged. "Spectators man," he said. "I loved them to begin with, but the ones who went to the Whisky went on to the great gig in the sky. Hell, the whole damn shithouse went to hell. Life ain't what it used to be. Why don't you read little Danny's book?"

"I have," I said.

He seemed impressed. "Good ain't it?" he asked. "That boy sure can write. He did better than me."

"Isn't that often the case?" I asked.

He looked quizzical.

"The pupil is often better than the master? That's what's supposed to happen surely? Otherwise no one would learn a thing."

"That's very profound."

"All I want is an interview," I said, almost begging.

"Why?"

"Because I want to be the one who writes the truth."

"You wanna be the man who rolled away the stone man?"

"I'm being straight with you."

"The Easter heist man. Hey, if you see Mary man, tell her I loved her. I know that now, right back to Clearwater, only I messed it up man. You wanna know something? I never told another soul 'cept her. She was my first; she made a man outta me. Man she was beautiful and she had the eye man. Sensible and strong, beautiful, we should have been together. I told her all my secrets man. That's me, soul of a clown and all that. The break-up wasn't because she couldn't handle LA. It was because she couldn't handle me. It was Pam – she knows that, and so do I, you ask her now."

"You could tell her yourself."

"Hey, she knows what I said to her that last night at the Whisky. It wasn't pleasant, probably because I was threatened by her success. You tell her I'm sorry man. Sorry she walked. Hey, I know better now. I was a shit man, a total shit. I was drunk. Man she could dance."

My mind was racing; this had to be Morrison, he had given me something personal which another living person could verify. Perhaps something another person could refute or substantiate, a kind of proof.

"Will you give me an interview?" I asked.

"Ain't that what we're doin' right now?" he replied.

"I mean with a tape recorder and photographs ?" I asked.

"No photos, no tape. I'll answer all your questions, but not today."

"When?"

"Day after tomorrow."

I sensed he might vanish again. He sensed what I sensed.

"I'm not gonna disappear man. Doug picked you in Paris man, back at that bar with The Lizard Kings."

"I don't remember seeing him," I sounded childlike.

"That's because you don't see, when you look. Hey, do you listen?"

"Of course."

"Can we trust you?"

"Absolutely."

"I got a wedding to go to and then I'll speak with you man, but not here."

"Whose?"

"Somebody special to me."

I didn't press it. "Where then?" I asked.

"The pergola on the breakwater. No cameras. If I see press or cameras or any other shit like that, I'm gone."

He extended his right hand and for the first time offered it to me to shake. I noticed he only had half of the wedding ring finger and virtually no pinkie. His hand looked like it had suffered major trauma. His forearm had suffered a major burn which had left the skin wrinkled and hairless. I was shocked.

"I give my word," I said. "No outside parties." I figured that a long shot photo might be possible from the beach. I also figured my girlfriend not to be an outside party. "I just wanted to ask what the Greek is above the door. You know, below Ninth Life. What does it mean? I don't know."

He chuckled. "I don't care."

I was shocked by his blunt response and wondered if I had overstayed my welcome and whether he had tired of me already.

"My apologies," I started. "I didn't mean to upset…"

"No man," he smiled. "That's what it means, I don't care."

"Oh it means I don't care?"

"Hey," he laughed. "Quick, ain't ya?" I noticed that he seemed to do a lot of that – laugh. "You don't listen do, ya? I hope your eyesight's better man."

* * *

It was a Monday, a day like any other day and I was waiting, always waiting. I'd expected the man to show at 11.00am, just like he said he would, but he didn't. I'd expected him to show up casually, walking along the concrete breakwater, but he hadn't. So I sat and waited.

My girlfriend was on the beach with a zoom lens trained on me. Her small bikini was pink and her skin white, her bright green eyes shone. Everything in my world was in balance, but the panic was beginning.

11.00am came and went – no sign. At 11.40 a small dingy with an outboard motor purred into the north bay. My pink-clad accomplice was seated and sun-bathing in the south bay. There was an eventuality I hadn't planned for.

A voice called as the boat approached the side of the concrete jetty. It was only then that I realised this was no local fishing boat. It was Morrison, complete with a Van Gogh style straw hat and sunglasses. From where the camera was, there was absolutely no chance of a close shot, telephoto lens or not.

"Hey man!" he yelled. "Tie me up." Today he didn't look quite so slim. The clothes were tighter.

A rope whistled past my ear, almost hitting a woman with an ice-cream who just happened to be walking past. He apologised and then with four double step leaps he was up and seated in the pergola with me.

"Ok," he said, "ready." It was as quick as that.

"Don't you want a drink?" I asked, hoping the signal of me standing would be registered by my trigger happy camera woman.

"Don't drink these days," he said, "AA and all that. Got my fruit juice here."

He pulled a bottle from the side pocket of a baggy, sand-coloured jacket he wore.

"Doug says you're all right," he offered, "so fire away."

I wondered if they had spoken, if the notion that Morrison had alluded to, that of them choosing me, was true. Then I realised that Morrison always seemed to be able to reflect back at people what they wanted to hear. Had he worked me out? And so quickly too – how?

I launched. "In 1971 you left Los Angeles for Paris, why?" I was off and running.

"We had a six record deal with Electra. *LA woman* was number six so technically we were free to do as we pleased. I wanted to write and get back to where I had been in '66, in Venice," he paused, "so I left. I needed some time to regroup and get my shit together."

"You just left? For a vacation?"

"No man, I left the band. The Doors were over. I was twenty seven, too old to be a rockstar."

"But you could have carried on?" I ventured. "John did. Didn't he quit one night in the studio and then come back the next day, and simply play as if nothing had happened?"

"He came straight back, yeah," his voice deepened, "but I'd have ended up like Elvis man. Maybe doing those films, you know?" He paused, thinking, *Blue Hawaii* or whatever. I could have been in Caesar's too." He paused again, "Only Elvis didn't have a sentence hangin' over his head now did he? It was Ok for him to do Las Vegas; me, I'd be doin' hard time, and they'd have had me bustin' rocks. "

251

"You seriously think they'd have jailed you? You were a star."

"For sure man, for sure." He paused again and then added, "Don't you?"

"So what happened to Pam?"

"After the burial, we went back to Sausalito. We had a house boat up there on the Indian named dock. Mr. and Mrs. Alvarez and we kinda hid out for a bit. Took a long holiday." He started laughing at his recollections. "Pam dyed her hair black man and I got some of those joke glasses. Like the ones Robbie had, only these had plain glass in them. I cut my hair man and regularly dyed that blonde. We looked really crazy. But it was fun. Hippies on a house boat. "

"You created new images for yourselves?"

"Yep and Pam she got to eat anything, anything she wanted. Hey, you know sometimes she didn't eat for two days man, when we were in LA. That's how she stayed slim." He was chuckling, "We ate tacos man and swam in the sea and kinda got clean."

"How long were you in Sausalito?"

"Must have been nine month." He paused again, "And then some guy started askin' questions and tryin' to fuck Pammie." His level of seriousness increased. "So she took off back to LA, a kind of diversion and I split for a while. At first everyone wanted a piece of her. Everyone wanted to talk to her about Jim. You know the kind of shit. What was he really like? Did he have a big slong? Could he get it up? Was he really a pervert who drank blood during sex and..." He stopped. "You know the kind of crap. You write it everyday. Sensationalist shit, nothing about the music man," he paused again, "nothing."

He was referring to himself in the third person. That I found interesting and also highly alarming.

"Where did you go?"

"India man. I did the backpack route. Actually got a job grape harvesting in the Dordogne. Went all round Italy too. Little bit of time in Africa, you know just looking around."

"Weren't you afraid you'd be recognised?"

"No, we had that nailed. Everyone was looking for the

Lizard King and he was dead. I played him man and then killed him off. He was my Sherlock Holmes and I did him on the fall from Chateau Marmont, not some waterfall. Nobody thought a fat blonde man was Morrison." He paused in deep thought this time. "See, a couple of times some guys asked me if I was from Miami. One even said if I had dark hair I coulda been Morrison. Said I even sounded like the man. I laughed a lot at that and he laughed a lot and then we got stoned. Next day he'd forgotten."

"How long were you in India?"

"Six months I think," he replied.

"Were you worried about the FBI?"

"The little blue men in their little blue suits?" he replied. "No man, to be honest that was a kinda spent thing by then."

"Really?"

"Well yeah cos they thought I was dead and the guy they were after was. But me, I've never been so free man. Perhaps being dead gives you the ultimate freedom. "

"Where did you go after that?"

"Italy, like I said; Nepal, and I spent two months in Sweden. White nights baby, white nights and the northern lights."

Not once did he mention locations in Africa.

"So you travelled a lot?" I questioned.

"Yeah."

"And Pam?"

"In LA man, playing the grieving widow. We had a place in Stockholm and a place in Nevada up near Lake Tahoe. A cabin where we could hide away. Pam and me would meet up and things would be fine for a while and then the arguments would start again."

"She go off to Paris?"

Morrison became sheepish. "Why ya askin' that?"

"Hyacinth House and that bit about throwing the Jack of Hearts away?"

"Yeah, the symbolism was the thing, wasn't it?" he snorted disparagingly.

"Weren't all your songs like that?"

He didn't reply and considered the situation.

I pressed him, " 'The End' was about Mary Werbelow, wasn't it? What about 'LA woman', that was Pam, surely?"

He smiled his reply but said nothing.

" 'Cars Hiss by My Window', that's about your own death." I stated.

"Hey, don't read too much into the thing, I was only twenty seven at the time."

"Did you ever think you had a premonition?"

He shook his head. "No man. But I'd love to be able to see into the future. Wow, imagine how far-out that would be."

"Have you written any poetry since 1971?" I asked.

"Not much," Morrison replied. "I kinda gave up on the world, or the world gave up on me. Shoulda become a gun runner. War always pays well."

"True," I agreed. "So why Greece? And when?"

"1974, after Pam died; as to why? Well why not? It has everything man, everything. It's like the cradle or crucible of enlightenment. They had temples carved of stone while you and I," he paused, "you Irish?"

I nodded. "You guessed by the name?"

He nodded too. "Well we, we Celts," he continued, "we were crawling around in mud huts and sleepin' with our cattle."

"I know, that's what my father used to say. He came from Irish stock and called himself a bog trotter."

"Great guy," he laughed. "A comic?"

"Army," I laughed in reply. "Worked his way from promotion to promotion."

"Mine was navy."

"I know."

"Was he a nice guy?" Morrison asked.

"Not always," I replied in earnest.

"What he do?" Morrison asked.

"Marched me down to the barbers to get my hair cut. Enforced hair cut."

"Mine too, holy shit!" he exclaimed. "They got a real bug up their arses," he paused, before spitting out the words, "military crap."

"So what happened with the Pam thing?" I asked in reply, trying to deflect his involvement. It worked.

"Well sometimes people die by accident, sometimes by design and sometimes," he paused again, "sometimes they just die and there isn't a reason."

"The autopsy says heroin."

"Well then that's the reason."

I was trying to get things out of Morrison and he wasn't really giving me much. The problem was, I was expecting too much and he knew it. He told me precisely what he thought I needed to hear. Jimbo, the rootin' tootin' son of a gun, had gone and instead there was a very cautious man who acted like a mature adult. Mature adult – he was more like a fugitive on the run. Which, technically, I suppose he was.

That day we talked for over two hours and covered many subjects, but the one I wanted to get to, and the one the world needed to know, was how he got away.

"You know there are some people who say you were mentally unbalanced." I threw the accusation straight at him. "Somebody said, I can't remember who, that you were just a paranoid schizophrenic on the edge of collapse." I continued, "Some critics said that you should be pitied and not admired."

I was surprised that he said little. He remained totally calm – listening.

"Wow man," he replied and then thought for a bit. "You know what, they're probably not far from the truth – whatever that may be." He looked straight at me. "The thing is, all those people lookin' right back at yer. It's kinda scary, like you're gonna shit yourself in public. I suppose the drink helped and then it cursed."

"Would you like to have been unsuccessful?"

"No, well suppose not. But I'd have liked a little less of the constricting, all consuming, choking fame we had. In the end I couldn't go anywhere, in the States anyway."

"What would you rather have been?"

"Mmm," he murmured, "maybe a truck driver who wrote poetry. But hey, they don't want poetry these days. It's all cheap thrills and TV."

"So what happened in Paris?" I finally asked.

"I came to realise that I didn't want to be Mr. Mojo Risin, or Jim Morrison of The Doors. I'd been playing that part all day everyday for five years and I knew all the lines. It was a trip, but I wanted to get some peace."

"So you stopped the drinking."

"Yep and Jimbo went away."

"So the drink was part of the act?"

"No man it was the act. I got drunk so I could sing. It made sure I didn't have to sing with my back to the crowd. You know, I used to get really nervous. The booze got me through it. Now I don't need to be Jimbo – I don't drink."

"Just how nervous did you get then?" I asked.

"Terrified." He paused and then threw in the comparison. "You like the movies?" he asked.

"Of course," I replied.

"Well think of the scariest movie you've ever seen."

I thought of *The Exorcist*.

"How scared were you?"

He gave me no chance to reply.

"That's how scared I was for five years man. The night before the Hollywood Bowl '68, I threw up for about two hours. Couldn't sleep. Walked a lot and boozed until I was so goddamn drunk I passed out. Rock an roll huh, pukin' and drinkin'? Only it ain't fun. It ain't. It's like you're on a rollercoaster and every time it slows and you think you can jump off, it suddenly speeds up. Everything clenches and every time it slows, when it starts again – it starts faster. So round and round you go until you fall off – me, I fell off in Paris."

It was my turn. "What happened?" I asked.

"I died," he laughed as he replied.

Then, without pushing, he began to tell me the detail. It was like an unburdening.

"Well Mickey and me, we had a real time. When Babe came over from the States even he couldn't tell us apart?"

"You set him up?" I said.

"No way, Babe an me, well we had a real good time. Mickey

played his part by being Morrison when it suited him. I gave him clothes and stuff and then the stupid bastard went to that club and some spade gave him some smack. Maybe they really thought he was me. Anyhow, he up and dies; dies right there in the girls' shithouse."

"Let me get this right?" I paused, hardly able to grasp the simplicity of the story. "Mickey Alvarez dies while impersonating you?"

"Yeah man and didn't he like the pussy that got him. He went crazy man. He went through those French women like a stud dog. One after another and those bitches acted like they were on heat. Ridiculous to watch, can you imagine that, women so desperate to fuck ya, just because you're famous."

I wasn't allowing myself to be sidetracked. "So that night?" I asked again.

"I'm at home with Pam. We'd been out for some food and seen a movie and it's late man, really late. There's a knockin' at the door. Pam goes cos I'm crashed out. They got Mickey supported under each arm and they say he's out cold. So they plonk him in the bath and off they go. They think it's me, so the rumours start. Maybe a couple of people saw Morrison carried out dead. Maybe one of the girls goes and squeals to the pigs. Well Pam says to me that she has a plan."

"So you changed places permanently?"

"Ain't that a gas?" He reflected, "Only now they'd say I killed the guy and I'd have a murder rap next. Only I didn't kill him. But they'd say I did. Hell, they wanted to toast me."

"Things have changed. Time has moved on."

"The hell it has," he snapped. "I might be Jumpin' Jack Flash, but it ain't a gas anymore. I listen to the news man. Greece ain't Timbuktu. Things ain't changed, like Townsend says." He started to sing, "Won't get fooled again no no."

"The Who?"

"Yep."

"So what did you do next?" I asked.

"Pam calls Ronay and they arrive and see the body and they say Morrison is dead. The body doesn't go anywhere and it's packed in ice until the Monday. Then that goes into the coffin and me, well I gotta stay outta sight for a while."

"You make it sound so easy."

"It was. Pam said it was me, Ronay said it was me. Bill doesn't check cos he's blown away. Agnes, she's took scared, so it becomes *Last Tango in Paris* and that is that. They bury the body and I'm gone. Bill clears the apartment and Pam goes home." He paused. "You know it took me three weeks to get back to the States. First over to my house in Stockholm and then on a plane to Toronto. I got a car and went down to the boat and we hung out."

"If you told the truth, you could go back to the States." I naively chirped. I hadn't considered his reply.

"Why though? I don't want my old life back. Hollywood's all changed and you can't turn back the clock."

"But you could be famous again," I expounded.

His reply was quite precise. "Why? Don't you listen?"

I had no real answer, except perhaps to say being famous must be great. That notion he would find ridiculous.

"Would you like a coffee?" I asked.

His reply was affirmative. So I trudged across to the beach hut which served a sort of Brown Windsor Soup style coffee, before trudging back. I hoped there were at least some photographs. When I got back, the man had gone. I cursed my own stupidity.

Then I noticed him back in the boat he'd arrive in – he seemed to be looking for something. I thought he might be leaving.

"Coffee," I said sheepishly. "I didn't know if you took sugar and milk so I brought both."

He joined me once again. Only this time he sat with his back to the water, almost as if he were watching the pier in case someone else arrived. He was nervous.

"Is there something wrong?" I quizzed.

"It's not my boat man. I don't want the cops coming over and finding any of my stuff down there."

"I thought it was yours."

"Nope, I kinda took it on a short term loan," he chuckled.

"Isn't that dangerous?"

"Well no more than any other hobby."

"You were talking about fame," I said.

His reply was direct. "No you were." He paused. "You wanted to find out exactly why I left and why I don't wanna go back to that life." He gave me no chance to answer. "See that's the problem. It's just like Warhol said man. Fifteen minutes. Anyhow, bein' famous is a bunch of bullshit. You know what the real important thing is?" I shook my head. "Love man, love and happiness and," he paused again, "and health man. Fame is a crock," he continued, "power is a crock. Who the hell wants that? Freedom man, freedom, enough money just to be," he paused again, deep in thought, "yourself. No acting, no image, just be. Can you dig that one? Getting up when you like and doing what you like. Dress how you like. If you have somebody who loves and supports you and doesn't want a piece of you?" He considered, "That's probably as good as it gets man."

"Dude-ism?" I laughed.

"Right on man. Those Coen brothers, they were on to somethin' there. Enough money not to have to work at all, or just do the things you want to do. You gotta be healthy enough to enjoy stuff." The tone of his voice changed. "See that's what killed me, and Jimi, loneliness."

"What about Janis?" I asked.

"Accident man, just an accident." He waited for a response. "It happens, like auto wrecks and plane crashes. Shit happens."

I laughed and he laughed and then winked.

Pointing at my feet, he drawled, in a pure Alabama accent, "They look like a really comfo'table pair of shoes."

He had me laughing with his references to films and his love of comedy. This man was a man who knew how to laugh and seemed to be more at one with his existence than me. He had had fame and rejected it. That must have taken real nerve, real steel.

"You know what?" he asked.

I was still laughing as he became thoughtfully reflective.

"Bob Dylan, he's on the road nearly all the time. Has a place in Malibu and two failed marriages and five kids and he's on the road all the time. Wanna know why?"

I nodded.

"He's lonely man. Fame don't give you happiness. I should know, I lost Pam and hey that..." his voice trailed away. "Dylan ain't got anywhere else to go but the road, lessen you consider the grave."

"What happened to Pam?" I asked.

"Accident man, just an accident, pure and simple." He became philosophical, "And people say I'm lucky. You know what luck is?"

I shook my head.

"There," he pointed, "that's luck, worth more than any fame."

I looked and all I could see were an older couple. They were strolling along the sand at the water's edge. As they approached, I could see both of their faces – they were smiling and holding hands. They appeared to be in love. Then I got it. Still in love after all the years. All of the stuff about fame suddenly paled into insignificance.

On that day Jim Morrison gave me one valuable lesson upon which I could hang my hat. Jim Morrison knew the nature of love. I am not really a romantic, but I understood exactly where he was coming from. I place here the simple question he placed before me: define love. We spent ages on it and he seemed to enjoy that discourse more than anything else. It wasn't an interview and it wasn't an argument; it was, if you'd been an observer, two old friends discussing their lives – trying to make some sort of sense of it.

His voice was soft and low as he spoke, "You know, some people never get it. They search and search for it and then for some reason it gets snatched away."

I could feel a lump in my throat.

"It's like those people who really want a kid, they get the one shot and the kid dies. Hey man, can you imagine that? You know that real certainty usually comes once in a lifetime?"

Now this may sound really crazy but that's the problem with

being a legend – isolation. Nobody wants to marry and have a legend for a lover. Just imagine that, a woman thrown over for a younger one, after years of marriage, because the legend has choice. Or having to spend sleepless nights guessing who had hit on her and where she might be, if you were a man. These are issues many of us carry and Jim Morrison, for all the bravado, had them too. I could relate to him.

I was learning fast that the wanton world without lament brought problems. I thought of Grace Slick, she of Jefferson Airplane, and her way of screwing the whole band. To be honest, I think that initially I'd have reacted like Morrison, but even I think it would have churned me up. Could I have dealt with it? I'd like to have had the chance to try. But the awful truth is I'd probably have run around in circles and then just disappeared up my own arse.

"Money doesn't give you happiness," he growled. "In fact, the most happy times I had were down on Venice Beach. I was poor man – no food."

"Yeah but money…" I started.

"McCartney," he interrupted, "you'd call him lucky?"

"Of course," I replied, "he's big time."

"Well the woman he loved more that anything else in the world died. Is that lucky? She gave him his kids and then she died. Some luck there." He paused in thought.

"Everyone condemned him for the Mills marriage, but nobody took the time to ask why. Perhaps he was just trying to get back what he had once. You can't," he paused again, "you can't. So how is that lucky?"

"So now you paint and sell pots?" I changed tack.

"Yeah and I kinda got this thing goin'. Maybe if Pam and me had a baby, things woulda been different. But she was kinda fucked up inside. She wouldn't talk about it much, but it stopped her having kids. Her sister Judy stuck it to her once. Though Pam could be a real…"

"So you knew that kids were not possible?" I asked.

"I knew, she told me, well sort of," he paused, "not in so many words. Pam said her mom may have had an issue with

Judy cos she was only eighteen when she was born. But Corky knows, you ask him. Pearl certainly does."

"But I thought Pam's mother married young at sixteen?"

Jim Morrison shot me a look. "You better do some checks," he said. "Pam and Judy I mean, sisters?"

"Maybe I will," I replied, though I had no intention of doing so. I wanted more about The Doors. "So the band, how did that happen? Was it like Ray said?"

"Look, we just bumped into each other in Venice and it seemed like a good idea at the time."

I wanted more. "And then?" I could sense he was growing tired. I changed the subject. "You know they got a sort of shrine outside your old place on Norton. There's a bust of you there. It's silver in a case."

"I know, it's crazy isn't it?"

"And in the Hard Rock Café on Hollywood they've got your pants. The old brown leather ones that you ripped at the crotch."

He whistled through his teeth.

"And a copy of the lyrics for 'LA woman'. The ones you used at the recording session. Large."

"You know those leathers were worn out," he said. "One of the waist ties just ripped off and they split one night on the way back from Barney's. I got to the Cienega and had to get Pam to find me some other pants. Only she wouldn't, so the girl in the office there stitched them up, or maybe Danny did it. I kinda don't remember, things got a bit blurred toward the end. Anyhow, Pam threw them out the window in Norton and that was the last time I seen 'em."

"Well, when you are next in LA you'd best go take a look."

"I ain't been to LA for some time man. Hell, things are different now; what a ride man. I liked Laurel Canyon. You know I wrote 'People are Strange' up on Mulholland, on a lookout."

"They've got your star on the walk of fame too. Over the doors at the Whisky they've got a guitar with 'Light my Fire' on it and down in Venice there's a giant mural on Speedway."

I showed him pictures.

"You know the Alta Cienega Motel, your room? The Morrison Room?"

"What room?"

"Yeah room 32 has a big sign on it. The Jim Morrison room."

"But I didn't always stay in the one room."

"The one on the end of the first floor landing?" I added.

"Yeah, well sometimes I was in the room second from the end. Don't know the number though," he paused, "who cares anyway?"

"Well in the end room they've got a black and white photograph on the wall." I continued, "and there's graffiti everywhere."

"What, like at the grave in Paris?" he asked.

"That's been cleaned up and they've got a security guard who sits there all the time. Your grave, I feel stupid saying this, is one of the most visited sites in all of Paris. I got deported once," I added. Don't ask me why I said it, I just did.

"Why?" he asked.

"Busking in the street."

He roared with laughter and clapped his hands together. "What do ya play?" he asked.

"Guitar."

"Any good? Robby was so good he could pick up the tune I sang and play it back. Ears like a bat man."

"Average to bad," I offered.

"Modest too," he licked his lips.

"I've never been accused of that before." I expressed genuine surprise.

"I like that man. It says…" he stopped as if a brake had been applied. He began singing, "I can change the course of nature." Then he stopped just as suddenly once again. "Music is wonderful, like language – intense and erotic."

"Erotic?" I queried.

"Yeah man, erotic, hypnotic, chaotic, all the things that life really is are in the music. Emotion, devotion, what a potion – explosion."

It was like someone was pouring warm oil into my ears. It

was soothing and spilling out on the concrete at my feet. In that moment I knew why Ray Manzarek had put a band together. The voice was amazing and I knew this man was Jim Morrison. That was my Venice Beach moment. My unique experience and one I shall never forget.

"Yep." He whistled through his teeth. "It feels good to sing. I ain't sung in years. Man, even after you're dead they want a piece of ya. Everybody wants a goddam piece. "

"You knew that would happen though, didn't you?" I asked.

He smiled. "Well let's just say I was experimenting with the possibilities, ticking the boxes and watching the experiment. Now it's down to someone else to write up the conclusion. It looks like that's you."

I wondered if I had been set up as a patsy. Maybe Morrison was just manipulating the story one last time.

"Everybody loves a conspiracy," he blurted, "everyone. Look at the Kennedys, Jimmy Dean, Marilyn, Jesus. Why do you think he was so famous man?"

"So you staged it?" I didn't want to get into an argument about religion, well not at this present time at least. I knew where he would take it and I'd not be able to get the story any further forward.

"Good trick though?" he asked.

"I know, it's like you started a religion or something."

As I spoke, the penny dropped. That was precisely what he had intended all along. He had looked into a mirror called the future and found the new religion: fame.

"I think you had everybody fooled for a while, including me," I said blandly.

* * *

We sat drinking coffee, all the questions, all the research, all the piecing together had now come down to this moment. To be honest it was disappointing. What I was expecting didn't happen. We were just two old guys drinking coffee.

I was sitting with a man whose face and body appeared to

have suffered major trauma. The voice was in tact, the brain was functioning, but there was a deep sadness in his eyes. For years I had wanted to be him and then like him and now I was glad I wasn't him.

"If you don't want me to, I won't reveal your whereabouts," I blurted out.

"It won't matter now," he said. "Just don't bring in other people so they don't get hurt."

"I won't."

"I know," he replied, as if he knew precisely what I'd do.

He stood up and calmly stated, "It's time man."

I thought how does he know, he's not wearing a watch? Time for what?

"Can we meet again?" I asked. "Tomorrow perhaps?"

"Sure," he replied casually, almost too casually. "This beach is a great place ain't it? The air you breathe, the food you eat."

I thought it was a lyric or a clue, one of his, and yet I couldn't place the song. My mind was racing, trying to find the reference.

"Where?" I asked, trying to seal the tryst.

"How about here?" he offered. "Seems as good a place as any. They do some tacos over there." He pointed. "You dig Mexican food?"

Nodding, I agreed. "Adore it. Margaritas are so great."

"The ocean is blue and your friend, she can swim too. Let's a get a bottle man and blow our goddam heads off."

I was stunned and, the lyric forgotten, my mind wondered just exactly what he knew about me. How did he know she was there? Or had he just taken a lucky guess? Why the drink? He had told me he didn't drink anymore. I was confused, stunned, elated and yet apprehensive, my emotions rolled and tumbled like the lyrics of the Muddy Waters song.

"She's beautiful," he smiled, "lovely eyes, great smile." Then he paused and looked straight at me. His voice was grave and very serious. "Make her the most precious thing you own, or lose her," he said. "If you love her and she loves you in return, you can take on the world." His voice had a tremble in it. "That's the greatest lesson you'll ever learn man," he paused again, almost as if reaching for a more profound closure. The final word came out like a whimper, "Ever."

"Tomorrow then?" I said, half hoping yes – and half suspecting no.

"Uh ha," he grunted.

It was as if all the words had finally left him and the bank of lyrics run dry. Perhaps he had nothing else to say. Maybe I had nothing else to ask. I wanted to talk with him about poetry and which of the beats he loved the most. What the 60s had meant, as if he knew himself. How the imagery of his songs hung together. Ginsberg and the magic bus. What turned him on. Having reflected now in the writing of this account, I think I know: Pamela Courson, plain and simple. Whether she was the cat and he the mouse, he loved her; together they functioned as a wailing banshee against the system; alone they were two sides of the same coin.

I watched him slowly walk away. My heart wanted to believe I would see him again; my head was telling me I probably wouldn't.

A strange and sad set of circumstances mixed into the being of this enigma. I had only just started to understand and don't profess to fully 'get it' now. I saw him walk off alone and turn the corner of Avenue Singrou, walking into the suburbs of Athens. He didn't look back. His eyes were firmly set on the road ahead and I knew he'd be alright.

As he turned the corner and disappeared a Doors song arrived in my subconscious: 'The Changeling'.

* * *

That was the last time I saw Jim Morrison.

Twenty one

Que sera sera…

When I got back from Greece, I went to my publishers with the story. Ballistic isn't the word best used to describe the reaction, but it's close. What I had was more than a story, it was a history. Everyone thought I was crazy; at times I did too. Well not everyone – there was one person who believed in me.

Some said I was mad, others bad, to the bone I hope, and several that I was dangerous. Don't ask me why – you work it out.

Nobody believed the story of course.

I might as well have said I was the son of God or the Devil, or that Elvis was abducted by aliens and living on Mars – but I know the truth and to some extent that has to be good enough, for me at least. Then there were the critics and the fans. Some said it was sacrilege, others that I was a monstrous aberration. Some wanted to thank me and others burn me at the stake as a heretic. In response I echo these philosophical gems: "That's all I have to say 'bout that."

That's the nature of aftermath, it cannot be explained: it just is.

I took five years to complete the research. And the book? Most of the writing took place over the final years, 2009-2011.

Now it's your turn .You can choose to say phooey or that it ticks off the possibilities. The choice is yours.

* * *

When I went back to France to see Doug and show him this text, his apartment was empty. It was as if he had never been there. The tapes, the instruments and all of his personal effects had gone. There was no forwarding address and no way to find him, or them. I suspect that one day, years from now, someone will find the canisters in the bottom of a box of bric-a-brac and maybe, if we're lucky, they'll be 'discovered'. I sure would like to be the lucky devil that gets to that auction. If not, then they'll burn on some celebratory kid's bonfire and I expect Jim would laugh at the irony in that.

Some of the neighbours said they thought Doug had died, and described a frail old man in his nineties; while others said he'd moved to the States, a young man with long blond hair. Most of them didn't know who he was, even fewer cared. In fact their recollections varied so much that I wondered if we were discussing the same person. Whatever people had seen, the apartment ended up being cleared. A life in boxes. Some kids told me they'd seen Doug with a friend, moving boxes, a grey-haired man with a beard and they'd been laughing. Somebody upstairs said she'd heard men talking about Nebraska one day, on a landing. Another said Oregon, and another Nevada, they were probably all red herrings – knowing Jim.

And me? I sometimes doubt my own sanity and grip on reality when I think about these men.

The Ninth Life Gallery mysteriously closed shortly after I left Athens. The shop lay empty for nearly six months, until a new venture started. At the present time the place sells tee-shirts, and the irony is, Jim's face appears on some of those too. Not the Jim I knew, but the Jim of legend – The Lizard King. I bought one.

The new owners have no forwarding address for the previous lease holder, though they think he has returned to America. The dark-haired girl, who worked as the receptionist, it turns out she was his daughter all along. I'd missed that completely because I hadn't considered it; there isn't a day goes by that I don't kick myself over that one. She had married just before the shop closed and was living on one of the islands now. Pregnant too – they thought. Santorini was the favourite guess, but they had no married name and no address.

After all said and done, James Douglas Morrison is an enigma wrapped in a conundrum, shrouded in a riddle.

And I for one wouldn't have it any other way.

* * *

The only item I have is the note.

Jon Blaine is still insane and in a clinic in Switzerland.

The Lucky U restaurant in Kalamaki has been sold again and renamed.

Most of the places in LA have been torn down or altered beyond recognition.

The remaining Doors are still playing great music.

* * *

I sincerely hope Jim is living a long and happy retirement somewhere in Nebraska, or California or wherever; and that he finally finds peace and that Doug is there with him.

That's what I like to think anyway.

Pancardi's Pride

Out of the darkness and through the rat infested sewers of Florence; under the ancient treasure houses of the Palazzo Pitti and into one of the strongest bank vaults in the world; the best cracksmen in the business are on the take.

They have done the research, analysed the problems and now they are ready to make the biggest score of the century. But something history has forgotten, a myth, a legend; only this is no fairy tale, this is for real – a dream come true. All they have to do now is get away clean.

The score is every safe-crackers dream, the big "A" number one, the last job before retiring into luxurious obscurity – only this dream is about to become a full blown nightmare of insatiable greed.....

"More ups and downs that a scenic railway; more twists and turns than a high speed rollercoaster ride. A must read book!"

"for once with a book I couldn't guess the ending"

a measure of wheat for a penny

If you had something valuable and lost it – what would you risk to retrieve it? Would you lie for it? Kill for it? Even dice with death for it? Some things are worth a sacrifice – the skill is knowing that someday you might have to choose. The nerve – knowing that you might lose.

The hunt for mastermind and lethal beauty Alice Parsotti is on. Months of tracking, searching, watching and listening are about to pay off and Alex Blondell is now ready. Ready to follow her down any rabbit hole into which she may run.

But there are other forces at work too, forces that have their talons in family histories and roots in hidden political prophecies.

The recovery of the missing Romanov jewels is about to unfold in a tale of death and destruction, double dealing and dark demonic deception.

Alice is back and this time it's not Wonderland she's in.

"Ron Clooney takes us to places where only those with the stongest psyche dare to venture - another triumph"

"Dark and sexy and un-put-down-able: Ron Clooney's writing is breathtaking"

271

gothique fantastique

Two novels - eleven stories - thirteen in all.
All linked and designed to play a cat & mouse game.
Tales to make you wary; tales to make you jump;
tales that make you want to lock all your
doors and windows at night.

"You should never be afraid of the dark -
just the things that lurk within it."

"Multilayered sub-text which can only lead
the reader to one inevitable conclusion."

Read them in any order and find the
clues which tell you the bigger story,
but be warned these are tales to
make your emotions twang and
your mind swirl. From the very
start to the very finish, each
tale sets the blood racing
& weaves & constricts
like the strands of
an intricately
woven web.

"a master story teller"

gothique
fantastique
and
other
tall tales

ron clooney